To De

from Jereyer

Eleanor's son

To order additional copies of this book, contact:
Xlibris Corporation
1-888-795-4274
www.Xlibris.com
Orders@Xlibris.com
106115

CONTENTS

Dedication

This book is dedicated to the many people who worked on the project.
Dr. Tyre Alexander Newton
Professor of Mathematics, Washington State University who we lost
in 2009 and to all the people who think there must be a better way.

Tyre Alexander Newton
http://www.math.wsu.edu/Events/tnewton.php

Introduction

The book is a fictional story. However, the project it is based on is not. So, you may ask which part of this story is real and which part is fictional. The story is based on the 1147-01 Space Exploration Project and the story was produced to explain how components of the project work and why it is to our advantage to consider their application. Full explanations of the components and fact sheets are not offered in the story and not everything about the project is presented in the story. The project is a new way to look at the development of Space Exploration. A perfect example is the Navcomm System and other devices that we don't have in application in our current plan. Such as hull repair, long term journeys, and the EOS system. There are over 100 components in the project that are designed to make Space travel a safer and more economical effort. The project is designed to save Money, Time, and Effort as to the correct way to go into Space. This story is staged over a forty year period chronicling the life of the main character, John Alexander, who just like now exists in a technically active world which is changing around him. The concept of an International Space Administration is a fictional concept but, might be a concept that may need to be considered. Space exploration is not cheap and this may be the right way to approach the cost factor. The AADG project is divided into five steps. The story of 'A Short Trip to Mars' is based on step D but represents steps A-C in retrospect. Step D is the manned exploration of the Martian surface. The story presents a false image of the project with the presentation of mistakes that are made in the development of Space Exploration which can and should be avoided. The conclusion of facts presented by both books 'A Short Trip to Mars' and 'Jovian Space the Space Train' shows incites that we should use and mistakes we should avoid. Also it's doubtful that the first Mars surface exploratory mission to Mars will be more than two years at the most. We estimate that the first mission of man landing on Martian surface and returning to Earth will most probably consist of a very short amount of time on the surface, less than 6 months and will probably not be accomplished by convicts. However an AADG consultant made a significant point during the development of the project. In exploring space great time and distances need to be realized. If we are not prepared to go to distant Planets then for safety reasons we should not go. Hopefully this book will shed a light on our future as far as Space Exploration is concerned.

The International Space Administration—fictional.
The concept of convicts being the first people on Mars—fictional.
The concept of the crew being international—possibly fictional.
The concept that the first mission's duration is six years—fictional.

Real Components from the Beginning

The earth lift vehicle—real.
The XPLM and CMP vehicles—real.
CTU-concept
Tri-Starr System—real
Navcomm System—real
Re-generative power supply technology—real.
Pods—real
Jumper—real
Rover—concept
Ariel—concept
Ariel float—concept
Space bathroom—real
Kitchen—real
Auto cooker—real
Module Interior Design—real
Electronic detective—real
EOS—real
Ion plasma propulsion engine—real.
Sensors application—real
Imagery and media—real
Lunar Starr concept—real
Orbital Platforms—real
Balloons—real

Lunar habitat development—concept
Facts on cryogenics—real
Hull repair—real
Expansion struts—real.
Panel construction—real
"Glass" panels—real.
Robots—real
Hydroponic systems introduced—real.
Air and system handlers—real
Theory of the Martian orbit and history—real

So as you see, there is more real than fiction. All the concepts are the property of the AADG 1147-01 project. So intensive descriptions of how the components are built are limited. The principle story occurs on the equator of Mars in the region known as the Marineris Valle and the Olympus Mons and surrounding areas.

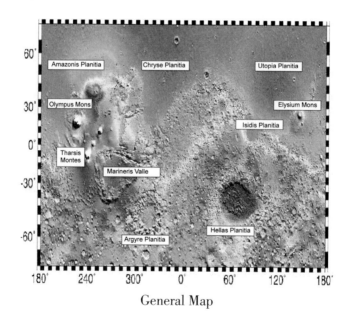

General Map

For further information on the project and its components, contact AADG at http://aadg.info. Enjoy the book.

Fcreyer—Consultant AADG

The Navcomm System   AADG

As it is explained in the book, the Navcomm operational system plays a major role in the 1147-01 Project. This project upon which the book 'A Short Trip to Mars' is based, is a five step program which, is an entirely new way to look at the process of Space Exploration. The idea behind the project and step one which, is a 'The return to the Moon', is to deployment a series of mapping probes throughout the solar system to serve as space information buoys. The deployment of these units will complete a navigational vector web (navcomm) which will assist exploratory vehicles in their journeys and operations. They also serve as watchdogs and emergency assistance units. Personally, I wouldn't leave home without them. There are eight different types of Navcomm units containing different components. However, the main unit discussed in the book is the T-111 mapping probe, sometimes called the Trex. This unit, as are all the units, is a combination of many different components. But, it's main function is to keep track on a section of space, monitoring the area and changes that occur within our Solar System. To do this, a series of T-111 units must be deployed in strategic locations throughout the Solar System. Once these Navcomm units create the vector web they can work as a single unit for traveling exploratory vehicles. Every vehicle launched in the 1147-01 project contains a Navcomm navigation unit. The vector web supplies mapping of the planets and their moons as well as large sectors of unoccupied space. Eliminating Mercury and Venus and including the Kuiper and Asteroid Belts as a sensor and signal booster cluster, the web establishes itself as a solar orbital safety guide.

*31 Moons		E—1	M—2	AS—N	J—64	S—62	U—27	N—13	KS (P) Kuiper SYS
Total 169		Luna	Phobos	Ceres	Ganymede	Titan	Titania	Triton	Ceres
			Demos	2 Pallas	Callisto	Rhea	Ariel	Proteus	Pluto
Regular				4 Vesta	IO	Iapetus	Uberiel	Naiad	Eris
Unstable				Hygiea	Europa	Dione	Miranda	Larissa	Makemake
Retrograde						Tethys	Oberon	Galatea	Hauma
Dwarf									

As you can see we have 31 primary locations selected for orbital anchors. The Six major planets Earth, Mars, Jupiter, Saturn, Uranus, and Neptune and their Moons, however we predict the deployment of over 60 Navcomm units, to be deployed with 5 units apiece for the asteroid belt and the Kuiper belt. One of the main concerns with this plan is the longevity of the units. The Planet Neptune is approx. 4,553,946,490 Km away (yes that's 4.5 billion 53 million km or 2,829,691,159 miles.) The Kuiper Belt extends another two billion miles past that point which is a considerable distance estimated at 5 billion miles. To get to Neptune at the speed of 186,200 miles per hour which is, 3103.3 miles per minute or 51.7 miles per second, it would take you 633 days to 1 2/3 years. At 100 million miles a year it would take a little over 28 years. Current standards of our systems today estimate a trip to Neptune to take 13 years. The longevity problem is that the units need to be constructed to remain operational for a minimum of 20 years. Power supply and fuel concerns top the list of problems that were addressed. It is speculation whether or not we will get to a time where we would get as far out in space as the Kuiper Belt System. However, I can see the eventual establishment of a Saturn Station for scientific investigation. But even Saturn is almost a billion miles out and Mars, who is our closes planet, is *48,541,996* km (36 million miles in Perihelion) away, which under current circumstances scientist estimate is a 8 month or a 250 day voyage. This would make

Jupiter 30 months away or 2.5 years and Saturn at twice that, or 5 years out. If it is five years out, then it is five years back which would be a stretch under any circumstances. That would mean a round trip of 10 years health issues would be a primary concern including radiation sickness, muscle control, insanity and mental fatigue. This venture would require ten years of food, water, and atmosphere plus other utilities to support such a mission. In the 1147-01 project the supplies are launched before any manned effort is made. The Navcomm system acts as the guidance system with safeguards against collision with debris and other space hazards. Everything has to have a beginning, and the beginning for the 1147-01 Project is establishing a permanent lunar base on the moon, next Mars, and then to continue out into Jovian space. As the Navcomm units grow older the older units will be refurbished and sent toward the Kuiper Belt. In the deployment of Navcomm in Jovian space application most of the units will be placed in orbit around planetary moons however in some applications the units can be anchored to the moon body such as on the Martian moon Phobos and certain asteroids. Although as we've explained the Navcomm units contain different components for different applications, some components are universal to all Navcomm units: the transceiver, the OS, and the regenerating power supply. Other components that may be similar are the sensor array, the maneuvering thruster array, internal system integration, antenna, and data storage. When the units are fully deployed and operational, the vector web which is produced forms a security web inside the solar system, nothing inside the web that moves will be undetected. Wherever the units link it forms a communication data conduit. These conduits will exist on both sides of the Sun with range of 5 billion miles. The Operating System used by the Navcomm System is the most important system in complexity and importance.

Tycho Brahe (The Navigator)   Solar Orbital Clock

The Operational system is quite complex but, here is a brief explanation of how it works. First, I must state that in designing this program we used an application called Mtronics an AADG product in development. We changed the value of the Astronomical Unit (or AU). An Au is commonly noted as a unit of measurement of distance, being 149,597,870 kilometers or 92,955,807.3 miles which is supposed to represent the distance from the Sun to Earth approximately. Well, this has not a relative concept for us so we changed it to 161,000,000 kilometers or 100,000,000 miles (NAU). This changes the values of the solar system measurement to be 29 Au instead of 30 AU (standard) but the conversion is easier to calculate. If it would be said one half Au it would be easier for you to understand 50 million miles or 80.5 Km than 46,477,903.65 miles or 74,798,930 Km. By changing this value it allows us to use scaling in macro generation which is a Mtronic concept. One of the Primary components of the Navcomm Operational System is the Solar Orbital Clock (SOC) which exists in the programming as a set of map grids on a time scale (calculator). Because we used Mtronics, the program also as a variable (sliding) base meaning I can get the time from the clock on a Jupiter base where a year is 11.68 Earth years or the Earth base of 365 days, or any other clock that exists inside the web on the map. Given a speed Navcomm can tell you how long it will take you to go from point A to point B and the position the planets will be in when you arrive at that destination and plot the course. It can also calculate circular orbital rotation and the velocity of planets. The grid maps are based on basic unit information.

✦	☿ (M)	♀ (V)	⊕ (E)	♂ (M)	♃ (J)	♄ (S)	⛢ (U)	♆ (N)
Aphelion	69,816,900 km 0.466 697 AU	108,942,109 km 0.728 231 28 AU	152,098,232 km 1.01671388 AU	249,209,300 km 1.665 861 AU	816,520,800 km (5.458104 AU)	1,513,325,783 km 10.115 958 04 AU	3,004,419,704 km 20.083 305 26 AU	4,553,946,490 km 30.4412506 AU
Perihelion	46,001,200 km 0.307 499 AU	107,476,259 km 0.718 432 70 AU	147,098,290 km 0.98329134 AU	206,669,000 km 1.381 497 AU	740,573,600 km (4.950429 AU)	1,353,572,956 km 9.048 076 35 AU	2,748,938,461 km 18.375 518 63 AU	4,452,940,833 km 29.7660709 5 AU
Orbital Rotation	87.969 1 Ed .2408y	224.700 69 day .615y	365.256 days 1y	686.971 days 1.8808Y	4,332.59 days 11.8618y	10,759.22 days 29.4571y	30,799.095 days 84.323y	60,190 days 164.79y
Oriibital velocity	10.892 km/h (3.026 m/s)	35.02 km/s	29.78 km/s[	24.077 km/s	13.07 km/s	9.69 km/s	6.81 km/s	5.43 km/s
Mass	3.3022×10^{23} kg 0.055 Earths	$4.868\ 5\times10^{24}$ kg 0.815 Earths	5.9736×10^{24} kg	6.4185×10^{23} kg 0.107 Earths	1.8986×10^{27} kg 317.8 Earths	5.6846×10^{26} kg 95.152 Earths	$8.6810 \pm 0.0013)\times10^{25}$ kg 14.536 Earths	1.0243×10^{26} kg 17.147 Earths
Density	5.427 g/cm³	5.204 g/cm³	5.515 g/cm³	3.9335 ± 0.0004 g/cm³	1.326 g/cm³	0.687 g/cm³	1.27 g/cm³	1.638 g/cm³
Gravity	3.7 m/s² 0.38 g	8.87 m/s² 0.904 g	9.780327 m/s²	3.711 m/s² 0.376 g	24.79 m/s² 2.528 g	10.44 m/s² 1.065 g	8.69 m/s² 0.886 g	11.15 m/s² 1.14 g
Atmosphere	Sodium Hydrogen	CO2 Nitrogen	Nitrogen Oxygen	CO2 Nitrogen	Hydrogen Helimum	Hydrogen Helimum	Hydrogen Helimum	Hydrogen Helimum
Meridian Orbit	11.9m km	.73m km	2.45m km	21m km	37.95m km	79.5m km	36.45m km	50.5m km

Meridian orbits (midpoint obits)—Meridian values are midpoint values of the orbit, which would be the orbit if it was completely circular with no Aphelion (+) value or Perihelion (−) value. The values of dx/dy are + − of variance.

Meridian orbit values from **Sun.**

M	V	E	M	J	S	U	N
57,901,900 km **35,978,572 miles**	108,206,259 km 67,236,252 miles	149,548,290 km 92,924,999 miles	169767100 km 105,488,385 miles	778,523,600km 483,752,137 miles	1,433,072,956 km 890,470,251 miles	2,876,679,083km 1,787,485,511.4 miles	4,503,446,490km 2,798,311,914 miles
Orbital Velocity							
3.026 m/s	35.02 km/s **21.7m/s**	29.78 km/s **18.5 m/s**	24.077 km/s **14.9 m/s**	13.07 km/s **8.1 m/s**	9.69 km/s **6m/s**	6.81 km/s **4.2m/s**	5.43 km/s **3.3m/s**
Orbital Circumference							
181,869,867.9 km 113,008,696 mi	339,875,857.5 km 211,189,066 mi	469,731,178.9 km 291,877,422 mi	715,108,329 km 444,347,714 mi	2,445,342,628 km 1,519,465,464 mi	4,501,282,155 km 2,796,967,059 mi	9,035,648,998 km 5,614,491,990 mi	14145325-10km 8,784,970,000 miles

Distance of Orbit Solar point (A to B)

This is a very important chart it tells you the mean distance from one point (A) to the other (B). It also sets up the orbital rotation for the clock in time sequence. Also included would be a map of navcomm stations and their orbital velocities. (Timescale)

Uppergrid—Meridian Orbital Distance (International Engineering Standard Metric (IESM)) in Kilometers—Distance Between

	Mercury	Venus	Earth	Mars	Jupiter	Saturn	Uranus	Neptune
Mercury	1	50304359	91646390	169767100	778532600	1375171056	2818777183	4445544590
Venus	*31,257,679*	1	41342031	119462741	670317341	1324866697	2710570924	4395240231
Earth	*56,946,426*	*25,688,747*	1	781207710	628975310	1283524666	2727130793	4353892000?
Mars	*105,488,385*	*74,230,705*	*48,541,996*	1	55085460	1205403956	3104348083	4275777490
Jupiter	*483,752,137*	*416,515,885*	*390,827,138*	*342,285,170*	1	654549356	2040253583	3724922890
Saturn	*854,491,678*	*822,997,861*	*797,545,251*	*749,003,293*	*406,718,113*	1	1443606127	3070373534
Uranus	*1,751,506,938*	*1,684,270,686*	*1,694,560,512*	*1,928,952,469*	***1,267,754,801***	*897,015,260*	1	1626767407
Neptune	*2,762,333,342*	*2,731,075,662*	*2,705,383,062*	*2,656,844,956*	*2,314,559,777*	***1,907,841,663***	**1,010,826,403**	1

Lower grid—American standard of Mechanical Engineering (ASME) in miles

These charts are a demonstration of two of the variable charts used in the SOC. There are over 10 charts per planet including moons and satellite rotation and orbits. The primary calculation which is point A to point B navigation is

Location (A)—Direction (X)—Velocity (v) = TIME it will take to get to loc (B) and where location (B) will be when you arrive at that point and how much fuel you will need to get there. The T-111 contains a dual projection sensor which allows the creation of a 3 dimensional image maps of sections of space. As the Navcomm system progresses into space certain areas where two units can be linked together can create virtual maps allowing for a virtual tour of the Solar System and its planets. This is most common when the vehicle modules which, all contain Navcomm units, link together to form an orbital platform. To get the location value of current planets look here: http://www.fourmilab.ch/cgi-bin/Solar

For an illustration of SOC design look here: http://lab.aadg.info (aadg pages)

The Navcomm system allows operators on Earth and other Navcomm stations to view images in 3d from anywhere in the web at anytime. All Navcomm transmissions are encrypted and restricted by Navcomm Central/ Earth to protect the system. Imagine this: You and your crew of eight are on your way in the first exploratory vehicle to the planet Jupiter. You're going to need food, water and air for 2.5 years and reserves for the 2.5 year return. But, after you pass Mars and are approaching the asteroid belt. A large stone impacts your vehicle putting a hole in your hull and your fuel tank. Venting your internal atmosphere and disabling your craft. You're a year and a half from Earth and you don't have enough fuel to return. And even if you did, you don't have enough oxygen to last but a few months. There is an emergency station where you can pull over and fix the problem. It is solutions to problems like this that hinders our exploration into space. Before we can start thinking of interplanetary space travel we need to find solutions to potential problems which could occur, navcomm offers these solutions. Suppose your seven months out on your way to Mars and one of the crew spills coffee it the main control panel shorting it out and making it unusable. Now what do you do? Well the solutions simple, don't allow coffee in the control room or make sure you have good cup holders (no those are not the solutions), however EOS offers solutions. And then there are always first contact situations such as, what to do if we encounter an alien race, what is the procedure?? You and your crew are a few billion miles out in Jovian Space and encounter an alien space vehicle they attempt communications and docking. What do you do? Anyhow the 1147-01 project solves a lot of these problems so we hope you enjoy the book. If you like to know more about the project and the Story feel free to visit the website http://1147-01.aadg.info

"3d maps are important because there is no 2d space, only 2d applications"

Dr. Tyre Alexander Newton—AADG Consultant

Chapter 1

The Beginning

The alarm clock went off as usual at 7:00 a.m., but it had to be put on hold. Twenty minutes later, it went off again. Reality stirred Jason Greene to consciousness. He knew he had to get up, but lately energy had been elusive and getting out of bed had become a major chore. He had no idea why his energy was low, but whatever was causing it wasn't of concern right now. He had a meeting with the United States director to the International Space Administration at nine this morning. He had gotten the call yesterday around 3:00 p.m. As an assistant to the United States director, these meetings were not uncommon for him however; most of the work came over the links via the wallboards. Communications had come a long way since he was in high school in 2014. Sure, there were wallboards (they called them TVs then), but they weren't as affordable or sophisticated as they were now, around 2018 three D screens had come of age. In the last ten years, over three-quarters of the world had boards that operated on the World Global News Network (WGNN). Most general meetings were held via the link; however anything that required security had to be done in person. This evidently was one of those things. Jason shoved some food down his throat and gulped down a, bit too hot, cup of coffee and was out the door down to the street.

Montreal was well into its morning stir. It was a brisk September day with a slight wind. The leaves had just started to change into their autumn colors, and Jason's energy picked up instantly. He caught the tram downtown; it was cheaper and faster to take the tram than personal transportation. Ever since the International Space Commission had located their headquarters here in 2022, Montreal had grown by leaps and bounds.

The Commission was composed of six independent groups or consortiums: the Europeans, the Asians, the Russians, the Chinese, the United States, and the English concern which included Australia and Canada and their lobbies. The lobbies were made up of business factions and conglomerates pushing their initiatives in order to make a profit off space exploration. The committee was originally designed to coordinate the ventures and the regulations of the exploration of space but in the last few years had become more like a political court puppet show. With over sixty representatives and four hundred lobbyists, the moods on the council floor changed every day, depending on who and what was going on here and millions of miles away in space. There was the construction on the Lunar Starr and its operational issues, and space tourism and mining concerns were also being addressed. Issues such as space debris and the establishment of space regulations were constantly a topic. And of course, there was that fiasco which still had not been resolved and was a constant ongoing topic. A few years ago, the Europeans had launched that robotic drone probe toward the center of the galaxy. That didn't go over well with the Committee or the United Nations. There was a chance that it may have been approved if the Security Council had known about it, but the Europeans had launched it without telling anyone. This had become a major safety issue, with the committee saying that this assembly was established to regulate space exploration and all parties need to learn to work together and follow proper procedures. The committee had condemned Europeans action on the basis that it had jeopardized the security of the planet. The position was stated that without knowing what lay outside our solar system, that giving an alien race a look at our current state of technology may not be such a great idea, regardless of what information we would gain in the process. The Europeans tried to save face by explaining that the probe was dropping telemetry relay probes at regular intervals as it traveled on its journey, and this would be to Earth's advantage. The Security Council was only partly abated by this and demanded that the manifest and specifications be turned into their security section. After two weeks, the council ruled against any actions being taken outside the solar system without their pre-approved consent. No information was released to the general public. Sanctions had been imposed against the Europeans as far as mining and tourism, which Jason agreed with. However, something in the back of his mind told him that the Europeans had come out on top in this one.

Jason arrived at his office at 8:25 a.m. He quickly loaded his briefpack with pertinent files and hurried off to the meeting. He assumed that the meeting was about the construction of Jupiter Platform, but he kept an open mind as he entered the room. As he approached the table, the U.S. director of operations Robert Milroy turned toward him.

"Jason, how are you? Haven't seen you this much this week, so how are things?" he said as he extended his hand. Jason spent most of his time doing research and preparation and wasn't on the floor as often as Bob was. Jason nodded, shook his hand, and took the seat to Bob's left.

"Any idea what this is about, Bob?" Jason asked as he put his briefpack on the table and shifted his attention to Bob.

"Nope, not a clue, I got a call yesterday and had to come back from New York early for this. Got in about nine last night," Bob replied.

Jason nodded. The door on the left of the room opened, and the big six of the Committee walked in: Representative Yangimata of Japan, Representative Jordan of the UK, Representative Misner of the European Alliance, Representative Petrov of Russia, Representative Chang of China, and the United States Representative Alan Todd, they took their seats.

"Gentlemen," Representative Misner began. "You're here today to be briefed in the latest decision as to the colonization of Mars. As you know, there has been a lot of lobbying as to the establishment of an explorative mission to Mars. Ten years ago, we produced the launcher package and the space exploratory module, which allowed us to establish the Luna Port and the Lunar Starr on the Moon. Mars port and Jupiter station are under construction, and we are pushing further out to the other lunar satellites and the belt. It is 2028, and it's time that we turn our attention to establishing a permanent presence on a planetary surface, i.e. Mars. There have been many proposals as to establishing a base on the surface. However, without a return vehicle and a adequate plan, these people would be marooned on the surface for an indefinite period of time. Also, there is no reason to go, without a manned landing and exploration of the surface. If we should land on the surface, because of the planet's orbit the crew that will go will be there for a minimum of two years. There have been proposals suggesting to implant an investigative group on the surface and to drop supplies to them at regular intervals. Then eventually have them construct or modify a vehicle for a return flight from Mars. However, these ideas have been disputed because there are no guarantees or dates as to when this could be accomplished. Without this, we as a governing party have not been able to give consent to this plan. Up until very recently, this has been a thorn in our foot. However, now a proposal has been suggested, and we are of accord—Representative Todd." Misner sat down, and Todd rose from his seat and cleared his throat.

"The points Representative Misner made are valid. We cannot ask free citizens to be doomed on a foreign planet with a small or perhaps no chance of returning to Earth. The whole idea is just too much of a gamble, and there are too many unknown variables. If things go wrong, and we can't for some reason retrieve them, they will be doomed to live out the rest of their lives in conditions which we can only guess at. It's true that we have entirely mapped Mars and we have the Mars Platform in orbit around the Martian moon of Deimos. We have as yet been unable to access the surface except by probes which only give us limited information. As Representative Misner stated, a proposition has been approved for the surface exploration of Mars." As Todd said this, Jason could feel the air in the room grow a little tense with anticipation.

"Basically, the proposal is to establish the first exploration of Mars from criminals serving prison sentences here on Earth." There was a faint rumbling among the crowd.

"We have given consent to the interested parties to choose and drop three candidates to the surface who are facing terminal charges here on Earth, in other words, death row or life inmates." Todd paused slightly to let the impact sink in. You could hear people shifting in their seats as they glanced around the table attempting to gauge the reaction of the others.

"Each of the six Committee groups will select a representative who will be responsible for picking and screening three candidates. Let me stress this," Todd paused again, twisting the cap on his pen. "We are not looking for serial killers or psychotics. We are looking for educated people who could be trained fairly easily. They need to be basically psychologically stable and fit enough as far as age and physical condition to make the trip. Also, the selection in the first manned mission is to be exclusively men. In the future, women may be used to implement the colonization, if that should become a reality. As compensation for their commitment, we will authorize payment of a basic service wage for the time spent on Mars and in preparatory training. If they never return to this planet, they will have no need of the money. The compensation will be paid to a designated recipient of their choice here on Earth."

Todd reached down and picked up a manila envelop that was on the table.

"This is the file pack for the mission and contains the contracts and stipulations. The supply vehicles will be staged to drop from the Mars port station every two years. They will be supplied with a full complement of supplies and facilities, including transportation and exploratory vehicles and tools. The objective of the first mission is to determine the feasibility of a colony, the location, investigation of pre-designated sites, and general exploratory work. Now, on a more somber note, if for some reason that it is determined that Mars is uninhabitable. The project will be terminated and the three individual members may be marooned on the planet for an extended length of time. We will of course continue to supply them and work on a way to retrieve them, and who knows maybe in the future, they will be able to return to Earth." Todd held up the manila envelope as a secretary passed out copies around the tables."

"In this package is the basic timetable and pertinent data of the project, including our legal stance and the forms required. Now, let me say that this project is a closed-mouth project. In other words, we would wish to avoid the news and the attention for right now and the hype that would be involved by public disclosure at this time. So, before talking to potential candidates, make sure that your picks fit the enclosed profiles. After the project is explained, the candidates will have to be interned in a separate facility, regardless whether they accept or not. We intend to make a public announcement over the WGNN, a short time prior to the candidates going into space. The actual time of the launch is yet to be determined. However, our window is approximately one year from now. Most of that time is required for training, and we'd like to have a little more. Out of the eighteen candidates that are selected, three will be picked for this first mission, some will be processed out and replaced, and the rest will continue training until it is decided when and if they are to go, are there any questions?" Todd said, looking around.

A delegate from the Asian consortium stood up, either Japanese or Korean, Jason couldn't tell which.

"Suppose, something does go wrong and let's say the transport vehicle gets hit by a meteor or crashes on landing, is there a backup plan?" Mr. Yangimata, the Asian representative, fielded the question.

"The selected individuals will be transported in a craft which has been specially designed for this mission; it's a modified XPLM. There is a second unmanned vehicle in orbit which can be brought in if needed. Also, this offer to the candidates is strictly voluntary, and they don't have to accept. They will be spending some preparation time prior to the mission at the Mars Platform until the drop sequence for the journey to the Martian surface is approved. Supply vessels have been dropping supplies to the surface for the last five years successfully. Such an incident as a crash landing hopefully will not occur. We would have a problem trying to explain sending another three volunteers. Activists would be screaming about their human rights. However the XPLM is the most sophisticated space vehicle ever built, and we have great confidence in the engineering and construction of the vehicle."

There was a mutual agreement about this from the rest of the delegates seated at the table. Jason thought that this was because the Lunar Starr, which was created by these vehicles, had been successful.

"Any more questions?" asked Todd. "Further details will be sent to you shortly. The meeting was adjourned, and Jason and Milroy left the room. As they were leaving the building, Bob turned to him and said,

"Jason, this is your baby. I need you to do a good job, and I want you to keep me apprised of your progress on a regular basis."

"Yes, sir, I'll do my best, sir," Jason replied.

Five days later, Jason had read all seventy-five cases the FBI had sent him and had narrowed his picks down to ten. Tomorrow, he would be on his way to Leavenworth Kansas. It seems military training was a profile plus. In Leavenworth, there was an ex-marine pilot, who was convicted of killing his wife's lover in a fight and was sentenced to die in three months. Next stop would be San Quentin; he had two inmates to see there: one who had murdered his wife and the other who had shot and killed a clerk in a holdup. He called Milroy and advised him of the schedule.

"Okay, Jason, let's hope we find three that will accept the deal. In short order, this thing gives me the creeps. A Justice Department agent is going to meet you in Kansas to handle the negotiations with the legal department. He has the full authority of the president, a clinical psychiatric profiler I'm told, and he'll be working with you throughout this project. So try to get along and make friends."

Jason didn't have a reply to this but thanked Milroy just the same.

Chapter 2

The Pick

The next day, he was on a plane to Kansas. He arrived at the Kansas airport sometime after 2:00 p.m. and proceeded to claim his baggage. He was waiting for his bag to come around when a voice came from behind him.

"Jason Greene, I'm Special Agent Morris, Department of Justice." Jason turned around to find a rather attractive brunette standing behind him with her hand outstretched.

"I have a car waiting." She turned, extending her arm pointing toward the door. Although her appearance was quite taking, there was something in her voice that told Jason this girl was all business. Jason picked up his bag and followed her through the exit onto the street. It was late September now but quite a change from the temperature from Montreal. The sun shone brightly in what must have been 80 degree weather. He was about to mention that fact to make conversation, when he realized that she probably had just arrived here also. Jason placed his bag and briefpack in the backseat and settled himself in the passenger seat.

"I've made accommodations for you at a conservative hotel here in town," she said as she started the car.

"Been here long?" Jason inquired.

"Three days," she replied without looking at him.

"I've already met with the warden and the state Supreme Court judges and have worked out the details of the transfer if needed with them. Including the cover stories for the press, they promised full cooperation. I'm staying at the same hotel. I'd like to ask you a few questions about your picks and go over your paperwork tonight. I'd like to present a unified front as far as the procedure, which we can use to present the proposal. I want the 'pick' to feel we have their best interest at heart."

"Something like good cop bad cop?" asked Jason, smiling slightly.

"Not quite, understand something, Mr. Greene. We will be dealing with people that have committed the ultimate crime, the taking of life, regardless of why they did it. You know everybody's got a story, whether it was a moment of rage or a situation they couldn't deal with. Or just a situation that accidentally presented itself and that the taking of life was their only way out. The act, in my mind is still the same, whether premeditated or not, and I don't feel sorry for them. The fact that they have justified their actions in their own mind prior to committing the action shows that they have no consideration for life or the society that they live in. My society, the one which I am sworn to protect and serve for the betterment of all parties involved. I feel that turnabout in this regard is fair play. Most of the people that knew their victims, believe that they should pay the ultimate price for what they've done. If they had not been caught, they would be living out their lives attempting to be normal and convincing other people that they are good normal people."

"Now, your people have developed this program by which you're going to make them into heroes, instead of receiving the punishment they deserve. So let's understand something here. I'm not mad at your people. Your program is born out of necessity, but don't expect me to go soft with these people. They have been judged guilty of their crimes, and that thought will not leave my mind. Now, there's a small quaint restaurant nearby the hotel. We'll meet there for dinner tonight, say around seven? I have some calls to make first."

She turned and glanced at Jason.

"How can I refuse a date for dinner with attractive women on my first night in town?" Jason replied.

She smiled slightly. "All right, Mr. Greene, seven it is, I'll meet you in the lobby."

They pulled up at the front door. Jason nodded okay and picked up his briefpack and suitcase out of the backseat. He picked up his key at the desk and took the elevator upstairs to the room. The hotel was old, probably built before the turn of the century and had no direct link for the briefpack. It's a good thing that briefpacks have a wireless modem built into them. Jason dialed up the WGNN link to the council to check any recent developments and checked with his office link for messages. There was one from Milroy, telling Jason to let him know of any developments.

The Asians and the Europeans had already selected their first candidate. He decided to shower and shave and catch the evening news on the miniature wallboard that came with the room. It was only 32″ wide, not much in comparison to the five foot board he had in his office. Two hours later, he met Agent Morris, whose first name was Joanne, in the lobby. She was conservatively dressed in a suit and jacket. Thoughts of a pleasant evening left Jason's mind in a hurry. They left the hotel, crossed the street, and entered a small Tex-Mex restaurant a few doors up. They sat down and waitress approached with two glasses of water and the complementary salsa and chips with their menus.

"Do you know what you want? Or do you need a few minutes?" Joanne asked. "I've been here before, the enchiladas are good."

"A few seconds," replied Jason. He decided to take her advice and ordered the combination plate.

"I don't think you gave the program the benefit of the doubt when you said that we're going to make these people heroes," Jason stated. "I mean, the people will know that the individuals are convicted criminals and that as punishment they are being exiled to a hostile planet. You're not giving the people credit for their God-given intelligence."

"Those convicts," Joanne defended, "will be exposed to massive media coverage. From the time the mission is announced till the time that they should die on the surface of Mars. In the beginning, the media will expose the details of their assorted crimes in every format available. During the seven months it takes them to get to Mars port, every facet of their life will be examined. Psychologists will be drawing conclusions, pointing out Freudian concepts as to what made them commit their crimes and justifications of their actions, bringing up the age-old point that society, as a whole, could be responsible for their crimes. By the time they land on Mars, the media will have them painted in an entirely different light. The fact that they will be the first members of mankind on a foreign planet will portray them, in many people's minds, as heroes."

Joanne paused as the food was delivered.

Jason started to say something, but Joanne held up her hand until after the waitress left. As soon as she was out of earshot, Jason said

"I think the fact that they are convicts, and the fact that they are being sent there as an alternative to execution would be enough to put a sizeable ding on their armor."

"The press is going to make those people martyrs, and regardless whether they live or die, they will go down in history. Children in the future will have to memorize their names for tests, statues will be erected to them, towns named after them, and God knows if they discover anything, it will probably be named after them too. Now, shut up and eat your food." Jason grasped the idea that Joanne really wasn't particularly happy with this assignment but, he let the subject drop, remembering what Milroy had said about keeping things friendly. After dinner, they went back to the hotel.

"Before we drive out to Leavenworth tomorrow, I'd like to see your work and draw up an outline. I'll meet you in your room in twenty minutes. This guy at San Quentin who killed his wife in a deliberate act, is he your third pick?" Joanne asked.

"Not necessarily, why, you have someone else in mind?" Jason asked.

"See you in twenty minutes," she said as she left the elevator. She headed toward her room as Jason headed to his. He set the briefpack up on the small table which had two chairs located in the corner of the room by the window. Shortly afterward, there was a knock on the door. Joanne entered briefpack in hand, and set it up on the table.

"Your people sure know how to pick 'em," Jason retorted. "This hotel is the definition of no frills, not even a link jack."

"I picked this hotel. It's standard operating procedure in cases like this. The less information that goes over the link, the better, and I picked this hotel for that and other reasons. But there is a jack on the bottom of the wallboard, it's an old-style plug-in type," Joanne replied.

"Okay, let's get down to it. Tomorrow is the first pick. I've read his profile: ex-pilot shot the wife's lover, act of rage. He's okay in my book. However, I've got a question about the two in San Quentin. I like this pick in Texas as the second. He shot and killed his boss when he was fired, also an act of rage, but I have a question about his ability to react correctly when things don't go his way. My third pick is this Samuel Johnson in the New Mexico State Penitentiary. He shot and killed his neighbor over a dispute, also military training as a Marine. As for two in San Quentin, the one who killed his wife, which was a premeditated act," Joanne paused and looked at Jason.

"I didn't pick the wife killer," she continued. "He had previous medical experience, three years as an EMT. His training means that he knew what he was doing. I picked this Robert Dunn in Attica instead, the holdup candidate because he's a college graduate with good grades in math and not necessarily was the holdup shooting a premeditated act. You would have to prove that he entered the store with the intention of killing the clerk, which may not be the case."

"I've read the police report about the holdup. The robbery was drug related, and he had a string of priors for drugs before the holdup," Jason pointed out.

"Well, he's not going to be doing a lot of drugs up there on Mars," replied Joanne. This got a visible laugh out of Jason.

"Point taken, all right, it's your call."

"So what's it going to be after Leavenworth: San Quentin or New Mexico next? I hope that we find the three we need without having to interview much more than five. The cover story will hold water only if it's not questioned too closely. The more people involved, the harder it will be to cover," Joanne pointed out.

"New Mexico's fine with me," Jason fired back. They went over a few more details and made arrangements for breakfast tomorrow morning before Joanne said good night.

Jason met Joanne the next morning in the lobby. They had a short breakfast at nine, and then he accompanied Joanne to the car. The trip to the penitentiary took about thirty minutes. Joanne instructed Jason with directions to the warden's office. The warden was a short, stout man and rose to greet them. He and Joanne went over a few details, and the warden promised full cooperation. He then called for a guard to show then to the conference room. Joanne gave him the name of the person they wanted to see, one John Alexander. Jason agreed that Joanne would go first in the interview, so he settled down with a magazine to pass the time. He saw when Alexander was brought in. About thirty minutes later, Joanne appeared and signaled him to come in the room. They took their seats.

"Agent Greene, I've explained the offer to Mr. Alexander, and he has agreed to the terms but would like to hear a little more about the details. Mr. Alexander; Mr. Greene represents the International Space Administration. They are the sponsors of the program. He will go over the details with you, Mr. Greene," Joanne said, pointing to a chair.

Alexander was now staring at him. Jason started,

"Okay, here's the deal. After you sign the contract, you will be transferred from this location to the NASA Space Center where you will be interned into the ISA training program for this mission. You will learn a large amount of information of various fields, which you will have to memorize, including languages. While you are in training, you will be under ISA regulations and supervision. Remember that we can cancel the agreement at any time, if things don't work the way we want them to go. If you are chosen for the mission, you will be compensated for your training and your time on Mars and a participation basic award paid as soon as you go into space, as specified in the contract. When you launch to Mars, you will launch from the Luna Starr. Within a week, the payment will be issued to you in the amount of $1,000,000 USD tax free. You may either have this amount placed in account for you or you can have the award transferred to another party like family or friends. When you get to Mars, you will be required to perform certain tasks to complete your end of the contract. You will be on the planet's surface for at least six years, perhaps longer, that point has not been settled as of yet. However, you will be reinvested for your time of good conduct at the rate of $250,000 per year. This means, that if you return to Earth alive in six years, this deal represents to you 2.5 million dollars tax free. Also, you will receive a pardon for your previous crimes here on Earth. There is also a clause in the contract that specifies a payment of $1,000,000 dollars in case of death. I know that this is a sudden turn of events, so we will give you twenty-four hours to consider the details. We will return tomorrow for your answer. If, for any reason, you violate the terms during training, you will be returned to custody here to serve the rest of your sentence, any questions?"

John looked down at the floor and shook his head.

"Oh, and one more thing," Jason continued. "Tonight you will be placed in solitary confinement, and you are not to mention this event or any details to anyone, understood? Not even the guards."

John nodded, and Joanne reached in her briefpack and handed John the packet. They said good-bye to the warden and proceeded back to the hotel. The next day, they had another meeting with John.

John sat down and handed the packet to Joanne, who went over the details.

"I see that you want the participation award to go to your son in trust, starting in payment at the age of eighteen. How old is your son now?" Joanne inquired.

"He's fourteen. I really feel bad about the way things worked out. I won't be there when it's time for him to go to college. But going to Mars is better than my fate here. You guys really know how to play hardball."

"I also see that you would be obligated to pay some type of child support if you weren't on death row, so we will take care of that as well," affirmed Joanne.

Joanne called for the warden to serve as witness, and the contract was signed. Joanne and Jason left for New Mexico the next morning; the procedure was pretty much the same in all the other interviews, and in two weeks' time, they had their three contracts signed. The candidates were held in solitary confinement until they were transported to the training facility at the NASA Space Center in Florida.

Chapter 3

The Prep

The alarm clock chimed; it was seven o'clock again. Jason shifted around and then rose from the bed, heading to the bathroom. Today was an important day, and he had to be up and on the mark. He had a ten o'clock plane to catch to take him to the NSC (NASA Space Center) for a meeting with the trainers of the Mars Mission. During the past months, eight of the convicts have been undergoing training for the mission, and now it was time to pick the three that would be going to Mars. In order to qualify for the program, they had to take a battery of tests, including IQ, creativity, mechanical aptitude, physical, intelligence, psychiatric, and memory. The project had started with eighteen candidates—Russian, Asian, English, European, and American. One by one, they were sorted out to leave just eight candidates remaining. Two of the candidates Jason had interviewed were still in the running John Alexander and Samuel Johnson. Shower done, clothes on, he staggered out to the kitchen and popped open the auto cooker to remove the morning meal consisting of: eggs, hash browns, bacon, coffee, toast, and orange juice. Everything was ready in the auto cooker, which cooked the meal completely, to be served at a desired time. In his case 7:10 a.m., except for the toast which he did himself, because he liked it hot to melt the butter.

He caught the tram downstairs to the airport. Forty minutes later, he was boarding the plane. The standard security search was waived because of his status. His ISA (International Space Administration) card pulled a lot of weight, including hotel and the transportation which he would be acquiring in Florida. The trip was uneventful as he arrived in Florida right before lunch. He decided to wait and grab something for lunch at the hotel. Maybe he could go swimming that afternoon. It certainly was hot enough, and he didn't meet with the training crew till tomorrow, although he still had to pick up the car.

At nine the next day, he arrived at the training station, which was within a stone's throw from the NASA Administration Building and checked in at the security desk. A few minutes later, a man approached and introduced himself as Michael Dunstan, the head of the training program.

"We need you to take a look over what we got here and give us your opinion as to who's best qualified to go. We've got it down to the top five, but what concerns us is the grouping: two are Americans, two Russian, and one Asian. All have learned to speak the three languages involved. The Asian, Hitu Ashita, who specializes on electronic systems, is Japanese. One of the Russians is from the Ukraine former Russian Navy specialist in mechanical applications. But the other is from the Chechnya, a Russian Army veteran. They won't be going together. So, how well the others react to them is the decider in this case. I understand that you interviewed John Alexander last year and know his history. We think he is the correct choice for mission commander, partly because of his pilot experience and military training. This bumps the Chechnyan, Yuri Olesky. We don't need two mission commanders. The other American is Samuel Johnson, specialization systems integration, also former military training. We want you to fill in the blank for us."

"Well, I'll do my best, but sounds to me like you have already filled in the blanks. Set up an interview with the men, and I'll talk to them." Jason replied. Three hours later, he had already interviewed the Ukrainian, the Asian, and Samuel Johnson, who seemed in better spirits from the last time Jason had talked to him. The door opened, and John Alexander stepped in and nodded at Jason. Jason gestured to the seat; Alexander sat down.

Jason started, "Well John, you look better than the last time I saw you."

John smiled. "Well, the food's better," he replied.

"Let's get right to the point. The ISA is looking for a decision as to who is going on the first launch and who is going to be in charge. The staff recommended you for both. You'll be 6.5 months or 195 days in space prior to reaching Mars, where you'll dock with the Mars Platform on Diemos. You will stay at Diemos station until the location and approach pattern is verified and the entry command is given. Your vehicle information as well as your landing site location is set in the navcomm guidance and navigation system control, so there won't be a lot of actual piloting involved unless there is a problem. Now, I have already affirmed Samuel Johnson for one of the other two positions. This means there's one space open. The council wishes to have this team reflex international cooperation, so I have three candidates recommended by the staff here, the Chechnyan Yuri Olesky, the Ukrainian Alex Gorkov, and the Asian Hitu Ashita from Japan, any thoughts on the subject?"

John looked up and then said, "Look, you're sending us to die as far as all things considered rates. It will take around seven months to get there and a month to slow down and confirm the site before the drop. And when we land on the surface, we will be completely on our own, depending on periodic drops of supplies to keep us alive. If something does go wrong, it will take the same seven months for any help of any kind to be able to reach us. Now, according to the contract I signed, it stated that among other things, the ISA will keep us well supplied, but there are so many things that can go wrong. However, that's not what bothers me."

"Okay, exactly what bothers you, John?" Jason asked.

"Well, just the fact that there is no plan to get us back and that any time someone down here gets tired of feeding the criminals on Mars, all they have to do is quit sending supplies. The press release might say that there was an explosion or something and we all died. Nobody would be the wiser, and there we would be starving to death on Mars."

Jason got up from his chair and went over to look out the window.

"John, you know this program was offered to inmates who were serving a life sentence or death row convictions. And the compensation for the mission is a good rate. In your case, I believe you requested that the money go to your son, right?" John nodded.

"Well, would you rather not go? I mean the decision is up to you. If you don't want to go, we will stop it right here and you can go back to jail and rot in a holding cell instead. Like I said, it's up to you. We are four months' away from the launch. In one month, the 'GO' team must be picked. Forty-five days before the launch, the press will be told, and the crew will be celebrities for a month, living it up, so to speak. Hell, you'll be on TV and the media. You'll get to spend some time with your son, here at the base of course. But that is, if you are picked to go."

Jason turned to look at John.

"Look, I know it's going to be tough. You and the other members of the crew will be together for at least six years, if not longer. You'll have to depend on each other. It would be better if you were friends or at least got along. Or you can simply opt out and go back to your cell and stare at the four walls until you can't look at them any more. Now, I leave here in a week. I'll need your answer and recommendation by then. Oh, and as far as a plan to get you back home, I understand they are working on that, and I understand they have something, so?"

"You won't have to wait that long. I'll go, I want to go," John said rising from his chair.

"And do you know where I'll be going?" he said as he shook hands with Jason.

"To Mars, I hope," Jason replied.

"Let's just say into the wild blue yonder." John smiled and left the room.

"The wild blue yonder, huh? Never quite thought of it that way," Jason said to himself. Even though these people were criminals and not to be respected by society, Jason found himself gaining a different kind of respect for the people who would be picked to be the first crew. They would be going to a place where no one had gone before and asked to endure harsh and uncustomary conditions and hardships for an unspecified length of time, perhaps dying in the process. They will be the first men on Mars.

But beyond all that, Joanne was right. They would become heroes, and their names would go down in the history books regardless how the mission turned out. The children of the future would have to memorize their names. It was a fact that this mission would become a historic event.

Jason had a couple of days left before he was expected back in Montreal and with not much to do. He decided to sit in and attend a few classes with the candidates. The next afternoon, he went down the hallway till he came to the classroom and opened the door. The course was just starting, and the instructor was giving a review of recent history. He found a seat near John and sat down. The instructor had noticed his entrance and paused momentarily.

"Mr. Greene, can we help you with something?"

"I just thought I sit in and try to get some education," Jason replied with a smile on his face.

"Okay," the instructor replied, "Welcome. Last week, we discussed operational systems and their components. This week we're going to discuss Cryogenics, Cryogenic production, power requirements, storage, uses, propagations, and attributes.

Cryogenics is the process of converting a gas into a liquid and refers to gases below −150° Centigrade and lower. As you can guess, the process of converting a gas into a liquid state has to do with two functions, temperature and pressure. Any gas can be turned into a liquid by lowering its temperature, but there are some gases that are essential for life in space. These gases are HeHOxN (hey oxen) which is a comment you might say to a group of oxen standing along side a road. However, it stands for Helium, Hydrogen, Oxygen, and Nitrogen. We give them in this way because they are given in rating from the coldest in cryogenic temperature to the warmest. For instance, the melting temperature for Helium is –272°C; Hydrogen is –259°C, Oxygen at –218 °C, and Nitrogen at –210 °C. For those of you who need a Fahrenheit translation, that's Helium and Hydrogen at –400°F and oxygen and nitrogen at –300°F, which is very cold but not as cold as space, which, to our best estimate, is three Celsius degrees above absolute zero or –275° Centigrade or –455°Fahrenheit. Absolute zero is where molecular activity is said to stop. Helium is our coldest cryogenic gas, but you say, why do we need helium? We can't breathe it, so what's its purpose?

"When cryogenic liquid is produced, such as Oxygen or LOX, which we also use to ignite propellant fuel, it needs to be stored in a container that keeps it below –361.82 degree Fahrenheit. In order to do this, we use a device known as a Dewar's flask, more commonly known as a thermos. However, these thermoses are a little more sophisticated than the ones you use to store hot coffee in. They are pressure seal vessels that operate with the use or three main components: a double cylinder, a glass reflective interior, and a vacuum. The vacuum in this case is the main operator, invented in the last half of the 1800s, when a Scottish physicist named James Dewar noticed he could retain liquid nitrogen longer by containing it in a vacuum shield. This has been the method of cryogenic storage for over the last two hundred years."

"On Earth, it doesn't stop expansion of the gas completely but it will slow down the natural temperature heating. Up until a few years ago, no improvements were made in the basic structure of the Dewar's flask. After about three days, the gas starts to expand, causing a problem. Pressure release valves were incorporated to stop the gas canisters from exploding. Then when the engineers who designed the current modules looked over the design, they realized something. In space, keeping things at that temperature of –260°C is not a problem. In some cases, you have to stir the cryogenic canisters to keep the liquid from freezing into an unusable block."

"The Mars Mission will put you on the Martian surface where even though the average temperature is –120 degrees Fahrenheit, it's not enough to keep oxygen in a liquid form forever. So a system needed to be developed to re-cool the LOX, and here's where we come to this device known as the Sterling engine."

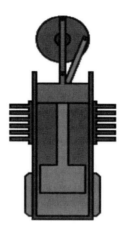

"The Sterling engine is a sealed one cylinder engine which produces heat on one side and cold on the other. This understanding is important because it and a few other components are used to heat the inside of your module. By taking the LOX out of its canister and running it to the cold side of a Sterling engine. You can achieve a re-cooling of the liquid and re-pressurization of the cryogenic canister, thus prolonging its storage life of the cryogenic gas. While the cold side is cooling the cryogenics, the warm side is supplying heat to the module's interior. Normally, on Earth, the heat is vented into the air, but you're going to need that heat in space."

"When the Mars Module designers realized that you're going to need several cryogenic canisters up on Mars and that re-pumping them would be a big time maintenance concern, they decided to design an alteration of the Dewar's flask and the adaptive handler. This system works on just one canister but services all of them. These new Dewar's flask canisters have another vacuum or a double vacuum system instead of just one. Inside this second vacuum is a coil that wraps around the cryogenic containment tank. There is an inlet and outlet valve that attaches to the Sterling engine and the air handler. The system can attach to several tanks at the same time. When the liquid starts gaining heat, the system auto starts pumping liquid helium from the helium containment canister. Since cryogenic helium is 40°C colder than Oxygen. This process of re-cooling the Oxygen is a rapid cooling technique. The other tanks such as those of Hydrogen and Nitrogen can be cooled by this process as well. The only canister you have to worry about is the Helium canister, which when it gets to the end or the line is re-cooled by a second Sterling engine. The order of the re-cooling canisters is hey oxen. Making nitrogen last after exiting the nitrogen canister the helium is re-cooled and restored in its cryogenic canister. The hoses that are used in this system are Dewar's hose lines, a relatively new product."

"The module that is going to Mars has two tanks located on the bottom of the module which will contain eight hundred gallons of liquid Oxygen a piece. This is not fuel Oxygen. This is the Oxygen you will use to breathe during your trip. First, a living person needs 550 L of normal non cryogenic Oxygen per day when at rest. That is equivalent to 14.5 gallons of normal oxygen per day. Over a period of a year's time, it would be fifty-three thousand gallons per year per person. One liter of cryogenic Oxygen is equivalent to 860 liters of breathable oxygen at 20°C (or 68 degrees Fahrenheit). You have a difference here of about three hundred liters, but let's think of this as every person uses one Cryo liter per day."

The instructor reached down and picked up three one-liter bottles, two were clear probably containing water, and one was a pale blue, probably a vegetable die. He picked up the light blue bottle.

"Suppose this is one liter of cryogenic oxygen. It will create 860 liters of breathable air. Over a period of one year, you will require 365 liters of liquid Oxygen, which is equivalent to 96 gallons of LOX per person. The Mars Module is designed for three people, so your yearly consumption of cryogenic Oxygen would be 288 cryo gallons, and over a six-year period, it would come to 1,728 gallons of cryogenic Oxygen. The storage tanks hold eight hundred gallons of cryogenic oxygen apiece or sixteen hundred cryo gallons total. Cryogenic Oxygen weighs approximately 9.5 pounds per gallon. This gives the cryogenic lift weight with tanks at sixteen thousand pounds. That amount of Oxygen under ideal conditions would last a crew of three for the entire six years, with hydroponics and electrolysis which are essential, perhaps longer."

"But you also need this," he said, holding up the two one-liter bottles of water. "Water is the most important substance in space. Not only is it required that we drink two liters per day minimum, but it also through electrolysis can be used to produce Oxygen and Hydrogen. When you do, you will produce twice as much Hydrogen as Oxygen, hence H_2O. In other words, it requires three gallons of water to produce one gallon of Oxygen and two gallons of Hydrogen. In order to supply enough Oxygen for a day for one person you must process 42 gallons of water. There was a scientific study of water consumption that makes the point that human consumption of water should be at a minimum of one half US gallon per day. This includes all beverages: coffee in the morning, juice, soda, tea, and just plain water. Half gallon per day is 182.5 gallons per year. For a crew of three, it would be required to supply 547.5 gallons a year. Water has a weight on Earth of about 8.35 pounds per gallon. Over a period of six years, a crew of three would require 3,285 gallons, which would have an Earth weight equivalent to 27,922 pounds. So, as you can see, 16,000 lbs of cryo Oxygen and 27,900 lbs of water result in 43,900 lbs. This is a minimum requirement weight. Actually, the payload weight for the Mars Module is seventy thousand pounds. However, there is also something else you need, and that's food. The average person consumes two and a half pounds of nutrients or food a day or 912.5 pounds per year. Multiply that by a crew of three equals 2,737.5 lbs of food per year. Over a period of six years, it will be equivalent to 16,425 lbs."

"Now while you are in a weightless condition in space, you will not cook as much as you will want to, mainly because cooking in space is messy. That's why the kitchen has sealed doors and a filtering system. Once a drop of anything gets out of the kitchen, it will float around indefinably. When you reach the surface of Mars, you will have a gravity which will hold your coffee in a cup rather than floating around in the module. Your module is equipped with a device called an auto cooker and a microwave oven which will allow you to cook on the Martian surface and certain products in a weightless environment. The microwave will cook food and beverages in a specialized device called a weightless cup. However, there will also be paste, lots of paste, and other approved weightless snacks like power bars, nutrient bars, and granola. Now, some of this food will be pre-installed in the module, and some will be dropped at a later date. Nitrogen is also an essential element: common air is 78 percent, nitrogen 21 percent, oxygen. When we breathe we extract the Oxygen but we don't affect the Nitrogen which contain trace elements including some Hydrogen and Carbon Dioxide gases."

"Your air handling system handles the mix of the air. Your air handler system is the major component of your life support system. There are other components systems that are equally important included in the life support system. You need to learn these other component systems as well."

The class went on like this for a while. The instructor demonstrated liquid nitrogen and its effects and explained that tomorrow they would be going to the shop to build a Sterling engine and a few other thermocouple devices. He instructed them to read about the air handler and the life support systems and what they had gone over today. The class lasted about three hours but definitely gave you the impression that you had learned something for the time spent.

Chapter 4

Back to School and the News

Jason returned to Montreal at the end of the week and filed his recommendation report with the ISA processing division. He had a meeting with the boss the next day.

Not so much a meeting but a debriefing over lunch. They met at 1:00 p.m. in the Committee cafeteria, and Jason ordered the daily special.

"Well, how did it go?" Bob asked as they waited for their food to arrive.

"It went okay, a couple of rough spots that needed a little sanding, other than that not much to report."

Milroy seemed on edge, and Jason was wondering why.

"You still are going with this John Alexander for mission commander on number 1?"

Jason nodded; there was still an edge in Milroy's tone.

"Ah, Bob, what's going on? You're acting as if there is instability between space and time that you're wrestling with."

Bob looked down; he was polishing the fork with a napkin, something he did you know.

"In the week you have been gone, the council has had a few meetings. Since there is a security cap over the mission, I wasn't allowed to send any of the information over the air to you. They suggested I wait for you to return before I said anything, that way there would be no chance of an unauthorized leak. The mission topic has come to a head with just six weeks till the pick of team 1. There is a large support for a fully international crew. Both the Russians and the Chinese are upset. The Chinese are even more upset because they don't have a candidate in the first mission selection. We tried to explain that the crew will be picked by the candidate's qualifications, not the sponsorship, but that didn't really appease them. So, we had to guarantee them a candidate on second lift if there is one. I would think that the approved mission language to be English, but I've been told 'not necessarily.' I may have to fight for it. This may mean a cram language session for John."

"Well, that's okay. John's not stupid. He has shown good learning skills during training. Besides, they will have six months to learn how to talk to each other. He should be able to pick it up, whatever it is," Jason replied.

"Well, you know some languages are harder to learn than others, but there is something else. One of the cargo modules has been, what we believe, struck by a meteor. Information about how much damage is involved is not disclosed, but evidently it knocked out the control robotics and punctured one of the fuel tanks. It put the module off course, heading for a round view of the asteroid belt. The hull has been repaired by the automated hull repair droid. However, because of the fuel that was lost, the module has only enough fuel to turn itself around and will follow the Martian orbital path. There is, from what I understand, a plan to have it alter course and cross over to the other side of the sun to intersect with the Mars Platform in about a year."

Bob hesitated as lunch was delivered.

"Is this a major snag? I mean I know it's a problem, but is it serious enough to cancel or delay the project for another two more years?" questioned Jason.

"As you know, the orbit of Mars makes it impractical to launch vehicles every year. The planet is only within range once every two years. That module contained oxygen and water mainly. If the XPLM is damaged on landing and loses its Oxygen containment, the CMP was the backup, now there is no backup. The lost CMP will now have to cross over the path way to the junction point halfway on the planet's way out. This is why three years ago we launched four CMP modules equipped with specialized equipment to prepare the planet for this mission. Two years ago, we sent another four more modules with equipment based on the findings given by the equipment of the first four. The four CMPs contained drilling and construction parts, machinery and of course food and water. The information gained by these crafts has been beyond our expectations. The second wave was to supply the hardware for the Mars habitat. The module that got hit was the backup that means that right now, there is no backup supply. A cargo module is supposed to accompany the crew module anyway. However, now that module has to be stocked with backup supplies, which will remain in orbit at the Mars Platform. The equipment that has already been dropped contained five 12×12 foot bubble packs per unit of specialized products, some of which have been working on the planet for the last five years, robots as you've probably heard. They have built two landing sites and are currently drilling a large cave in a cliff.

Jason was now staring at Milroy with a blank look on his face.

"Why are they drilling a hole in a mountain? And no, I hadn't heard," Jason replied.

"It's not really a mountain. A cliff is more like it, and they are drilling because the preliminary test results predicted that it was a likely location as a base of exploration. A little south about two hundred miles from our primary target the Valles Marineris. Plus, it will provide protection from the elements and radiation and other concerns."

Jason shifted position.

"I thought that the plan was we were to launch them with a habitat that they would have available to live in."

"We are, and it's going to fit inside the shielded cave that the robots are building now, in other words, a cave with an air lock seal. It will produce a rather large internal structure. This is much more habitable than just a module and has room for the hydroponics. I mean seriously, Jason, you didn't expect them to live for six years in a little metal box, did you? These robots that are on the planet are not small robotic units. They weigh a ton and a half and are built like a four-foot block cube with extendable hydraulic arms and come with a variety of attachable components, including a drilling rotor. It only took them about a month to grind out the landing strip and remove the debris. They are also self functional. They can change out their own bits and change their own batteries, but they are strictly work bots, no intellect."

Jason was now perplexed. Bob had played his hand well and established a dominate position over lunch, but the question in Jason's mind was how were they going to get a module inside a man-made cave but decided to change the subject instead.

"Is there any plan to get them back yet? Because even though we said maybe not, the contract states that we will try. This recently became an issue with some of the personnel."

"Of course, we are going to try to bring them back," Milroy added, "but no guarantees. Just like there are no guarantees, they will get there to begin with. I understand that the company that designed the modules has some kind of plan they are now working on. But I don't know the details, so I'm not going to speculate, and security mandates no disclosure, so mum's the word. Look, we will have another meeting when they announce the crew. I may know more by then."

Jason nodded. It looked like the meeting was over.

Approximately four weeks later, Jason was notified that the crew selection had been made. It was to be John as mission commander, the Alex Gorkov from the Ukraine as Co-operator, and the Asian Hitu Ashita from Japan as mission specialist and technical support engineer because of his knowledge of electronics and computers. Jason had met with Milroy and had been informed that the language selection would be English because all three knew how to speak and understand it. The crew would continue specialized training until the press release in a week.

A week later came press release day, and Jason was expected at the base. Tomorrow afternoon, Bob would be handling things in Montreal, and Jason's job was to keep the press away from the crew at the Cape. It was going to be like a shark feeding frenzy with them. He would be handling a lot of controversial questions, so his answers had to be formed so that they wouldn't be misinterpreted. He was going over the details and wording so that he would give the just the basic information, something that would or could not be taken incorrectly or cause any problems. The phone rang, and it was Milroy. Jason toggled the accept switch, and Milroy's image appeared on the wallboard.

"Director Milroy, I've been expecting your call," Jason said as he looked up from straightening papers.

"I just want to touch base and go over a few things with you before tomorrow. First, you don't let the candidates out of your sight with the press. You will be their 'guard dog' for the next six weeks. You wake them up and put them to sleep. Defiantly, under no circumstances, are you to leave them in a position where the press can talk to them alone. They are not to answer any technical questions about the mission, and they are not to answer any questions about their past life. Make sure they understand this: they are to field all of those questions to you. Also, you are not to say anything about a return plan. You're to say that they are on a four year mission and will be returning in six years but that you don't know the details at this time. Okay, any questions?"

Jason remembered what John said at the launch site and realized he may not want to be with the program in six years when they didn't come back.

"No, I've got it pretty well, check me. They are going for six plus years. They will be building a permanent habitat structure on the planet's surface and doing exploratory work on the Martian surface. They will be in constant communication with the Luna Starr and Earth station control. Most of the supplies have already been transported, but more will be sent in intervals every two years. They will always have more than they can use and ah, we are expecting good things. How do you intend to handle their police records because that's going to be a main issue?" Jason asked.

"Drop the plus it is six years period. Don't worry about that when the release goes off tomorrow, for it will contain all the information that they need to have. The ISA council heads are going to tape an interview session where their personal stories are presented in an edited version, doctored, and a representative from each government will be there to answer the questions, including your friend Joanne from the Justice Department. The stories have been doctored pretty well, so it's going to look like they volunteered and were not pressured into the mission. In one case, it says that our Japanese member wasn't in for murder but instead was serving time for computer embezzlement. John's record, of course, we couldn't change, your girl Joanne wouldn't allow it. Okay, are we clear on the information? And if you get in trouble, just say that it's classified or, better yet, that you're not authorized to speak on that subject."

"Yeah, I guess, and quit calling Joanne my girl. We just had meals together that's all," replied Jason.

Bob laughed. "Okay, give me a call in a couple of days and let me know how it's going down there at the Cape." Jason nodded, and the wallboard clicked off.

Jason was up early the next day. He had a ten o'clock flight to catch and three hours in the air before landing in Florida, which should be around 1:00 pm EST. He thought to have lunch before going to the base and the meeting with the crew. He did not particularly care for the military food at the base, even though it was better than standard.

After lunch, he proceeded to the base and checked with the mission training supervisor, Michael Dunstan. The crew meeting was scheduled for three. And at three, Jason found himself face to face with the crew in a small conference room. He then proceeded to go over the publicity outline that he, Milroy, and the ISA had approved. Jason was sitting on the table as he spoke.

"Let me emphasize that you are to have no unsupervised contact with any people who are not in this room, regardless of what kind of uniform they may be wearing. If questioned, you are to say you don't know and refer them to me. And you are not to discuss your former crimes or circumstances. And by no means are you to mention or in any way refer to the fact that there is no retrievable plan in operation at this time. The people, who are the press, are to believe that you are going on a mission to Mars for six years and will be returning in six years. Understand me, say you don't know the details at this time and refer to me. Now, according to your contract, if that becomes a reality and you do return to Earth, you will be granted a pardon for your crimes and be free men again. Okay, any questions?"

The Russian Alex Gorkov raised his hand, which caught Jason unprepared.

"Just go ahead and ask your question, Alex. You don't have to raise your hand."

Alex shifted in position and said, "What if the President asks me a question, and do I answer it or refer him to you?"

"First of all Alex, the President or upper management personnel are not going to ask any questions," Jason replied. "All nationalities, including yours, have agreed that no questionable information will be offered from them publicly. This will be the protocol policy for the mission, including prior information as of your past. So, when the press asks you how you got chosen don't answer, refer them to me. For that reason, your governments have issued a cover identity and have blocked people who knew you. Here is their statement, memorize them. The announcement of the mission will be on the 6:00 p.m. news here in the United States and won't be actual news till tomorrow, which will give you twenty-four hours to get in tune. From this time on, you will be in a non-communication status, which means no outside communications."

"Now, tomorrow at 3:00 p.m., there will be your first press conference here. The press will take pictures and have a small Q&A session. When I think they got enough I'll end the session, explaining that you still are in training for the mission and that exposure to public media will be limited. Your lift will be in six weeks to the EOP (Earth Orbital Platform), then to the Lunar Starr. For now, concentrate on what you need to know to present a unified credible story."

Jason passed out their cover folders, and the men adjourned to learn their scripts. Jason had dinner at the base, and a room had been provided. At 2:30 the next day, the second meeting with the crew commenced with a general Q&A of the information in the folders. Jason felt it went fairly well, so no problem with the three o'clock conference. They entered the room together and took their seats as they were introduced. Jason stood up and started,

"Hello, my name is Jason Greene, and I am the assistant to the United States director to the ISA. I'm here to answer any questions you may have about the upcoming project expected to start in approximately six weeks, regarding the first manned mission to the surface of Mars."

All the hands went up; Jason picked an attractive-looking female in the front row. "Yes?"

"How long is the project going to last?"

Jason replied, "Approximately six years, next."

"What will the crew live in during this time?"

"The crew will transport to Mars in the artificial habitat module that has been being built for the last two years," Jason replied. "They will leave from Earth to go to the Lunar Starr, where they will board the spacecraft on the Lunar Platform (LP) and then proceed from there to the Mars Platform around Deimos, one of the moons of Mars. The trip is scheduled to take a little over six months, after which time, the habitat will be dropped into the Martian atmosphere to land at the designated landing site on the surface. They then will move the habitat, which also serves as a rover to the assigned location, next."

Jason pointed to a press member he had met before.

"Where is the assigned location, and how far will they have to go to get there?"

"As you probably know, for the last four years, we have been lifting cargo supply modules to Mars. These modules contain supplies: food, water, fuel, support utilities, and also included two robotic construction vehicles. These robots or 'bots' have built in the last four years a landing strip and are currently in the process of drilling a cave in the base of a cliff located approximately two hundred miles from the landing area. The cave is located at the southeastern opening of the Valles Marineris, where the rover habitat will set up shop. The first job will be to install the air lock inside the cave to increase the internal useable space and to serve as an atmospheric seal. The robots will do most of the work, and I understand that they have already finished the opening and have drilled an inner cavity of 100×30 feet. We are still eight months away from the landing, so it is hoped that they will accomplish much more by then, next." Jason then pointed to a portly man he knew worked for the New York Times.

"You said the trip would take six months, and now you say seven months, which is it?"

"They will leave here in six weeks to go to the Lunar Starr, where they will be orientated with the habitat module. They will be there for approximately a week, learning everything they need to know about the craft. They will then go from the Lunar Orbital Platform to Mars Orbital Platform, a trip that will take six months approximately. They will stay on Mars Platform for two to three weeks with the habitat and the accompanying CMP. The CMP will then drop its cargo to the surface. After the CMP drops its supplies, it will be integrated into Mars Platform. Three of the CMP shells will continue on to the Asteroids and Jupiter's moons to start formation of the interplanetary vector web. Then the crew will then drop in the modified module to the surface, next."

The next few questions were to the crew on how they felt about the mission.

The guys stuck to the script until someone asked the Russian Alex how he felt about the mission, to which he replied, "I was happy to have been chosen for this adventure. I am proud to represent my country and my planet on this mission, regardless of what the outcome is. I believe that this exploration is a necessary development in our future, and I am happy to be included."

After a few more questions, Jason called a stop, and the conference was over. The next day, while the crew was attending classes, Jason received a call from Milroy.

"Yeah, what's up?" Jason responded.

Bob seemed a little excited. "We've been barraged with calls, and everybody wants the boys on their TV show. Russia and Japan are sending film crews for a personal interview with the ISA Representatives. We were hesitant at first, but we are going to allow it as long as they are compliant with our pre-specified conditions. Number one, that all film and pictures will be taped and censor edited by us, and that we retain ownership of all publications and images. Also, we will have a translator present during all interviews, which works for us. So, I'm shipping you some extra security to work the crowd control. The translators will be sent by their governments and will probably have a security agent with them. The first interview will be in three days by Japan, and the next day will be the Russians. The interviews will be at the base. Now, the TV shows got a news filler to do, and I've got five talk show requests. The late-night and early-morning shows want an interview with the crew. They will be filmed at the base also. So no one will have to go anywhere. I expect the hype to ease up after about two weeks," said Bob. "Oh, you can expect me at the cape about the same time along with other ISA representatives okay?"

"Two weeks, huh, got an actual date?"

"No, just try to keep things on an even keel so that nobody gives us a funny look," Bob replied.

"Can do out," Jason acknowledged.

And the wallboard went blank. The next two weeks went by pretty fast, thinking back on it. Of course, during the time Jason found himself pretty busy. They were setting up one of the conferences when Jason heard a familiar voice from behind him.

"Getting things together for the big day?"

He turned to see Joanne coming toward him.

"Joanne, hey, what are you doing here?" John replied.

"I'm here to give a psychiatric viewpoint to the mission and the effects that six years of close confinement will have on the mental health of these men."

A look came over Jason's face. "No, don't worry. I've been fully briefed as to what to say and what not to say," she continued. "My bosses and your bosses have stressed to me how important this mission is to everyone concerned and so well, you know."

"You mean you're going to lie?" replied Jason.

"I think the words you're looking for is present a 'restrained credible viewpoint '. Jason, it would be against my moral integrity to straight out lie."

They both smiled as if there was a silent joke.

"So how have you been?" Jason proffered.

"Okay, but it's been a little hectic recently. You know when I signed up for this detail, I don't think I realized how much would be involved and how much the exposure and publicity would affect me. These media people don't leave you alone. They want to talk to me, but I'm as busy as they are. They don't seem to take no for an answer," Joanne replied.

"Well, it will all be over soon," Jason said with a sympathetic tone. After about a week, the media blitz slowed down. Jason was with the crew every day, even attending some of the courses with them. Shortly into the last month, Michael Dunstan approached him.

"I'd like your crew to go with me to hangar 34-B to view the CMP that will be accompanying them before it's loaded. They can talk to some of the engineers, and see the structural design in raw form. Get acquainted with the rail and how to fix it, and so forth. It will take about two days. Can you clear their schedules?"

"Sure, no problem, I'll take care of it right now," Jason replied.

The next day about seven o'clock, Mike showed up at the dining room, where they were having breakfast.

"Okay, is everybody ready to go? The taxi is outside, let's mount up."

It was a five-minute ride to the hanger. As they entered the hanger, they got their first look at a live CMP standing inside. Dunstan started with the vehicle introduction.

"The CMP stands for Cargo Module Prototype. It was designed and developed out of a concept design produced by a company named Altered Atmospheric Design Group, who also designed your XPLM. The XPLM you will be going to the Mars in is a modified version of the XPLM used at the Lunar Starr. The CMPs and the XPLMs are similar in structural design, both inside and out."

"The framework is the same, the internal setup is basically the same, and the systems are about the same. However, the CMP is designed to transport cargo in space, and the XPLM is designed to transport personnel. But don't write the CMPs off, they serve as your hardware store and your emergency rescue stations. Also, in deep space application, it is your only source of assistance. Another capability of CMPs and XPLMs is that they can be linked together to form large multiple unit structures, which can be rotated to develop an effect of artificial gravity. This CMP is being loaded with supplies that will be dropped to your landing site on the Martian surface. The packages that they drop are encased in a bonding structure, which is sealed inside a twelve-foot double sphere or bubble to protect the cargo. The sphere which at this time is not inflated will inflate during the drop sequence, which is controlled by the onboard Navcomm system. The packages once loaded will be placed in the internal framework inside the CMP on a device called the 'rail.' The rail will release the packages one at a time, when directed to do so by the onboard navcomm unit. The water bubbles are wrapped in the triple impact sphere and are five feet in diameter. The water spheres contain 188 cubic feet of water or approximately 1400 U.S. gallons, which weighs 11,600 lbs on Earth. It is enough water for 1.5 years for a crew of three, based on regular daily consumption of half gallon a day.

The Japanese candidate interrupted, "Mr. Dunstan, a bubble that weighs that much, wouldn't it break apart on impact with the surface?"

Dunstan kind of smiled. "To answer your question, you forget that the CMPs drop bay is not pressurized or heated, so the water freezes as soon as it enters space. It makes the trip in a frozen condition inside the sphere, and for the drop, it is contained inside the double sphere, which is highly pressurized. The drop sphere, which is twelve feet in diameter, pressurizes just prior to the drop. The containment sphere has a bounce insert that works like a spring to keep the water sphere stable during the landing. Also, a point to note that 10,000 lbs only weighs 3,800 lbs on Mars however, even so our maximum drop weight is 12,000 lbs Earth weight or 4,560 lbs on Mars. When you leave for Mars, you will have two of these bubbles onboard your XPLM."

"As they explained to you in class, water is the most valuable substance in space. It's your Oxygen and fuel and is something you can not live without. You can't live more than three days without water. Hydrogen which you can get through electrolysis is your fuel cell power supply and the second part of your fuel. A CMP can lift five water spheres (60,000 lbs.). You shouldn't have to worry because there are already two spheres on the surface. CMPs also carry fuel, more fuel than they generally need or use, because they are in no hurry to get to their destination. They are robotic and are not generally in a hurry to get anywhere. Your flight to Mars will take a little over six months. This CMP will launch from here two weeks before you leave for the Lunar Starr. It will be ahead of you for the majority of your flight. About half of the way to Mars, you will pass it, arriving at Mars Port or Mars Platform ahead of it. It will arrive shortly thereafter and drop ahead of your landing then link at Mars Port. Let's take a look at the drop bay. Each CMP carries 5 bubble packs in the rail assembly. The main bay or payload bay is sixty-eight feet in length with a 32 x16 foot loading hatch on the top of the craft. The drop bay panel, which opens for the drop is 16×24 feet and contains a launch chamber which propels the spheres out. Standard length of a CMP is one hundred feet, but the rail can be any size. The main drop bay can be pressurized after the cargo has been unloaded. On the roof on top of the loading bay are sixteen 4×6 foot solar panels and a magnetic walkway with tether guide. Now, let's take a look at the inside." They proceeded to the front of the CMP and passed through the air lock. Dunstan still held the floor.

"All CMPs are basically the same. They contain the same systems and framework. You have your basic systems navigation, computer control, detectors, life support, and others. Standard length of CMPs and XPLMs is 100 feet. Your Mars Module is a modified unit, and is eighty-eight feet in length. The bay of a CMP, called the rail, being sixty-eight feet leaves thirty-two feet of usable space in the front of the module. Those thirty-two feet are divided in half, producing a top and bottom. The center is divided in the middle, producing sections on the left and right sides, twelve 9 x 8 x 8 foot compartments, six upstairs and six downstairs. The cockpit and external air lock are also separated by a pressure door, creating a pilot pit. All the sections are eight feet in height, eight feet in width, and nine feet in length. That nine feet accommodates area for four life pods and nine feet for internal support, including water, bathroom, enclosed kitchen, secondary control panels, air handler, and backup systems. The downstairs is accessible through any of the rabbit hole hatches or the elevator in the dining room," said Mike, pointing at the three foot (one meter) in diameter floor hatch.

"It is the storage and support systems area. The CMP contains three air lock seals, five pressure seal doors, and four rabbit hatches including the extendable docking hatch on the roof. The main air lock on your left is one chamber with two internal pressure outlets and an exterior outlet. You have two air locks that divide the payload bay from the front section, one upstairs and one downstairs." Mike turned, pointing at the space between the pilot pit and the system control station copilot's pit.

"The pressure doors allow you to enter into the other rooms. The idea behind this is that if there is a hull breach, the damaged section can be sealed off."

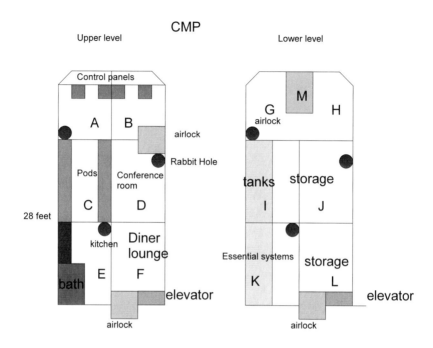

CMP

Upper level   Lower level

Units on upper level 8 x8 x9 2 airlocks and 3
pressure doors. Bathroom (4..5 x 4.5).Kitchen
(4.5x4.5) three rabbit holes one overhead docking
hole not shown.
Lower level sections G-L second airlock to rail
airlock M extendable dockink conduit.

"There is a pressure door that separates the co-pilot pit from the pilot
pit. The sections are labeled: Pilot room is A, Co-pilot B, Pods room
C, Conference room D, Kitchen and Bath E, and Dining room F. The
downstairs section under the pilot is G, the right section is H, the mid left
is I, mid right is J, under the kitchen is K, and the section under the dining
room is L. The downstairs ceiling is only six and a half feet high because
of the fuel tanks on the bottom of the module. They run down the drop
bay and stop just before the engine section. So, from the left front upper
level, we have a cockpit area of 9×8 feet, two chairs and control console,
system control board plus a rabbit hole to bottom level. The pressure door
access connects to co-pilot pit, which contains secondary system control
panel and exterior air lock entrance. The conference room is accessible
through the air lock pressure door which contains a desk and a large screen

wallboard, then pressure door going to the dining room and kitchen and air lock doors to payload bay, then the pressure door to the pod room."

"Now downstairs," Dunstan said as he spun around and disappeared down a rabbit hole. The crew and Jason followed.

"In the storage area here, is stored your food supplies, spare outer suits, electronics replacement parts, extra sensors, light bulbs, gas canisters also your air handler, hydroponic tubs, interior controllers, and other system controllers."

Alex raised his hand. Michael pointed at him, "Yes, Alex."

"I noticed that when you went through the upstairs doors, you did not open them. They opened as we approached and closed after we were inside, how?"

"It's because of this, Alex," Michael said, pointing at a plastic card on his uniform. "It's an identification chip. It tells the computer where you are at all times. It turns things on and off to save power. It even affects the air handler for instance. A large amount of Oxygen is not needed in the lower floor during flight, so Oxygen is not supplied. Should you go down there; the Tri-Starr will signal the handler to release a small amount of cryo Oxygen. The Oxygen is cryogenic and has a rapid expansion once it is heated by the internal temperature. It's always good idea to wait a few seconds before going into the unused rooms. During unmanned flights such as the one this module is going on, significant air is not required, neither is heat or light, so the systems will be put in a non-active mode. No heat, light, or atmosphere until activated by the approach of another vehicle or the destination. With the navcomm system, all the vehicles in the solar system know what's going on with each other and where you and the others are at all times. They even talk to each other."

"For example, if your XPLM is damaged on the way to Mars and you are in need of assistance, the information goes through the Navcomm system signal relay, and all the operational units know instantly, including us here on Earth. They will also know the module's location. Navcomm will do a little calculating and select the closest unit able to assist, depending on fuel, position, and supplies. Then it plots the course to intercept your vehicle. If your navcomm on the damage vehicle is working, it knows that the assisting unit is coming and even what time it will get there and has given a full account of the damage to be repaired, including internal status conditions. It is also important to know that the system has a fail safe program with an override. In other words, suppose the hull has been breached and normal systems are down, the emergency operating system

(EOS) would be activated, and access to the damaged section may be denied. Example: opening the air lock or a pod into a unexpected vacuum. It is a protective feature of the system like planning a trip using Navcomm and not having enough oxygen or fuel for the round trip."

"Navcomm won't activate, but like I said, there is an override. Here's another good example: CMPs are designed for operation in weightless conditions. When a CMP is in gravity, like at the Lunar Starr, navcomm will lock the upstairs rail bay air lock, and only the downstairs air lock will work. This is so no one falls the eight feet to the floor because they forgot they were in a gravity field."

They were now in the front of the downstairs section of the CMP.

"Mike," Jason asked. "What's that 4×6 foot section with the pressure door on the front of the module?"

"I'm glad you asked that, Jason," Dunstan replied. "Even though there is one on your Mars Module, you will probably never use it. That is the extendable linking conduit designation M. It extends out ten feet and can auto connect with other module conduits. Modules can be linked together two ways through the right-side air lock or with this conduit. Here's a good example: two unmanned CMPs have dropped their supplies and are going to be converted into an orbital platform. The navcomm units line them up for docking with this conduit. The conduit then extends as does the conduit on the other CMP. They dock by linking the two conduits together. For a platform of four units, one of the units must be carrying a Hub connector, which serves as an interconnector for the four modules. These Hub connectors have four pressure doors. They are eight feet in diameter octagon structure with eight feet in height and a rabbit hatch on the top and bottom to allow a conduit connection to other Hubs. The Lunar Starr was formed this way as well as the Mars Lunar Platform. When a CMP drops its supplies at the Starr or on Mars, the four units can be used to form an orbital platform. Right now, the Starr is celebrating its third year since completion. It receives three CMP supply runs a year. The CMPs were then used to form the Lunar (LP) and Earth Orbital Platforms (EOP). Four of the CMPs that dropped your supplies on Mars formed the Mars Orbital Platform (MOP), and two went to deep space to set up a navcomm link for Jupiter and Saturn Platforms. The advantage to an orbital platform over a lunar based station is that they are more cost effective. You can set it up to orbit a planet or a moon. You don't have to waste the fuel to effect docking or launching of supply ships. It can be moved at your discretion without much fuel consumption, and that orbit can be changed and maintained without much expense, which is important in deep space applications like Jupiter and Saturn. Instead of orbiting the planets, the platforms orbit one of the moons, in Jupiter's case Europa and in Saturn's case Titan. It requires less fuel to maintain the orbital platform than a surface based station. Investigation missions are then sent to the moons surface, and in some cases, a temporary vehicle is landed on the surface. Once the moon has been fully investigated, they can move the orbital platform to the next moon without expending a large amount of fuel and repeat the process."

"Mr. Dunstan, how much food and water do CMPs carry?" asked the Japanese crew member, who John and Alex had learned in class, was to be addressed as JP.

"Well, let's go to the kitchen and find out." Everybody followed Michael to the kitchen. Mike reached down and opened a door hatch and pulled out a box.

"JP, open it," JP released the clip which held the box together.

"Okay, what is it?" asked Dunstan.

JP pulled one of the packages out. "It looks like a sausage egg and cheese biscuits," replied JP.

"That's right, and there are twelve in that box. Downstairs, there is a pallet with one hundred boxes on it or twelve hundred breakfast biscuits. Let's say that you each eat one biscuit a day. That would be enough to supply a crew of three for over a year. Plus there are other quality foods packs and, of course, paste tubes, granola bars, freeze dried fruits, and other things. Basically, all CMPs carry a supplement food supply of weightless food products. I'd say that a crew of four could live for a year and a half on what's stored on a CMP perhaps longer. All these foods you can cook or eat in a weightless condition. In fact, since CMPs are not designed to come out of space, the foods that you would find stored on the vehicles are predominately weightless food items and last a long time. Do you remember I told you for the three of you to have enough water for normal consumption for a year is 547 gallons? CMPs carry a water supply equivalent to one bubble sphere, which is 9,000 lbs or 1,078 U.S. gallons of water, which could keep your crew alive for about two years. The water in the internal tank freezes upon entering space. In order to use the water you have to defrost it. Inside the internal water tank is a micro heater which will defrost the water into liquid form when activated by a navcomm signal," Michael paused. "Even though all vehicles have solar panels on the roof for power, hydrogen is also used when necessary to power the onboard fuel cells in case extra power is needed." Mike continued. "Okay, let's take a look at some of the vehicle's other features."

The crew followed Dunstan outside. He stooped down to point at a tank on the underbelly of the vehicle. This tank is your electrolysis tank where your waste water is turned into hydrogen and Oxygen. It doesn't look like much, but without it, you may not be breathing. There's a backup unit on the other side, and here's one of your three Sterling engines," Dunstan said, pointing at a tube on the belly. As they proceeded to the rear of the vehicle, Dunstan pointed out the propulsion systems.

"All CMPs and XPLMs have two different propulsion systems. The main engines are two LOX-driven engines; the secondary engine is a radio plasma ion engine, which is used for long-distance travel and maneuvering. When the vehicle is being propelled by the ion engine, you have slight propulsion gravity in the inside of the craft, not much but enough to pour a cup of coffee. This tank here," he said while pointing to the undercarriage. "Just above the plasma nozzle is your mix and/or expansion tank which excites the fuel into plasma before ignition. The navcomm calculates how much fuel is needed pressurizes the feed tank and feeds it to the expansion tank. Then the fuel is excited by radiation developing into plasma and spun into a vortex coil. The plasma is then fed to the dual pulse igniter, which feeds it to the nozzle. The process produces a blue white vapor flame instead of your typical flame, which is because of a more efficient combustion.

"This," he said, pointing to a three-foot box on the undercarriage, "is your EOS unit, your black box. However, it does more than just record vehicle functions. It is also your emergency navcomm backup. This section here" Dunstan said pointing to the main hull of the craft "is the rail. It is the cargo storage and transport section of the CMP. The cargo drop bubbles are loaded and placed in the unit through the top Load Port, on the top of the vehicle. The bubbles are secured on trays which are attached to a slide. The spheres are also tethered to an upper rail. When it's time for the drop, the tray delivers the spheres to the drop port, and the tray then retracts. The bubble is now being held by only the tether. When navcomm gives the signal, the tether is released, dropping the bubble and on the way to the surface the bubble auto inflates."

They then went up on the roof to look at the solar panels, the eye or communications disk, and the tether magnetic walkway. JP had noticed a panel section separation in the area over the pod section.

"What's this for, Mr. Dunstan?"

"That JP is part of your EOS pod ejection system. When a condition exists and the EOS feels it is unsafe and needs to eject the pods, the EOS will pop the panel and eject the pods through the opening. However, this is only in extreme circumstances under normal conditions you are much better off staying with the vehicle. Dunstan went on to describe the automatic hull repair device and how it operates. To demonstrate, he alerted navcomm that there was a hole in the craft. He placed a magnetic six-inch pad on the ship's hull, and they watched as the repair device responded. The tour of the integrated systems went on for another two hours till lunch and continued the next day.

Chapter 5

The Starr

Breakfast for the crew came early at 5:00 am John got his tray and joined Alex and JP at the table.

"Today's the day at 10:51 am we will be in the module headed for the Lunar Starr." said John

"Don't forget, we go to the Earth Orbital Platform (EOP) first, which would make me happy," JP commented.

"I don't mind so much going from one point to another in space. I only worry about the takeoffs and landings, same with АЭРОПЛАН (*aeroplanes*)," remarked Alex.

JP nodded. "Once we are in the Mars Module, where we will be for the next six months, things should be fine."

"Yes, you're right, but when it comes to the Mars drop, I just hope this modified module they built for us holds together and is okay after the landing," John said between bites.

Alex and JP nodded.

"Hey, you guys ready for the lift?" It was the other half of the lift crew, the re-entry vehicle pilots that would be taking them to the EOP. The re-entry vehicle was a Constellation class ship, designed for a crew of eight: Alex, John, JP, the pilot and co-pilot, and three other crew members who were going to the Lunar Starr for some work project there. Two of the men were seasoned veterans; they had been to the Starr before. The mission commander, Richard Mathews, had over twelve launches under his belt and was designated to report to the Lunar Starr to take over system transportation there. Everybody greeted each other and John said,

"We are probably just nervous because this for us is our first lift."

Richard took a sip of his coffee.

"Well," he started, "don't worry about that. I'll get you there, unless something goes wrong and the vehicle blows up." Richard smiled and got a laugh from his copilot. The crew got a blank look on their faces for a second.

Richard continued, "I really envy you guys. I mean to be the first men on Mars, what a deal!"

JP stressed a point, "You overlook the fact Commander that we may be the first men to die on Mars as well."

"I hear that the average temperature on the planet's surface is minus 120 degrees Fahrenheit, and that the storms on Mars are particularly bad, with no trees to stop the wind which can generate gusts over 100 mph. I also hear that they have built you a cave to park your XPLM in, so that may help you survive, but you guys are going to be there awhile, I mean six years is a long time. Standard tour on the EOP and the Lunar Starr is only a two-year contract," Richard replied.

JP interrupted, "I just hope they keep dropping food and supplies."

When breakfast was over, they all adjourned to the ready room and final briefing at nine o'clock. Traveling in space required the usage of an inner and outer suit. The inner suits were to be worn at all times with helmet and gloves close at hand, they were an airtight safety requirement. Outer suits were required for extended excursions and landings, and in this case the takeoff. After they finished putting on their suits they were on their way to the lift vehicle. A Constellation class lift vehicle named the 'Morning Star' was poised on the gantry, ready to launch. A small vehicle, only thirty-two feet in length, it resembled one of the old-style space shuttles of twenty years ago. It was actually a one quarter scale model of that craft, with several main alterations. It was not designed to carry more than a couple of hundred pounds of cargo on board. Total lift weight including craft, cargo, and crew, with maneuvering fuel, was 60,000 lbs. Dead vehicle weight was 42,000 lbs. Ninety percent of the cargo lifted to the EOP, and the Lunar Starr were transported by CMPs which had a payload capacity of approximately 120,000 lbs. The CMP that would be joining John and the crew on their mission to Mars had already been launched a week earlier. The schedule was pretty simple: a lift to the EOP, a transfer to a lunar jumper, a two and a half day ride to the moon landing at the Lunar Starr, a brief orientation there, and then a jump to the Lunar Orbital Platform (LOP or LP), to get acquainted with the module that they would be living in for the next six years. Next would be the launch of the module from the LP to Mars Orbital Platform, and then the drop to the Martian surface. The countdown for the Morning Star was under way when John noticed that the veteran sitting next to him was reading a book. The vet looked up.

"You're reading a book?" John couldn't help himself.

"Yeah, it's a good book besides; this is old school for me. This is my third lift."

Less than ten minutes later, they were on their way.

"Up we go into the wild blue yonder," John thought to himself.

The launch and the trip to the EOP were uneventful, thank God. They arrived at the EOP and disembarked the Morning Star, to be received by the station's crew, who seemed very interested in talking to them. This lasted for about two hours. The Jumper to take them to the Lunar Starr was already there and ready to go. Within two hours John and the crew along with Richard and the three others bound for the Lunar Starr were on their way. The Jumper was also designed to carry eight people, and that's about all. It consisted of a crew cockpit and a total operational space of twenty-nine feet, including air lock, bathroom, small cargo space which contained food and water, and a secondary upper hatch. The pod section, which contained eight pods, was two sets of four, taking up sixteen feet of that space, storage three feet, cockpit four feet, and a seating area of six feet, which included four chairs and the air lock. The seating area also contained a wallboard which toggled images from the outside cameras. In this part of the journey, there was nothing to see but space. Anyhow, there were monitors in the pods.

ISA rules required that all passengers in a weightless environment, called free space wear an interior space suit, when in operation unless in a pod. In case there was a hull breach and the cabin were to lose atmosphere pressure. The ISA also required that a system pilot be awake at all times of operation, which would be either Richard or his co-pilot on alternating shifts. They were just there for emergencies because the navigation and the fuel usage were auto programmed by navcomm. There wasn't any actual piloting involved. During the first couple of hours, John and the crew, including the extra man of Richard's party, were in the front section having dinner John had got the impression that Richard's man was some kind of mechanical engineer. Paste was the service for weightless conditions, and after that, JP and Alex decided to adjourn to their pods to watch television and maybe get some sleep. They wanted to watch footage of the takeoff on the six o'clock news. The co-pilot went as well, because in ten hours, he would relieve Richard at the helm.

The next two days, John didn't see much of the crew. Everyone, when not required, stayed in their pods. John had grasped that it would be the way things would be on the journey to Mars as well. The pods were quite comfortable: TV, DVD player, radio, computer, thermostat, direct air and memory foam cushion. Alex had brought a couple of Russian music CDs and was watching movies in Russian from the media link, which was a library of media in a variety of languages. John caught a glimpse of it when Alex had opened his pod door. After two days, they were coming into lunar orbit in preparation for landing at the Starr. The Jumper made several orbits to align before initializing landing procedures. The landing alarm sounded to awaken everyone. Another ISA rule was that all personnel on an in-flight craft must be awake during any docking, landings, or takeoffs, and in outside suits, regardless whether they were in pods or not. For the lunar landing, pods were recommended. If the Jumper were going to have a hull breach on a rough landing, the pod was the safest place to be. This time the landing went like a clock, and safe landing at Lunar Starr became a reality. John and his crew parted ways with Richard's crew when they were greeted by Alan Groton, Lunar Starr supervisor.

"Okay guys, we are happy to see you here on the Starr. Your station pods are located in module C. You'll be here for three days before being transferred to the Mars Module on the LP. We will have a few orientation meetings here before you go, which will be hosted by myself and Tech Officer Mark Jensen, who is up in your module right now installing some final equipment updates. The module arrived fully equipped, but that was nine months ago. We've had both programming and tech updates since then. Okay, have you had lunch yet? We run on an Earth normal clock here (Greenwich Mean Time) EST in space means Earth Standard Time (Greenwich). Here we also have an orbital clock or planetary clock which is somewhat different. But you would probably enjoy a little normal food instead of the paste, eh?"

Groton smiled. The crew agreed and went for the meal. After lunch (hamburger), the crew was treated to a tour of the Lunar Starr. The kitchen was in module 'A' along with most of the tech equipment and recreational area. The Starr was composed of three CMPs (B, C, and D) and a XPLM (A) module joined by a hub which normally housed an average of eight occupants per mod. Right now, there were twenty-six people on board; six had gone back to Earth on the 'Morning Star' after it had been serviced at the EOP. Unit 'B' was the hydroponic module which also contained the air processing pumps, filters, and purification system, including waste management system and water recycling equipment, mostly machines. A very small area was designated for a tool shop and lab. Units 'C' and 'D' were crew quarters which had been modified to hold 12 pods apiece in the pressurized rail section. Alan went on to explain how 'B' unit was able to supply enough oxygen to maintain a atmospheric presence for the modules, and how used water from the kitchen and bathroom was purified by the filter system and used to supply both oxygen to breathe and hydrogen for the fuel cell electricity generation during the non-light periods. All together, while summing it up, the Starr was a well designed structure. Unit 'B' the hydroponic lab was impressive with large amount of plants. Unit 'B' had one feature that the other modules didn't an integrated lighting structure to support growth of the hydroponics.

The hydroponic unit contained a great variety of plants besides the Oxygen generating plants. The unit had an abundance of food plants: tomatoes, cucumbers, melons, onions, peppers, and others. Alan explained that the food plants were hybrid rapid growth and dwarf plants with a ninety-day yield which, when planted in sequence, delivered a small continuous flow of food products. There was a small processing section even a small amount of poultry. Chicken hens for eggs were raised to supplement the food supply. The tour ended at unit 'C' as Alan described that the modules were approximately sixteen feet high and sixteen feet wide. The pods were stacked three high in three columns with a sliding ladder rack to get in and out. The CMP rail section had been converted to a living space and pressurized. Alan explained that when you wanted to get out of the pods, you pressed the inside button in the pod and the rack will slide to your pod and allowed support for the upper bunks. The bathroom was a vacuum-sealed compartment. In case you were taking a shower and the cabin lost pressure. Alex couldn't contain himself and asked, "Well, if that happens, wouldn't you be trapped in the bathroom?"

Alan stared at him for a second and replied, "Yes, you would, and you will stay in there until the pressure is restored in the module or someone on the outside manually overrides the lock. It's the same with the pods. However, there is a manual override from the inside, but that removes the air from the bathroom and the same in the pods. Okay, let me explain how the shower and sink water usage devices work because they are the same on your ship. In the shower, when you go in, you'll need to dial your preferred water temperature. A mist is sprayed and the vortex engine will start to form a water cyclone of mist that slowly falls to the bottom. Use the liquid soap it' has an alcohol base. It will smell a little odd, but you'll get used to it. Use the body mop that we issue you. You will be given tags to indentify your products for private use. Do not use someone else's product. This goes for the toilet, shower, and food items. After you soap up, press the exit button and clean water will be sprayed for the rinse then dry off with your towel. Place the towel in the recycle bin where it will be cleaned and sanitized for the next use. While you are in the bathroom, a dehumidifier runs constantly to process random water. It may impress you to know that it takes less than a liter of water for your shower and most of it is reclaimed. In fact, tests show that in this sealed application, only three tablespoons are lost."

"On the Starr, we shower every other day to remove salt mainly, now the sink and shaving. In your issued gear, you will have a canister which is soap in an antibacterial solution. When you go to wash your hands, use this." He pointed to a covered vase. "Pass your hand over the red light on the left and stick your hands in. A small mist will spray. Remove your hands and scrub them. When you wish to rinse, pass your hand over blue light on the right," Alan instructed, pointing at the small lights on the top of the vase. "The second spray is the rinse. Dry your hands with the air gun and you're done, got it?"

Alan turned as a gentleman approached them.

"This is Jeff Robins. He's your section 'C' chief. He's responsible for maintenance and repair of this section and section 'D.' He also works in 'B.' If anything needs to be reported or assistance is needed, then he is who to talk to."

"Hi, guys," said Jeff as he handed them each a packet. "These are your issuance packets which contain the following: your identification card, your identification tags, and pass key. When you are not in your pods, you are required to wear your ID card at all times. They open your pod and the bathroom doors. They also open the module doors. Without them, you can't go to the other modules. You need them to access other sections and to operate the doors in the linked modules as well. This area over here is the library. It contains," Jeff said, pointing at a group of computer panels. "all information on the features and systems which make the modules work. It also contains information on maintenance and system repair, so get acquainted. I understand you will be here for two more days. All XPLMs are designed and built with the same basic utilities. In some cases, certain modifications are adapted for special applications. Your XPLM is a modified

XPLM. First modification is the length standard XPLMs are one hundred feet in length standard. Yours is eighty-eight feet and designed to serve four people instead of eight. It contains all the basic features, plus a few more modifications, but you'll be learning all of that in the next two days. While you are here, you'll be taking eight hours per day of prep instruction. You will need to learn the basic systems of your modified XPLM module. So, that if you have questions about the operation of a system. You can ask me, Alan, or Mark, class starts tomorrow. Later, you'll be going to your ship with Mark Jensen for four to five days until you launch for Mars Platform, any questions? No, okay, go tag your issuance. It's in your locker. Use the card to open the locker, the locker numbers are on the card. Take a shower and change into Starr wear, and wait for dinner."

The crew turned toward the section, which contained the lockers when Jeff said,

"Oh, Alex and JP, we have three Russians and one Japanese crew member onboard. I'll introduce you at dinner. They are all on assignment right now. The tags were small but thick pieces of plastic and were to be placed on all personal items, bath towels and utilities. John clipped on his identification card and headed for the shower 5 minutes later he came out with an amazed look on his face. Alex was waiting to go in.

"Wow," said John. "That shower is something else. I feel really refreshed, it doesn't last to long but the whirlpool effect really gets into your pours." Jeff walked up,

"You can stay in there for quite some time if you want. The vortex will continue to work until you press exit," Jeff looked down at Alex.

"Where's our identification card Alex?"

"I thought I'd wait until after I shower," Alex answered.

"Oh no, Alex you must have your identification card on at all times. The computer that controls this station is part of the navcomm system. It scans constantly and it knows who you are and what you are doing, and it requires your card to know where you are. It won't know it's you, without the card and will send and alert. For instance, if I need to find you I can just ask it. Where is Alex Gorkov, and it will tell me what section you're in and will even contact you if I wish. But without it, it may deny you access to the bathroom and to the other modules."

Alex went 'Oh' and went to put his card on. At dinner the crew was the main attraction. Each sat with their home members and every one enjoyed the food which consisted of a Salisbury steak with gravy and mashed potatoes and broccoli with a tasty sauce. After dinner they went back to their section. There was a staff meeting in 'A' section. When they got back to the pods Alex, who had a strange look on his face remarked,

"Do you know what they are doing here?" John and JP both shook their heads. "Did you think it was a little odd that 16 of the onboard crew are construction personnel? They are in the process of encapsulating a crater."

John stopped in his tracks, "What? You're kidding?"

"NO I swear! I don't know the details but they have already been successful in forming a air pressurized seal over the top and are currently building the interior infrastructure which, I understand is multiple unit housing, housing for a one hundred person habitat. So, while we're on Mars, they will be transporting people up here to the Lunar Dome that's what they're calling it."

"Well, that's progress" said John "gives you something to think about."

The next day they met with Mark Jensen who had just gotten back from the Lunar Platform and the Mars Module. After breakfast they went to their first instruction course, where certain aspects of the mission were to be explained.

Mark stared with a summation "Ok here we are. I'm going to explain some things about the conditions on the Martian surface. You probably already know most of it but, just bear with me. First of all, the average mean temperature is minus 84 degrees Fahrenheit and during the wind storms, the winds can attain a velocity of over 100 mph. In those storms the wind will pick up sand and small rocks and transport them along with it. It could actually bury you or one of the robots if you were out in it. Secondly, the temperature can go as low as minus 200 degrees Fahrenheit which is not as cold as space however, it's still very cold. The Martian day is 24.62 hours, or 37 minutes longer than an Earth day. You will have an average of 12 hours 15 minutes of light, more during the summer months. Onboard you will have a Martian clock which is a stretched version of an Earth clock by adding 1.59 minutes per hour to the minute hand. During dark periods the conservation of power may become a concern. You may wonder how come it took the robots as long as it did to drill the cave. They didn't allow the robots to work during the night. The robots operate off a solar powered charger and the robots need to recharge every 4 hours which takes 30 minutes to do. Thus, the robots worked for 10 hours per day. When the robots first landed they built a storm pit at the landing site to protect them from the storms. The robots are not allowed to work during the storms. When a storm approaches, the navcomm system will alert them and the robots will stop work and go into the pit, which is underground. The navcomm sensors are known as "lights" as well as the solar power generators also sink into the ground for protection. When the storm is over they come back out. We can view the robots progress over the navcomm link which, I want you to monitor periodically. According to the most current information the robots have carved or tunneled the cave approximately 130 feet length and 36 feet in width and are now working on enlarging the width to 100 feet. You will be in space for approximately 6 months during the trip that will give the robots time to finish their project. You will be accompanied by a CMP with a surface rover for your surface exploration. The index menu is listed in your mission folder. Your sponsors want you to investigate certain locations; take pictures and samples of the surface to bring back to the module for analyst. The cave the robots are building is not to far from the majority of these sites. Also, going with you are two (T-111) mapping probes to join the two already in orbit. They will be able to keep track of weather conditions and supply navigational information. If you are in the rover and get caught in a storm, you will have some advanced warning. Find a spot that is shielded from the direction of the wind and sit it out, do not try and move during a storm. The Gravity of Mars is 38% of Earth's normal gravity so, if an object weighs 100 lbs on Earth it ways 38 lbs on Mars thus your XPLM weighs 180,000 lbs on Earth so figure approximately 64,000 lbs or 32 tons on Mars. Mars is primarily made of sand and rocks which can be dangerous in wind gusts. The robots clear the landing runway when required to remove debris left after the storms, okay any questions?"

Alex raised his hand, "are we going to have enough supplies to survive the conditions there for 6 years?"

"Alex, we dropped 4 CMP's to begin with and 3 more 2 years ago there are supplies from seven CMPS already on the ground plus you're going with another CMP which will drop before you do and you have the supplies in the XPLM. So right now there are 35 bubble units on the ground, one CMP accompanying you and the XPLM. Yes, I'd say you will have enough for the two years before we send the next three CMPs. Since the solar rotation of Mars has a solar perihelion of 128 million miles and its aphelion is 154 million miles. It is only close enough to Earth every two years. At that time Mars can be as close as 36 million miles. For that reason you can only receive supplies every 687 days which, is the amount of time it takes for Mars to complete one solar orbit. There is a differential ratio between the orbits of Earth, which has solar orbit of 365 days and Mars which completes its solar orbit in 687 days, the difference is 43 days. Which means the Earth's position is not the same every two years when Mars is closets. Some years the Earth is on the other side of the Sun and can be out of phase. Also, about communications, while you're on the planet and in range there is a slight lag when you talk to the Lunar Starr in voice as well information programming. This will increase as distance increases. As the distance increases so will the lag which can become as much as a minute or more. When Mars is at its farthest point form the Sun (its aphelion 154 million miles) and the Earth is on the opposite side of the Sun the distance can be as great as well, 154 + 93 or 247 million miles. That's over two and a half Astronomical Units or two and a half times the distance from the Earth to the Sun. Your signal will come through the Mars Orbital Platform where the signal will be boosted and sent to the lunar platform boosted again and then sent to Earth. When required that procedure can take up to two minutes because of the distance. When you're out on the far end of the Martian orbit you're over a year away from any help, not 6 or 8 months as you would be when you're only 40 million miles away, so understand that. When you're closets in distance we will be loading you tri-star computer with tons of entertainment and information to keep you entertained but, we don't really know about long distance communications because we've never sent that type of information that far before. We've tried it before with the CMPs that we had in orbit but, it didn't work very well. We believe solar flares caused interference which may have been the problem. The conference lasted another three hours with Q & A and various working examples explained. It was the same thing the next day. Just before dinner John was summoned to section 'A'. The section chief for 'A' informed him there was a telephone call for him so, he went to the comm.

"Hey John, just called up to see how it's going?"

"Hey Jason pretty good, I guess we are leaving tomorrow for the Lunar Platform and to see the module, so that what's up?"

"Just called to check up, how are the rest of the guys?" Jason asked.

"Their okay, I don't guess there will be any fan fair for our take off from the lunar platform and then six months will be nothing but space. However, I really like the way the Starr is set up. It's spacious and has just about everything required but, it doesn't have a swimming pool," John laughed.

"Well," replied Jason, "Maybe sometime in the future. Anyway, the ISA is sending someone to see you guys off. They are sending a documenter and a camera man to record the event. Now John, these are ISA documenters not news people. They are going to be taking pictures of you and the ship. Their questions will be more on a technical nature than news documenters but don't worry Mark Jensen will be with you. They should arrive within a day or two but, I understand that some news people are also coming up to get footage for public television. Don't get the two mixed up and say anything wrong. I'll call again before the launch and a few times during the flight. Jensen will be your mission coordinator at the Starr. He will be the person you will speak to the most of the time. The base for your mission control is the Starr. They are in charge of what information from your mission gets sent to Earth."

"Say Jason, do you know anything or heard anything about the encapsulating a crater?" John asked.

There was a silence on the other end of the line, and then very slowly Jason said,

"You see that's just what I mean, you must be very carful about what you say or suggest. Ok, but since you asked and we are such good friends, here is my response. I know nothing about such a project, I haven't heard anything about that subject and neither have you so, we couldn't possibly answer that question and any answer we may give would not be based on anything factual and are probably incorrect, OK?"

"Yeah I got it, ok," Jason replied with hesitation.

"I'll call again in a couple of days, Greene out."

There sure a lot of left hand, right hand stuff going on with the ISA, and of course Jason knew more than he let on to. For all John knew Jason may be in charge of the project, something to think about. The next day, after breakfast Jensen instructed them to say good bye to the Starr crew and to meet him at the Jumper docking bay in an hour. Alex went to say goodbye to the friends he had made while JP and John went to their pods to collect their personal items, which took all of 2 minutes. 45 minutes later they met Jensen at the Lunar Jumper loading platform. The platform which was just an enclosed room was attached to the Starr by a walking tunnel. In the room was the door to a crawler that would take them to the Jumper approx. 300 yards away. On the way out the crew noticed the two other Jumpers parked together. There were a total of 4 jumpers stationed at the Starr. One was on the lift site, two were parked on the side that made 3, and one was not here, probably at the Earth Orbital Platform which had replaced the faded ISS about seven years ago. Their Jumper was ready to go. The Jumpers can carry 8 people but, this time only the crew, Jensen and a Lunar Platform operator were on board. As they entered and took their seats the platform operator signaled John over to say something to him.

"Your the pilot right?" John nodded.

"Well then, why don't you sit in the pilot's chair and take us to the LP?"

John put his bag in the lounge compartment chair and sat down in the pilot's chair as the operator directed.

"I've never flown one of these before what do I do?" stammered John.

"Ok," said the operator. "Watch me very carefully because I'm going to do this only once."

John glanced up and caught Jensen tap JP on the side of his arm. They where both smiling so, he new something was up.

"The first thing you need is a key, all assigned vehicles require one." The operator placed his Starr key in the lock and turned it, the control panel lit up.

"The next thing is to turn on your onboard navcomm. That toggle switch there," he said pointing at the upper panel. John flipped it on. The LCD navigation panel lit up

"Ok, see in the panel is a 3D map of the moon created by the T-111 mapping probes of which there are 4 circling the moon at all times. Notice the ball on the right hand side, if you move the ball it will navigate the map. You can use it to view a circumnavigation or orbital image of the moon. Once you fine the location you wish to go to, you can press select and lock it in. Notice that the dark side of the moon is lit up by light. Notice also that this map shows only the moon and that the surface is all lit." John played with the rotational mouse.

"To see the solar rotation press the button on the right below the screen." John did as instructed and a shadow appeared on half of the moon.

"Right now, the Starr is in sunlight, find the Starr." John rotated the sphere backwards until the image of the Starr was shown on the screen.

"Ok, now we want to go to the Lunar Platform. So, on the right hand side you'll see 8 preset location buttons in a panel. One is marked LP press it."

John pressed the LP button a lighted panel came on with three sets of three number bars.

"That button you pressed," the operator explained. "Is a preset button for the Lunar Platform there is also one for the Earth orbit and Earth's

Orbital Platform. John noticed on the panel that had just lit a series of clocks he pointed to them the instructor nodded.

"Those are your time vector clocks. The first one tells how long till take off. When you are in motion it will switch to display arrival time to destination, travel time from activation, and current velocity. The second clock tells you the location of your point of origin and your destination location. When you are in space it is the destination vector and the orbital velocity. The third clock displays fuel usage, in this case in lunar time if you want earth time press the button lower right side." John looked at the takeoff clock it said 3.45 minutes. The operator reached over and pressed a button. The map screen split into 4 pieces. The operator continued to instruct.

"Ok, the first screen is an image of where we are, taken by navcomm, actually taken by a T-111 or 'Trex' as they are called. See, it can be viewed in the second screen which is the image from the Starr's camera. The third image is a picture of the Starr and the T-111 taken from the Lunar Platform. The forth image on the screen is the front camera of this Jumper. This Jumper and all Jumpers including your module have 7 orbital cameras front, back both sides, two orbital fully rotational on the bottom, front and back and one fully rotational on the top middle. You see 7 buttons on right hand side but, don't key them right now, we are about to take off and I'm sure the passengers will want to see themselves take off from the Lunar Starr. He looked behind him all were watching the screen behind the cockpit door. John looked back to the launch clock it said 30 seconds.

"OK, what do I do?" The operator turned and smiled at Jensen all of a sudden the Jumper began to lift and with out so much as a shudder headed up in space.

"Great bunch of piloting there admiral," the operator exclaimed. Jensen and the crew laughed. The instructor went on to explain.

"When you turn on the "activate" switch the Jumper performs a series of operations including a navigational track, when a destination is selected. Navcomm then selects the course and calculates other vehicle functions including fuel usage. Then calculates the minimum amount of fuel it will take to reach that destination and pressurizes the engines. Then it sets the take off time, when time is up the vehicle takes off and proceeds to the designation site, with out the need of human assistance. Now, that's a pretty good explanation, but in actuality since navcomm was born in application of space navigation, it has grown. It learns and it runs calculations constantly so, if you want to go from point A to point B and both are in motion.

Navcomm is mapping them constantly and can tell you exactly when you should take off. If you have a window it will pick the least expensive time within the window. It can even do this when there is a mass between the two points by creating a vector map of the orbits. As I said it learns; every vehicle currently in space has a sensor package that transmits data to navcomm. For example; when landing at the Lunar Starr the navcomm unit has performed that maneuver over 100 times. The first efforts were a little bumpy but, ever time a Jumper or a CMP lands on the lunar surface it collects the sensor information, until it can perform the task perfectly. So, the system which controlled our take off time knew when the platform would be overhead. It lined up the Lunar Platforms vector coordinates and velocity. Loaded the correct amount of fuel into the expansion tanks and fired the rockets to take the shortest course to the destination. Without us doing anything in fact, the operator at the Lunar Starr can do this without a crew being onboard. For example; if the Jumper is needed to go to the EOP, Earth can order it to take off and go to the platform unassisted Earth has priority. They can do this without even notifying the Starr. However, the Starr has a lockout on two of the Jumpers which only answer to Starr's control. The reason I'm telling you this because your vehicle works the same way and so do all of the modules of the ISA. The Modules and the Jumpers will not take off if they don't have enough fuel to get to the designated destination. When, for instance you plot a course to the dark side of the moon. The navcomm calculates the fuel and time for the round trip and won't launch if there isn't enough fuel."

John had a look on his face that defied description. Then said

"If the vehicles don't need any piloting, why did they take all that time teaching me to land one, vector math and the emergency procedures."

"Well John, not all the time do things work right and if an emergency situation should come up you may need to take manual control of the vehicle. At that time you may need to know what to do. The ISA requires that if the vehicle is manned, that a pilot or operator be present at all times of operation unless a vehicle is operational in an unmanned mode. That goes for all passenger transports regardless of designation. By pilot, I mean an onboard licensed technical operator, which is what you are or soon will be," The operator explained.

"Those courses you took at the Cape were over and above the normal requirements to be certified as a tech operator or Pilot. They have sent this ahead of your arrival; congratulations." The operator pulled a case out of his pocket and opened it. There was a small circular pin with a wing through it. JP, Alex, and Jensen applauded.

"Look I've got one too ok?" The operator pointed to his uniform where the operator's insignia was pinned.

"Here comes LP, helmets on everybody." The docking was flawless and soon they were onboard the LP station. Jensen noted the point that this station, 'ain't no tourist hang out'. And that the crew would have to stay on their ship, in their pods, during their stay.

"Let me show you to your ship." Mark suggested.

They went through a hall way to an air lock and arrived at a service bay. Here they got their first look at the Mars Module. The craft was enclosed in the service bay which was pressurized. Mark started talking about the construction of the bay.

"We didn't have anything like this when the Lunar Starr project started three years ago. This bay was a dream that came true. The bay was constructed with the use of 196 panels plus the doors. The panels were lifted by two CMPs carrying 120 panels apiece and the framework. The panels are the same kind of panels you'll be using on Mars. It was easy to assemble the panels except for the door which had to be custom formed.

"Boys welcome home, at least for the next 6 years," Jensen said gesturing towards the module.

The crew looked up at the modified XPLM that loomed before them. It was quite impressive gleaming with a shinny coating. The Module was gloss silver with a picture of Mars painted on the side and the lettering AADG Mars Module painted on the nose.

"I'll give you an hour to get settled in and then class will begin. Don't press any buttons until I get back." Jensen left and the boys went to claim there pods. The LP had a little gravity, not moon gravity but, things didn't float like in weightless space. They fell but very slowly. Jensen had explained that the platform which, is made of linked service modules (CMPs) same as the Starr, were in rotation to create the artificial gravity. The CMP's had been converted into a habitat mode containing housing, workshop, recreation area and machine shop. Vehicles from the Starr where sent here to the LP for repairs. It was easier to work in a weightless condition. Jensen showed back up an hour later. The next 3 hours were spent going over the ship's main systems and sub systems. How they work, and how they are repaired. Jensen stressed that they needed to learn everything about the two main systems which were, the Tri-Starr computer system and the navcomm system and how they relate to the other systems. Then he talked about the Tri-Star computer system.

"The Tri-Starr computer system besides maintaining operation of the ship and the right hand of navcomm system has recreational features as well, and can store: movies, programs, TV episodes, news, weather, sports, and games which, you can access from your lounge panel or from your pods. The actual storage capacity of the unit's hard drive is 200 Terabytes of which 20 Terabytes is module applications, another 20 Terabytes are sub system maintenance and navcomm and navcomm back up. Your onboard Tri-star has already been loaded. It contains over 5000 movies 2000 TV series and 100 games. New material can be added on daily or weekly basis. Recent news, sports and live content will be available until such time as the Sun is between your position and the Earth. When the Mars Module has a direct line of transmission, Navcomm Central Station (NCS) on Earth will transmit the data using the Starr as a signal repeater and booster. So, according to the map you will be out of contact for about 2 to 6 months a year. During that time you may not be able to get live media feed, after that a wealth of media awaits you as you try to catch up for the months you lost. The navcomm system is like a second link to the Tri-Starr sys. Both systems have a smaller back up emergency systems in the EOS (Emergency Operational System) which can activate the craft to return here. Example: if the ship is hit and you have a hull breach and everyone dies and the ship is void of life adrift in space. It will advise us of the onboard conditions and request permission to return here. If the module can it will, if not it will request assistance from the nearest source. It will if it can, attempt to repair the hull and turn the ship. The EOS navcomm unit will activate and will set course for here. Ok, for the next 4 days you are to study every system of this ship. If you have any questions we will be able to answer them and provide explanation of the correct procedure before you takeoff. You're welcome to join me and the rest of the LP crew of four for breakfast and dinner in the platform diner. We don't celebrate lunch here so for that you're on your own. Before you launch to Mars we will have a small party at the Starr. If you need anything, this button is the 'will call button'. You can also communicate through your pod link and of course you can access the Tri-star data base. So, you can study, read, watch media, access the computer, and talk to us, or the Lunar Starr, or each other from your pods. A complete listing of what you can do from your pods is described in the module manual and systems on the Tri-star database. Ok, I guess that's it for now, see you in about 3 hours that's 6 p.m. Earth time. Breakfast is dealt at 7 am, if you don't want to cook it yourself or reheat it; you need to be on time."

In the next few days they spent most of their time studying. Jensen showed up and was there for three hours every afternoon and went over their questions and demonstrated aspects of the module that he said were maybe not clear in the manual. One afternoon Jensen said that he was going to have dinner with them and he wanted Alex to cook meal #207 for four which was beef stroganoff, potatoes, and vegetables with rolls. Alex got the meals out of storage and followed Jensen's instructions to operate the auto cooker. Later Jensen took the crew downstairs to go over the supply locations.

"These three 50 gallon barrels contain your hydroponics. Notice the hose hookup one in and one out. Two contain Cyan bacteria or blue green algae. They are your high oxygen producers. In the other containers is a variety of plants germinations cups which include Sansevieria, Dracaena, Philodendron and others. They are dormant status until activated. They all fit into the trays after germination. They looked to the wall where he saw a rack of plastic trays 8 feet long 2 feet wide, 220 trays and 200 covers with racks and frames. On your way to Mars you will need to install four algae trays in the upstairs compartment. Now in these 10 drums are sea water and these two contain growth soil which expands when wet. While you're on Mars you will take a volume of pills to sublimate your diet, vitamin C, Garlic, fish oil and this."

Jensen produced a small blue green pill

"This is the blue green algae. You can make these pills with this machine." Jensen showed them to a small pill making machine. "Your first order of business once you get in the cave is to install an atmosphere and set up your hydroponic units. This is important there are a couple of boxes of seeds over by the trays. When you're on the trip the tanks will be maintained by a CO_2 concentrator which feeds through the air handler. The internal CO_2 that you produce is fed through your air handler to your hydroponic systems. The light source for the hydroponics is automatically regulated. You'll need to check the live plants every other day. Hydroponics has been overlooked in the early days of space exploration, even though we don't depend on the hydro's to produce oxygen, they have another important function. The plants work as atmospheric cleaners which make the oxygen atmosphere cleaner and healthier."

Jensen appeared about mid afternoon on day three. He instructed everyone to stop what they were doing.

"Guys, I have about two hours before I have to go back to the Starr and there some thing we need to talk about, and that would be the pods. Now, I know that you know a lot about the pods because you have been sleeping in them for the last couple of days. However, there may be some things you probably do not know. As you know the Tri-Star and navcomm units are separate systems which are combined to operate together. The Tri-Star contains your programming and history; it is the brain and mission recorder. The navcomm controls your navigation and propellant usage. The two systems working together control almost all of your ship functions velocity, your water, your cryogenics, your waste management and many of the other operational systems of the module. One of the systems that it also controls is your Life Support System which is your module interior oxygen content, sensors or encoder systems and the pods" Jensen toggled the display on the control panel and continued.

"Like I said, you're already familiar with the attributes of the pods. The pods are 4 feet wide, 3.5 feet in height and 8 feet in length. The pods contain the following; media display, communications link, internal atmosphere control, memory foam pad, sensors, alarm notification, maneuvering system and a small navcomm unit. But you may not know that the pod system contains an inactive emergency operational system (EOS) which when activated turns the pods into life boats. Let's suppose that your three and half months out of Earth and three and a half months to Mars. A large rock the size of a truck hits your module, completely disabling the front control section of the module. The EOS system will then activate. EOS navcomm and Tri-Star will attempt to access and repair the damage. What you may also not know is there is a back up to each system at the rear of the module that activates whenever the link is lost with the control navcomm. Once the damage is been assessed the automated Hull repair system will attempt to fix the problem by resealing the hole and re-pressurizing the module. If for some reason the EOS cannot fix the problem it will switch over to a secondary system control. This involves the sending of an emergency notification signal through the navcomm link to all navcomm units including Earth. At that time Earth station will authorize the operational procedures for the module. This may include separation of the pods from the remaining module structure. As you know the pods are attached to the internal grid framework which is connected to the walls. During EOS notification, the pods can be disconnected from the grid and use mini maneuvering thrusters to exit the module through the roof patch. Now, even though the pods are three and one half feet high, you have probably noticed that there is only two and a half feet of usable space, when you are in them. That is because the first foot is taken up by the following components," Jensen pointed to the display screen.

"Four cryogenic canisters two Oxygen, one Nitrogen, one Hydrogen, and one water canister, also you have 3 1/2 inches of memory foam. You're navcomm and mini tri-star, a regenerating power supply, transmission signal booster, waste handling unit, and your thermal sleeping bag. The pod also contains in the 1 foot catch above your head an EOS reserve helmet and gloves and a variety of weightless food stock mainly granola bars and paste. The pod is designed to keep you alive for a minimum of 8 days however, 12 days would be stretching it. I have to say at this point that even though your vehicle may be severely damaged it is much better to remain with the vehicle than to be marooned in a pod. However, if you're heading into the asteroid belt or entering an atmosphere this may not be a good idea, in such case your module navcomm will probably eject you in a direction away from the danger. While you are marooned and inside a pod this is what you have to look forward to. You can use the communications link to connect you with the other pods including, if you have a signal, other navcomm stations. The pods are a well designed Dewar's flask vehicle for thermal protection, plus you have your thermal sleeping bag and an internal heater. After you launch for Mars it is your responsibility to setup your pod. You can change your food storage supplies to your tastes and the flavors you like, select a preference of media and download it. The pods have orbital cameras one of the top and one on the bottom. The front and back sides of the pods are solar panels to generate power for storage and use. And finally, if at any time during your trip you notice that maybe the side entrance door isn't working right, or the pod is not pressurizing correctly, or the air handler is not operating correctly. Do not stay in that pod. Your module has four replacement pods in storage. Remove the old pods and hook up the replacement, do not put it off until later. You may go to bed that night and never wake up. The ISA says the safest place to be is in your pod during a potential hull breach situation, which includes your landing on the surface. Understand, your module may break apart on landing but, if your pod seal is still intact and you have the robots you may still come out alive. Okay, I've got a Jumper to catch I won't be back for two days but I will be back to see you launch." Jensen left a few moments later.

The press showed up the next day and a series of interviews were filmed first in English then in the crew's native languages. They would ask a question in English and instructed JP to answer the question in Japanese and the same with Alex of course John only answered in English. Three days later the press informed the media services on Earth (WGNN) of the launch of the Mars Module on its way to Mars.

Chapter 6

Welcome Home

The trip was rather uneventful. The crew divided up the watch detail into rotating eight-hour shifts. On the second day, John disembarked from his pod to find Alex hanging from the ceiling in an upside down position.

"Look John, magnetic floors. They didn't activate until after we had left the LP. There is a pathway on the floor and ceiling, and on the exterior roof and sides. Your inner suit packet has a controller on the upper side that regulates the amount of magnetic pull you wish to exert. There is a map showing the pathways on the Tri-Starr. Evidently, they don't activate until someone is in contact with them. This way I'm not just floating around. I can control the shoes magnetic grip to enable me to walk normally."

The interior of the module was coated with foam panels, and there were no sharp corners as a safety concern for weightless travel. The internal system displays were covered with a clear protective sheet so that someone didn't break them by bouncing into them. John had read the EOS manual. In order to repair the hull on the interior side, you had to remove the foam and if necessary cut the hull to make a flat surface. Then using the EOS-HR gun (emergency operational system hull repair gun), which actually looked like a gun in a weird way, repair the hole. The gun repaired holes up to twelve inches in diameter. After that, you had to hand weld the patch and use an 8 × 8 foot sheet from storage, cut it, and put it in place yourself. The external hull repair was conducted by an external service droid. John was impressed with the magnetic strip idea and gave it try. Sure enough, it worked fine and would probably stop the crew from bouncing around in the cabin. The crew spent most of their time studying or watching media in their pods. There wasn't very much to do but study. They were about

1.5 months out of the LP when the proximity alarm sounded. This was the first time anyone had actually heard the alarm, the module's maneuvering engines powered up and fired. The alarm then stopped, and JP came out of his pod.

"What was that?" he asked.

"Proximity alarm," said John. "We evidently were on a collision course with some kind of space debris. The navcomm corrected our course to avoid it. Look here, you can see it on the playback."

They all watched as the navcomm identified the approaching object, corrected speed and course, and started the engines to avoid impact with the object.

"You know, if we didn't have this system that could have been the ball game. The only one of us that would still be alive would be JP because he was in his pod," remarked John.

"JP, what would you have done?" asked Alex.

"Well, I guess I would have continued on to Mars Platform."

"You're out of your mind," said Alex. "What would you do by yourself? I would have turned this mod around and gone home," said Alex.

There was a silence. JP went back to bed.

"You know, John," said Alex. "What you said is right. We would not have known about the possible collision, and if the collision had punctured the hull, we wouldn't have had any time to put helmets and gloves on. The atmosphere would have vented in a matter of seconds, and we would have been quite dead. That would have left JP locked in his pod until the module's auto hull repair had fixed the problem and re-pressurized the internal atmosphere."

John agreed, "The main thing is that we, you and I, wouldn't have known anything until we were gulping for air like a fish out of water," replied John.

"Hey, have you seen this?" John pushed a button on the control panel. The image presented was an image of the interior of the ship.

"See there?" John pointed to the front of the ship. There were two infrared images posed near the control panel.

"Is that us?" asked Alex.

"Why don't you wave and see," replied John.

Alex waved his hand, and the infrared image waved back.

"That's nothing, watch this." John pressed another button on the panel, and the image suddenly became a real image and in 3-D.

Alex was taken aback "Where's camera? Behind us right? There has to be a camera."

"I don't know. I've looked around, and I can only find one camera, that's the one directly above us which is focused on the control panel area. Look, this can see right through the floors and walls like they weren't there. I don't know how it works, but look, here's a picture of our backs." Alex looked at the screen and a picture of the back of his head. He turned around to look for the camera behind him.

"No, don't bother," replied John. "I've already looked. There's no camera on the back wall."

Alex started for the back wall, turning around every few steps to check the image. He got to the spot where the camera should have been, and there was nothing there but the wall.

John continued, "Notice that Jensen didn't bother to show or explain this to us. I found it by accident. The program probably dumps to a transmit file, and they probably can see and know everything we are doing."

"We should talk to Jensen and let him know we don't like it," Alex suggested.

"No, Alex," John corrected. "I'd prefer that they didn't know that we know. We'll have JP see if he can disable it," Alex agreed.

The next day, John showed the program to JP and recommended that he see what he could do. JP agreed.

Five days later, Alex and John cornered JP at the kitchen table.

"Well," said John "what did you find out about our visitor?"

"Keep your voice down and don't let them see your mouth move." JP said looking at the table "If they can see us, they can probably hear us also," suggested JP.

"What did you find out?" John asked.

"You were right. The program dumps into the navcomm transmit pack, and you were right again, it isn't done with cameras. Fact is, I don't know how it's done, but it's integrated into the navcomm system, which means it's automatic. We are like a program to navcomm, which means they can see everything we do just like a navcomm map. And I don't know how the images are produced, so I don't know how to disable that part of the program. But, we are dependent on the navcomm system to land us on Mars and for a lot more. I'm scared that if I monkey around with it, I may disable the navcomm unit, possibly making it unusable for the landing. That might not be to our advantage. We have a saying in Japan. If it's not broke, don't attempt to fix it, and I agree." JP got up and went to his pod, leaving Alex and John staring at each other from across the table.

"We have same expression," suggested Alex. "It was invented in Russia," Alex said as he got up and went to his pod.

A few days later, John came out of his pod to find JP at the control panel studying the systems file instructions.

"What are you doing?" John inquired.

"Well, you know that investigation you had me on? It got me curious about the navcomm system, so I thought I'd read up on it. This thing's really remarkable. The system is a collection of components: a laser distance sensor and imager, radar, a compressed wave transceiver, a mini Tri-Starr brain, an encryption algorithm generator, a re-generative power supply, and it goes on, but get this, do you know how many individual navcomm units there are?

"No," replied John, "how many?"

"Seven and they are indentified by letter. Okay, there's the Series 'B,' which is the big units on the Earth and the LP. There is Series 'M,' which is incorporated into all the modules and Series 'T,' which are in the majority of the T-111 units. Series 'Rs' for relay signal booster station found on special T-111s. Series 'H' is a handheld unit. Series 'F' for a float, I don't know what that is and Series 'C' which is a contact repeater. We have on board 1M, 6Rs, 48H, 64F and 288 Cs. I think I'll go downstairs after I get through reading this and take a look." John agreed and suggested,

"We should know what we have and how to use it."

An hour later, JP reappeared back in the control room with a thirty-inch cylinder in his hand and a sheet of paper.

"What you got, JP?" John inquired.

"According to the manual, this is the unit we will mainly use on the surface. It's the H-series handheld navcomm unit," JP replied.

"How does it work?" John asked.

"It is a combination of components, but basically, it's a 3-D laser imager. It also has a variety of other components: a transceiver, a computer interface, a re-generative power supply, and a series of sensor encoders. But that's not what's so interesting about it. What's interesting about it is the microelectronics and the integrated programming. It is really a well-designed piece of equipment. It has to be activated, but I've already activated this one, actually the modules navcomm did. Okay, let's test it. Walk to the back of the room, turn around, and walk back." JP turned on the unit and held it vertical. John walked to the wall turned around and came back as JP turned the unit horizontal.

"Let's see what we got," suggested JP.

He went to the control panel, opened the navcomm program, and pointed. "You see the module's navcomm has identified the H unit. Let's see the file." JP toggled the controls to display the file, and there was John in 3-D walking to the back of the room and turning around.

"Very impressive," John admitted.

"That's not what's impressive, John. What's impressive is look here at the bottom," JP said, pointing to the line at the bottom of the image. "It's a recording feed line. See it gives the date, time, vector location, vector sequence, temperature, atmospheric content, and even identifies who you are. See here, John Alexander."

"How does it know who I am?" John asked.

"It's your tag, John, which I found out is a C unit or contact repeater. When a navcomm signal hits it, the unit sends back a reflex signal. The signal sends whatever code it is programmed to send, in this case, your ID code. According to the manual, the unit, when it uploads to navcomm, it also initializes a confirmation security scan to determine whether or not you are supposed to be here. It also identified the module from modules navcomm which it has on file in its file vault. However, what's really unique is that the unit contains a motion detector program. Not like the motion detectors you're familiar with for home security but an internal program that identifies motion by comparing captured images. It has image recognition. When it does its first scan, it captures the image. The scan takes like a nanosecond. The unit is in off mode now, but it still scans three times a minute to detect any changes. If there are changes indentified in the scan, it will cause the unit to reactivate and take a magnified image of the motion or the change in image. This is an internal program. The same program that does this will tell the unit when someone or something is approaching. Your card will tell it that it's you, and it will wake the unit. Navcomm works on a master-slave structure with a pecking order. Units M, T, and RS have priority over the other units, but if the units can communicate, what one unit knows, the other units also know."

"You mean like a large robot?" questioned John.

"Exactly, and a robot that doesn't forget and there is a file explaining that navcomm has a learning program. That means every time it completes a task, it makes a file on that task or more like a map. It will adjust the file code to do the task more correctly the next time. This is related to its input feedback, which mainly comes from the sensor encoders, or its eyes and ears."

"I'm sure it will come in handy on the surface. You need to tell Alex about it," added John. "Good work, JP."

John woke to the sound of the type-2 proximity alarm in his pod. He went to sleep late last night; the clock said that it was Thursday, May 9 and 12:00 pm, EST Earth. Well, it just said 1200 hours military EST (Earth Standard Time: Greenwich Mean Time (GMT)), but without a point of reference, that was meaningless. He popped the door of his pod and floated out. Alex and JP were in the kitchen, having coffee out of their "weightless" cups, a very essential component to weightless food consumption. John turned on his magnetic grips and walked out to the kitchen.

Alex uttered "Well, look who's up. We were just going to get you. We've been up for the last couple of hours, join us." John greeted Alex and JP. They slid over to make room. John got his cup and injected it with an instant coffee shot, then the water, nuked it and joined them at the table.

"What's going on? I take it we are approaching Mars Platform," said John.

"We have been in orbit for the last three hours, and that alarm means we are on approach for docking with the platform in," Alex said looking at the clock. "Fifty-two minutes."

"Okay, let's finish our coffee and get into outer suits for the docking," John instructed.

"Can't we stay in our inner suits? Why do we have to have both on?" asked Alex.

"ISA rules, didn't you read the regulation book? This is procedure, which means that's the way it goes. If that's what the book says, that's the way it is," John replied.

JP looked down and said, "The book says that all passengers must be in outer suits during takeoffs, landings, and dockings. An inner suit during traveling is okay, as long as the attachable helmet and gloves are within ten seconds of their position. Right now, your helmets are at your stations, and mine is at the comm link at my station. We are in inner suits, and the helmets are within two seconds in a jump, two seconds to attach, so we're okay."

"Well, I think we should be at stations for this linking, so let's go," John emphasized.

They finished their coffee and rinsed their cups, placing them back in their holder brackets and went to suit up. Ten minutes later, they were at their stations. John was in the pilot's chair, Alex in the copilot/navigation position, and JP was at the comm and systems panel reading the signals from the sensors.

"Time; now thirty-one minutes and counting till dock," John advised. A notification he really didn't need to give, as everyone had that information displayed on their panels.

"Wow guys, look at Mars, that's really something." They spent a couple minutes looking at the view.

"JP," John said. "Do you have the surface landing location marked? And will we be able to see it?"

"It's on the equator, John. We are too far north right now. We will be able to see it from the platform in great detail. The platform has a high-definition telescope. Deimos and the platform came into view, and the module completed final maneuvering for the docking. Ten minutes later, they had docked and were taking off their outer suits inside the platform. The platform was constructed by the linking of four CMP shells, which had dropped their loads to the Martian surface and linked here in orbit around Deimos. The same way the Lunar Starr and LP had been formed. After they settled in, John called a conference.

"We are going to be here for two to four weeks. They gave us a list of things to be done to update the platform. Remember, we are the first people to be here. The automated systems need to be secured to bring the platform up to operational requirements." The platform consisted of sections A through D. Only A had atmosphere which had activated upon their approach.

"So, it's pretty much self-explanatory, but take a look and select the order of installation. Some of them will require two people. First, we need to call home. They already know we are here, so let's turn on the comm and see what they have to say. JP, it awaits you."

JP turned on the comm and set up the tuning and functions, and sure enough, a picture of Jensen came to life.

"You guys made it, nice of you to call. I thought we would hear from you before you docked, but I see we are too late for that, so how's it going?"

"Well, as you know, we just got here so we're trying to get organized and looking over the list," John replied.

"Okay," said Jensen, "I'll be here or Bob will, if you need assistance. If we are not on the comm, they will page us. Also, we have directions from Earth online, so there shouldn't be any problem we can't handle. I need to explain your trip, which has been six months sixteen days, has taken Earth to the far side of the Sun. And soon we will be going around to the other side. At that time, we will be out of direct communications for a few months. We would like you to drop before we go out of direct contact. Mars is on its way to its Aphelion (farthest point) from the Sun. It will take you approximately a year going out and a year coming back. In the meantime, we are going to be on the other side of the Sun twice. So, your signals will have to be relayed or bounced through the asteroid belt. We have a CMP that dropped six years ago in orbit near the asteroid belt and is now behind you but will be able to link us to bounce a signal to you. The CMP that went with you will soon be dropping supplies to the Mars surface. It will also be launching a series of T-111 probes toward the asteroid belt. These probes will serve as signal repeaters for the Mars Platform in order to transfer your signal and ours. Even though it will improve our signal reception, there will be a lag in the transmissions. During solar flares, there will most probably be some signal corruption in all communications and programming signals. You will have to verify content before installation to your Tri-Starr system, JP, that's your job. Oh, and about the two T-111s in orbit around Mars that have been in operation since the start of the project, we need you to do a small repair job. They will be docking with the platform soon. The navcomm will bring them in through the upper load port on one of the CMP sections. We need you to refuel them and change out the battery packs. Navcomm will then re-launch them and re-pressurize the bay when you're done."

JP nodded "Can do, Mr. Jensen."

"One of the most important fixes that you need to address is the senor array from the four corresponding units on the roof and a directional setup of the disks. This will require a space walk on the roof. The upstairs of unit C has no upstairs living quarters. It is sealed, and there is a rather large series B navcomm unit contained inside. Remember, you are the first actual people to be on that platform. Navcomm and the robot did the best job they could in assembling the platform, but it needs a human touch. Oh, and by the way, the robot which is a small service robot is located in section D. It has been recharging since you have docked. It will be coming to see you as soon as it is fully charged. We will have to re-adjust the programming so that it can to assist you."

"JP, there are some adjustments we wish you to make with the robot. We also have a few chores for you before your drop to the surface. We will be sending a packet, but first, let's get the platform in order, that's about it. You are to contact us every day, so keep in touch, any questions?"

"No, sir, we will contact you tomorrow, Alexander out."

They started the upgrade immediately. The first order of business was to pressurize the three modules. First, the air handler lines had to be joined, same with the electric lines, data lines, and sensor lines. This was accomplished by joining the tube transporters through the link hub and the regulation meters. JP was trapped at the control panel of unit "A," re-programming and integrating the systems; the robot was helping. Then they needed to attach the emergency Oxygen feed line to the main air handler. Then the electronic detective and components needed to be joined. Alex and John handled that, while JP went over the computer attachments and the comm system components. When everything was done, they pressed the button, and a faint hiss was heard as the sections pressurized. Once the sections were pressurized, extra oxygen and air pumps were turned on. They could enter the other sections without a helmet now, and the sections were now acting as a single unit through the hub control.

In the next few days, they set up the pod bays, kitchen, water system, shower, lounge, storage grids secondary control station, auxiliary, power systems, and more. The hydroponic growth vats, including lights and thermostatic controls were set up. The T-111's showed up and docked themselves in the rail of unit D. John and Alex handled the repair. First, they had to deactivate the probes and refill the fuel tanks, then unfasten the battery packs and insert the new ones which they had located in unit D's storage hole. Once that was completed the units were reactivated, and after a few seconds, they beeped and lifted out of the bay. The setup was then complete. John, Alex, and JP got ready for the space walk. In order to do so, they needed to put on back on their outer suits. This would be the first time that John would wear an outer suit except for the launch and the docking. The outer suit fastened over the inner suit in the same manner with a front zipper seal. In order to get into the outer suit you needed to remove your inner suit shoes and replace them with outer shoes. The helmet locked into the collar of both the inner and outer suits, forming a double pressure seal. JP assisted them in getting suited up. John noticed a metal grip plate on both arms. He had noticed it before, but he hadn't said anything about it. Since JP was here, he thought he would ask.

"JP, what are these for?" JP looked at John once and then approached him with two 6″ x 2.5″ items which looked like calculators.

"You really need to read your system manuals, John," said JP. "This one is your navcomm controller; it fits into the sleeve of your right arm. The other one is the suit controller, which fits into the plate of your left arm. The navcomm controller controls all navcomm functions. The system is integrated into your suit. For example, the navcomm controller has a two-inch display. By toggling a button on the controller, you can project the image inside your helmet. It also has a magnifier to magnify the image and many other applications. The suit controller on your left arm controls everything that has a do with your suit. It controls the internal temperature, the oxygen flow, the water jet, waste handler, and just about anything else that has to do with your suit, including your magnetic grips.

"Navcomm monitors the suit. When you turn it on, it tells navcomm central where you are and what you are doing. These units link your inner suit with you outer suit including your internal sensors which tell your respiration, body tempeture, and bio functions. Navcomm can access and transmit through your suit's online cameras, just thought you'd like to know. You know John, you really should read more of the technical information that is supplied, especially for your outer suit. Not knowing what you're doing outside could have hazardous effects. Okay, now here's the plan. You and Alex will go out the air lock up the ladder to the roof. When you get up there, the first thing you need to do is to attach your tether to the tether rail. Next, you need to adjust the knob on your left panel to adjust the magnetic strength of your shoe grips. The top of the module has a magnetic walkway on it, just like in the interior of the module, and so does the hub. All you need to do is to stay on it, if you slip or fall the tether will catch you. Now, I'm going to be coordinating the signals from down here in the control room and working the operational integration of the system. So, I will be online the entire time, if there is any difficulty, be sure and let me know."

John and Alex walked into the air lock, and a few seconds later, JP heard it hiss. JP followed their progress from the control room. The first thing they needed to do was to release the locks on the navcomm directional sensors. To do this, they needed to cross over the hub to all four units. Alex and John disconnected the hold locks first A, then B, then C, and finally D. The units had to be coordinated with the large navcomm unit in B making B the master. Once the units were unlocked JP pressed the integration button. The sensors started to cycle around until they emitted a beep. JP Okayed the setup, and John and Alex relocked the systems. When they were done, they returned to the inside of the platform. The CMP that had been dropping to Mars arrived within eight days. Jensen called in; it was time to take a space jump. According to the packet Jensen sent, there were four rocket packs in the storage area of unit B, which they had started calling the basement B. John and Alex went to B bottom level to see if they could find them. The hub conduit attached the four basements of the CMPs together. John went first, Alex followed. The storage area was filled with food and supplies. Alex went to the right, John went to the left, and after a few minutes, Alex said,

"John, here they are."

John went over to where Alex was standing. The rocket harnesses were there, but there were no tanks attached. The instructions called for them to attach fuel and Oxygen canisters, which would have been quite large and heavy on Earth. However, here in weightless space, they weighed next to nothing.

"You know, Alex, I remember these packs. They were invented in the middle 1900's. They never became popular," John commented. "They could only carry enough fuel for a couple of minutes of operation on Earth. These are not the same units. These unit thruster packs have been modified for space, and they carry four times the fuel that the original units carried."

John and Alex located the appropriate canisters, filled them, and attached them to the harnesses. They transported the rocket packs back to section "A." Jensen was on the comm.

"Okay, guys, this next mission is a little more complicated. We want you to install a navcomm unit on the Martian moon known as Phobos. The unit is in the basement of module 'D.' it is Series Rs unit. Here's the plan, you are to take the rocket packs and the navcomm unit back to the Mars Module. Then activate navcomm to match the speed and direction of Phobos, placing you in orbit around the moon. Once in orbit, you will use the rocket packs to descend to the surface of Phobos. On the surface, the navcomm will indentify the location for the unit's deployment near the moon's South Pole. Once completed, you'll return to the Mars Module and prepare for the landing drop to the surface. It is believed that Phobos is not a Moon but a rouge asteroid that became entrapped in the gravitational pull of Mars. It is also believed that the moon came from the fifth planet that exploded, creating the asteroid belt. The gravitational pull of Phobos is non-significant, so you should not have any problem landing on the surface with the rocket packs."

"The orbital velocity of Phobos is significant, because it is much faster than Deimos. Phobos makes a planetary rotation every seven hours and forty minutes, which is very fast. Also the moon's orbit is unstable, and it is predicted that Phobos will one day crash into Mars sometime in the future. When, we don't know. We feel that implanting this sensor will give us a better control grid over the planet's surface, which will be important to you when you are on Mars. The idea is to use the rapid rotation of Phobos to form a relay base, which will operate on both sides of the planet. The installation of this navcomm unit will create a vector web around the planet with the T-111s and the platform. This should give us constant contact with you and the surface."

"Now, here's the procedure, suit up in your outer suits and use the rocket packs to transport to the moons surface with the navcomm unit. You will probably have to use a tether to transport it. When your module is close enough John, you and Alex will proceed out the airlock and institute a navcomm control drop to the moon's surface. You will then need to install an anchor for the unit on the moon's surface. Implant the unit and then return to the module, and that's about it. We will begin tomorrow; say around 10:00 a.m. Oh, and remember Phobos is traveling at a high velocity. Time is of the essence here. Otherwise, you may have a hard time returning to the Mars Platform even though the module when in orbit around

Phobos will keep up with the moon. Phobos will continue its planetary orbit around Mars. Not that I don't have confidence in navcomms ability, but if you take to long you may end up on the other side of the Planet from the platform. If that becomes a reality you may have to spend another seven hours to re-dock with the platform after circumnavigating the Planet. So, every minute you're on the Phobos you will be a little farther away from the Mars Platform. After you land on Phobos and implant the unit, we are hoping that it will take you less than thirty minutes, you're done. After that navcomm will take its shot to re-link you with the module, so don't stop to admire the view."

John activated the module navcomm to proceed to the approach position around the Moon. At nine o'clock the next day, they put on their outer suits and attached the jet pack harnesses and the Rs navcomm sensor unit. Jensen came over the comm about 9:45. John and Alex proceeded through the air lock to the outside. Once outside, they scaled the ladder to the roof of the module.

John turned to Alex. "Are you ready?"

Alex nodded. John reached to his left arm, turned off the magnetic footplates, and pressed activate. The navcomm activated, John went first with a push off the top of the module. Alex and the sensor pack followed next. As they got closer, the rockets fired to slow their descent. The gravitational pull on Phobos was considerably less than the gravitational pull of Earth's moon. They landed on the surface with a mild bump and headed towards the Pole. When they reached the Pole and the navcomm unit beeped signaling they had arrived at the location. They began to set up the anchor unit. It didn't take long. They drilled the holes and mounted the anchor plate to the surface. Alex then fastened the sensor to the plate and backed away. The sensor beeped, and the solar panels expanded. Then they turned around and started moving across the surface. In approximately a minute, they were on the other side of the moon. John pressed the activate button on his sleeve. They lifted from the surface at an accelerated velocity. Phobos faded away underneath, and they were adrift in space. John addressed Alex over the comm,

"Quite a view", John commented over the comm.

"Yes," said Alex, "but where is module? I can feel the gravity of Mars pulling me down. I don't want to enter the planet's atmosphere and burn up."

"Alex, you're not going to enter the atmosphere and burn up, and the gravity is not pulling you down," John reassured him. "You are imagining things. Hey look! Here comes the module."

The module was approaching slowly, and within five minutes, they had landed on the roof and re-entered through the air lock. Jensen congratulated them on a job well done. They then returned to the platform for a short stay. Jensen called the next day.

"Ah, guys, we are going behind the Sun in ten days. We need to know that you're safely implanted on the surface and in the cave before we go. So you're going to drop in the next seventy-two hours. Make sure you finish what needs to be done on the platform. Remember, there won't be anyone there for at least another two years."

Within seventy-two hours, they were in the module and on their way to align the link for the drop to the Martian surface. An hour before the drop, the proximity alarm sounded. They put on their outer suits and locked themselves in their pods. Navcomm and Tri-Starr were now in control, and all they could do was cross their figures. They all felt the retro rockets fire and the module bucket a little as it entered the atmosphere and the landing gear extended. Then the landing rockets fired, and then came the bump that signified that they had landed on the surface. All in all, it was a pretty smooth trip. It was a full minute before they popped their pod doors. Alex was checking for internal pressure and asking everyone else to check their sensors to be sure that the landing hadn't caused a leak. After it was confirmed that the module's internal pressure was the same, a relief was heard, and tension faded. The crew disembarked their pods to take their first look at the Martian surface. Alex jumped to the floor. He was definitely excited and said,

"I can't believe it. We have landed on Mars and alive; hey gravity." Alex turned off his magnetic shoe plates. The rest of the crew followed suit. JP was the first to say it.

"Well, it doesn't look very appealing. There's nothing but rocks and sand as far as the eye can see, and all of it is Red or Orange." The crew took a few moments to take in the view of the Martian surface.

"We need to call Jensen. I mean, they know we landed, but we need to confirm it for them." JP raised the Starr on the comm Jensen's face appeared on the display.

"Well, you made it okay, that's great. You need to get to the cave and get set up while you still have some light. Give me a call when you are tucked in. I have a list of things that need to be done." John could hear a bunch of people yelling and cheering in the background, and he turned to Alex and JP.

"Well, they seem pretty happy."

Alex retorted, "I'm pretty happy too."

"Well, of course, they're happy they're not here," JP pointed out.

"Okay, we need to get this thing to the cave ASAP," said John. "We don't want to be caught in a storm." After a few changes and calculations were made, they put the module in drive and headed toward the direction of the cave. At the end of the landing strip, they noticed bubble packs of supplies that had been dropped by the CMPs. Alex counted fourteen bubble packs on the way and pointed out that two of them were water bubbles.

They continued on the pathway that the robots had built, which led to the entrance of the cave. When they reached the cave entrance, they noticed that the robots had built a drop site for the bubbles on the left-hand side of the roadway. There were eleven bubbles standing to the side of the pathway at the cave's entrance. The robots' solar recharging units with their solar panels were located a few hundred yards further down. The module's top speed was only 45 mph. It had taken them just under four hours to get to the cave, approximately 168 miles from the landing site. According to the instructions, John announced they were to back the module into the cave as far as they could so that there would be enough space to move in supplies and create a work space. Alex and JP put on outer suits and grabbed the required gear.

"Alex, take the side navigation with a series H sensor. JP, take the back and set up the navcomm light. Let me know when you are ready. Also set up a portable light tower so you can see what it looks like. But let's first get the robots clear of the cave," John instructed.

"*DA*," said Alex.

JP said, "Wait till I say okay, before you signal the robots to come out."

"Yeah, okay," John replied.

The robots had carved a 24×24 foot hole in the side of the cliff. They had installed the framework guide into the sides inserting six-inch bolts into the rock of the entrance hole. The air lock panels would fit inside the frame and then be sealed. The module once sealed inside the cave would not be coming out again. Alex was with JP on their way to the back of the cave, with the navcomm 'H' series sensors operating, to create a map of the cave.

"JP, let's get the light tower up and running so we can see what we're doing. See if you can find a flat spot for the tripod out of the way of the module's path so John doesn't back over it," said Alex.

JP laughed. "Okay, got it. Let me hit the switch."

"Yeah, John probably would run,-" JP stopped in mid-sentence. Alex said some expression in Russian.

"John," said Alex, "you really need to come see this." John glanced at his screen, which had just activated. Evidently, JP had turned on the light tower. It showed the entrance extending twenty feet back and the tunnel continuing back another hundred plus feet in length, expanding in width.

"I'll be right there. Let me get my suit on," John replied.

Five minutes later, he joined Alex and JP at the rear of the cave.

"Wow, they really did a job on this. I didn't quite expect this. Well, they can stop drilling. This thing got to be 100ft. × 100ft."

"120 by 111," said JP, looking at his arm navcomm, "but I'm not complaining."

"No, John, this is very good," remarked Alex. "Plenty of room for the supplies, and I think the hydroponic garden will fit well, which will give us a nice interior space."

"Okay, let's back the module in here and see what it looks like. We've got a lot to do," John replied.

The module docked itself in the cave with ten feet in the front between the module and the twenty-foot entrance tunnel and ninety six feet on the side. The first thing they had to do was to hook up the exterior comm link. The signal would go from the comm link inside the module to the external link. It was then boosted to Mars Platform, from there to the Lunar Platform, to Jensen and Earth. A familiar face came on-screen.

"Well, boys, how does it look? All tucked in?" Jensen asked.

The crew explained what they had found.

"That's great! It will make things a lot easier. Okay, let's go over a few things. On the computer, there is a file that you need to call up. It is code encrypted, but JP has the codes available, so look for file pack 2487 MLP. It's your schedule, which is listed by priority and importance, so do as many as you can the next couple of days. When you get the lock installed, make sure the robots are inside. There's a ramp that attaches to the air lock which you need to install so that they can get in and out. Talk tomorrow, it's just two days before we go behind the Sun. We will try to bounce to you but don't know how that will go out, Jensen out."

JP pulled up the list.

Find package (7) inside structural foundation for cave. Follow instructions for installation.

Find package (10) outside air lock panel and installation.

Find (11) air lock and install follow instructions.

Install temp Atmosphere, package 5.

Implant temp. 80 degrees, package. 3.

Transport package. 1, 2, 3, 4, 9, and 12 to inside.

"Install and set up hydroponic garden.

"Package (13) contains robotic conversion equipment.

"Package (8), (17), and (18) contains personnel supplies."

And so on it went, listing contents of all the thirty- five packages located at the landing site and the outside of the cave. John had JP go outside and run a hand scanner on the bubbles that were located at the cave's entrance. The bubbles had a set of patches on them that identified their labels to a navcomm signal when scanned. JP came back in shortly with the report.

"Most of the packages out there contain the cave sealing equipment, framework, air lock, and machine components, which means that the bubbles at the landing site are mainly food and water. I wonder how these bubbles got here. Do you think the robots brought them from the landing site or were they dropped here? I'll have to ask Jensen about that. Anyhow, we have the equipment to seal the cave and reinforce the interior. The rest of the supplies will have to be brought here by the robots and broken down and brought through the air lock. Six of the eleven packs that were outside the entrance contained product for sealing the cave. Inside two of the bubbles are the framework supports and the 8×8 foot panel components, which will have to be assembled. It will require both the panels and the air lock to complete the seal. Also included were two extension ladders."

John adapted the robots to handle the panels by attaching a hydraulic extension arm. The arms extension was twenty four feet, putting the top panel of the seal within reach. The framework installation came first. It took about two hours to complete the panels and one hour to install the air lock. John then attached a sprayer to the extension arm. The robots then applied exterior coatings to the panels, an epoxy ceramic sealer. The panels were then sealed, both on the inside and outside of the cave. The air lock was a different matter that wasn't exactly 8ft. × 8ft., more like 7ft. × 7ft., with a prefabricated insert that would fit inside the frame. Once the seal was completed, it had to sit for twenty-four hours before it could be pressurized. The crew and the robots went on to unpack the rest for the remaining bubbles outside the cave. JP and Alex were working on a large one, when John heard JP say.

"What is this? It's got wheels?"

John stopped what he was doing to go and take a look.

"It looks like some type of mobile machine," said John.

Alex added, "Hey, here's the disk."

John suggested, "JP, go into the module and see what's on the disk. Alex and I will take the rest of the equipment out of the bubble and lay it out so we can see what we have."

JP returned about three minutes later. John and Alex had and laid out most of the parts.

"What is it?" asked John.

"It seems if I understand it right, to be an expandable cart," JP replied.

John looked confused, "What do you mean expandable?"

That's what I don't really understand. It has a basic frame structure which evidently can be modified. This disk," JP said holding the disk up in his right hand. "This is the computer assembly disk. Let's put it in the robots and see what they do." JP revolved around to the back of robot #1 and inserted the desk. The robot stood there for a few moments and then it started beeping. JP accessed the robotic interface.

"What's going on?" asked John.

"It appears they want me to change their tools. They want a tool called WR-34 and SW-19. I know what that is," JP replied. "That's a multi bit screwdriver set and the multi bit ratchet set." Another problem is the extension arm which was still attached to robot #2 had to be removed. After the corrections were made, the robots proceeded towards the outlaid parts. The crew stood and watched, within 25 minutes the assembly was complete and operational. It looked like a wall panel with wheels.

"Okay how does it work?" asked John.

"I will ask the robots for a demonstration," replied JP.

He then pressed his right arm navcomm, communications switch and signaled the robots. The robots demonstrated the cart by removing the sizes. Then they expanded the 8 x 8′ foot frame which folds out of the base in both directions making the base 12 feet wide. They replaced the sides then unfolded the back increasing the length by 4 feet. The rear extinction also functioned evidently, as a hydraulic lift.

"That's what they mean by expandable," prompted JP. "However, this unit has a very limited navcomm transceiver it's more like a remote control. It does have a signal transceiver that works on a navcomm frequency but has very a short range. It activates to the navcomm signal when flashed. However, it has limited motor propulsion so, it cannot move any great distance on its own.

"Okay," said John. "So, it expands from an 8 x 8 foot cart to a 12 x 12 foot cart what about it? Are we supposed to use the pull it, the robots?"

"Yes John, I think so," Alex replied. "You don't expect the robots to transport all the bubbles from the landing site. The water bubbles weigh 11,000 pounds you expect them to transport 11,000 pounds 170 miles without some kind of tool?"

"Those bubbles only weigh 4180 lbs. here on Mars but, no I get your point," said John. "That's still a lot of weight. Well, JP, tell the robots to go to the landing site and get a bubble."

"I'll tell them John," JP replied. "But, I need to tell them what type of bubble I need a bubble number."

"Tell them to bring a water bubble here," suggested John.

JP entered the operational code to the robots. One a robots turned and then backed into the cart. The front extension arm of the cart locked with the grip on the robots rear side and the robot proceeded to go to the pathway. It then started off into the direction of the landing site. Jensen called again that night with some more news.

"How's it going?" Jensen asked.

John gave an update on the progress that had been made that day.

"Ah, one thing I didn't mention yesterday. There is a CMP that was launched a little after you left. It should arrive in about 70 days. It has a special present for you guys. Take good care of it. You won't be getting another supply drop for two years so, they packed it up. We are going behind the Sun in the next 72 hours we will be out of direct communications according to the scientist here for approximately six and a half months. We will come back into direct communication for a period of nine months as Earth comes around the other side of the Sun. We will go back out for communications afterwards for 6 months and will remain out of direct communications till we circumnavigate the Sun. At that time, you will be over 249,000,000 miles away. After that we will be in direct communications for over a year which including the time of the drop. So, for the next four months concentrate on getting the cave setup and secured. Let me stress that the less time you spend outside the better off you are for right now. We can't afford an accident at this point so use caution."

"Are you going to tell us what the surprise is?" John asked.

"No, but it will drop before we come back around the Sun. I'm going to leave it as a surprise however; I will say it comes with instructions so follow them. Anyhow, you probably won't hear from us for while but, we will try to link just to see if we can. If some thing happens we should know about. Send it on 'Alert' and we will get it faster. The Mars platform will store it until we can retrieve it. Good luck guys, and don't take any unnecessary risks, we would like to get you back alive, Jensen out."

"Wonder what they are sending?" JP questioned. For the next three months the crew was busy getting the cave set up which was becoming fully operational, structural supports were secured, and the hydroponic garden was just starting to produce its first crop. Interior lighting and atmosphere had been established, and all packages had been opened and stored. Also, there had been some modifications made to the interior of the cave. Things were working out quite well. And the other CMP had signaled it was in orbit and ready to drop. The drop activity signal beeped and the track image was produced on screen. No one was to be outside during a drop. After 16 orbits all packages had been released and were on the ground. JP sent the robots and cart to collect and transport the bubbles packages back to the cave. There were 5 bubbles in the shipment.

"What's wrong with them? They know the airlock dimensions. We will have to break them down out here and move them into the cave in sections," complained Alex.

JP agreed, and started opening the first four packages the robots then transported the contents inside. John assisted in getting the supplies properly stored in the cave. JP joined Alex outside to access with one of the double wrapped units when John's voice came over the comm.

"You'd better make this quick, we got a storm coming in."

Alex stopped "how long do we have?"

"Looks like about 5 minutes," John replied.

"We'd better leave this until after the storm passes. It has enough weight to remain in position even at 80 mph gusts. They turned and headed for the airlock. The storm took two hours before it was completely over. At which time Alex and JP went back outside to continue to unpack the package labeled GWKSRL 1334. As they opened it they could see frame pieces inside, JP found the disk package.

"Looks like some type of machine," remarked Alex as it was unpacked. But its purpose was not obvious.

"I'd better look at the disk before we go any farther," JP suggested. He went back to the module Alex followed. JP put the disk in the Tri-Star read drive and a picture came to screen.

"Hi, my name is James Gruhler. I'm the head engineer of Gismo Works Robotics Laboratory. The 1334 unit is your transportation vehicle for your exploratory missions on the surface. The unit comes with all robotic functions that the AADG modules have and some they don't. But, the most important feature is the navcomm link. Of course, with the navcomm unit you can go a thousand or more miles in distance and still maintain a link with your home base, and the T-111's, and even Mars and Earth lunar platforms. The vehicle is at this time in parts. There are four major sections; the framework, the wheels, motors and electronics. They will be packed in separate bubbles. You must assemble the framework yourself. To do this insert the second disk into the robotic programmable drive. Then follow the enclosed instructions. Be sure and convert the robotic equipment according to these instructions. Now the rover is too big for the airlock. When completed the rover will be 22 feet in length and 10 feet in width and 6.5 feet in height. It will have to remain outside. But don't worry; the robots will take care of it. The rest of this disk is the operation manual keep this in the vehicle after it's assembled. JP stuck the second disk into the CD /DVD robotic programming player and both robots sat there for a few moments and then went out of the cave and started assembling pieces. John and JP went to make sure the parts were screwed on tightly. Alex headed for the pod he hadn't gotten a full nights sleep because of the drop. Twelve hours later Alex's shift was due he came out to find JP starring at the view screen which was odd because there was nothing to see but rock and sand.

"What's going on, have robots finished the rover yet?" he asked JP.

"The robots finished putting the machine together several hours ago. It was really something to watch. The framework slid together and locked in place. The completed framework and wheels took no time. The package included a machine or tool that allowed them to put it together in a snap."

"Well, if they have put the machine together what are you watching?" asked Alex as he came to take a look.

"They dug a hole approximately 24 by 24 feet. Now they are constructing some kind of panel frame work, out of the extra panels we had left over. I guess that the rover will go in it when they are done. It is night but I have a light tower on out there so that we can watch. They watched as the structure was completed and the rover backed itself into it. Then the door panel closed the structure with the rover and robots inside.

"Now," exclaimed Alex "that's smart!"

JP said, "I'm going to bed."

Six hours later John got up. "What's going on?" Alex repeated the details of last night. John had a blank stare on his face.

"Where are they now?" asked John.

"They are inside the cave. They have some kind of spray and they are coating the inside of the cave with it. When they started a Warning came up on the monitor not to go outside. They are on the second coat. Robot 1 is coating the walls and ceiling including the area behind the module. All, I can figure is its some kind of sealant."

"What about the hydroponics?"

"They sealed them in a cover, so it shouldn't have any harmful effects on the plants."

"You can go, I'll take over." Alex thanked him, and shuffled of to his pod.

When JP got up to relieve John, the outside fans, air handlers, and heaters were on and running at high volume. The robots were resting together in front of a hydroponic bubble and the Sun was coming up. JP set up to go over the files on the disk. A meeting was called John, Alex and JP met at the kitchen table.

"One of the files I found on the index is a description map of the group of missions that they wish us to accomplish in the next year," JP stated. "It points out various locations they wish us to investigate. One is of course the face of Mars and craters. The locations are not more than a day or two away and two of us are to do the explorations and one is to stay in the module. The rover is electric powered and has a re-generative drive so fuel is not an issue. The EMF power should be enough to get us there and to investigate these sites. However, one of the sites is the Olympus Mons which is the highest spot on the planet. Fourteen miles in height, and 345 miles wide at the top point called the caldera. It is not a day away; we are about 9,000 miles away from it."

"Look, we aren't going to do any rock climbing. It's to dangerous and even though it says that it has a moderate slop, how are we supposed to get up there? We don't have any rock climbing gear? We're going to have a tough enough time going down into this Valle," John said pointing at the Valles Marineris on the Map.

"We are here." said John pointing to a mark on the page "Eos Chasma. And Olympus Mons is to the Northwest approx 9,000 miles on the other side of this Marineris Valles. The three other mountains are about 6,000 miles away but, we are within 200 miles of the entrance to the Valles Marineris and the Valle is 3000 miles in length. So add that 3,000 miles to the distance and they become slightly out of our reach. Look I'm okay with the short trips and after that maybe the trip to the South Pole, and that's about it, as far as I'm concerned. I've just figured this out. This isn't a new list this has been planned for along time. The Valles Marineris is approximately 4,000 km in length that's 2480 miles and is deeper than the Grand Canyon at 4 miles. In fact the Valle is as long as the United States is wide if you include the labyrinth at the northwest end. Top speed of the Rover is 45 mph it would take 55 hours to reach the other side and on rough terrain and believe me, that trench is going to be rough terrain. We won't be able to sustain 45 mph more like twenty so now that's over 100 hours. If we were going in the module it wouldn't be so bad but in that rover it's out of the question."

"John, we should send the robots first to carve a path way through to the other side. Anywhere we go on this planet it's going to be that way," suggested Alex. "Anyway, it's going to take over a week to get to the other end and the same to get back plus Oxygen, water, and food. Plus, in that terrain, we will only be able to drive during the day which means we would have to sleep at night in a bio-tent or in the rover. So, let's make that one or two months."

"Look, there's no hurry but I agree we should send the robots first," John replied. "We will have to convert them for the mission and they will have to carry their recharge kits, and a navcomm unit with them. JP you'll have to set up the program."

JP had been looking over the map and programming details in the file manual. JP looked up with a confused look on his face.

"Did either of you see this section about component installation, what is this second section they are referring to?"

Alex and John took a look. Sure enough there was a section in the Exploration file on the attachment and operational usage of section 2.

John looked up, "This doesn't look like part of the rover. Are all the drop packs opened?"

"No," said Alex. "There are still two left outside."

"We'd better open then up." John and the crew put on there outer suits went back outside and started unpacking the remaining two bubbles.

"It would be in the last one," remarked John. As he was opening the side panel, he made a discovery "Hey, here's the disk. JP, go take a gander at it while we unpack the rest of the bubble."

"John," asked Alex "what is this gander, is like goose?"

"No Alex, a look, you know 'like' you take a look'."

JP took the disk back inside the module he returned in a few minutes later

John was asking Alex what he thought it was. Alex was saying that he thought it was some kind of plastic bubble. When JP interrupted, "It's a helium inflatable mini-blimp."

"A what?" John retorted.

JP handed him the pages he had just printed off the disk to John.

"There should be a few gas cryogenic canisters for fuel around here" he said.

"Yeah, right there." John said while pointing at the canisters stacked to the side of the cave entrance.

"Ok," said JP "here's how it goes, we fill the balloon with helium till it begins to float then we attach the enclosed air handler, the battery pack, combination thruster array and harness to the connectors and secure the anchor till were ready to use it. Since, we are not going to use it for a month or so, there no reason to have it floating around inside the cave." It was agreed and the robots carted the blimp inside and stored over by the hydro bubble.

The next day instructions were made to the robots and they were sent off to the Valles Marineris entrance on the south eastern side. The crew was able to monitor their progress over the viewer.

John was watching with JP who was reading the blimp manual as he was supervising the road construction. When JP said,

"Now I know why they sent us here instead of a qualified crew."

"Why's that?" asked John.

"I've been studying this blimp and I believe it is unsafe. It may go up and down ok and have a propulsion system and a collision avoidance system, to control the thing for speed and direction. But, I don't think it has enough thrust to navigate in one of these storms. If you're airborne with 80 mph gusts you will probably wind up on the other side of the planet. They say that in such a case the 1 mile of tether wire that came with it can be used to anchor the unit, but I don't know. The safety conditions say a maximum payload weight of 250 lbs. It has a navcomm, Air to ground distance notification, and so it pretty much flies itself but it won't be able to weather these storms. In this application we are the Guiney pigs."

"I guess we better be on the ground when the storms hit then," suggested John. "But if the blimp turns out to be unsafe we won't use it."

Two months went by. Jensen and Earth were just coming back into direct communications. John updated Jensen on the Marineris project. Jensen approved the details and the robots involvement. After words, John called a meeting about the Valle. They all met in the kitchen.

"The robots will be done sometime this week. The road way will be completed so we will have to decide what we are going to do."

Alex was the first to comment. "I've been thinking about this for some time. In the rover at 45 miles an hour it would take us around 50 hours to go from this end to the other end at 12 hours per day that's 4 days, more like five days up and 5 days back. Let's just say two weeks. To get to the Olympus Mons and back would take 174 hours there and 174 hours back and we would have to carry enough water, food, fuel, Oxygen, and specialized gear required for the trip on board and that's a lot of luggage. The water alone would be over 28 gallons for two people plus food, plus we will be unable to travel during the night. In Oxygen we'll have to take 8 canisters and we will need two extra canisters just in case."

"In case," echoed JP "In case of what?"

In case we have a flat tire, or in case of an emergency," retorted Alex.

"Look," interrupted John. "How fast does that blimp go? JP you've studied the manual how does it work?"

JP went to the console and put the manual on screen "Basically, it's a simple structure, it has a mini navcomm, and a maneuvering system. There is the blimp section which is shaped like a rounded triangle and a utility pack which attaches to it. The pack contains a shoulder harness with a battery pack, the navcomm unit and a carry basket. There is the control panel, the mini-thrusters pack and the canister rack, which will support 4 canisters, in this order, 1helium, 1hydrogen and 2oxygen. Last but not least are the cameras."

"The balloon reminds me of the shape of the spacecraft in movie 'War of the Worlds'," said Alex.

"Let's start at the beginning" suggested JP. "In order to assemble this thing we must first anchor and fill the balloon with helium using the automatic meter pump, they sent with it. The balloon will levitate to a height where we can attach the harness and framework. Every time we add weight, the pump will compensate the balloon pressure and tempeture. When we put the harness on, the pump will apply enough pressure to equalize the weight. When we tell navcomm that the blimp is fully loaded it will lift us ten feet off the ground and it will do this several times while it calibrates its thruster and navcomm values. After we put the harness on, the navcomm control panel is on the right arm of the harness. Your right arm fits into the sleeve. The left hand sleeve is your operational controls. Such as cameras, magnification, water, and air just like your outer suit it integrates with your outer suit by navcomm. On the panel you will see a square which is a small viewer. Then you have your manual navigation with four triangles forward, left, right, and backwards and then the two larger triangles one blue (UP) and one red (DOWN). Then there is an emergency button orange hexagon for rapid descent and the manual override functions. For the cameras there is an auto rotate cycle that moves the camera around in a circle making navcomm map of the voyage on all sides. The video is produced in two quantities one on your control panel monitor and the other to the navcomm mapper, where it gets transmitted on the navcomm link. Understand the Ariel as it is called, is the same as a navcomm handheld unit. We don't have a camera in our module that's taking our picture. What we have is a navcomm mapper, which maps our location and image. When we are inside the module for instance, we are within the sensor range. They then know that we're all in the kitchen, whether or not they can hear what we are talking about is another question. There is probably a file pack that has been keeping track of all activities since we landed whether it has audio or just images, I don't know. But while we are using the blimp, they will see and hear everything that the blimp maps or photographs and hear everything that's said when it's operational. We could just send the blimp unmanned and watch it on the monitor thru the navcomm link instead of actually going to Olympus Mons."

"OK I've got it but, I want the decision to come from them," John replied. "But, I liked that last idea."

"Meanwhile, I will look for camera. When I find camera, I will rip it out." Alex said while looking around.

"I strongly recommend you don't start pulling out wires Alex" JP stated with some resolve in his voice "I would have to oppose that idea. The people, who designed this module, the blimp, the rover, and just about everything else involved in this mission, didn't think the same way that you or I would normally think. The way they designed these packages to fit together is just different. So, is the internal engineering design of the module and for that matter so is their programming. Before them there was no navcomm or tri-star system and let me remind you it's a long way to a repair station from here. If we accidentally rip the wrong wires out, we could be here a one very long time."

"OK," said Alex. "I let them have their camera. Before, in space walk, they go out and dance around like women. Now, we go out and just push buttons much better." That got a laugh.

"Anyhow I think we should take a test run of the blimp just to see how effective it is."

The crew had now been on the planet over five months with the 6.5 months of travel time and the three weeks on the Mars platform a total of over 12 month's mission time. The next day they all were together making the blimp ready for its first test run. They unfolded the balloon from the package. The balloon was 30 feet wide and was made of a fiber mesh. Alex pointed out that when the Ariel was inflated it wouldn't get through the airlock so, they put on outer suits and took it outside. Turned out the assembly was fairly simple. They raised the balloon to 4 feet and attached the harness and fuel pack. The Ariel re-adjusted itself every time a component was added. JP had volunteered for first flight and put on the shoulder harness and fastened the safety belts. They placed the weight panel under his feet as instructed and the blimp raised and lowered him three times and then returned him to the panel.

"Ok, where should I go?" asked JP.

"Go to that hill, in the distance looks like about three miles. Go over the top turn around and come back. I'll monitor it on the module console," John instructed.

"OK here I go," JP said as he entered his and destination location to navcomm and activated.

John and Alex watched as the blimp rose slowly, picking up speed with a blast from its mini ion turbofan engine and JP was in a gradual assent.

John went inside to monitor the event on the display. It held the image of JP and the blimp from the exterior nav. link. John pressed to activate the blimp monitor. JP was talking through the helmet comm. The image came up on the screen. It was in auto cycle and John could see the hill ahead, then the cliff sides and finality the cave, with Alex standing out front.

"JP can you take the camera off auto-rotate. I'm getting dizzy," asked John

"Yes I think I can. There is a button with a dial here on camera"

The image slow and finally stopped facing front. John noticed there were a group of buttons on the display on the Ariel's navcomm link; one said camera John pressed it. A circle appeared with a XYZ grid John guessed (X for forward velocity, Y for altitude, and Z for direction) John entered 100 feet in Y and the blimp began to loose altitude.

JP yelled "Hey, what's going on?" John quickly explained what he had done to which he got a rather brisk response from JP.

"Well, don't do it again, you hit the override. Wait oh; I see I have a button that cuts your command off. Your command is for unmanned operation only. I'll have to fix that."

JP was circling the hill now rotating at an altitude of 1000 feet and 900 feet orbital distance from the hill.

"Do you feel it's warmed up yet?" John asked. JP said he thought so. John said as he was reading the instructions. "I'd like you to take it up to 2000 feet and pick up speed by using the thruster controls. Press it and hold it for three seconds," John instructed.

"OK, here we go," he was pointed it the direction of the cave. John heard the thruster fire through the monitor as he watched JP gain rapidly on the base position. In approximately 90 seconds he was over head.

"My god," John exclaimed. "Do you know that you're going 120 mph plus. That hill is 3.69 miles away and you covered the distance it in 95 seconds"

JP had gone past the base and was now turning around to come back. John instructed JP to try it at a greater altitude and suggested 3000 feet. JP then repeated the event this time at a faster speed. Alex said he was going back outside. JP brought the blimp in for a landing. Alex said he wanted to try it and put on the harness while JP came back inside.

"OK, but just one trip we don't want to use all the fuel." John said to Alex over the comm. While Alex was doing his run JP said, "you know its funny the way that thing is designed."

John was now watching Alex. "What do you mean?"

"Well, according to the manual when you want to gain altitude you don't do it with the thrusters. The blimp fuel is helium which gives it buoyancy of its own but inside the balloon is a frame work with a heater/ fan in it. When you press the altitude button the heater which, is powered by a DC current, heats up and gives the balloon greater buoyancy lifting it up. If you want to go down toggle the switch to reverse position and the heater becomes a cooler thus causing the vehicle to slowly descend. However, it isn't fast more like sluggish the same with turning. In other words if your at 2000 feet it would probably take you several miles to drop to the surface, but if your on navcomm autopilot it will work fine."

"That's not all, did you read the sections on the development," John handed over the manual to JP. "See what it says there, that they tested it on Earth and achieved moderate success as far as elevation and maneuvering but, atmospheric density inhibited the operation. It gives a payload weight of 125lbs Earth they estimate 280 lbs Mars. Also, that they tested it on the Moon at the Luna Starr and got more positive results there."

"John," JP countered. "I understand the physics involved Helium by atomic weight is lighter than Oxygen and CO_2 and when heated it will cause the blimp to rise but there is no atmosphere on the Moon so why does it rise there?"

"The question you asked is same as asking me why there is no water on Mars, I don't know. I would guess that it would most probably be the thrusters. As far as the water goes, it is suggested that at one time there was a lot of water on the surface, and there is evidence of that for instance the rippling effects in the sand in places. Then something happened that caused the planet to lose matter density and the planet could no longer hold the lighter atoms to the surface. The free Hydrogen that might have been part of the atmosphere at one time simply floated away. The same would be true about surface water on the moon. Here the free Oxygen atoms bonded with Carbon to form CO_2 and Iron Oxide which gives the planet its red color. Even though there is still some Hydrogen in existence in the atmosphere most of it is retained by chemical bonding. When they tested the blimp on the moon, the density couldn't hold the Helium and with the help from the thrusters it was able to lift itself and quite a bit of weight. Since the moons gravity is 1/6 th of Earth's. The Ariel payload would be 6 x 125 or 850lbs, on Mars it would be about 300 lbs. I want to say that without any atmosphere as on the moon, the Ariel has zero resistance and it would be quite easy to place the unit into LLO (Low Lunar Orbit) without requiring very much fuel. The only problem with that is keeping the systems from freezing while in operation which was probably solved by the internal heater. But regardless, if they tested it at the Starr, they must have found a way around that problem."

Alex had returned from his jaunt and was pretty excited. They waited for him to come inside. They talked about it for a while. Alex suggested that the blimp should be able to navigate the Valle in 10 hours maybe faster if unmanned.

But then John said "I don't want to use it until I talk to the Starr about it. So, we should store it in a protected area until then. We should be hearing from them soon. The robots are on there way back but, it will be 2 weeks before they get here, so we need to bring it inside. They put on their helmets and gloves and went outside to take it apart. A week later the comm panel signaled an Alert. It was Earth or more correctly the Lunar Starr. John and Alex were awake and answered the call, it was Jensen.

"Hey guys how's it going?"

John gave Jensen a rundown of the mission accomplishments to date including the completion of the Valle Marineris road and explained that he was a little unclear how they were to proceed. Jensen cleared it up quite quickly.

"Look guys, the rover was just for you to have transportation in case something came up. Our idea was to develop it for exploration of the nearby area. The Ariel was the big deal. In 29 hours you could use it to go to one of the poles and back, which is what we had in mind. In 70 hours you could circumnavigate the planet. We also have in mind a few other locations which you can visit but, now that you have a pathway in the Marineris Valles. We think the rover road trip might fit the ticket. You wouldn't be able to see much detail from a fly by with the Ariel. Alex went over the time and supplies required but Jensen had the answer. Look we are not in a hurry. I'll send the list you pick them but, if it were me I'd take the Ariel to one of the poles and get that out of the way. For the Marineris take either the robots or the Ariel to plant supplies at the half way point and the turn around, to lighten the carry load."

"It takes the robots three weeks to go 2000 miles and three weeks to come back so this is going to take a while," replied John.

"Like I said no particular hurry, you guys have been there now for eight months. Mars will be turning around and be coming towards the earth in approximately four more months. We need to have an update as to supplies you require in the next half year so that we can load it and ship it to arrive for drop on time, when Mars is closet to the Sun. Look; I have someone here that wants to talk to you, one at a time." The screen blinked and an image appeared; it was Joanne.

"Ok boys," she said. "It's time for your mission check up. I want to talk to each of you one at a time. The two not being interviewed should be in their pods, John you first."

John was followed by Alex then JP. The questions were about how they were getting along with each other, how they felt about things, and personal stuff. The next day there was a meeting. They decided to convert the bots to carry supplies into the Valle but, were hesitant about the pole excursion. The robots were dispatched the next day to implant the supplies on the Valle roadway. Jensen was still talking about the exploration to the poles. They kept putting him off every time he asked about it. One day Alex cornered John on the problem

"John, you know we are lying to Jensen eventually he's going to catch on that nobody wants to go to the poles by himself what are we going to say?"

"Look Alex, we will put him off as long as we can. Besides, this Valle trip will hold their attention for a while" replied John.

"John, I'm not saying anything but, they know when we are awake and when we are asleep. Where we are at all times even outside the cave and what we do. They may even know when we go to the bathroom and how long we take and even more. Eventually this South Pole thing will come to a head some one will have to go. If we refuse they may not provide us a way home, you know it's in the contract."

"We'll cross that bridge when we come to it," but John knew Alex was right. "The bots will be back in a week and we need to get organized for the Valles run."

They advised Jensen of the bots success in the supply run "The bots placed food and Oxygen and water at midway and at the end turn around before the Noctis Labyrinthus section and a power supply station was placed at each point. The power supply stations were solar re-generative units with a navcomm application. A sensor pole that the bots drilled a hole for and inserted into the surface, during storms the Trex would notify the station. The station would then close its solar panels and sink into the ground. When the storm passes it rises and re-extends. They drew straws to select the crew John and JP lost so, it was decided that they would start the mission as soon as they were sure that they would have good weather, which came in three days. John and JP got the rover loaded and charged up and took off for the entrance of the Valle which was approximately two hundred miles away. After a little over four hours they entered the Valle's gate.

Chapter 7

The Valle

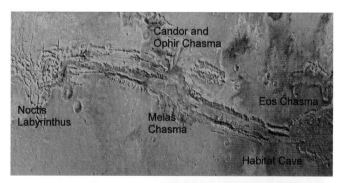

The bots had done a good job on the pathway. It had been cleared of rocks. They had been up and down the pathway twice now. In the next eight hours, John had traversed three hundred miles, but the sun was starting to go down. John wasn't happy about traveling during the night hours, so they stopped traveling as soon as darkness fell. As far as sleeping went, the rover had adjustable seats which weren't very comfortable. On day two, they made some real-time, completing over three hundred miles and would soon be approaching the Melas Chasma. Day three arrived, and John wanted to get to midpoint station, the beginning of Melas Chasma before night, which was still over four hundred miles away. Starting before dawn, they should be able to reach it before they lost the Sun. John was pushing to get there. The navcomm had already recorded the pathway and had developed a 3-D map of the route from the information. The T-111's had also gathered images of the Valle during the making of the pathway. The Navcomm had transposed the data to the rover's directional control. However, a flat tire at this point would be a disaster. John was using manual control to operate the rover. At the end of day three, the sun was going down but, they were still sixty miles out of the midpoint station. John decided he didn't want to risk it and pulled the rover over for the night.

The next morning, they proceeded on their way. An hour and a half later, the vehicle pulled up at midpoint station. JP hooked up the recharge line, and they gathered the supplies, had lunch, and watched a movie while the unit recharged, which took about an hour. They were in the deepest part of the Valle now, nearly four miles under the Martian mean surface. At this point, the Valle was over 320 miles wide. However, the pathway was close to the northern cliff wall. JP mentioned it would take them a full day to cross the Melas Chasma. The pathway in the Melas was smooth, almost like a riverbed. They were about one-fourth of the way across the chasma, when JP pointed to something in the direction of the cliff to the north.

"John, what's that over there?"

John looked, "I don't know, let's take a look." John swung the rover toward the cliff as they got closer they could see that it was a hole in the cliff.

"Looks like a cave," John replied as he stopped the rover about a hundred feet from the entrance.

Alex came over the comm. "A cave, a real cave, or just a depression on the cliff wall?"

JP was now outside the rover, looking in the entrance to the cave.

"Looks like a real cave. I can't see a back wall. John, what do you think, shall we go in?"

"I don't think so," said John slowly. "I'd say this if we were on Earth as well. We don't know what's in there." JP looked and went to the rover; he came back with a portable spotlight. Then Jensen came over the comm.

"If you're going to go inside, take a handheld navcomm scanner so I will be able to see also. We will want footage of the inside."

Then Alex's voice interrupted, "Have you been watching the entire time?" There was a lag of about thirty seconds, then an affirmative.

"Yes, and yesterday as well, and the footage is being viewed, and command says that it's a go. As long as Alex can pilot the Ariel for backup in case something goes wrong. Well, Alex, what about it?" There was a pause.

Alex said go ahead but asked, "What do you want me to do?"

"If they need some assistance, you may need to take the Ariel to them." Jensen replied.

Alex was slow to respond. "Okay, I understand." JP started talking,

"Look there's not going to be anything in there. This is a barren world with no life."

"That we know of, but my concern is we don't know how stable the cave is," John replied. He retrieved a camera and light from the rover. JP was already five feet into the entrance, when John yelled for him to stop.

"Look, if we are going to do this, we are going to stay together." So together, they proceeded into the cave. For the first forty feet, it looked like any other cave, and then the floor started to tilt, and it was downhill. Now, they had gone a quarter mile and were still going down. They started to notice stalactites and stalagmites formations clustered on the sides in some of the larger areas of the cave.

JP commented, "John, this is the first time I've seen something like this here on Mars."

"I know this is quite unexpected," John replied.

They were still going down. They continued walking for another twenty minutes. John's watch which had an encoder as one of its features, indicated that they had now gone down over three quarters of a mile.

"We will go down another quarter of a mile, but that's it. This thing could go on forever, and besides, we have lost our comm link to the outside."

JP agreed but added that if they didn't get to the bottom they would have to come back later, which John knew to be true. They continued on, and all of a sudden, the wall on the right-hand side became slick. They stopped to examine it, it was ice. JP picked up a stone from the ground and smashed it against the ice, creating a cracking sound. John was visually upset.

"Didn't we agree that we weren't going to make any unnecessary vibrations? Once again, we don't know what's on the other side of that wall."

John cautioned, "When the ice begins to break back away, we don't need a hole in our outer suits. We're too far from home."

John picked up a rock and joined JP. After about three hits, there was a distinctive crack and a chunk of ice fell out. John instructed JP to back up about twenty feet. John threw the stone at the area that was showing damage. Then he took JP's rock and repeated the toss. The wall cracked a little more. John picked a larger rock up off the floor. Quite a bit larger, the rock would have weighed over 30 pounds on Earth. It weighed a little over 11 pounds here on Mars. John threw it with all he could muster. The ice broke, revealing an extension of the cave on the other side. With their pickaxes, they chipped away at the hole and made a hole large enough to walk through.

"What do you know?" said John. "One side of the cave looks just like the other side of the cave."

But JP was busy looking at his watch.

"John, check your watch. What's the temperature?" JP suggested. John looked at his watch; the temperature registered 24 degrees Fahrenheit. John had noticed when they started down the cave that the outside temperature was minus 80 degrees Fahrenheit.

"Seems like that ice wall worked as a temperature shield," John pointed out. "This area is probably heated by magma of what's left of the planet's mantle. At some time moisturized vapor traveled up the cave till it connected with cold air from the surface, thus creating the stalagmites and freezing at the curve. The vapor formed the ice wall when it came in contact with the cold air from the surface. They continued down the cave, and then John looked at his watch. They were now one and a quarter miles down.

John stressed, "We've got to go back. I'm not going any farther. We've lost our daylight, and we have a one and a half mile trip back to reach the surface. Plus, I haven't heard anything on the comm for over a half hour. Maybe we will have to come back, but that's it for this trip."

JP held up his hand. "Do you hear that?"

John listened and turned up his outside microphone. "What?" Then he heard it. "Yeah, sort of a gurgling, and it's not far away. JP, we have to see what it is," John said. Since they had been on Mars, they had become accustomed to silence. There wasn't any noise except the wind on the surface. They followed the cave and came to another curve. They rounded the curve John nearly dropped his camera. What was before them was a small stream which was bubbling up from a hole in the floor. The spring measured a foot wide and about a half foot in depth.

"John, this doesn't look like carbon dioxide. It looks like water," remarked JP.

"That's not all," said John looking at his watch. "The temperature is going up. It's now 46 degrees." John reached into the utility bag and produced a small metal and glass box. He pressed the side switch; the hole opened and then closed. A light blinked for a second. "Well, just as I thought. There's Oxygen here."

JP gasped, "What?"

John continued, "Where there is water, there is usually some Oxygen, and that is true most everywhere. Normally water, as it travels, will release a few atoms of Oxygen after several hundred years; it would build up in this sealed chamber to form a detectable presence. In this case, about 10 percent or that's what the mini-spectrograph says, however not enough to breathe. Now, let's test the water." John stuck the mini-spec into the water to gather a sample. This time, the light flashed longer.

"Well, it's water of a sort, with a few other chemicals, one of which is iron, another is lime. Okay, let's collect a few test samples, and get back to the surface."

It took them over an hour to reach the surface; it was the middle of the night. When they got within a quarter mile from the entrance, the comm started going off; it was Alex and Jensen.

"I am very happy to hear your voice. I thought that something had happened to you, and I was going to be here by myself for the next five years," Alex emphasized.

"Yeah," added Jensen. "You could have at least put out a call and let us know you were okay. What was in the cave?"

"It wasn't possible," explained John. "The comm went dead about a quarter of a mile down, and we couldn't get a signal out. What was in the cave? We are not sure, and we won't know till we get back to the module. But right now, we have got to get some sleep."

The next day, they didn't wake up early. John woke up, turned on the autopilot, set the speed at 20 mph, and went back to sleep. When they did wake up, they had traveled a forty miles. They found no more caves on the trip. In two more days, they reached the turnaround at the end of the Valle. They recharged and started back the next day. Jensen had left instructions to leave the navcomm unit at the end of the Valle pathway. JP was monitoring the navcomm recorder, which was making electromagnetic images of the Valle. They arrived at the module six days later.

Alex was happy to see them, overjoyed would have more like it. John now knew him well enough to tell that he was really scared when they had lost contact. Five years on Mars by yourself was enough to scare anyone. John unpacked the samples, while JP downloaded the Valle files to the Tri-Starr and Jensen. Alex set up the test equipment. They had brought back samples of rock, the water, the atmosphere, the sand near the water, the ice, and the stalagmites, and just about everything else they could carry. Jensen was on the link, waiting for the test results. He blurted out, "Test the water first." So they did; the water was loaded into the tester.

"Okay," said John, "here's what we got: Hydrogen and Oxygen bonded H2O, but we've got a significant presence of iron, lime, and other trace elements. It's not safe to drink in its natural form. It would have to be processed and filtered. But Jensen had a smile on his face.

"That's just great, guys, extra goodies for you guys on a job well done." All of a sudden, the screen blinked and split into two half screens. The new faces were from Earth. It was Jason, and he had a few tech people with him, who were introduced as ISA engineers. A rather portly gentleman introduced himself as Dr. Chambers, the projects chemical engineering supervisor.

"Boys, ah, we have looked at the tape of your cave exploration, but the camera was a little dark during the water segment. I have a question, where did the water come from and where did it go?"

JP was quick with his response.

"It came out of the ground. It formed a small stream which ran down the cave about twelve feet, where it seemed to disappear under a rock."

The scientists started talking to each other.

"What would you say was the temperature of the water as it came out of the hole?" Chambers asked.

John's turn, "Well, we don't know, but the water was in liquid form, meaning it had to be at least 32 degrees Fahrenheit plus. The cave, before when we broke the wall, had an ambient temperature of 46 degrees, which was our first measurement."

"Okay," said Chambers. "Where the water disappeared, what was after that point in the cave?"

"That's about as far as we could go. The cave got narrow, and there wasn't enough of an area to continue the cave exploration."

"Okay," he said, "I want you to keep your eyes open when you go back through the Marineris Valles for unusual rocks or rock formations, especially when you're in the cave. Also, I want you to keep your Geiger counter on when you are exploring."

The crew agreed, and then it was Jason's turn.

"Guys, we don't want you going back to the cave for a while, about two months. We are going to borrow your bots, so we will give you a week with them. Then they will be gone, till it's time for you to go back to the cave. In the meantime, we are on hold, so take a vacation, Jason out."

The left screen closed, but Jensen was still there.

"Okay, guys, let's get on with the tests. Let's try the solids and the internal atmosphere next." John set up the tube to test the atmospheric sample next. The spectrograph produced a reading of 72 percent CO_2, 10 percent O_2, 4 percent N, 6 percent H, and 8 percent inert and molecular gases.

"Well," remarked John, "it's not breathable, but there is Oxygen there. Maybe it can be processed. However, I think a better question is how much is there available. I mean we only found this sample in the last hundred feet of the cave when we broke the ice wall. It's probably leaked out by now. It's my opinion that the water which contains H_2O plus a lot of other things like iron, lime, sodium, and inert elements comes out of the deep hole at a higher temperature, creating a vapor pack. The vapor saturates the ceiling and walls, dripping down and creating the stalagmites and the stalactites. When the vapor hits the cold air coming from the surface, it froze. This caused the construction of the ice wall because it is a smaller cavern than the main cave," John pointed out.

"This is possible," agreed Alex as he handed John the rock sample from the cave, that JP who was sitting by the samples, thought looked funny. John put it in the grinder, which produced a burnable test sample which was then placed in spectrograph. When the tests were concluded everyone was pod bound. John and JP were really exhausted, and it had been two weeks since they had slept in a non-movable bed. The rover wasn't really very comfortable. Most of the rest of the week was uneventful. Until one day JP buzzed John. The pods have a small twelve-inch screen and a micro camera which you can turn on or off at your digression. John left the camera off. He was still asleep but woke up when the buzzer went off.

"Yeah, what's up, JP?"

JP's image showed he was in the module's control panel.

"John, the robots are gone. I was out having them help me with the hydroponics in the outer cave, and all of a sudden, they turned and made for the lock. By the time I realized they weren't around, they were gone."

"Where does navcomm say they are?" asked John.

"It says they are headed for the Valle."

"I'll be right out." John joined JP at the control panel. "Is that them?"

JP nodded. "They are not too far away. See if you can raise Jensen," John instructed. JP boosted a link, and a few moments later, Jensen came on-screen.

"Jensen, our bots took off on us. It was like a stampede," protested John.

"I told you last week," Jensen replied. "That they were going to be busy for a couple of months and that you would have to do without them. But, you're right. I should have told you they were leaving last night. I didn't trigger them, the ISA directorship did. On the lighter side, it means your vacation just got longer. You won't be able to do anything much until they get back in two to four months, so relax. Of course, you could take that trip to the pole, which is a one-man trip in the Ariel?"

John looked at JP and responded, "No, we will wait."

"If you want to watch the bots, you can view them through their cameras, but you can't talk to them, as their receiver is blocked. You guys have been there just about a year now. It's time for you to assemble your shopping list for the next drop which will begin in eleven months. Let me say that there is already a lot coming in your direction, so try to stay out of the way when it starts. In other words, look at the navcomm before going on any outside excursions."

For the next few months, they did nothing but take care of the habitat. The Earth was going behind the Sun again for five months, and live comm was intermittent.

Jensen called, "Your supplies are being compiled, and the CMPs are being put together. There are going to be a couple of extra CMPs this time and another rover and a XPLM module."

"Great," said JP. "Now I can have my own module."

"They are not for you. They are for the other team," Jensen replied.

"Other team what other team?" John said with his voice not hiding his surprise.

"I didn't know how to break it to you. I guess that was as good way as any. Yes, you remember the scientists you talked to a few months back.

They have decided to send you help. Well, not really, they are sending a second team. The team will be located in the Valle, at the cave. It's a team of three, like your team, but who have been trained to do drilling and mining operations in the cave. They will be doing excavation work and sample testing. We want to see where the water comes from and where it goes. They are the same as you, just trained in mining techniques, and their deal is the same. But to supply them is going to take a lot more supplies. There is a manifest of equipment related to their supply in file pack A27—GWKS on the Tri-Starr under supply. Now, you still have five years there. You will still have your own mission schedule, but we would like you to assist the other team whenever needed. We would like you to offer any and all the assistance you can supply to Team 2. We don't know exactly if we are going to be sending anyone to take your place at your location after you're done with your mission. It may be decided that your site is expendable and may be abandoned. Like I say, it hasn't been decided. The designation code and information as to Team 2 is in the file also."

"So are we going back to the cave?" John asked.

"No, you will not return to the cave until the second team gets there. We have some other projects for you that we would like you to accomplish. I'll send you the list tomorrow."

John and the crew spent a lot of the next five months with the Ariel and rover investigating sites close to the habitat. The main site of their investigations was the Ganges Chasma to the North and the Argyre Planitia which was to the south, not to far from the habitat. One of the main problems with the investigation of the craters and the Argyre Planitia was that the storms had given a false layer of sand on the floor, which made it hard to find exposed samples. This was true in all the craters, and there were a lot of craters in that particular section. There was no talk about any great missions now. Jensen kept trying to get JP to go to one of the poles for samples of the ice. That was all there was at the poles. JP kept avoiding the idea. John argued that they shouldn't need to go because of the cave, which was a good argument, but it didn't win in the long term. It came to a head one night about three months before the drop. Jensen and the crew were talking about the new crew that would soon be arriving and discussing the schedule. Jensen mentioned that their schedule would change and that pretty much the focus would be on the new crew. Unless they wanted to make an exploration of the other side of Mars, there wasn't too much left for them to do. Of course, JP could always go to one of the poles.

Alex mumbled, "There he goes with the poles again." Which Jensen, I guess overheard.

"Look guys don't be mad at me. It's not my idea. The sponsors want to know what the ice is and what's underneath the ice. They figure that since you are just sitting around eating their food and living in their module waiting for the next drop, that you could make the effort."

"Well," said JP. "I don't want to go, but I don't want to sit here for three months having people think I'm lazy. The main thing about the trip that bothers me is the fact that I have to go alone and that I'll have to spend three nights in a bubble. If something does go wrong, there is no way that John or Alex can reach me. The pole is about 9,600 miles away. It is way out of range for the rover or anything else we have, and I have never slept in a bubble before."

"JP," replied Jensen. "The navcomm will keep you in communication constantly. John, Alex, and I will split the watch so that you have someone to talk to the entire time. We'll have navcomm plot the course, and we'll monitor your progress. As far as sleeping in a bubble, it's pretty simple. Take the memory foam pad with you, unlock the rabbit hole, and climb in. Seal the rabbit hole and set your emergency system on active before you go to sleep. If there is any change in the Oxygen content, the mini-handler will make the adjustments. A loss of air pressure will set off the alarm, but you'll be in an outer suit. Just close the helmet. That's all there is to it." Jensen paused. "Have navcomm plan the whole thing for you. Of course, it will take a week for the Ariel to place the supplies en route, but it shouldn't be a problem."

JP hesitated, and then said okay. The trip was scheduled to start in eight days. The next day, the navcomm punched out the plan and supplies needed to make the flight. The crew took most of the day loading the Ariel. They put the foam mat and supplies in the carry box on the Ariel. That way, JP wouldn't have to transport it with him. When they had it all loaded, they went over the checklist the navcomm had provided. Shortly thereafter, the Ariel took off. It rose straight up and disappeared. John watched it disappear, and then went inside with the crew to monitor the flight. John and Alex went to the kitchen to make a pot of coffee while JP went to the control panel to monitor the Ariel's flight. John was putting sugar in his coffee when JP said,

"Hey John, I think you better look at this."

John strolled over to the panel. "What's up?"

JP sounded concerned. "The Ariel, it's not going the way we planned it to go. It's off course and it's really high according to the navcomm. It's at 100,000 feet in altitude. John, isn't that—?"

"Yes," finished John, "Outside the atmosphere? As a matter of fact, the atmosphere here stops at about eighteen miles, which is just less than 100,000 feet so it's close. I hate to say this, but that thing's in orbit." They all watched with disbelief as the Ariel proceeded to gain and gain rapidly toward the South Pole.

"Look at the velocity. It's going well over 300 mph, actually 385 plus. I didn't know it could go that fast," Alex exclaimed.

"Probably in the atmosphere, it can't, but seeing how it's way above that, who knows?" John offered.

Seven hours later JP, who was glued to the screen, noticed a change in the Ariel's velocity.

"I think its coming down," JP shouted. John and Alex came back over to the panel. JP pointed to the velocity was at 300 mph and falling, and the altitude was 70,000 ft. and falling.

"It's coasting in for a landing at the pole. Look, it's only six hundred miles away. The altitude was dropping slowly, but dropping."

"They don't expect me to make that trip, do they?" JP asked with a quiver in his voice.

"I don't think they knew, JP," John offered.

"They know now, I'm not happy about going into orbit in that thing," said JP.

"No JP, this is good," Alex suggested. "Now you can go and come back in two days instead of four, so only one night in bubble."

JP stared at Alex, and John decided to go somewhere else. The Ariel returned the next day. Upon JP's request, they dialed Jensen up for a little talk, but Jensen was prepared.

"JP, now I had the design engineers looking over it. They say it's safe. You should have no problem with the altitude or the re-entry into the atmosphere with the Ariel. The navcomm course compensates for the planet's rotation. You'll actually be going to the other side of the pole, where the Ariel dropped the supplies. Collect the samples and return over the top with just one night in the bubble. You can leave all the supplies, including the bubble, at the site. Wrap all the supplies in the bubble and close the rabbit. However, the cryogenic tanks you'll have to bring them back."

"What about heating during re-entry?" asked John.

"The engineers have assured me that there is no significant heating because of the slow rate of descent. They said that heating should not be noticeable, which is good."

Jensen argued with JP for about twenty minutes before he got JP to agree. They synchronized the event so that they could schedule their watches. JP was to take off the day after tomorrow.

At 6:00 a.m. that day, JP and Alex were outside checking the Ariel over for the journey. John was in the module, watching on the control panel. Jensen was on the link, as well as some of the design engineers and ISA senior staff. They made their presence known by verbally giving JP their support. At 6:20 a.m., JP activated the Ariel and off he went. He was only visible for about five minutes. Alex came inside, and they watched on the screen for about a half hour, talking to JP and having him give a conditions report.

"I'm at 65,000 ft. and still going up. So far it's okay, and the power's good. The Ariel waited until I got in the upper atmosphere to fire the thrusters. The navcomm says I'm going about 325 mph, but I don't feel it because there's no atmosphere. It's kind of like floating in space. Navcomm gives my arrival time to destination as six hours. I think the fun part is going to be coming down."

"Well, whatever you do, don't fall asleep," John emphasized.

"John, don't worry. The proximity alarm will wake me when the descent starts," JP responded.

"Okay, I've got your sleep watch, and Jensen will wake you up. So I'm turning you over to Alex for the rest of the trip. See you in the morning."

John turned off the microphone and turned to Alex.

"If anything happens, wake me immediately," he said. Then he turned the microphone back on.

"Here's Alex," and went to bed. Midnight came early. When John got up at 11:30, Alex advised him that JP had already landed and was in his bubble, asleep. JP had taken images and map plates of the surface. Alex pulled up the pictures. John spent thirty minutes going over them. JP had found a crater to set up the bubble in and had set up the camera so you could see him crawl inside the bubble. Then he set up the bed and had dinner. Jensen came on at 8:00 a.m., but JP was already up and collecting samples, John was supervising. JP had collected ice and atmospheric samples. JP remarked to Jensen that this trip may have been a waste of time because all that was there was ice. He pulled out the drill and took a core sample, which didn't take long. Then he asked Jensen whether he was satisfied and whether he could start for home. Jensen said okay, and after he put on the harness and pressed the activate button, he was on his way home. He arrived back at the cave at around 5:00 p.m. and John started the analysis of the samples that he had brought back.

After a couple of hours, John said,

"I hate to admit it, but I think JP was right. There's nothing here that might be considered unusual. The ice is frozen CO_2, the atmosphere is the same as outside, and the core sample is routine stuff. However, it doesn't seem to contain as much ferrous oxide as normal, but that's no great find. So JP was right. The trip was a waste of time."

"Not entirely correct," remarked Jensen. "We got a good test of the Ariel's abilities, and the navcomm got map data of the pole, from which it is developing a model as we speak. And we got a reading as to the thickness of the ice cap. Not a total waste of time, but the main data on the Ariel's ability means we can explore the other sides of the planet without any major problems."

"That may be, Mark," replied JP. "But I'm not going on all these missions."

"What about Alex or John?"

"I can't go," replied John. "My responsibility is to the module. It will have to be Alex."

Everyone then turned to look at Alex who stood up and went towards his pod.

The next three months were uneventful. JP had really expanded the hydroponics, and both John and Alex complimented him on his job. They had melons, lettuce, tomatoes, peppers, broccoli, and a variety of other fruits and vegetables, which did a lot to spice up the meals. Even Jensen was impressed with the amount of food that the hydro units were producing. JP explained that even though they produced enough for them during certain times of the season, what he really needed was a food process system. The exterior temperature was perfect for flash freezing the product, but a canner and grinder would be a nice addition if they wanted to have things like jellies, jams, and tomatoes year round. Jensen agreed and said he would see what he could do. One night, John was at the control station when the comm lit up. The face in view wasn't Jensen but was familiar. It took a second for John to place it as Yuri, one of the candidates from the training program at the Cape. He had competed with Alex for the first launch, but Alex had won. John thought it was because he was not really Russian, but a Chechnyan. Chechnya and Russia had been engaged in a dispute for over four hundred years, called The Four Hundred Year War, and Russians considered the Chechnyans extremely unfriendly and hostile. John didn't know him very well but remembered that he was pretty well briefed in class. John had spent most of his time with his roommate, Samuel Johnson. He, Sam, Alex, and JP used to sit together in class.

"Yuri, isn't it? How are things on Earth?" John was wondering how he was being able to use an encrypted navcomm signal to contact them.

"I don't know. We left Earth a little over three months ago. We are on our way to see you. We should be at the Mars Platform in about three months."

"Oh yeah, who's with you?" John countered.

"I have a Frenchman named Lefluere and a representative from China called Xiao. You remember Xiao from school, right? We are coming to do work in the Valles at your cave." Lefluere's and Xiao's images appeared, and they both waved at John. John waved back. Alex had heard the conversation from the kitchen and joined John at the console. Alex started a conversation with Yuri in Russian, which lost John for a while. He understood about one in every five words. Suddenly, Yuri turned back to John.

"The drop should start on your end in about two and a half months, slow to start. Is there anything we should know as far as surface conditions and the landing site? I mean, I have it on navcomm however, it's always good to check your sources," Yuri hesitated.

"Our landing went fairly well. Except for the bump when we impacted the surface, everything else was fairly smooth."

"That's good to hear, John. How far will we be in time from the Valles entrance?"

"We are approximately two hundred miles from the entrance to the Valles on the edge of Eos Chasma. The place you're going, which is just before the main section of Melas Chasma and the widest place in the Valles, is about halfway up the Valles or about 1,700 miles from our location. You're looking at about four days in the module or rover. This includes the 168 miles from here to the landing site. We have a device here called an Ariel which is able to cover a large distance fairly quickly. Let us know when you're getting ready to drop, and I'll have one of the crew meet you at the landing site to guide you here. We'll do lunch."

Yuri laughed, "That's a good one, John. But for you to know, we have Ariel also. They are becoming quite popular on the moon. We tested ours there. They are quite the deal."

The conversation lasted another forty minutes, with Yuri and Alex talking in Russian at the end. The crew conversed with Yuri's crew every other day and seemed to be getting along pretty well. Alex advised John that Yuri had made it clear to him that they were not coming to do any exploratory work. They were coming to mine the Marineris Valles and the cave, and to develop a permanent water source from the cave. The drop was mostly their supplies, including tanks and pumps, for this purpose and other supplies. Yuri also informed him that the majority of the drop would be at Melas Chasma.

Chapter 8

Visitors

It was a couple of weeks later when the notification alarm on navcomm sounded.

"Sounds like a microwave," remarked John from the kitchen. Alex came to the control panel to see what was up.

There was a ship in approach orbit. The signal was coming from the Mars Platform and the T-111s in orbit. The MAP camera enlarged to give them a better image.

"Looks like a CMP coming into orbit," said Alex.

"It will be ready to drop soon, so don't go outside without checking. You wouldn't want one of those bubbles to fall on your head."

It was a few days later that the alarm sounded again. The first CMP hadn't dropped yet, and now there was another CMP coming into orbit.

"What are they waiting for?" John muttered, mainly to himself.

"Remember, when we dropped John, it took the navcomm a couple of days to line us up. I don't know why," JP replied.

"Then I'm not going to worry about it until the product gets on the ground," John replied.

The next day, John got up and went to the kitchen. He was having breakfast when Alex came out of the bathroom. He had been taking his shower. The rule had been formed between them that showers were taken every third day to conserve water. The next day, it would be JP's turn, and then John's.

"Have you seen our guests outside yet, there on the comm?" mentioned Alex.

John looked up from his sausage, egg, and cheese biscuit to the view screen. In the image, there were two robots at the recharge station. Then he noticed that their structure wasn't the same as their crew robots.

"They started dropping last night. They went all night, and I think they are through. The robots made a beeline for here and have been here about two hours. They should be finishing soon. Also Jensen called. I didn't wake you because it wasn't urgent."

Alex cued the screen to display Jensen's message. The instructions were to refit the robots with extra battery packs and to send our bots, which had returned recently to the drop site, to unpack some luggage."

"Where are our bots?" John asked.

"Playing with JP in the garden," said Alex, pointing to the air lock door.

John went to the door and looked out of the window. In the two years they had been there, JP had outdone himself with the hydroponic garden. Of course, the robots had helped. The garden now filled the cave. The original garden from the design plan was supposed to be a bubble with a pressure door measuring 16×16 feet with three hydro trays, but JP had carried it a step farther. He had abandoned the bubble and constructed the hydro pans and frames extending throughout the distance of the cave. The habitat cave was 120 feet long × 96 feet wide. The module took up 88×24 feet approximately. This left not much in the front, with twenty feet being used by the entrance but left 84×100 feet on the side of the module. Of course, there had to be work space and a place for the bots to park during storms, but this still left a good sized space, and JP and the bots had transformed the area into a natural garden. The cave consisted of Oxygen-generating plants and vegetables, there were even a few small hybrid dwarf trees, and the Oxygen content of the outside was probably better than inside the module. But the module and the garden seemed to work together.

The waste from the bathroom was separated into two process tanks, liquid and solid. The liquid was separated by membranes and, through electrolysis into hydrogen and oxygen. The hydrogen powered the fuel cells, creating extra power and heat when needed. The oxygen, which was breathable, was pumped into the cave with the Carbon Dioxide from the module and the pods. The higher Oxygenated air was then filtered by the hydroponics and fed back into the module's air handler. The system was so successful that it supplemented the Oxygen enough to slow the consumption of the cryogenic Oxygen by 25 percent. The cleaned air was then fed to the internal air handler and interior compartments of the module. When no one was using the command facilities, in other words when everyone was in the pods, the handler cut the feed. When a person entered the control section Cryo-Oxygen was injected by the air handler, the same for the basement section. This maintained a lower but effective atmosphere, and when a pod was not being used, the handler didn't continue to supply Oxygen. However, since the pods are air sealed, they are able to maintain their Oxygen supply for long periods of time. John opened the lock and went out to talk to JP.

"Did you read the instructions?" JP nodded. "Okay, I have to get a hold of Jensen to activate the bots and send them to the landing site and do the unpacking, so, as soon as you're ready."

"They have just finished mixing the growth mix, and as soon as they pour, they'll be ready to go," replied JP.

"Okay, how long will that take?" John asked.

JP reached over and turned a valve. The mix filled the supply canisters. After a few minutes, JP replied, "They're done."

John hesitated. He was looking at some cantaloupes that were growing in the garden.

"Can we get one of those for the meal tonight?"

JP agreed and said, "I also got some lettuce, tomatoes, onion, garlic, and cucumber ready to go, but you know what I miss?"

"No, what?" replied John.

"Olives," exclaimed JP. "We had some in the freeze packs when we first got here, but they've been gone for three months. I can't grow them here and there are other things I can't grow here. I put in a request for them on resupply. Hope they send some."

John went back inside to call Jensen. Jensen came online. He approved the dispatch of the bots and John then asked Jensen what the schedule for the drop was.

Jensen said that the list was already posted and added,

"You know, the other crew is on their way. They launched six and a half months ago. They should be getting to Mars Platform sometime this month. Actually, within the next week, however, all the cargo will drop first."

Seven days later John got a call from Yuri.

"Alexander we are docking at the Deimos platform in 15 minutes however, they have sped up our time scale and we will be coming to see you within two days. We will only be at Deimos for a one night, and then we will be going into drop orientation."

"Ok we will be waiting to see you," John replied.

The crew watched the landing on the navcomm split screen. They had the camera from a T-111 and the land camera from the landing site and the camera from the XPLM that was landing, plus the image from the Martian Platform. It was quite a show seeing the landing from four different angles, a real treat. Alex had taken the Ariel to the landing site in case he was needed, which he wasn't. The landing was almost flawless.

"You know, I think that their landing was smoother than ours John," said JP. John agreed they had that rather abrupt bump on their landing, but it didn't appear to happen on this landing.

"The navcomm is learning," said John. "The more landings, the better it gets. Our landing was based on mathematics not experience."

"Alex, are you going to lead them back?" asked John.

"*DA*," Alex responded.

"Let me give them a call," John toggled the comm "Hey, Yuri, everyone okay?"

The face of their mission commander, Yuri Olesky came up on the display.

"Yes Alexander, we are happy to be here and in one piece."

"Alex Gorkov is at the site and will lead you here. Help him bring the Ariel inside."

Alex and crew arrived at the cave about four hours later, and the crew in outer suits parked the XPLM in front of the cave. Once they were inside the air lock, they could take off their helmets and relax. JP had prepared some food and refreshments, realizing that Olesky and his crew had been mostly on paste for the last six months. The meal was steak with noodles, vegetables and salad with fruit salad for desert. He had also prepared a nice package of vegetables for Yuri's crew to take with them. Alex and Yuri were having a rather avid conversation in Russian, but then paused as Yuri turned to address John.

"Nice trip?" John asked.

"Boring," replied Yuri. "We have been in training since you left. We are now considered highly skilled in mining application. I remember when you launched two and a half years ago. I and the team, Xiao Cho and Antony Lefluere were picked approximately a year ago but, had been in training since before that, as you know."

"I understand that you will be going to the cave for your mission?" John prompted.

"We will be spending our entire six years in the Marineris Valles in that cave you found and other places in the Valles. We have a rover too and one of those blimps. We will come and visit occasionally. But most of the time, we will be drilling and testing samples. I had thought that you would be helping us, but they said that you would be doing crater jumping and collecting samples out here. If you find something out here, be sure and give us a call or bring it to us. You probably noticed that we have almost three times the amount of the drop in comparison to you. Mostly because the extra packages contain the drill, test equipment and other required construction material, including an atomic spectrometer for accurate diagnoses of metallic elements. Along with supports and struts, we have four packs of panels for exterior construction. You'll have to come over for the house warming when we put them together, somewhere near the cave."

"We had some panels with us, about thirty-two, I think. We used them up or rather, the robots did. The robots built the rover enclosure and an exterior storage bay for exterior supplies and the power module for protection from the storms."

"Our packs hold sixty panels apiece and struts, John. The mainframe units are in another pack," Yuri replied.

"My god," commented JP. "You've got enough to build a small city."

"Not quite," Yuri explained. "The panels are set for construction of a structure that they wish to have built. Come, I show."

Yuri went over to the control panel and pulled up a file in their sub-domain CDG 141 structure. The image came to screen.

"This is the structure they want us to build. It is a square with equal sides with an open section in the middle and a storage rectangle on one end." Yuri said pointing at the screen.

"This," Yuri pointed out, "is the storage bay for the rover and this is the internal structure. This shows the main framework and floor plan of the unit's interior, showing layers of component assembly water systems, electricity, furnishing, and system structure, which will be added in the final steps. When we are through, we will be moving from the XPLM to the square, and the XPLM will become the main vehicle for exploration in the Valle. JP, I understand that you are responsible for the hydroponic garden outside. Will you assist us in setting up ours? They want us to set up and finish the base as soon as possible so that we can begin working the cave."

"We will all help. When do you think you'll be ready?" asked John.

"About a week or so, we have to prep the cave and complete a small mission with the water. Then prep work for base form, then we build."

Yuri and his crew left the next morning. They were looking at a four day trip, so they got an early start. Their XPLM also had a top speed of 45 mph, and that was only over cleared ground. However, even with the roadway the bots had built, you couldn't go 45 mph continuously. With twelve hours of light, the module should average 540 miles a day. However, 460 miles was more like it. John and the crew kept track of the module as it moved down the Valle roadway until it arrived at the destination. A couple of days passed. John hadn't heard from Yuri, but Alex talked for a little while every night with whoever was on duty. It was John's duty shift. Both JP and Alex were in their pods when the comm chimed an incoming call. John looked at the identification code and punched receive to accept.

Yuri s image lit up the display.

"John, we are about ready for your help. We are going to start on the foundation tomorrow. We will have the bots level the site and fill in the bad spots. This should take them a day or so, and then we will start to assemble the panels. It will take you three days to get here, and we should be ready then."

"Okay, I guess I'd better get some sleep. We'll leave early tomorrow." He posted an "Alert" on the comm and headed off to his pod. When he awoke it was 7:00 a.m., JP and Alex were in the kitchen.

"When did Yuri call?" Alex asked.

"About eight o'clock last night. That's why I didn't finish my shift, I'll be driving all day. We should get started as soon as possible. We need to load the rover with oxygen and hydrogen and check the helium and nitrogen for the Ariel to make sure they're full. We will be going to their site and coming back, however we can refuel there." The crew had the rover ready to go at 8:30. John left instructions for JP.

"Wait till we get there and then bring the Ariel over. You should be able to get there in about seven hours. So, keep the comm manned as much as possible, in case we need your assistance."

John and Alex closed the rover hatch doors and off they went. Three days later, JP activated the Ariel and headed to the cave. He had gotten John's permission to leave early because the rover was almost there, and he couldn't be any help from where he was. He left early and arrived at the cave around 3:00 p.m. The rover with Alex and John showed up about an hour later. Yuri's crew had been busy. The ground had been leveled, and they had used a mixture of cement (Goop) and Martian sand to graph a foundation. Also, the anchor holes had been drilled, and they had put together a 24×24 foot structure, which would eventually become the rover and storage garage. The robots were busy welding the garage framework when they pulled up. Yuri, Lefluere, and JP were standing outside and waved when they arrived. Yuri signaled them to go to the module which was parked outside the cave, about one hundred yards from the building site. Inside the module, Xiao was on the comm, and a meeting was called in the kitchen to discuss the procedure of construction.

Yuri started off by bringing up the construction diagram on the display. Everyone took their places as he preceded with the construction procedures.

"Here is the structure we are to build, and this structure is designed by a computer whose instructions we will follow to the letter. The structure is 64 feet × 64 feet with an open interior, which is 48 feet × 48 feet. First, the panels are in internal and external panel sheets. The panels fit into a frame and are separated by eight support cups, 3 7/8 inches in height. These fit into clips on the interior sides of the panels. The interior panels have a clip so that when the interior and exterior panels are pressed together, they lock. Then the completed panel is then slid into the frame and Gooped on both sides in order to form the vacuum seal. The panels are 7 and 15/16 inches by 7 15/16 inches by 3 and 7/8 inches in thickness. When they are placed in the structural framework, they make an 8×8 foot panel four inches thick. It will require 192 panels to complete this structure. Plus 16 panels for the roof over the center section, total 208 panels, of which we've already put together 68 panels. This includes the floor, walls, ceiling, and interior cube, which will have a natural floor. We also have internal panels for room separation. The standard rooms will be 8×12 feet with a four foot walkway. We also have windows, pressure doors, and two air locks. Pressure doors separate the four sections and the two air locks, one on the east side and one on the west side. They are pre-assembled and need simply to be inserted into the structural framework. The specialized panels for the windows are half panels two 4×8 foot clear sheets placed together with out internal supports. The window section is comprised of a 2×8 foot steel sheet then a 4×8 foot clear sheet and a 2×8 foot steel top. The exterior sheet of the window panels are one-way glass. There are seven eight foot windows, two in the control room, one to the west, and two in the dining room facing south toward the cave. Two panels are reserved for the inside, looking into the center square. The panels used in the center square ceiling are also clear panels and must be supported by support struts every sixteen feet in other words 6 interior struts. As we build these panels, there are inserts for water, ventilation, and electricity and data lines in the framework which need to be connected as we're putting them together. After the structure assembly is complete, the robots will transport the panels to the structural framework, interior and exterior and apply a sealant. All of the structural modifications have been made, so there is no cutting involved. If it doesn't go together, you probably have the wrong parts."

"Okay, I need two people for panel assembly. How about John and JP with Antony and Alex for exterior structural assembly? Xiao, I need you to man the control room, and I'll take over assisting the robots. We've completed the rover garage so that we can use it for the assembly. Okay, so let's eat. Oh, and John, we have some foam cushions for your crew tonight. It's going to be an early day tomorrow."

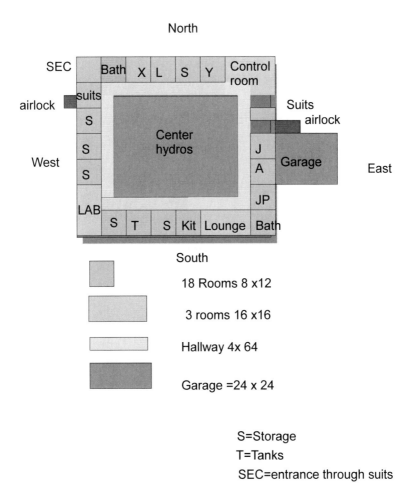

As soon as it was light the next morning, Yuri was up and organizing everyone. The panel sheets and frames were loaded in the garage by the robots and a work station had been created. The outer door was closed and a portable air handler pressurized the room. John and JP could open their helmet shields and take off their gloves. It took them a few trials before they got it right, but they started to pick up speed once they got the hang of it. They were producing a panel every 1.25 minutes. The sealing was done by a machine which had been dropped for the construction along with a press and other required construction tools. With a completed panel and frame, JP had constructed an eight foot table for the construction assembly. John was inserting the internal structural supports. The two sides were then pressed together by a press which arrived via the drop and then the completed panel was slid into the framework a finished panel was ready. Meanwhile, Alex, Yuri, and Antony were assembling the main structural framework outside by placing the completed panels into the pockets in the foundation frame. Where, the robots were welding them with an extension welder. The floor was completed first, then the walls and then the ceiling. After about five hours, they had completed the floor and three-quarters of the walls. Yuri called lunch. The robots needed to recharge, and they had run out of completed panels. During lunch, Yuri remarked that the process was coming along pretty well. They were at the end of their panels outside, and the robots weren't very far behind. They had completed an L-shaped structure. They weren't going to be able to pressurize it until the next morning. Everyone would have to stay in the module again that night. He asked John how far along he and JP were.

"We've already completed a hundred panels. We still have about sixty to go. From what it looks like, about another hour before we get to the clear panels, which won't take long. We should be finished in about three hours."

Yuri said, "**гоод** (good), then we should be able to complete the structure today and finish it up tomorrow. We have about two days of installing fixtures and connecting lines. JP, you're still going to set up the hydroponics as soon as the interior square is sealed, right?" JP raised his right hand. Yuri continued,

"The robots are still working on the exterior welding. However, the interior welding we will have to do because the robots are too heavy to roll on the floor. We'll then need to test for leaks and do corrective welding for minor structural leaks that the robots may have missed. This should be most of tomorrow anyhow. The installations, including hydroponics, should be completed the day after. We should be able to move in, in three days."

That turned out to be a pretty good guess. Two days later the main structure was finished sealed and pressurized the inner square was also finished. Yuri suggested that JP start on the hydro unit for the interior. With the base framework completed, John went out to the center space to assist JP in putting together the hydroponic units. JP was reading the instructions that he had downloaded off the database.

"Well, what do we do?" John asked.

"The first thing that we should start with is the fluid panels and rack frames for the trays," he said, pointing at a group of ten two-foot wide and one-foot deep plastic trays.

"So how does this thing work?" John asked.

"Okay, John, here's a brief understanding of the hydroponic process. The majority of oxygen produced on Earth is produced by sea plants or algae. These trays will run a fluid mix to support the growth of the algae for the air handler. Regular plants such as vegetables and fruit plants don't produce a lot of Oxygen however they do clean the air. Depending on what you want to grow. You place the seed in the germination cups and place the cups in the germination tank. For example, you will need more space for melons and squash. However, tomatoes and other vegetable plants are fine with a twelve-inch separation. Most of the food plants we have are rapid growth high yield hybrids. Air on Earth is 78 percent nitrogen and 21 percent oxygen, which adds up to 99 percent. The one percent of normal air consists of a mixture of other elements and inert gases and so on. To live off the Oxygen produced by a hydroponic garden, the plants must produce a minimum amount of 550 liters of Oxygen a day per person. Thus, three people would require 1,600 liters of breathable Oxygen a day. It takes approximately 1,200 regular plants to make that amount of oxygen or around 400 plants per person. Our garden at the habitat cave now produces about 700 liters a day, but when we started it, the production was only 10 liters a day. As it grew, the auto regulator reduced the oxygen feed from the cryo tanks by over 30 percent. Presently, we draw only 60 percent of our oxygen from our cryogenic tanks. However the main function of the hydroponic units is to filter and clean the air. The time when part of the crew is out of the module, for example, when we are on a mission. The hydro unit produces an abundance of Oxygen, creating Oxygen-enriched atmosphere where the Oxygen content is over 21 percent. The excess is cryogenically stored in the module's cryo tanks."

"The regulation of the atmospheric values is important. Too much CO_2 reduces the Oxygen output of the plants. The atmospheric values need to be as close to Earth normal as we can make them. Fortunately, the regulator does that by bubbling the atmosphere through the tray using a micro bubbler like in an aquarium. The chemicals additives and nitrates are fed along with a small flow through this tube. The plants clean the air and gases like a CO_2 scrubber." JP pointed to the end of the tray. John looked where he pointed to the 3/8—inch hole.

"This one's for water and this one's for air," he said, pointing to the ¼-inch tube. "Okay, now the way they designed these trays are very smart. For the food plants, you need to have a space between the rows. The way to do this is to place two trays side by side creating a two foot space so you can walk between the rows. The trays are meant to fit in a rack which houses three trays, one at two, four, and six feet. Now, this is what's smart on the bottom of the trays." JP turned the tray over. "You'll see a clip set on the bottom? This clip supports the tray in the rack. The clips also support the application a variety light strips. Actually, three strips which are controlled by the regulator. The strips contain three different light radiations: ambient solar, which is a mix of radiations, growth light which is ultraviolet, and a high-end light, which is pulse-emitted infrared. That plus this," he said as he pointed to the other end of the tray, which had a circular disk on the end 'An underwater signal generator'.

"What's that for?" asked John.

"It was found during a growth studies that vibratory effects keep plants healthy and stimulate growth production. After eighty thousand tests, they determined that both audio frequency and radiation frequencies effect plant growth and production. The results varied depending on the plant species and frequencies used. Also, it is proven that algae production of Oxygen is better or higher if the alga exists in a higher Oxygen atmosphere of over 21 percent. Alga usually grows together, since it is our major Oxygen producer, we need to keep the conditions stable."

John was now staring at him. "Like I said, what do we do?"

"Help me set up the support racks on the walls. Then we can set up the frames and ground framework."

It took them about three and a half hours to get it all set up, and by then, it was dinnertime. They would come back after dinner to adjust things and place the germination cups in the germination tank.

When they entered the interior of the building, they could not believe it. The inner separation panels had been installed and the station had been incredibly transformed. To their right was the control room, with a total area of 16×16 feet in dimension. The room connected into a four foot wide hallway with sleeping rooms of 8 to12 feet in a row and a bathroom at the end. There were another three bedrooms and another bathroom on the opposite side. There was another 16×16 foot room with a large-screen TV and computer and dining tables in the third section. The adjoining room was the kitchen with a serving counter. Then, there was a work room or lab with equipment in it and a machinery room housing the air handler auto systems. The fourth side contained two more bedrooms and four other 8×12 foot rooms for supplies and specialized equipment storage. They were not filled at this point because the crew was waiting to bring the supplies in from outside. John guessed that it would be the order of the day for tomorrow. The dinner was good JP had brought a large batch of vegetables from their garden including mushrooms which they grow in a tray inside their cave. Pork chops with fried onions were the main course with mashed potatoes and broccoli with a sauce that Lefeure had mixed up and a salad. After words everyone was a little tired and retired early. John opened the door to his bed room. The room was similar in appliances to the pods. The beds were memory foam on a frame approx 2 feet off the ground, an LCD HD viewer was suspended from the ceiling with a dual rotator controlled by a universal remote. The bed framework was adjustable whereas you could raise or lower the top or bottom of the bed. There was a chopped half circle desk with an LED reading light in the corner. Next to that there was a two foot closet and a three panel dresser drawer on the other wall.

There was a panel that extended from the wall which contained a USB port and wireless keyboard and mouse. It didn't take but a few minutes before John was asleep. He was awakened by a beeping from the comm

Xiao voice came over the speaker, "Sorry John, call from Jensen."

"Hello John, still asleep thought you'd be up and going by now."

"Jensen it is 8 a.m. here ok?" John replied.

"I just called to say good work, and offer a special reward for your successful completion of this part of the mission. We won't be able to see the base completely for about two more days. The internal and external cameras still have to be installed and activated. Look, I want you to remain there until they finish with your robots which, should arrive there today. Two programmers here will help with the final touches. Ok, now for the big reward as you know ISA rules say alcohol is completely forbidden upon flight vehicles in any form. We thought as a reward and since your not actually in flight, that we maybe be able to see our way clear to pack a reward for a small celebration. In bubble 22 which is about 200 yards away from you is a small container of spirits. You may enjoy it, because at 8 pm tomorrow night I'm going to be jamming your signal for maintenance repair so have a good time. Oh, don't open it until Yuri is with you and split it, as a show good faith. And don't drink it till your done working for the day, I won't call until late the next day so use in moderation, Jensen out."

John went to breakfast. Yuri had already eaten, JP was just finishing and Alex was still asleep. Lefeure was up and hooking things together.

"What's up for today?" John said when Yuri turned to look at him.

Yuri pointed at Lefeure, "Attaching connections and a little time in outer suits with the robots but, first we have to convert them. We need to attach to one a sprayer and the other to the pump but, that won't be until this afternoon so as soon as you're done we will start completing the list."

"Hey look, here come your bots now," Yuri remarked pointing to the display.

John looked up to see his bots coming over the hill towards the base from the east. Everybody worked on the connections till lunch time. After lunch Yuri needed someone for outdoor work.

"Alex and I will take it, what do we do?" John volunteered.

"We have to convert two of the bots. Then we have to get the mixer setup on the eastern side and we have to get the mix out of the packs. We can use your bots for that. We will mix the sand and the premix in the mixer then feed it to the sprayer. You will need to use the snow shovel to load the mix. And listen, when the bots are spraying use the plastic suit covers, that's what they are for. They are 'use and throw away', but we will probably try and keep them if we can. The mix contains a strong adhesive epoxy and other components. Then added to a fiber alloy mesh and mixed with Martian sand to give it a natural look.

"Ok, let's get the bots in the rover garage and get them converted," instructed Yuri. Converting the bots was no big deal, the grinder and the plow were detacher and the sprayer and extension arm were added. The rotor arm for the mixer was added to robot #2. John and Alex went to put on their outer suits and then met with Yuri in the rover garage.

"I'll be online so let's discuss the steps before we start so we know what we are doing. The mix packs are piled up on each of the four sides. I'll talk to you over the comm for instructions from inside. We are going to mix the spay in the mixer and feed it to the robots."

Yuri stepped back inside and closed the airlock door. John and Alex waited as the atmosphere was removed from the garage. When the pressure equalized the main 24 x 8 door opened allowing them to venture outside. Once outside the door closed. In the center of the wall sat a big mound of Martian sand and a pile of mix bags and twelve 5 gallon containers. The robots took there positions. Yuri's voice came over the comm.

"Here's how it goes. The first coat is just a primer mix. So add 2 gallons of goop out of the 5 gallon containers to the blender and 1 bag of mix #2 to five gallons of sand. Then put your protective covers on."

The wall was 64 feet by 8 feet, and the mix was turning Yuri cautioned them to stand back.

"I'm going to start the sprayer," he said.

The robot with the sprayer moved to the side of the wall on the left and there was a hiss and the mix started to spray out the nozzle. The robot, which was being controlled by Yuri, was spraying from bottom to top, and finished in about 8 minutes.

Yuri continued, "On the next layer you have a bag labeled PB-06. Alright add 2 bags of mix # 1, 1 bag of mix #2, one bag of UPB-06, 5 gallons of Goop and 3 buckets of Martian sand also the same for the third layer. The boys finished that wall and were moving onto the next wall when Alex stopped and pointed to the wall they had just finished.

"John look, the wall we just finished its gotten bigger." John looked and sure enough the wall had grown in size and was now about four inches thick.

"That's the urethane," Yuri said over the comm "It takes it a couple of minutes to activate. That combination of ingredients that you have applied is an expandable coating, which will seal the structure of the base making it become nearly invisible from the air and creates a radiation shield."

On the next wall they had to tape a precut mask over the windows. The first wall had already been taped. John guessed by Xiao who had been out here before, doing some of the set up to work. The windows had and interior automatic storm pressurized seal. John and Alex finished all the walls in about an hour. The building looked a lot different. Instead of it looking like a metal box, it was now the same color as the Martian surface. Alex was remarking on this as the pressure was being re-established in the garage. Yuri came in through the door and joined the conversation. They re-entered the control room. JP was on the control console.

"Well, you know Alex," Yuri remarked. "Space is a big place. I can easily make this statement; it is a place we know very little about. We don't know what's out here nor do we know if what maybe in this area now or in the future. Either way we don't know how it will relate to us. For all we know they may want to eat us. Anyhow, we haven't had a first contact situation yet, although we've certainly produced a lot of bad movies about the subject. The ISA voted that this unit be masked from the sky as well as possible, and that there be windows on every side along with cameras, navcomm detectors, a scuttle hole and armament.

"What is a scuttle hole?" asked Alex.

"In the old days Alex" said John. "Sea travelers would sometimes create a hold where, if they were attacked. They could store valuable cargo in the hidden room so that the pirates couldn't find it"

"We are not at sea," said Yuri. "But we have a hidden room on the other side of the western airlock which is 8 by 8 feet. While we are here the navcomm knows everything we are doing, it knows right now what we are doing. It knows if anything comes within ten million miles of the planet, and if anything does come near the base and it will alert us. You can't even pick up a stone outside and through it without navcomm knowing. It will set off the silent alert and the base will seal and arm itself. The navcomm system has an operational response program that automatically locks down the base and arms the access points including the 3D interactive hologram. If that alarm should go off we are to go to the room which has a complete access to the interior and exterior monitors. This system will allow us to talk or watch the intruders and find out whether they are hostile or peaceful before making actual physical contact. When this base is armed to defend, it possesses plasma and electric field generators, tasers, and lasers."

"What if that doesn't stop them?" asked JP

"Oh," said Yuri. "That will stop them, that plasma gun produces enough juice to fry your cookies. It works like electricity; it passes electrified plasma through the base which envelops into a plasma wave which would cook a regular person in less than 20 seconds. So you can relax JP, no buggy men are going to get you."

Alex interrupted, "you mentioned a holographic how does that work?"

"Let me see if I can explain it correctly," continued Yuri. "When an object approaches the base the security system which is integrated with the navcomm system will alert us. We will go into the security room, it will also alert Earth. The navcomm which monitors us will scan the approaching creature and create a very life like image which, it projects into this chair, the chair is the projector. So, if the creature enters the control room it will see one of its own at the control panel. This system also contains a program that duplicates response of course language is a problem, because we won't know their language. Here let me demonstrate, this process is newly developed in the last two years by AADG." Yuri typed in a security code and an image appeared in the chair.

"Hey I know that robot, that's Robbie from that old Si-fi movie 'Forbidden Planet'," said JP.

The robot hesitated then turned in the seat to face them.

"Good evening gentlemen, how are you today?"

"The image is produced by a projector in the chair and this program is now being incorporated in all vehicles and I think it's smart, it could fool me" added Yuri.

Everyone agreed JP couldn't take his eyes off the image "If I didn't know better I'd say there was really a robot here."

"They also have an image of the Alien from the movie 'Alien'. Hey how about this" Yuri looked at the directory for a few seconds and selected a file an image of John appeared in the chair."

"Hey it's John, how?" asked JP.

"Navcomm has files on all of us; these images can be projected into that chair. The chair can even move and it won't affect the image."

Yuri continued, "John I need you to assist me installing the solar panels on the roof tomorrow. In fact we will need everyone. Andre is going to finish the external structure to make it look more natural and there are still some small items to be taken care of."

They spent the rest of the day going over the documents on the station and making a duty roster for what was now being called Marineris Base. The installation of the solar panels required the attachment of a rail system on the roof of the base. The panels had been dropped along with the other supplies, however were already assembled. The rail was in sections which had to be put together and inserted with clip locks on the roof. Lefeure was designing and creating pieces of urethane foam inserts which he would be installing on the exterior to make the base look more natural. The next day John, Alex, JP, and Yuri put on outer suits and started fabricating the rail. Yuri moved the XPLM as close as he could get, to the base walls. The XPLM has a 100 foot rotational boom crane on its aft section which allowed them to hoist the rail sections and the solar panels to the roof. Xiao and JP, because of their lower body weight were assigned to the roof. Their job was to place the panels into the rail. At 2 p.m. all but 3 panels had been installed. John was thinking that they were almost through when Yuri came over the comm.

"Alex, help me with the shroud."

Alex stood there wondering what he was talking about.

When Yuri answered his questioning in Russian, "What's the shroud? It's the cover; it's in that tube over there." Yuri said pointing at a tube near the supplies. Alex joined Yuri as they unpacked the container inside was a wrapped cloth. Yuri instructed Alex to assist him in carefully unrolling the sheet.

"It's a ceramic fiber mesh cloth that fits into the rail," Yuri continued. "Okay, take this end and hand it to JP. JP inserted the ends into the rail."

The cover was the same color as the Martian sand. Once it was inserted, they finished off installing the last of the solar panels. Yuri attached the electricity to the rail and pulled the shroud over the top of the base. Lefluere had been outside attaching the foam units to the pre-existing walls and was getting ready to spray the final coat. Yuri instructed everyone to vacate the area. John watched Andre load the mix. It was a different formula than they had used for the walls, it contained more sand and a colorant. The spray was like an adhesive powder but with the same expansion properties. Once they were inside Yuri made the announcement that he believed that they were done. So, John decided to divulge the location of the spirits. Alex and Yuri went out to search for the bubble and returned shortly. Lefluere had finished outside and had come in. He was in the control room where he ran a test by retracting and extending the shroud several times explaining that he had to be sure the sealant didn't inhibit the operation of the shroud. Yuri was mixing the drinks in the Kitchen and Alex was passing them out. After which they all joined Lefluere in the control room for the demonstration."

"It's done?" asked Yuri "when can we see it?"

"In about twenty minutes," Andre replied.

Andre turned on navcomm tracking and everyone noticed a Trex heading in the direction of the Valle from east to west. It would very soon be entering the Valle. Yuri went on to explain that the solar panels wouldn't be needed if the Valle was routed south to north because the panels would not get enough sunlight to be effective. Since the Valle ran east to west, the Sun would be able to supply light to the panels for at least 8 hours a day. The shroud was connected to the navcomm system which has an effective range of several thousand miles from space and can detect any movement on the surface. During storms it has a picture of the surface and follows the process of the storm and takes an image of the surface. When the storm is over it highlights any changes on the map display.

Then Yuri said, "If there were any life out there we would know about it. Navcomm can pick up movement of a snail or a cricket on the ground from 1000 miles in space."

They were interrupted by Lefluere who said "Here we go. I've got the setting set to take a full scan of our location. I have the navcomm programmed to have the base respond as if the Trex is unknown object. We should be in view in about a minute."

They all watched as the Trex passed over their position. John was the first to speak "I didn't see the base, where's the base?"

"That's because we are invisible," prompted Yuri with a smile.

Lefluere played back the recording from the Trex in slow motion with the base location highlighted by its navcomm signal. They watched as the base came into view. Yuri was right you couldn't detect the base it looked like the rest of the surface. Lefluere's augmentations blended in the edges of the structure to make the base look like a raised crop of sand and rock like most of the rest of the surface."

"Without the location being given by navcomm I wouldn't know it was here," John admitted.

The party continued for a few hours more, before everyone was well oiled and turned in. John and the crew stayed at the base for another 5 days to help unload and store the supplies before returning to their habitat cave. The trip back to their cave took three days for Alex and John in the rover. JP arrived at the cave a day before they did and was attending the hydroponics when they entered. JP explained that while they were gone the Oxygen content in the cave had multiplied and all the cryogenic containers were now full and a higher oxygenated atmosphere now exists of 28% in the cave. Since, they couldn't use the extra oxygen. JP suggested the extra Oxygen be vented to lower a fire hazard that may be caused by sparks. John agreed however he recommended they postpone the vent for two days to see whether the Oxygen level would change with all three of them in the cave. Three months later the crew was called to the control room by an 'alert' bulletin. John toggled the display screen to produce a split screen image of Yuri and Jensen.

Yuri started, "We would like to announce the discovery of a new cave located approximately 150 miles east of our position. The new cave which we have designated as cave #2 was discovered by accident on a routine investigation of the cliff surface of the Valle. We as of yet have not done any intensive investigation of the inside of the cave. We have however positioned a navcomm repeater at the entrance to mark the location. We wanted to wait to produce a scan until we know more about the caves interior, which should come sometime this week. We plan to go into the cave as far as possible with a Navcomm scanner to create the internal Map. So far, there has not been any presence of water detected. We will keep you advised on the details of the exploration."

"Well" said Alex. "What do you know about that, another cave?"

Jensen was still online and said,

"Guys you might have to drop what you're doing and give them a hand. This is new information and they may need assistance in the exploration."

"Rest assured Mark we will do what we can," John offered.

However, no help request came from Yuri. The crew spent the next four months crater hopping and going to places that the ISA wanted explored. Bringing back samples to be tested with occasional conversations with Yuri's crew who confirmed that work continued in the new cave. It was during this time that John got an alert from JP who was with the Ariel investigating the section southeast of their location.

"John I found something," JP said over the comm.

"What JP?"

"I'm about 150 miles from the habitat east and about 80 miles north of the landing site. I noticed a crater and was just going to scan it but as I flew over and I noticed a hole in the caldera so I landed. I was right it was a hole about 5 feet in diameter. Here take a look through the Ariel camera."

John toggled the Ariel camera the image displayed was a malformed opening but defiantly a hole.

"Where does the hole go?" asked John.

"I don't know. I'm going to see whether I can scan it with the handheld I'm carrying."

"Ok, but be careful the sides may not be stable see if you can use some tether to tie yourself off with before advancing to the hole."

JP retrieved some tether line from the utility pack on the Ariel. He attached one end to the Ariel and the other to the tether clip of his outer suit. He picked up the handheld unit and slowly advanced to the edge of the hole. Standing at the edge he lowered the navcomm scanner into the hole and rotated it.

"Are you getting it John?" said JP.

"Yes," replied John. "But this can't be right the reading records the bottom is over 2 miles deep. I'm sure that you don't want to fall in. I don't think we have enough tether to reach the bottom. In fact I don't think we have anything that we can use to go that far down. We'll have to talk to Jensen about it come on back we'll put in a call tonight."

JP returned about an hour later. After dinner they boosted a link to Jensen. JP and John described the discovery and the problem of getting an accurate read out of the hole. John said that they had made a preliminary scan of the hole without any conclusive results and didn't have the equipment for further examination. To which Jensen replied

"Send me the scan I'll go over it with the engineers and see what we can come up with."

Then there came a call one afternoon from Yuri while John was on duty.

"Hey Yuri, long time no hear from," John answered.

"Yes, I know we have been busy here most of the time. How is your crater jumping going, and how is everyone there?"

John recanted the discovery of the crater hole and added.

"Everyone here is fine. I tried to get in touch with you last week ago but was told you were unavailable."

"Yes, I apologize" replied Yuri "I must have been in cave #2. The comm goes out at about ¼ mile down to much iron in the walls. Maybe, we will come over and join you for some crater diving later. Anyhow, what's your schedule look like. Think you could spare some time to come over for a visit of a couple of days? There' something I want to talk with you about."

"Yes, I guess we got the time. I'll have JP fire up the rover. We should be there the in about 3 days or so," John replied.

"No John, just you, and you need to make up a reason for coming and bring the Ariel."

"Yeah OK, but what's up?"

"I'll wait till you get here tomorrow night and we'll talk then."

The wallboard signed off the next morning John called a meeting with JP and Alex explaining that Yuri had called and needed his assistance on some installation of structural supports in cave 2. And that he would be gone for a couple of days. Alex helped him suit the Ariel and after setting the destination and clearing the journey with navcomm, he was ready to go. Finding the base without the Trex mapping was nearly impossible but, there was now a preset link of location in the directory. John pressed activate and the Ariel came to life. It rose slowly picking up speed as it went. Soon it was at 4,000 feet with horizontal speed of 250 miles per hour. The base according to navcomm was 1486 miles away as the crow flies. Approximately 6 hours of travel time. The destination time said 6 hours and 12 minutes. John settled in for a long ride. He arrived at the base in the late afternoon and parked the Ariel in the rover garage, before going inside to the base control room. He was greeted by Yuri and Xiao. Yuri asked him if he would like some liquid refreshment and directed him to the dinning room down the hall. Yuri prepared two coffees for them and sat down at the table.

"You know since we've been able to synthesize the water here we haven't had to worry about rationing our usage. We can basically have as much as we want. Plus the electrolysis keeps us in Hydrogen for the fuel cells and breathable Oxygen supply. We synthesize about 200 gallons a week more if needed. Make sure to remind me to give you a few canisters of water to take back with you."

"Good, we can use it," John replied. "So now, why did I travel seven hours to get here, and what did you want to show me."

"What I wanted to show you is in cave #2 and it is a little late for that today. It takes an hour and a half to get there by rover and about 20 minutes to walk down to the drilling site. It would be past dark before we got back. So, we'll leave in the morning. Tonight we'll just talk with the boys and have a good dinner. Go over the drop lists and I've got a surprise. Lefluere has built a still so, there will be some liquid refreshment," which caught John off guard.

He hadn't thought that they would be enough produce to support such a venture however; Yuri assured him that they had achieved good results out of the still and that John would be surprised by the results.

After a very nice steak dinner which was given two hours later, Yuri unlocked a cabinet to produce a gallon container and poured the drinks.

"Now John, I believe you Americans call this moonshine it's 180 proof," he said while pouring. "And I hate to admit it but it puts vodka to shame so, we limit ourselves to two glasses a night. We make it from potatoes and other vegetables from the hydros in cave#1. Yuri capped the container and relocked it in the cabinet. We've been cutting it with the soda syrup and a little carbonated water not to bad." John took a sip.

"Wow that has a kick."

After the second drink everyone had a buzz and Xiao retired. It was Lefluere's shift on the control room and Yuri signaled John to follow him to the lab. Once they were inside John figured that the alcohol had loosened Yuri's voice box because, the next word to come out of his mouth was

"I was going to wait until after we went to the cave but, I might as well tell you now. We found some things in the second cave that are going to have an impact on our status with the ISA."

"While drilling in the cave 2, the robots came up with this." Yuri opened a drawer and pulled out a bag of rocks and dumped then on the table. There were 6 rocks lying on the table but one caught John's eye immediately.

"Is that what I think it is?" John gasped.

"If you think that you are looking at high yield gold ore you're exactly right but, some of the others are more important. Here you have copper, zinc, lead, nickel and silicon crystal which is abundant because of all the sand. But what's important about these samples is that the zinc which is also very common has bauxite attached to it and in the bauxite is gallium. When we synch the water one of the chemicals we remove is lithium in small quantities. These two elements have changed the value structure of Mars. It means that it is possible to create and produce electronic components like integrated circuits and computer systems here on the planet. This is very good but, that not all, we have been finding other elements including chlorine convertible isotopes which can be used to create a vast number of products, a major discovery. But, that's not why I called you. We found two more interesting pieces, ones in this box." Yuri produced a small metal box onto the counter John reached for the box.

"No, don't open it," Yuri exclaimed. John quickly retracted his hand.

Yuri continued, "Uranium, high yield Uranium, usable Uranium and we didn't find it in the cave; we found it on the surface along with other samples. It happened by accident. Lefluere was taking the rover down the Valle in search of other caves. He pulled over to view the Valle walls with the binoculars, which were in the utility bag. When he heard something clicking he looked in the bag to find the Geiger counter and after scanning the surface. He located several uranium rocks of which he brought three of them home. They tested out good and I've already let them know, they were of course excited. To use them they will have to be refined but it's changed the prospective of Mars, if you get my drift. They now can build an entire community here and don't think it hasn't crossed their minds but even that isn't why I called you. I called because of this." Yuri retrieved a small bag from the closet.

"You'll see tomorrow but here's a small sample. He unfastened the drawstring and poured the contents onto the counter. John looked at the collection of stones the majority of which had a rose color. Some of them were actually red also; there were green and blue crystals of good size. Yuri was looking for a reaction out of John that didn't occur.

"Do you know what you are looking at? You probably don't recognize them because they're rough or uncut. John these are raw diamonds, the CO_2 on this planet had an effect on the formation and chemical properties. John diamonds are created by carbon and pressure, besides Iron, Carbon is the second most prominent element on this planet and this area the volcanic activity may have provided the pressure. The rose and red stones which are extremely rare on Earth are caused by carbon impurities, that effects the diamonds color when they are developing. It's my guess that the impurity is iron. It gives it the red color the more iron the redder the diamonds is, the same as this planet. Now, look at this one," John noted that it was green. "This color is produced by gamma radiation bombardment; the green color is the result. We are still looking for what caused this gem to have this bluish color."

"What caused the blue color?" asked John. Slowly turning a red stone over in this hand

Yuri waited till John looked up. "Boron produces the blue color which goes with this" he said pointing to the small lead box. "This is not a significant amount but because of this blue diamond, we know that there is boron existing on the planet. That means we have the components to build a small reactor, the Uranium, the Boron and the coolant water, which we are still producing at a rate of 250 gallons plus a day. We have requested a series of storage tanks for the gases and the water we are producing. If they send the components we may be able to construct a small generator. That means heat, light, and power. This will change the structure of life on this planet reducing our dependency on solar power. This makes us the dream team they will deny us nothing now, because we are sitting on their investment to the good. So what do you think, we didn't have these until last week so we haven't requested specialized equipment as of yet. Anyhow, I could use another drink how about you?"

John agreed; on the way back to the dinning room he couldn't help but ask a question.

"Yuri how can you run a still you need to produce mash, all of or hydro products we grow we eat, we don't have enough to support a still."

"I'll show you tomorrow. We have the plants and we've been cultivating yeast. You know John, we've now been here just eight months an even though we've been busy. We were still able to improve the living conditions here; the development factor of this planet is huge."

They finished there drinks and retired for the night.

The next day John woke up with a slight hangover. Xiao gave him some aspirins during breakfast. After breakfast Yuri suggested they get started by putting on their outer suits which took about 10 minutes. Yuri then produced 2 utility bags, handing one to John, and they started out the airlock. First stop was cave 1, whose entrance was only a few hundred yards away. John followed Yuri through the airlock entrance of the cave which they had sealed with panels. As soon as they entered John noticed that the cave had changed.

"My god," exclaimed John. "When did this happen?" The internal structure was flooded with plants and algae oxygen trays. The internal structure was larger, longer and higher than their cave and though JP had done a good job with the hydroponics, this was a step above.

Yuri removed his helmet John followed suit. The air was thick and was Oxygen enriched with high Oxygen content.

"This is really something and the air, truly impressive," remarked John.

"This is just part of it. The plants continue down the tunnel for about ¼ mile. The heat is generated by a Sterling engine and because it's sealed it remains above 70 degrees all the time. The water downstairs adds a vapor heat which we control with a tube fan. With the combination of the base hydroponics and the cave's, we actually have or produce more Oxygen than we can use. We bottle all we can but, when we are in the base the hydros here just keep pumping. The Oxygen generation has been estimated by the Tri-star on the module at 70 liters an hour of which we use just over 1600 a day. We pump in CO2 for the plants from the concentrator we have set up via the airlock. I'm sorry to say we had to vent some of the oxygen because we have filled all our available tanks. We are still producing an extra 60 liters per day that we don't use. We had it set up this way for over 2 months. The plants just keep growing and we had to modify the lighting. Yuri gathered two water canisters from the purifier and handed one to John.

"May need some water on the trip," Yuri suggested. He placed the canister below the valve on the 50 gallon tank and turned the valve filling the canister. When he was done John did the same. As he was filling Yuri said,

"John I remember you telling me about the spyware you discovered in your XPLM module. It's true they can monitor everything in the module or that comes over navcomm, like when we talk through our helmets. This cave is okay but in cave #2; don't say any thing about the diamonds or anything else we discussed last night okay especially, in front of the robots?"

"Yeah, I got it," John replied.

They put their helmets and gloves back on and proceeded out the lock to the rover in the garage. It was a little over a two hour trip in the rover to cave # 2. Yuri parked the rover outside the entrance of the cave and they gathered their gear to start the descent.

"Yuri," asked John, "how come you haven't sealed this cave yet?"

"We plan to, as soon as we get more panels. We didn't have any left when we got through with the base. The panels were just enough to complete the base and seal Cave 1. Hopefully, they will send enough for the work that they want done and maybe some extra in the next drop. We will have to call Jensen tonight and check supply so that we know what we will be receiving." They continued down the tunnel. Yuri halted for a second and pressed his comm.

"Yuri to Marineris base, Yuri to Marineris base," There was no return signal. "I think we are deep enough down, so you can speak freely. We got another half mile to go. We have the robots working down here round the clock. Every time I come down here, it's a new experience. After a few minutes, they came across a pile of extendable interior supports.

Yuri instructed, "Pick up a couple of those. We will probably find application for them when we get to the site." About ten minutes later, they arrived at an enlargement of the cave. The two robots were at work drilling out a new extension on the left-hand side. Suddenly, the robots stopped. One gathered up a large group of rocks, turned, and headed out of the cave.

"Funny how they are, they knew we were coming, and now know that we are here, so they're taking a charge break," Yuri remarked.

"We are too deep for the navcomm to be active, so who is telling them what to do?" John asked.

"The robots have an internal sensor program and memory that feeds from an internal basic root function which directs them to a certain protocol. What just happened is they detected our presence, and the program told them to stop working because the process could be harmful to our health," Yuri replied.

They continued a little farther, and Yuri stopped and pointed. John looked at the wall. There were crystals embedded in the wall, lots of crystals.

"There are a lot of crystals here. Are they all diamonds?"

"No, there are other elements as well. Diamonds are formed by coal or carbon. But this may just be the tip of the iceberg. We are just a short way from the three volcanoes and the monster Olympus Mons. My guess is that during its active era, the Valle was created by volcanic activity and possibly the eruption of the Olympus Mons. That action caused these stones to be pushed to the surface. Remember, the Valle is three miles below the mean surface. Of course, that was millions, perhaps billions, of years ago. Then time and pressure created the diamonds."

"What are we going to do with the stones?" John asked.

"We are going to continue mining and testing the crystals, and I imagine that it's possible that we may find a larger deposit. I mean we found this one by accident. This is that something that I wanted to talk to you about. When they find a way to transport these stones back to Earth, there is going to be a problem. At first, they are going to be rare because they are Mars stones and red, but the more stones that are transported, the less rare they will become and their value will go down. I've been collecting the super nice stones, and I'm starting to get a nice collection. But if there is a chance that you and your crew should get back to Earth, I want you to take the collection back with you without ISA knowing about it, of course. I'll give you the name of a person I know in Russia that can handle the retail of the stones, just in case. It should be worth several million a piece for everyone, Alex, JP, Lefluere, and Xiao and us, deal?"

"Well, I don't know how I'll get them past ISA security, but I'm game."

"You leave that to me," Yuri suggested.

John noticed a crystal with a dark forest green color and used his pickaxe to chip it out of the wall. It was two inches long and a very dark green almost black. They spent about another twenty minutes examining the cave and implanting some struts before heading back. They headed for the rover and the trip back. When they got back to the base, it was dinner time. Lefluere had become the head chef. That night, it was Salisbury steak with real baked potatoes, vegetables, and bread with a salad.

Xiao remarked, "I don't know why we have to have potatoes every night. Is there something else we can have in place of potatoes?"

Yuri replied, "Potatoes are carbohydrates. The other two main carbohydrates are pasta and rice. When we got here, we had rice, but every time you cooked, you cooked rice, and now we don't have any. And we can't grow rice and we can't grow wheat as of yet. It takes up too much space, but we can grow potatoes. There's a bunch of them in the cave right now. If you don't want to eat them, fill up on salad or vegetables, which we have quite a bit of. I hope you ordered some rice for the drop."

"I did, double supply," Xiao defended.

"Look," interjected Lefluere, "if you want, you can start rice in some of the oxygen trays, although I don't know whether the yield would be significant enough."

"Speaking of the drop," commented Yuri. "We are going to call Jensen tonight to talk about it, so if you have anything to say, you need to be there. John, you need to call your station and let them know so that we can present a united front." John nodded. "Okay, everybody, eight o'clock it is, and no drinking until after the call." After dinner, the boys were a little upset that there was no alcohol but knew it was for the best.

At eight o'clock, everyone was gathered in the control center. JP and Alex had linked on through navcomm, and Yuri pressed the internal comm active switch. Jensen's image appeared on the wallboard.

"Hey, guys, I suppose this is about the drop list." For them, it was still eleven months away, but the order had to be loaded and it took seven months to get to Mars. "I'll send the supply pack tonight, but first I've got some news for you. The ISA have changed the ball game. Okay, here's the new menu. Yuri, your team is still working Cave 2. They approved that, you're to continue with the cave and the investigation of the Marineris Valles. By that, I mean creating a graphic map of the Valle, covering every foot of the sides and floor. That should hold you for a while. We are recommending special equipment to this end. It is listed on the drop sheet. Now, John, your team is still investigating the craters. That got approved as well. There is a discussion about the habitat cave. It has been recommended that we close the cave and move you and your crew to the base. The base will be undergoing an expansion after the drop. We are sending panels to affect the expansion. There will be enough panels for you to duplicate the current structure, and you will have extra panels for other applications. The second structure will be a bigger work space. It will have a smaller control center with more rooms and more lab space, any questions?"

JP was the first to say something. "If we move to the base, what will happen to my hydroponics?"

"JP," replied Jensen, "I know you did a lot of good work bringing the hydro units up to speed, but you must realize that when you blow the exterior air lock panels, the plants will die. However, all is not lost. The scientists down here have come up with a plan to save most but not all of them. They are shipping in this drop a new handler that should maintain the plant growth inside the habitat cave unmanned. The handler is equipped with robotic arms and extenders with micro cameras that can be used as viewers so you can farm the site from the base via navcomm. They also have a bubble pack that will support some of the plants when you pop the door, it will keep the plants protected until after you reseal the entrance. So when it comes time load the module up with whatever you can carry and take all the equipment. The equipment has priority over the plants, and then head to the base. Yuri, they will be busy with this for a little while. You are to take a break and assist them if needed. Two of you can go over in your XPLM, and one can take the Ariel. However, this has not official as of yet and this won't be for eleven months. Okay, any more questions?"

"Are there extra trays coming?" Xiao asked.

"Xiao, you will have another full complement to play with, in the seed pack we are sending is an extra complement of plant seeds. We are sending some plants that the scientists here have specially cultivated. They are some dwarf hybrid trees and soy product which have been successfully implemented on the Moon."

Yuri interrupted this time, "Where are we going to put these trees? There's no room in Cave 1 for them."

"Don't worry; they're not real trees, more like bushes. Read the instruction pack and call me back if there are any questions, Jensen out."

It would take Jensen a few minutes to upload the information, so everyone went to the dining room, where drinks were being served. Yuri turned on the dining room wallboard, and they sat down at the table. JP remarked. "I'm very happy to be getting the soy plant seed that's good news" Xiao agreed.

"But if the drop is not for nearly a year, why do they need the shopping list now?"

"Okay," said John. "Let me see if I can explain this right. The orbital rotation of Earth is 365 days; however the orbital rotation of Mars is 687 days. We say that the orbit is every two years, but the orbit loses forty-three days every two years. So Earth and Mars are not in the same position every two years, when Mars is closest to the Sun and Earth. You have to take in the fact that every eight months, the Sun is between the Earth and Mars. It takes 6.5 months for the journey of a CMP from the Earth to Mars. On this year coming up, the Earth will be going behind the sun in six months. Mars has currently turned in orbit and is going back toward the Sun. We will be coming close to the perihelion and the drop will start this time

11 months from now. We will have direct communications with Earth for approximately sixteen months because of the orbit change. Earth then catches up and follows Mars around the Sun. They have to launch the CMPs while they are on the other side of the sun at the closes point. They will be out of direct communications, so they need the shopping list and the CMPs loaded before they come into the launch window. Also, you figure that it is eleven months until the drop. Seven of those eleven months the CMPs will be in transport. That gives the ISA engineers four months to design whatever it is that they are shipping to us so they need to know now what that might be."

"How do you guys feel about the news?" asked Yuri.

"Well," Alex said over the link. "I'm not too excited about moving but living at the base would be a step up. The pods are good, but they're not beds and I think they are right in combining our assets. There is really no reason we should support the habitat as a independent station." The wallboard chimed, which signaled completion of the upload.

"Let's take a look at it," Yuri said as he opened the file. The listing index was divided into two parts. The first part was for John and crew and the second was for Yuri's crew. Yuri's re-supply was 400 percent more than John's. The majority of the drop was closer to the base in the Melas Chasma instead of the normal site, down by John's habitat. The drop gave John eight balloons, whereas Yuri's drop contained thirty-eight balloons. John guessed that at least four of them contained panels, two would contain internal equipment, four would contain structural steel for the caves, and there would be four containing Hydrogen, Oxygen, Nitrogen, Helium and water and other sealed products. Four would be food, so that left 20 balloons with unidentified content.

"Let's see what's in those four." John suggested

"Yes, let's see," Yuri keyed up the package description. "Looks like the grinder I ordered, Bunsen burner, some chemistry equipment, another Geiger counter, a welder, chemicals, which I suspect to be acids, and other elements and glass works."

"Try the next one, Yuri," John suggested.

Yuri toggled the next one.

"What's that?" John said, looking at the list. There was a component designated as CRT parts.

Yuri pressed description "described unit is an attachable cart for rover which allows transport of secondary products."

"Another cart, it may be helpful in moving. This is good. We can use a second cart," said Alex.

"This one's coming to you," replied Yuri. "It's got your name on it."

Sure enough, the next one was on John's drop list.

"Looks like your hole diving equipment," Yuri said. "Let's see, float sensors, navcomm adaptors, tether reels, and wire, balloons, mini-canisters, more navcomm adapters, grapple device, tester, sample containers, and other stuff."

"Yeah, that's the hole equipment. What about the last one?" John replied.

"Capsule for surface lift from Mars," Yuri said as he viewed the description. That got everyone's attention.

"Look," said Xiao, "it's a launch capsule." And that's exactly what it was but just a capsule. A lightweight capsule made of beryllium alloy, ten feet in length with four seats, a fuel tank assembly, four fuel nozzles, view glass, and various components.

"Where's the fuel? How's this thing going to fly without fuel?" exclaimed John.

"Maybe they expect us to make the fuel out of the hydrogen and oxygen we have here?" replied Alex.

"Cryogenic fuel, for that?" John said, pointing to the diagram of the capsule on the screen.

"I don't think so, and how do they think we're going to keep the fuel cold enough until the launch, a sterling pump? And where's the fuel tanks? It says there fuel tank assembly, but I don't see any tanks."

"I don't know. We'll have to wait till it gets here John," suggested Yuri. "But I don't think we should say anything to Jensen till we have a chance to look at it."

John saw Yuri's reasoning in this.

Don't talk about things you don't know about, and agreed with it. John spent another two days at the base before taking the seven-hour trip back in the Ariel to the habitat. Yuri had loaded him up with a little water to take back.

Chapter 9

Olympus Mons

The next month Jensen suggested that they should start the first mission because they would be too busy once the drop started. Yuri confirmed that they had built up enough reserves and called for an after dinner conference. Jensen was online and started,

"It's come time for the Valles Marineris exploration and the Olympus Mons mission. The mission involves a high-level scan of the Valle walls and a navcomm implant on Olympus Mons. I've come up with a strategy for the mission, so I guess we need to go over the details."

"Basically, we'll take the Ariel's and send them up the sides of the Valle at low altitude and low speed with navcomm hand scanners. The alert is to be set for cave detection. Let's face facts, the Valle walls are about the only thing we're going to find on this mission, but I could be wrong, so keep your eyes open. Anything that looks different or not normal is game. Okay, the second step is to send Yuri's XPLM up the roadway to act as support, whereas after the team has completed their shift they can return to the XPLM module for food and sleep. We're in winter now, so the temperature will be below minus 120 Fahrenheit. The XPLM support will be necessary."

"John, you will drive Yuri's module. JP and Xiao are going to stay at the base and will handle the control room and base maintenance on twelve hour shifts. Yuri will serve as the third while continuing the mining of Cave 2. This means that the exploratory crew will consist of John, Alex, and Andre. Now, there are two Ariel's and one module. You can take turns, as the module can drive itself on the roadway. But the Valle can be wide, Melas Chasma is over three hundred miles in width, and I feel that someone should stay in the module while the Ariel's are scanning the cliffs. If assistance is required, it will only be a half hour away. We are to make a full map of the internal structure of the Valle. This means a very low altitude, about ten to twenty feet and the same with the distance from the cliff side. Your speed shouldn't be over 20 mph. The scanner will alert you when it registers a distance greater than the normal distance of the walls which would be anything greater than thirty feet. When you get an alarm, it means you need to land the Ariel and take a better read. If it turns out that you've found a cave, do not attempt to enter the cave alone. Alert the module and wait until another crew man arrives. Okay, now the Valle is 1,800 miles in length to the very end of the west section from the base. It should take about 8 days to reach the western end and the beginning of the Noctis Labyrinthus section. If a storm hits while you are in the Ariel, try to make it back to the road and the module. If you can't, find cover by the cliff and wait it out. One more thing, if you have to un-strap from the Ariel to take a closer look at something. Be sure you anchor the vehicle under partial pressure. I will need to go over the details with the logistics people here on Earth, but it sounds good to me. I was kind of figuring next week for the start time. You will have to do some preparation work and clean up the module, but how does that sound?"

"It's okay by me, but I'm driving. How 'bout you guys, Alex?" John replied.

"да"(yes)

"Lefluere?"

"Oui"

"Okay then, we'll wait for the 'Go' signal and then we'll start," replied John.

John and crew transported to the base. They had talked with Jensen, who confirmed that the plan had been approved. They set about cleaning up and performing maintenance on the XPLM. John helped JP set up some hydroponics and assisted Yuri preparing supplies until the departure day arrived. They headed the XPLM towards the Melas Chasmata, which started eighty miles west of the base. The robots had already mapped the area up to the entrance to the Melas Chasmata. They would not start mapping until after they had crossed into the Chasmata. When they got to the start site, Alex and Lefluere unloaded the Ariel's and strapped them on. Andre took off to the south, and Alex took off to the northern cliff. It took them forty-five minutes to reach the sides. Alex arrived first and after getting confirmation from navcomm started up the Valle northern side. Lefluere did the same thing on the southern side. They had gone a few hours when Lefluere got a bite. His alarm went off, he was about twenty feet from the cliff, but he didn't see any opening. He circled around, John was online.

"What do you have?" John said over the comm.

"I don't know. I don't see anything," Lefluere answered. "There's a cut in the rock, but I can't get in there with the Ariel on. I'm going to park it to view the other side of this rock."

He shredded the Ariel harness, remembering to anchor it, and proceeded to the cutout in the rock. Sure enough, as he got closer, he could see that the indention was an entrance to a cave. After ten feet, the cave turned sharply to the left, which made it unnoticeable from the outside.

"John, I'm going in," Andre replied.

"No, wait till I get Alex there," John instructed.

"That will take half an hour. I'm just going in to where it curves to get a better reading." Andre replied

"Okay, but no farther and don't touch anything. If a cave-in should happen, you'll be in dire straits. We don't have the equipment to dig you out, and it will take the robots over six hours to get here."

Andre proceeded into the cave with the scanner. As he approached the turn, he got a deeper reading. It was definitely a cave. The scanner showed an opening ten feet ahead. Andre continued till he came around the curb.

John's voice blasted over the comm, "No further that's it!"

Lefluere slowly turned the scanner from left to right very slowly to get a reading of the cave. John was looking over the information the scan was sending back. Suddenly, Jensen logged in. He had been watching. There was a time lag on the transmission of about thirty seconds.

"Andre, listen to John now. We made an agreement. No single person explorations, so wait till Alex gets there."

Then John's voice came over the comm.

"Alex is not coming. From the read I got, the cave ends in forty feet with no extensions or further openings. Lefluere, pull yourself on out of there. We'll send a robot to do the exploration."

Jensen agreed and Andre went out to strap into the Ariel and continued the cliff scan. They met back at the module that night around dusk. During dinner, John advised both of them that they had completed just less than two hundred miles that day and that was pretty good.

Marineris Valles

"If we can hold this rate, we should reach the end of the Valle in about ten days, covering 1,600 plus miles. Then Olympus Mons is another 6,000 miles from there and fourteen miles in altitude. The three sisters are about halfway or about 2,500 miles from the end of the Valles. The way that command has run the instruction for this phase of the mission is the northern sister and the center sister the first day. You're to plant your navcomm units on the top of Pavonis Mons and Olympus Mons if possible. If for some reason we cannot reach the top of Olympus, save the navcomm and plant it on the most southern sister, Arsia Mons. Now about the storms when we are in Marineris Valles, we don't have to worry that much about the storms because the Valle acts as a partial shield. We get partial gusts during the storms that run from east to west. The three sisters provide some shielding from storms coming west to east, but when we come out of Marineris Valles we will be exposed to the full impact of the storms so we must take precautions."

"If you are up on top of a Mons, especially Olympus, you don't have to worry too much about the storms. Olympus is fourteen miles high and you will be at the top of Martian atmosphere. With a good push, you could probably put yourself in orbit. You may even be able to circle the planet. If a situation such as this were to happen, set your destination on navcomm, which would either be the base or this module. You'll be carrying oxygen canisters and hydrogen canisters. Your breathable canister is an M-cryo canisters capable of supplying enough for three days (4 cryo liters). The Hydrogen canister and second Oxygen canister are for your propulsion and maneuvering, but in an emergency, you can use the Oxygen from the propulsion system to breathe by transferring it to the breathable Oxygen supply."

"This would be automatic with navcomm, so this is for a worst-case scenario that for some reason navcomm isn't working. On the top of each Mons there is a crater which can provide fairly good shielding. You are going to be out there overnight, so each one will carry a navcomm unit and a bubble to use for sleeping and food consumption. You know how the bubbles work, so no explanation is required, but let me say that when you're looking for a place to camp or to have lunch, try to remember how fragile they are. A small breeze can push them great distances, and if you're in them when this happens well, it may be a bumpy ride. And remember, don't take your helmet off in case you snag a rock and the bubble rips.

Alex interrupted, "John, okay, but what is snag?"

Andre came to John's rescue. "It means hook, Alex you know like hook something."

"Okay," said Alex.

"To continue, you guys will be working together in implanting the sensor units. Even though there should not be any or much wind at that altitude, the units need to be anchored to the top of the Mons. Navcomm will pick the setup locations for you and beep. You will be carrying a drill with special bits for drilling into the lava which exists in the calderas on the top of all four Mons. The anchor bolts are six inches in length. You are to use the drill and insert the anchors in the hole. The bolt you will be using has an internal rotor that expands the bottom of the bolt. Change the drill to the hex drive and run it until it stops. And finally, when it's fully installed, turn the unit on, and then use the sealer (goop) on the anchors. There are three bolts to each sensor anchor plate. When it's correctly installed and operational, the navcomm will thank you by saying A-OK, it will come over your internal comm link.

However there is one more problem at the end of the Valle is a section called the Noctis Labyrinthus. The Labyrinthus consists of a maze of channels most of which are two miles below the mean surface (Martian sea level). We will be going into this maze but thanks to navcomm we have a map. I wouldn't attempt to navigate this area without navcomm. You could very easily take a wrong turn and become lost inside the maze. But we need to find a pathway that we can use to exit the maze to the surface above. Navcomm has picked three main pathways we might be able to use to get to the top. Of the three, this one looks the best," John said pointing to the map. "Because the slope is the best and the pathway doesn't look obstructed. We'll try that one first. Okay, big day tomorrow. Let's get some sleep and start out about 7:00 a.m. We won't have actual light till nine, but the sensors don't need light. You of course have the Ariel spot light you can use to view the cliff walls."

They adjourned for the night and left the module before seven the next morning. Navcomm took them to the last area scanned and started them up the Valles. That day was uneventful. On the third day, Alex let out a yelp.

"Got something, Alex?" John voiced over the comm.

"Yes, John, I do something big."

John looked through the view plate to Alex's camera. The opening was at least thirty feet in width across.

"My reading is of an interior depth that is off the scale," Alex stated.

"Don't move. I'm sending Andre."

Andre arrived forty minutes later. He parked his Ariel next to Alex's and grabbed his utility pack.

Jensen had chimed in.

"Post one of the portable scanners at the entrance so we will be able to communicate with you while you're in the cave," Jensen instructed.

Alex got the portable transceiver out of the bag and placed it in the center of the entrance. Then both Alex and Lefluere proceeded into the cave. Alex turned on his scanner. The cave started expanding in volume to almost three times the size of the entrance and still no reading on the length. Lefluere had switched on his light.

"Gee," John exclaimed. "They should have sent us to this cave instead of drilling the one we spent three years in."

Alex uttered, "This place is huge. There are those stalagmites and stalactites everywhere."

John knew from previous experience.

"That means water, so keep your eyes open."

They had now traveled a half mile, and the cave took an abrupt turn to the right. The tunnel narrowed, and they found themselves on a narrow access pathway. It continued for about 1,200 feet before it opened again into a huge underground cavern. But Alex and Andre had reached the end of their journey, because at the end of the pathway was a cliff, from which there was no way to continue except down. As Alex looked over the edge, he thought at least three hundred meters, but he put the scanner on it.

"It's 1,187 feet to the bottom. Andre, get your scanner out, and let's do a double scan for the imager," Alex suggested.

"Way ahead of you look Alex," Andre replied.

Alex glanced back and Lefluere had pulled a float scanner out of the utility bag. He inflated it and tossed it over the cliff. It hovered for few moments and then started to sink slowly into the abyss, mapping all the way. In a few minutes, it had reached the bottom. Lefluere controlled the craft the way you would control a model airplane.

"That looks like ice and there's a lot of it," Andre observed. "The scan says that the bottom is over a mile and a half in length and three quarters of a mile in width. This thing is a small lake." Alex tried to see what John and Jensen thought of their discovery, but the comm wasn't working.

"The navcomm has a hard time reading water and ice. However, it will read the bottom of the lake but not the ice, so we don't know how deep it is."

Andre came to his rescue, "Yes we do. We will do a scan to gauge the distance of the bottom of the lake from here. Then we will subtract the reading of the distance where the probe stopped, which would be on the top of the ice. That will give us an estimation of the depth of the water."

After a few moments, Alex questioned Andre, "What have you got?"

"It is 859 feet on the probe and 1,187 feet on the bottom," Andre replied. "That would mean the water is 328 feet or 100 meters deep at this point, however the scanner at this point only has a horizontal read of about hundred feet, meaning it could be deeper in the center," Andre concluded.

"The comm is not working," Alex emphasized. "Must be the tunnel we went through. Let's finish the scan and get back to the entrance." They did just that. As they came out of the tunnel on the other side, Alex was talking about the establishment of a colony inside the cave when John's voice came back over the comm.

"What are you going to name it? The Gorkov and Lefluere cave? I mean, it's your find," John said with a laugh.

"No, John, we've already discussed this, and we have decided to call this cave, since it is the largest cave so far. The Cavern Marineris," replied Andre.

"He means the Marineris Cavern, John. Andre, why do you make it sound like some kind of restaurant dish, Cavern Marineris," Alex corrected with a touch of sarcasm.

"Well, that's just great. Would you mind sending your scan so that Jensen and I can get a look?"

Alex pressed the send button on his scanner. There wasn't anymore conversation until they exited the cave.

John came on again, "Boys, you topped mine. I'm having a hard time understanding the concept of a small lake under the surface of Mars, but according to the data it represents thousands of gallons of water just in the visible distance dimensions. The question is the water, is it stagnant or is there flow under the surface of the ice?"

"You need to get the robots here to get those answers, John," Alex retorted. "That cliff is a long way down. We estimate nearly nine hundred feet."

"The robots right now are exploring Andre's cave and will be on their way there shortly," replied John.

"Oh, by the way, Jensen is beside himself. This is like a huge step for this project. You'll probably hear from him in about a minute and a half or so." That got a laugh; the lag had been increasing daily. They put back on the Ariel's and retuned to cliff scanning. In the next five days, they found three more caves, none as big as Marineris Cavern, but one had a little stream of water on the north side. As they approached the end of the Marineris Valles, they were now going uphill. The Valle became shallower and the caves became less frequent. They finally reached the end of the Valle and parked for the night in front of the navcomm probe that the robots had set up on the original Marineris run. During dinner, John announced that the next day they would be entering the Noctis Labyrinthus. Navcomm wants us to relocate the sensor outside to a new location."

John pulled out the map.

"Approximately 120 miles from here inside the Labyrinthus and in a more direct location to the exit point of the Valle. That would put it approximately here."

John pointed to the spot on the map.

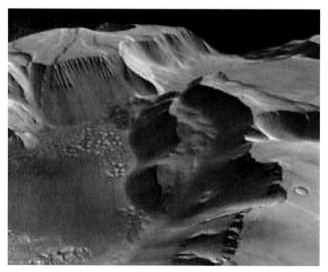

Labyrinthus Plato

Noctis Labyrinthus

Navcomm is going to guide us to the exact spot it wants us to plant the sensor, a highpoint Plato in the Noctis Labyrinthus section. It will take about three to four hours to get there. It's going to be an uphill trip in rough terrain and about a half hour to install the sensor and test the signal. Then we will attempt to find a pathway to the surface using Navcomm's directions. The problem with this is that once we get to the surface Olympus Mons is still over 6,000 miles away. It is over a thirty-hour flight to Olympus directly, and we want to stop at Pavonis Mons and secure a sensor there. It will take about another four-plus hours to get to Pavonis Mons from your first stop on Ascraeus Mons. In bought cases, we want to arrive at the Mons during the daylight hours. It is a six-hour flight to Ascraeus Mons and a four-hour flight to Pavonis Mons. Okay, let's say we get to Ascraeus Mons at 9:00 a.m. and leave at eleven. We then should arrive at Pavonis Mons around 4:00 p.m. or so. We'll lose light around 6:00 pm this time of year. That should be enough time to complete the operation on Pavonis and to find a place to park for the night, which means that you will have to leave Pavonis area early the next morning?"

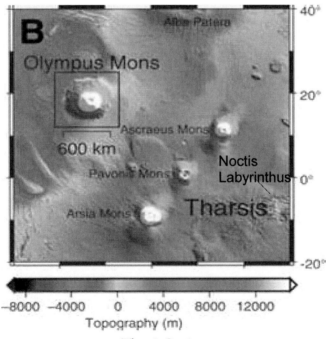

Tharsis Section

"It is a seven hour flight to Olympus, but afterwards you'll have to get to Arsia which is 8 hours away from Olympus. You can't spend the night on Olympus. It may be completely dark, but the area has been completely scanned by the T-111s. Command wants the Mons scanned for a 3-D display. To do this, the navcomm may alter your course to record the image. I'm going to move the XPLM another three hundred miles closer to the sisters, so the distance on the return would be shorter." There would be no pathway after they left the Valle and the surface would be rough. John would have to put the module into multi-drive (which is four wheel drive with 12 tires) but would only be able to travel about 15 mph. The module would still be about 1500 miles away from the sisters.

"You will not be able to communicate with me when you get to Ascraeus, but you will as soon as the sensor is installed and operational on Pavonis. You will be able to contact me through the unit's transceiver, the same with Olympus Mons. Okay, that's about it, so relax. Tomorrow all we have to do is detach this unit and transport and install it at the new location. You may want to go to bed early tomorrow night."

The next day, everyone slept in late. After the crew retired John got a call from Jensen.

"How's it look for tomorrow?" he asked.

"Okay I guess I don't think we will have any problem implanting the sensor on the Plato with the Ariel's. However, we will be inside the Labyrinthus under navcomm guidance. My main concern is the exit pathway to the surface, it has never been used before so there is a safety concern," John replied.

"John, navcomm picked the pathway because of the more gradual slope but your right we don't actually know if it's safe and we don't know what it's made out of. The best piece of advice I can give you is stay to the rising cliff side where you have a wall instead of a drop off. We don't need to lose you and the module in a 1 mile fall off the side. But, if for any reason it looks to be unsafe abort the trip to the surface and launch your crew from inside the Labyrinthus. If you are successful you should arrive at the surface within 2 days, good luck"

They got under way around 8:00 a.m. and arrived at the new location site at 2 p.m. Navcomm took them there and alerted them during the approach to the site. According to the map Navcomm wanted to place the unit on a Plato two miles above their location with a good view of the Valle. John and Alex suited the Ariel's and set out to implant the unit on the location which had been selected by the navcomm system. The lift was straight up landing them on top of the Plato. As they go closer to the site location, the unit started to hum, then it started to beep. John stopped for a minute there was a spectacular view of the Valles northwest entrance.

"We're here, put it down," said John. They drilled and installed the anchors and attached the sensor, then activated it. The navcomm issued the AOK alert and they went back to the module. They reached the starting point of the pathway that afternoon. Andre and Alex had entered a state of rapture and were both in the control room enjoying the views offered but the Labyrinthus walls with its many turns and features. They were marking locations on the map. John had the navcomm on full recorder. After a few hours they arrived at the entrance of the pathway to the surface. John stopped the module to take a look. The rest of the crew was also starring at the pathway which had an unusual pattern on it which was odd but somehow familiar. After starring at it for awhile Andre said,

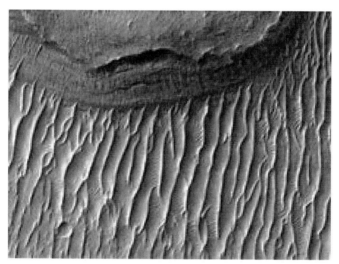

Noctis Labyrinthus Pathway

"John there is something strange about this. I've seen this pattern like this before on Earth. I've been starring at it, trying to figure out where I have seen it before. But I know I have seen it I just don't know where."

"Da, I also" offered Alex

John had to admit he had also seen a naturally formed pattern like the one in front of them before but, couldn't remember exactly where. Suddenly, Andre said

"I got it, water. This is the pattern that you sometime see produced when a current is retracting water like at low tide it forms a ripple pattern in the sand." As soon as he said the pieces fit together.

"Yeah it's created by water flowing downward," said John

"So, where's the water?" asked Alex. There was a pause.

"You don't think that the Marineris Valles was at one time filled with water?" suggested John

"I mean looking at the pathway the ripple pattern continues up which would mean that at one time water was at that level inside the Valle."

"John I think we need to take some samples of the pathway to determine what we are dealing with before we start," Andre suggested.

"Let me call Jensen and see what he has to say," John cautioned.

Alex and Lefluere went to the back to get their outer suits. Jensen came online a few minutes later.

"Hey John, I've been expecting your call navcomm says you're at the entrance of the selected pathway how does it look?"

John advised him of their realization and that Alex and Andre were suiting up to gather samples of the pathway. Jensen agreed but had another idea.

"The samples will give us an idea of what the pathway is made of but, I want you to send Andre and Alex up the pathway in the Ariel's. Like I said we really can't afford to lose that module right now it would put a serious dent in our exploration abilities not to mention you guys. But if the pathway base is loose sand we may have to cancel the ascent. The sand may collapse under the pressure of the modules's weight and take a journey off the side of a cliff."

Alex and Andre walked into the control room helmets in hand Jensen noticed their approach.

Guys we want you to take the Ariel's up to the top of the pathway. In other words the surface and carry a couple of shovels and pickaxes. Stop and test the surface every 200 yards and pick up samples when ever you see a change in the road surface. Carry some navcomm 'C' reflectors with you. Travel together and keep your comm active so we can see also."

Alex nodded and went to supply to pick up the gear. Five minutes later they were outside and activated their Ariel's proceeding to the beginning of the pathway. Going up the pathway they collected samples and tested the surface with their pickaxes.

Jensen and John watched their progress as they preceded up the pathway which navcomm said was 3.5 miles in length.

Alex came over the comm "It looks good so far we have cliff on both sides and the grade is not steep. The pathway is solid as far as we can tell. There seems to be rock under the sand that is firm."

About a mile up the Andre said,

"Hey look at this" the pathway had narrowed and was uneven with a slight drop of 12 feet on the left hand side.

"Take a measurement and make sure we have a clear solid 22 feet that the module requires," John instructed.

"Navcomm says we got 26 but that may not be true because the side may not be stable let me test it

Andre pulled out his pickaxe and moved towards the edge of the drop on the third hit the side slid down the drop.

"Well," said Jensen. "It may be safe enough to walk on but, a 28 ton vehicle is another thing. I don't like it, a twelve foot drop may not sound too terrible but if the module turns on its side it could wind up upside down and that wouldn't be good. Look John, like I said we can't afford to lose that module. Call the guys back and we'll come up with some type of solution."

John told Alex and Andre to come back in they arrived 5 minutes later took off their helmets and sat down in the control room.

Jensen started "Guys we can't afford to lose the module. That little drop-off you found and the fact that the surface is made of sand makes that pathway unstable. We are going to have to find another way, other wise we will have to launch the exploration from inside the Labyrinthus. Navcomm had pointed at a few other locations that might be acceptable. I think what we need to do is scout these other sites. We are looking for a site that is not to steep and does not border any drop-offs. But since this is the case maybe we should map the Labyrinthus. That will hold the mission up for a week however, I want to be sure we are on firm ground for the assent. I would have a very difficult time explaining to the ISA that I approved your climb and that the module fell off a cliff and was damaged and unusable. You guys can use the Ariel's to scan the walls and create the map. If we find one that is good you'll need to scan it form the bottom to the top to make sure it's safe, okay?"

Andre countered "Mr. Jensen can the navcomm give us a distance as to the length of the Labyrinthus channels if they were laid in a straight line.'

"Yes Andre navcomm gives rough distance measurements of over 8,000 miles but, you don't have to scan the entire maze just the parts where the Labyrinthus walls exit the maze, it won't do any good to find a pathway to the surface to wind up entrapped on top of a Plato. John you will have to keep the module stationary so they can find their way home, they don't call it the Labyrinthus for nothing. I've been going over the map you have two sites to the northwest of you and two directly north. I'm going to put this on priority to navcomm we should have their feedback by tomorrow morning."

Everyone understood Jensen's point of view to loose their only operational module would be a disaster beyond description at this point. Without that module long term exploration missions were out of the question. The next morning while Alex and Andre were suiting up Jensen came back over the comm.

"Okay this is how this mission goes, Alex you and Andre will take off and investigate these two sites to the southwest side each of you are to carry a 'H' series navcomm mapping probes recording every minute you are outside. Alright navcomm has made a map of the Labyrinthus section and your XPLM module's location and will download the map to your Ariel's and any other navcomm unit that within reception your suit and the H series handheld you will be carrying. Navcomm will create a mobile map setting up the locations you're going to and the stationary module as a preset destination. So, if you get disorientated on where you turned the time before last and need to get either to the previous site or back to the module, call up your navcomm map and press the preset location and the system will bring you back to the location including the module. And John, if for some reason while they are in the Labyrinthus and you have to move the module like a police officer pulls up and says 'Hey buddy you can't park here' make sure to let me know before you move the module. I'll have to send a T-111 overhead to map your new location. Also this is Yuri's module right? In the supply room there should be a case of CRs navcomm units. These units are signal repeater devices. Yuri was to set them up inside cave1 to transfer the signal down the cave to the drilling site but so far he hasn't gotten around to it. This unit differs from your standard 'C' unit in the fact, that it has a regenerative power supply and can transfer real data rather than just an identification code and the units are meant to be deployed in sequence. When you start deployment the first unit will line up to the nearest dominate navcomm unit in this case would be your module as you continue the navcomm will let you when it's time to implant another unit. You can place these units anywhere, but navcomm will tell you where. To plant a unit on a wall you will need a drill and a thermal tube for the Goop. Open the two pack epoxy and coat the wall and the unit. Place the unit on the location and use a drill to secure it. You should have about 200 units but only carry ten at a time."

Andre seemed to know what Jensen was talking about and disappeared for a few minutes returning with a thermal goop tubes and ten CRs units.

Jensen continued, "You guys are to travel together and map both side of the channels. If you find something that looks like a 'GO' be sure to alert us we'd like to take a look also. I have to get an okay for this assent mission from Earth ISA so I need a good presentation, okay?"

Andre prompted 'Oui' and the crew headed for the door. John stayed at the control room watching the mission through their Ariel cameras.

"You know Mark the navcomm system has really been an asset to this mission," John remarked.

"John you know without navcomm we would have never let you enter the Noctis Labyrinthus it would have been too risky. Even in the module you could have taken a wrong turn and wound up lost for days perhaps weeks. It's hard to believe that at one time before navcomm that mankind believed that it was ready for a mission like this. If it wasn't for navcomm you probably wouldn't be on Mars in the first place." Jensen replied.

Alex and Andre spent the next four days exploring the Labyrinthus and placing navcomm buoys at every turn forming a navcomm vector map of the interior of the maze. On the third day they returned to the module early. As they entered the module they seemed a little excited. Alex got his helmet off,

"John I think we found it." Alex pressed the send button on his handheld navcomm unit which transmitted the information to the module system. The file came up on the viewer.

"John look," said Andre. The pathway starts here and runs a slow upward path with walls on both sides but after two kilometers it levels out onto a platform. Which goes for about 500 meters then it turns into the cliff side and continues going up to the mean surface and I'm not talking about a Plato. I'm talking about the real surface. But, that's not the best news the pathway starts the same as the pathway here but, if we can make it up to the platform it turns into bedrock and we shouldn't have any problems getting to the surface from there." John was studying the images, when the comm chimed John knew it was Jensen and accepted. Andre continued describing the pathway as they went over the information. Jensen stopped him "Andre how wide is this platform that we need to take to the surface pathway."

"About a half of a kilometer you could actually turn the module around on the platform," Andre replied.

"Okay I'll turn it over to the navcomm engineers in the morning for their feedback. And if approved we will move the module to the pathway location for a better view. This will probably take a day or so but before we leave this location I'd like you to implant a few more CRs units in the maze. Up until now you've been planting the units on the North side I'd like you to spend tomorrow planting as many units as you can on the South side so, that we have some kind of functioning map of the Labyrinthus. And let me also say that while you're in that maze there will be no traveling at night, this refers to the module as well as the Ariel's, okay? So, give the engineers on Earth a little while to go over the information. and if it's a 'GO' we will move the module to the pathway entrance for further examination."

The next day they spent their time planting sensors in the southern channels. That night when they came in John was on the comm with Jensen. He turned as they came in,

"It's a "GO" we go to the pathway entrance tomorrow."

Jensen corrected him "it's not a 'GO' yet. They just want a closer look and John I think they want you and Alex to take that look. Andre can stay in the module. So, tomorrow early, start the module up and head to the pathway entrance and wait for us to come online."

The next morning did just that. The pathway was over 300 miles to the northwest from their location it would take the module over twelve hours to get to the pathway entrance because of the rough terrain. They reached the entrance approximately 6 p.m. and parked at the foot of the pathway. John dialed up Jensen to let him know they had arrived.

"Okay you guys just sit tight, we will map the pathway tomorrow it will be John and Alex to do the scan. But I need to say that something has come up, the navcomm engineering staff on Earth says we may have a problem. In the section of the pathway from the platform to the surface there is a spot which has an increased slope this concerns them."

John interrupted "This module got a lot of power in multi-drive. I looked over Andre's scan I think the module can pull it."

"From what I understand John, they aren't questioning whether or not the module can go up the pathway. There questioning whether the module can come down remember, after your through with your Olympus Mons exploration you're going to have to take that pathway back down in order to get back inside the Valle. Otherwise you'll have to go down the southern side to the Melas Chasmata to re-enter and that's some pretty rough territory. How many spare tires do you have on board?"

"I don't know, Andre this is your module how many tires do we have in supply?" John asked.

"We have not used any so, we should have 12," Andre replied.

"If you haven't used any you should have eight. True you have 12 wheels on the module the four sets of doubles in the rear that's eight and two sets of duals in the front that's twelve but, they only pack eight tires in the supply," Jensen corrected. "Anyhow, let's hope it doesn't come to that. You might want to read up on the procedure for changing a tire just in case. Tomorrow we go up the pathway with the engineers who will be directing the operation and we'll know tomorrow night whether it's a 'GO'. Oh, and you should go easy on your electricity use, we are going to need a full charge when we start up the pathway. So, I want you to start burning water and use the Hydrogen to supply your power needs. If we decide to go up the pathway we will be going up at noon the day after tomorrow so we will have full light for the solar panels. Remember that vehicle weights 26 tons and it's going to take some power to get up the pathway."

"Yes that's true Mark but as you know on Mars it only weighs a little over 13.2 tons," John corrected. "But, I get your point."

"Right, okay we'll start tomorrow about 10am that will give everyone time to go over the data, Jensen out."

The next morning there was a short review with the engineering crew on Earth one of the engineers who was introduced as Bracken pulled up the map made from the first scan.

"The main point we are concerned with is the part on the pathway where you start the assent to the surface from the platform the scan revealed that the slope may be to steep to be a safe descent which may result in you losing control of the craft and with its weight sending the module off the platforms edge. This was a main concern as to the rejection of first pathway; the sand would inhibit your traction thus causing the module to slide down the hill. It's a mile drop-off from that platform edge, so you understand. Mark did you take care of that matter we spoke about four days ago?"

"Yes I did they are just clearing the Melas Chasma now, they should arrive at the Labyrinthus in approximately two days," Jensen replied. "John, we are sending two robots to you to straighten out the pathway. There may be a slight delay in coming back down until they are finished."

"Okay," replied Bracken. "Let's take another scan of the pathway John we will be monitoring the scan here. We will tell you when we need to concentrate the scan to a particular area."

John and Alex finished putting on their outer suit and proceeded through the airlock to the outside. With shovels in hand they proceeded up the pathway to the platform; testing the surface as they went up the slope. They reached the platform they both agreed that the pathway so far was okay. Then Alex turned to John and said,

"Do you think we should name the pathway?"

"What are you going to name it" Jensen replied over the comm.

"Well Andre found it, how about the Lefluere Pass, how does that sound Andre?" said Alex.

"That sounds very good," said Andre over the comm.

They had reached the platform and Bracken requested they slow down for the surface scan of the platform for the next 1500 feet they were on a level plain. Then they came to the second pathway, the pathway to the surface. Not at the entrance but a hundred yards behind it was a rather steep slope. Now John could see why there was concern about the slope, it would be tough to get up and could be really hard to control the module coming back down. Bracken came over the comm.

"Yes that's the area we are talking about. John, I want to see if you and Alex can scale the slope without assistance. If you can we may still have a shot.

The slope must have been a 28 degree incline and ran in length about 800 feet. John and Alex started up the incline slowly and got about half way up the before they had to grab onto the walls for support. Once they reached the top the pathway leveled out to a 13 degree slope which was quite easy to navigate. They proceeded up the pathway till they reached the top. When they exited the path they were on the mean surface and could see across the top of the Plato's of Labyrinthus. The surface of the top appeared to be a little rough with rocks and sand mounds. It would be slow going but, not to much for the module in multi-drive. Jensen came back over the comm.

"Okay guys you can take the walk back and return to the module. However don't turn your scanners off, slow and steady going back down."

After they arrived back at the module Jensen came back on line.

"The robots have cleared Melas Chasma they should be at your position in two days you are to wait for them to arrive but it looks like the pathway is a 'GO'. When they arrive they will start structural work on the pathway to make it safer and you are to assist them. After they are done, we will attempt the assent. You will continue on to the Mons but, on your return you are to stop at the original site and load the robots in the rear bay for the trip back so, take a break, Jensen out"

It was two full days before the robots showed up John recognized them as his crew robots. Robot #1 had the circular grinder attached and robot #2 was pulling the cart loaded with struts, half panel, and a Goop tub. The robots stopped to recharge then started up the pathway. John and Andre followed while robot 1 ground the pathway and robot #2 follow mixing the sand with Goop and spraying it were necessary. The reach the platform and the robots re-worked the first 40 feet of the platform. Robot # 1 continued grinding until the reached the surface pathway. Then robot #1 went into high gear it went up and down the incline leveling the slope. Robot #2 was mixing the sand with the Goop and forming a speed bump at the end. This took awhile John and Andre returned to the module when they got back they noticed Alex setting up a navcomm unit and a recharge station a few feet for the entrance.

"What are you doing?" John asked.

"They told me to set this up for the robots to use while we're at the Mons. What are they going to do here while we are gone," asked Alex; John shrugged.

The next morning Jensen came online about 10 am the light was just starting to filter into the Labyrinthus. Light was hard to find inside the maze because of the size of the cliff walls on the sides, which were two miles high and not very wide the sun needed to be directly over head for light to penetrate to the floor of the maze.

"We've gotten an AOK from the bots we are going to start the assent at 11:30. It should take about a half an hour to get to the top. John you'll be running in multi-drive at a low speed so you won't have to actually do anything unless something goes wrong. Oh, and leave the remainder of the CRs units with the robots in their cart, it is at the recharge station. Also, you need to change out robot 2 to the plow on the cart. "

Alex took the CRs units over to the robots and placed them in the cart, then attached the plow shovel to unit 2. Shortly after he returned to the module the engine started and module started heading up the pathway. The module made it to the platform with no problem. Then they approached the surface pathway. Everyone was in their outer suits and John cautioned everyone to standby. The module turned into the pathways entrance. It had changed the robots had done a good job the 28 degree hill had be transformed into a 18 degree slope which the module had no problem with.

Slowly they reached the surface with no further problems and stopped the module on the side which gave a good view of the Labyrinthus.

"Good job," replied Jensen over the comm. "Relax for the rest of the day, we'll start for the Mons mission tomorrow."

Everyone turned in early that night. Four in the morning comes pretty early.

"There is no room for error here," John stressed. "So, we're going to double pack these bags like two drills and two sets of extra bits and don't forget the paste. You won't be able to use a bubble for lunch today or tomorrow. And look, there won't be any auto cookers, so it's cold food."

"They should invent a portable unit so that we can have hot food on these trips," complained Alex.

"Maybe you should take that up with Jensen," John suggested.

"I'll make some sandwiches," volunteered Andre.

"Before you guys take off, we need to check your suits, because you're going into space. So let's do the test in the air lock." One at a time they entered the lock while the atmosphere was emptied. John took oxygen and pressure readings, then you had to wait two minutes for the second reading. However, they both checked out. The carry basket was full with the bubble and the utility pack. The navcomm units were tethered to the frame. The units were approximately four feet long metal tubes and divided into sections. In the tethered bag was the navcomm power supply and battery pack. The transceiver pole was small enough to transport in the basket. John helped Lefluere on with his harness and then Alex. The Ariel adjusted for the weight and then slowly lifted into the night sky. John sat and watched their lights as they gained altitude and speed. After three minutes, they disappeared out of sight. He went back inside and decided to make a pot of coffee. At nine, he decided to call Yuri. Yuri's image came up on screen.

"Привет (hello) John, how's it going?" John said okay and then began to fill Yuri in on developments of the Valles exploration. When he got to the discovery of the Marineris Cavern, Yuri interrupted. "Yes, quite a find that Marineris Cavern. I read the report and watched the video. Tell Alex and Andre congratulations and hello for me. Our robots finished off Lefluere's cave and brought back some interesting samples. John look, our robots are here now, your robots however are still at the Labyrinthus. Ours were scheduled to go to the Marineris Cavern next, but Jensen vetoed it. He says he wants you at the location to coordinate the exploration, and our robots are to arrive there just before you on the return. So, the next time you pass that location, navcomm will send them out to you. He also wants Alex and Andre with you, so they can forget about taking the Ariel's back here. They have to suffer the ride back in the module with you. Things here are normal, JP's been working in the hydroponics every day and already has the plants singing, and since you've been gone, there is an excess of oxygen. Plus, Xiao has taken over the electrolysis and all the tanks are full. When you guys are gone, we don't use as much electricity, and of that, we also have a surplus. In fact, we've got a surplus in just about everything."

"Well," stammered John, "I'm glad to hear you miss us. Alex and Andre will be at Ascraeus Mons sometime this afternoon. Tune in and watch the celebration when they activate the sensor on Olympus tomorrow. I told them to record the mission from the beginning so that everyone can enjoy it. You know the placing of a man on top of Olympus is a historic event. The pictures of them standing on the top will probably be in history books for a long time." Around 10:00 am, the navcomm chimed. It was Alex

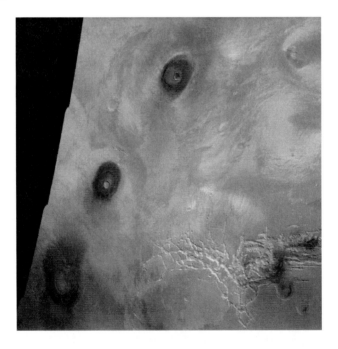

"Ascraeus landing successful, wow the view from here is really something! I mean, I know it isn't as tall as Olympus, but it is still really something. We are up on the eastern side on the craters edge."

"According to navcomm, you're eleven miles above the mean surface area of Mars. Where's Andre?" John asked.

Alex turned to show Andre looking out over the horizon.

John had a question, "You said you're on Ascraeus right now? How are you talking to me? You didn't install the navcomm sensor on Ascraeus did you, because the unit is supposed to go on Pavonis."

"No, John, we just turned it on for a few minutes," retorted Alex, "so we could talk to you. It did give us a beep but," Alex shrugged.

John activated a view through Andre's camera unit. They were right. It was quite a view.

"Can you see the Valles?" John asked.

"No," reported Alex. "It's too far. We can't see Valles entrance, however I think we can see part of the Labyrinthus. What's the curvature of Mars anyhow? Whatever it is, we're past it. We better get going if we want to make Pavonis before we loose light."

"Okay, let me know when you get to Pavonis. Can you see Olympus from where you are?"

"Let me turn on my glasses," Alex called Andre over to take a look also. Alex stared in the direction of Olympus. "I see something, but I don't know if it's Olympus or not, but it's still a long way away," Alex replied. "Ready, Andre?"

Andre nodded.

"Okay, we go. We'll call when we get set up." John used the camera link from a T-111 orbiting overhead to watch them take off. John settled back, offering an occasional comment. However, after forty minutes, there was no Trex available, and they began to fade. John was at the control panel. He eased his seat back to be more comfortable. The next thing he knew, the navcomm alarm was sounding. He had accidently fallen asleep.

Alex was signing in. "Alex, how's the view?" John offered while rubbing his eyes.

"What view? The top of this thing is a crater. We are about standing in the center of, what did you call it the caldera, and from here you can't see the ground or anything else. It's like a big crater and it's composed of lava, all lava, and it's hard to drill. We broke two bits installing the navcomm unit, and we got a fog which is also reducing visibility. Good thing we brought extras. The navcomm says the temperature here is minus 180 degrees C, and we would like to get out of here. I hope no frozen CO_2 falls on my head. Navcomm is making us circle each of the Mons to take an image scan, I guess for the map, but I've got something to say."

"You know those caves we keep finding? Well, we noticed two more near the base. We are not going to investigate them because it's getting late.

It's already five, and we need to find a place for the night. We had the unit we installed take a look at the path to our next stop, Olympus Mons. Well, it didn't look like the Trek image of it did. Anyhow, turns out Arsia has a large crater on the caldera that looks pretty good. After we get done with Olympus, we'll be heading there. I don't think that will be too hard, it's entirely downhill. Arsia is nine miles high and Olympus is fourteen miles high, so do the math. I'm sure that navcomm will calc this trip to be a boost altitude at take off and then a coast into Arsia. However, it will still take some time, and so we'll leave you now because we need to get set up for nightfall while we have light."

"Hello, John," replied Andre.

"Hello, Andre," replied John.

John watched the takeoff through the navcomm's eye. He noticed through the display screen that there was a Trex in the area, but it was too far south to get a good picture. However, it did enable a tracking guide for the Ariel's navigation.

John lost communications as soon as they passed six hundred miles, which took them less than two hours. He pressed to see what their velocity was, and it was over 320 mph. The partially downhill trajectory must have given them a little extra speed. The Ariel's can receive navcomm signals sent by the sensor units and, if close enough, transfer a message. But the Ariel transmitters have a limited distance complicated by the curve of the Martian surface. They do have an emergency signal which will call a Trex to come and operate as a communication transmitter. Each Ariel contains an ESG (Emergency Signal Generator), a separate unit which basically is a compressed wave flasher. He wouldn't be able to talk to them until they set up the navcomm unit on Olympus the next morning. They had a six-hour journey to Olympus and six hours back to Arsia. John went to sleep early and awoke early around 6:00 a.m. He had nothing to do immediately, so he checked to see whether a T-111 was in the area. There would be one at ten o'clock. However, he could get a partial read from Phobos and the Mars Platform. It revealed that Andre and Alex were about eighteen hundred miles east of Olympus in a small crater. He called Yuri and Jensen about nine. Both of them had read the navcomm report from the three sisters' transmission.

Yuri asked, "When do you expect them to get back, John?"

"I should guess sometime tomorrow, if everything goes right. However, I won't know when they make it to Arsia, not unless a T-111 passes this way." Jensen said he would send one over.

"I don't know what time they took off this morning," said John.

"Okay," said Jensen. "Give me a chime when they get in. I want to read the report when it's loaded." John assured them that he would.

Twelve o'clock came and went, then two. John started to become concerned. He couldn't find them on navcomm, which meant they were either parked somewhere or they were in a crater or cave. At 3:20, John got a navcomm signal. They had just landed on Olympus Mons and had just implanted the navcomm R-series unit.

"John, you wouldn't believe this. You can't tell you're on a mountain. We planted the navcomm unit on the eastern side of the caldera just like we did on Pavonis, but we can't see the ground, even from the edge, because the top of the Mons is covered in a light fog. It's kind of like being suspended on a platform in the sky. The caldera is completely lava and smooth except for a few small craters marks. Other than that, there's not too much to see. From where we are, we can't see anything but a large plateau. Take a look through the navcomm." John did and they were right. There wasn't much to see but 360 miles of plateau and the sky.

"Did you guys pose for the pictures yet?" John asked.

"Oh yeah," said Alex. "Andre, get over here, pictures!"

Alex grabbed Andre and pointed off into the distance. Then they shook hands, and then they stood by the navcomm unit. Then Alex posed as if making an adjustment. Then John stopped them

"Okay, that's enough ham. Do you think you'll make it back tonight?"

"I doubt that, John. We got a late start and encountered a high wind resistance as we approached Olympus, which used a little more fuel to get up the fourteen miles into space. Then we had a tough time implanting the sensor anchored and it's late. We've been looking at the navcomm map of Arsia. From my calculations, we are still six hours out."

"How much fuel do you have left?" John asked.

"Over a half a tank," Alex replied. "You know all these Mons all have craters at the top. That must have happened when the lava stopped coming out, but Arsia has the largest crater, which should be good cover for tonight. We will probably make it back to the module around noon tomorrow."

Alex and Andre suited their Ariel's and took off for Arsia. John watched their progress over the navcomm display. Once again, they were traveling much faster than normal with a velocity of well over 300 mph, but as Alex pointed out over the comm, they were using a minimum of fuel, mostly coasting. John watched their progress over a T-111 for three hours until the Trex was out of range. Jensen called the next day at noon.

"Well, where are they?"

"I don't know. I got confirmation that they had arrived at the Arsia caldera by a T-111 that passed over last night but haven't heard anything since," John replied.

"I've already dispatched a probe to that area. It should arrive in about twenty minutes. We will find out something then," said Jensen.

The T-111 appeared about twenty minutes later and showed that they were just leaving Arsia. They arrived at the module at 5:00 p.m. and pulled up about ten feet from the lock. They got themselves inside and then brought in the vehicles. As they were taking off their helmets, John said,

"What happened to you? I was beginning to get a little concerned."

Alex replied, "John, you should have been there. The top of Arsia is this huge crater. We got in just as the light was going and couldn't see much. We were pretty tired, so we decided to set up the bubbles and have something to eat and then some sleep, which we did. This morning, we were up about 5:00 a.m. and still couldn't see anything, a fog layer had settled inside the crater. What we did see was a massive cloud that entered the crater and brought visibility down to about sixty feet. Navcomm wouldn't activate the Ariel's, so we spent the next couple of hours walking around the crater. John, there were caves, about five of them; they go straight down inside the caldera. I got scan readings of them and pictures. We had several hundred feet of tether in the utility bag. Andre attached the scanner to one end, and we lowered into the caves for an internal read. When we were done, we went to take off around ten. Just after we took off, a wind storm came up. We turned around and went back to the caldera, so we were stuck there till well what, about one."

Andre volunteered, "You know they make a big deal over Olympus Mons John, but it was nothing compared to Ascraeus and Arsia. When you are on top, you don't know you're on a mountain. The navcomm says the Olympus caldera is over 360 miles wide. I think I liked Ascraeus the best."

"What about Pavonis?" John interjected.

"Pavonis is good if you want to get a view of the Labyrinthus," Andre stressed. "The top also has a crater, a deep crater, but not as impressive as Arsia. Pavonis has a little plateau in the center which would be a good place for the navcomm sensor, but the plateau doesn't clear the side walls.

In other words, you can't see Marineris from it. You have to go up the edge of the crater for that view."

"Sounds like you guys had quite an adventure," replied John.

"John," Lefluere said. "You know before, when we were preparing to go on this mission, I was a little hesitant because I didn't know what to expect. But now that it's over, I'd like to say that this little trip was an experience not to be missed. That, plus the fact that Alex and I were the first people ever to see it like this well, you will have to go see it for yourself sometime. I cannot put it into words the feeling I got from standing on the edge of Ascraeus, eleven miles up in the air. Looking over the surface of Mars was an experience that I can't describe."

"Tell John how you almost took a 5.5-mile unplanned trip down the side of Arsia," chuckled Alex.

John was taken by surprise, "What?"

Andre didn't answer, so Alex went on. "Yes, we got to Arsia, and in the morning found out that we were going to be there for a while. So Andre decided to pitch a bubble to eat. He was filling it up. It was at about three-quarters pressurized when this gust of wind from the storm came into the crater, picked the bubble up, and propelled it around the crater to where there was a shallow spot in the wall. Then it picked the bubble up, and the bubble disappeared over the rim. If Andre had been in it, it would have been a nice little 5.5-mile ride to the bottom of the Mons, so we're minus one bubble."

John was starting to put the Ariel's back in storage when Alex blurted,

"Ah, don't do that. We will need them for the trip back to the base tomorrow."

"So, you guys have this wonderful adventure, come back here. And then take off with the Ariel's, leaving me with the 1,800 mile trip back in the module. Which only gets 45 miles per hour, by myself. In the meantime, you guys will be relaxing at the base, huh? Well, there has been a change of plans," John replied. Queuing up the previous conversation with Yuri, John could see the hope fade in their faces like someone had put a hole in their balloon.

"So, it's a return to Marineris Cavern. Well, that's okay with me," Alex snorted. "Hey Andre, we are going back to our cavern."

"Hurray," retorted Andre with a depressed look on his face. John started up the XPLM module and turned it around. John wanted to wait till tomorrow to start back because the Tharsis region they were on the edge of was rough terrain and he didn't like to travel in rough terrain at night. The next morning they fired up the module and headed for Noctis Labyrinthus. They were to connect with the Lefluere Pass to return to the Valle. They were 300 miles from that point and it took most of the day to get to the Pathways entrance point for the descent. When they got within 3 miles of the entrance John noticed a navcomm 'CRs' series marker posted in the surface and the beginning of a road. John pulled the module over to the side,

"Hey guys take a look at this."

Alex and Andre came up from the galley to take a look.

Alex commented first "Looks like the robots have been busy since we've been gone. John, pull up navcomm map and let's see what else they've been up to."

John pulled up the map. The robots had been busy alright the map showed that the robots were inside the Labyrinthus planting more sensors on the northern side completing the vector web that Andre and Alex had started. It also showed that the robots had completed a road joining the Labyrinthus pathway to the Marineris Valle pathway.

"They must have started this the day we left because it's fully completed it even has 'C' markers on the sides like the Marineris Pathway does," John pointed out.

"Let's call Jensen and see what they want us to do. I mean he said we were to pick up the robots on our way back but he may want them to finish their work here."

John toggled the comm and Jensen's image came on screen. He was obviously doing some paper work in his office on the Lunar Platform.

"Mark we are here at the entrance point to the Pathway getting ready for a descent tomorrow morning because it is after five pm now and I'm not going to do that run at night. The robots have been busy and are currently at the bottom of the Labyrinthus. Are we to pick them up and transport them back to the base or what?"

"John glad you called I was going to call you in about an hour. Ah, yes you are to pick up both robots and the cart and transport them back to the base. Do you remember the original site that you went to first and we had to turn down? They will meet you there tomorrow morning. Load then up and head for the Marineris Cavern where Yuri's robots will meet you. But, before you turn that engine off for the night I recommend you continue down the Pathway till you get to the entrance. Then start down the Lefluere Pass in the morning. However, give me a call tomorrow when you pick up the Bots, okay?"

John said okay and the screen went blank. He started up the module and continued down the roadway for another three miles. Then he saw that a navcomm recharge unit they had left with the robots had been planted at the entrance point. John pulled the module over for the night. It was then Alex who had been in his pod announced that reception of the navcomm link reception had improved greatly. The module when away from the base could pick up media feed from the Mars platform, the T-111's and the Phobos repeater. However the link varied according to the position of the module and the orbit of the transmitters. John toggled the navcomm link and it showed good signal strength.

"John where is the signal coming from" Alex asked "Is it coming from the base?"

John was studying the link map "No it appears to be coming from the Rs unit you placed on Pavonis"

"John do you know what they are doing?" commented Andre.

"No what?" John replied.

"With the implantation of the navcomm units and the one on the Mons they have created a navcomm channel with the roadway. That starts at the southeast entrance to the Valle and ends up at Olympus Mons a channel and roadway that extends over 7,000 miles. Now, they can send robotic units from the base to the Three Sisters and Olympus without the need of human involvement. This is a realization vision of the future here on Mars. They will be sending big bots to do the work on the planet surface. And they will probably continue this plan all the way around the other side of the planet. The future of the people who come here will be under the surface like in the Marineris Cavern," Andre added.

"This may be so; a large community living on the surface would not work. The conditions are too harsh and the effects of radiation to dangerous." agreed Alex.

The next morning they started down the Pathway it took about 30 minutes to arrive at the bottom John could tell that the robots had worked on it after they had left and was impressed with the work the roadway was smooth and easy to navigate. When he reached the bottom he took a hard left following the new road towards the northeast where the robots were waiting. The next day they arrived at the site the robots were standing with the cart. John stopped the module and extended the boom crane on the top of the module. Alex went outside to make sure the robots were properly linked. John would then lift them into the rear load hatch. Alex attached the cart to the back of module. When everything was secured

John put the module in drive and headed for the Marineris roadway. It was the next day before they reached the Marineris roadway and John could put it on autopilot. Andre had fixed lunch in the auto cooker, and they sat down in the kitchen to eat.

"You know, we've been gone over a month. With the trip back, it will be over a month and a half, plus the amount of time that we spend at the cavern is there anything new at the base?"

"You heard Yuri's message. You know the robots went into Andre's cave and found some interesting samples, and JP's adventures in gardening seem to be working out. Other than that, I don't think so. I'll guess we'll find out all the news when we get to the cavern."

The module was on autopilot. You can only operate the auto function when you are traveling in a navcomm area, in this case the road which the robots built. They had planted the reflective 'C' sensors along the pathway for guidance control. Only one problem with that is top speed in auto was only 20 mph. At that rate, with twelve hours on manual means and twelve hours on auto, the module could cover 780 miles a day, which meant they could arrive at the cavern in approximately three days. But it usually doesn't quite get 780 miles a day, more like 650. John and Alex split the drive time with John taking 12 hours and Alex taking the other 12. With the added speed they could do 1000 miles a day. They might still reach the cave before sunset the second day. The module ran fairly well. There were some bumps, but overall it wasn't too bad. Sure enough they pulled up shortly after sundown two days later at the Marineris Cavern. They were now only eight hundred miles from the base. They would wait till dawn the next day to start their examination of the Cavern.

John was awakened by a navcomm alert, as was everybody else. He turned on his display to see what the alert was about and was shocked to see the image of one of the rovers with a loaded converted panel with wheels pulling up to the module. The screen split. It was Yuri.

"We thought we would come up and see what all the hubbub is about. Put some coffee on, will you? We haven't had breakfast yet."

"We, who's with you?" muttered John as he stumbled out of his pod.

"Hey John," It was JP.

"JP, what are you doing here?"

"I wanted to see the cave John, and yes, let's get that coffee going."

Lefluere and Alex spilled out of their pods. Andre set up the coffee and got the auto cooker going Yuri and JP entered through the air lock a few minutes later. Everybody parked themselves around the dining table while Andre poured and brought the coffee over.

"You got me this time. I wasn't expecting a welcome home ceremony. Did you drive twenty-four hours just to see the cave?" John asked.

Andre interrupted, "Hold it, before you guys get involved in a long-term conversation, what's the breakfast menu selection? Eggs, bacon, potato, biscuits, juice okay?"

"Andre, can I get sausage instead of bacon?" asked Yuri.

"Yeah, me too," said Alex.

John timed in, "Make that three."

"John, it's like JP said. We're here to see the cave. Jensen and the ISA will be online shortly. We are pretty far away from Earth right now, so there will be a lag, but they are pretty excited. They are already talking about establishing a colony here inside the cave and they will, if things check out. They'll be sending supplies to construct the basic structure on the next drop after this one. They're doing the design engineering now. This was a major find. It changes everything. Remember what they said in class? Water is the most valuable element in space. If all things go well, they will start construction after the next drop, but of course, you'll be on your way home by then maybe. And your replacements will most probably be showing up to put it together, and from what I understand, they are sending a massive amount of equipment."

"What do you mean if things check out?" asked John.

"They want someone to see if that's really water in that drop off, or if not, what it is?"

"How are they going to do that?" asked John.

"We brought with us a cabled tether and harness. But don't worry. JP already volunteered for the job. And we brought a bunch of other equipment loaded on the converted panel we put together. We needed something to put the equipment on to transport it here. So, we took a wall panel and put wheels on it, works pretty well, anyhow it got the equipment here. The equipment includes: special scanners, special lights, and panels with framework and navcomm units. They want us to seal the cave. We also brought our extra pressure door left over from the base construction. So if all things are good, we should have two days of work here, maybe three. The robots have been here for five days and have carved out the entrance for the framework insertion. Okay, as soon as we finish breakfast, we need to suit up and take a look at this lake of ice."

An hour later, they were leaving the air lock on their way to the cavern. Yuri pulled two utility bags out of the rover cart. JP picked up the tether, Alex took the harness, John took the wench, and they proceeded to enter the cave. Yuri was astounded by the size of the cavern's interior. He had seen the information and viewed the scan results. However, seeing it up close was different. The crew followed the pathway to the tunnel. It was single file till they reached the drop-off. The platform they were standing on was only approximately 4×8 feet. So John instructed Alex and Lefluere to hold back until they secured the wench. The robots weren't able to pass through the tunnel. It was too narrow and they stayed outside with Alex. Because of this the wench anchor would have to be drilled manually. Yuri pulled the drill out of the utility bag. After positioning the wench base plate, he began drilling starter holes. Then he switched to the ratchet to drive the six-inch expansion bolts home. The wench was then secured. Yuri also pulled out some adjustable ice cleats and handed them to JP.

"The original scan says there is a shore on the opposite side. It's not very large, about 20ft.×30ft., but we want you to head for it and set up the equipment there. If that is ice down there, you will need these grips for traction to cross the surface. The tether is only 1,200 feet long, so you will have to detach from the tether to cross the distance. If for some reason the ice should break, don't panic. You're in a space suit. It should be able to handle it." JP nodded. Yuri continued,

"Okay, here's the drop order. JP, you will go first. You will carry with you the drill, some specialized equipment, the sample tester, and some float sensors. After you reach bottom, and are secure, before you start for the outer side, we will lower the navcomm unit and the light rack. Now, as you know, your weight is about 130 lb. on Earth. Here, your weight is about fifty-five to sixty pounds. The navcomm unit weighs 60 lb. Earth / 25 lb. Mars. Together, you weigh less than one hundred pounds Mars. Here's a short tether line. When the navcomm unit gets to the lake surface, detach the wench line and attach the tether. You can use it to pull the unit across the ice, thus dividing the weight. Okay, got it? John, help him on with that harness."

"Oh, and one more thing," Yuri added, "try not to jerk or tug on the tether. If it breaks, you may be down there for a while. We have another line in the rover, but it would take an hour or so to pull the reel and insert a new line, so ease yourself over the cliff. We have a fifty-foot line of nylon rope you can use to ease yourself over the edge to start. Okay, ready?"

JP nodded. He grabbed the rope and then eased himself over the cliff backward in belay fashion and started down. John called for Alex and Andre to come in to watch JP's descent. JP descended about two minutes when they heard him yell to stop. Yuri stopped the wench.

"I'm about two feet from the surface. I got a light on. It looks like ice and it's solid. Lower me slowly so I can test the strength." Yuri lowered him slowly. Again JP said to stop.

"I'm on the surface. I'm going to apply my weight to the surface. It seems to be holding. I'm now standing on it with slack in the tether. Okay, I'm releasing the tether. Okay, pull it up."

Yuri reversed the wench and raised the clip. When it arrived, John attached the scanner and the light rack to the tether and lowered it over the side. A minute later, they heard JP say,

"Slow it down. You're almost there. Okay, that's it. Give me a little slack." Through their suit viewer, they could see the sensor and JP's light, which didn't show very much.

"I'm attaching the tether to the scanner. Okay, I'm moving north toward the shore. I can't see it yet. I'm pulling the scanner behind me about twenty feet back, so far so good." There was a pause of about forty seconds, then,

"I'm still going, moving pretty well. Still don't see the 'shore' yet." Another pause

"My personal scanner says I'm getting closer," Another pause.

"Wait, I think I see something. Just a minute, yes, I see the 'shore'. It's about eighty meters from where I am. I should be there in a minute or two. You can't see anything in here. I am lucky the spotlight is reflecting off something. Okay, I'm there. Give me a second to set up the light. The scanner's with me now." About a minute and a half later, the crew looked over the cliff to see a light appear on the other side, a quarter of a mile away in the cave below. Yuri pulled a pair of high-powered binoculars out of the utility bag and aimed at the light.

"JP, we can see you," he said. Then he handed the binoculars to John. Across the lake to the right of the light stood JP, who was working on setting up the navcomm unit. John handed the binoculars to Alex.

"JP, can you tell how big the dry area you're standing on is?" asked John.

"No John, but I will in a second." The navcomm scanner JP was installing was a medium navcomm T-series sensor recorder. The unit contained: a 3D image recorder, a zoom camera, laser distance recorder, transceiver, regenerative power supply, and a programmable system generator, which ran over forty different programs, including of course, code response. Since Yuri had a navcomm scanner and the codes, he transmitted the codes which instructed the unit to do a full rotational scan of the cave. Yuri warned JP to stay ahead of the beam. Otherwise, his face would be encoded as part of the cave's map. JP said he didn't care about that. The people on Earth needed to be reminded that there were people up here.

"JP," said Yuri. "We really need to get a first complete image scan without you, okay?"

"Besides, how are we supposed to see the Loch Ness monster when it surfaces and has you for a snack?" questioned Alex. Everyone turned and stared at him.

Yuri added, "No, but Alex is right. We may not have found any life on the surface since we've been here, but underwater life is not out of the question, so be careful."

"I wish you hadn't said that," added JP.

"Anyhow JP, see if you can get the light rack set up spotting over the lake in three directions. You have your back to the north and we are on the south side. The lake and the cave extend from the northwest to the southeast. That's what we need to see."

Yuri sat down for a couple of minutes next to the cave wall. JP went about setting up the light rack and then turned it on. After a few minutes, Yuri instructed JP to pull the drill out of the utility bag and attach the circle cutter to the bit housing.

"We need to take a sample of the ice and the water or whatever's underneath it, so we need to cut a hole in whatever it is so that we can extract the samples. We don't know how thick the ice is or how far we may have to drill. For all we know, it may be completely solid ice."

Yuri continued, "JP, go about twenty feet out over the ice and see if you can find out what's what, but if the ice starts to break, stop." The crew watched, because they could see JP setting the drill up. JP began drilling. The hole cutter was one foot long by six inches circular and had very sharp teeth. It didn't take JP long to carve the hole, except that he didn't come up with anything but ice.

"You may be right, Yuri. I so far can't find the bottom of the ice. What now?"

"Attach the two-foot extension. It's in the bag. It has a push lock on one end and drill housing on the other."

"I got it," said JP. "I'm attaching it to the drill. Okay, now attaching the cutter."

"Okay, here we go." JP's image appeared again and went back to the hole. He hesitated; the drill was now about eighteen inches down. JP all of a sudden said, "Something broke because I have no pressure on the drill. I'm pulling it out; woops got water at one and a half feet down. Okay, now how do I get to it?"

"In your utility pack, you have a wrapped four-foot hose with manual pump. Use that to gather your samples and place the ice in a separate container and you're done. Take a look around before you come back and see if you find anything else to take a sample of. Wait till I give you the signal and release your floats one at a time. JP waited for the signal and dropped two float sensors into the hole thirty seconds apart. Five minutes later, JP was being raised to the top. Yuri waited until JP arrived and suggested that it was time for lunch, and they adjourned to the module. Yuri had brought some food from the base, and Lefluere, who was the best cook of the group, started preparation for lunch. No one knew why Andre was the best cook. The main cooking devices were the microwave and the auto cooker, neither one of which required any particular skill. Yuri activated the comm and uploaded the scan data. It took about a half a minute, but Jensen's face appeared on the screen.

"Good, you're back, I tried to call earlier, but no one was home. How did it go?"

"Nothing to report, results turned out pretty good. It looks like water. I'm going to run basic tests on the samples after lunch," Yuri replied.

"Okay, have lunch. The ISA has a staff of geologists online. They, as well as I, want to go over the data you recorded and will get back to you in about two hours or three o'clock your time. So, hang loose till then."

The screen went blank and lunch was ready, which had a portion of pork fried rice, compliments of Xiao. After lunch, they hung around, passing the time of day. Alex and Lefluere accounted the Olympus Mons trip, Alex got to tell about Andre's near 5.5-mile trip, whereas Yuri added,

"That's not true, Alex. He would not have made it the entire way down. Something would have broken the bubble. It would have deflated and might have even thrown him out. Then he would have stopped on the first flat surface."

"Yes," agreed Alex. "Probably a snag."

John reminded Yuri of an old American saying, 'It's not smart to insult the cook.'

At three, Jensen chimed back in.

"Guys, our geologist friends are online and want to talk to you." The screen split, and an older portly man came to the screen, who was introduced as the head geologist, a Dr. Werner.

"Yes gentlemen, we have just a couple of questions to ask you. It won't take long. Ah, did you notice any mineral deposits in the cave when you were down on the lake?"

"No, sir," replied JP. "The only thing I did notice is that when I approached the shore, I got some kind of reflection from the far wall, but when I got there, I couldn't see the reflection."

"Another question, I understand you put a float scanner in the water?"

"Two, I put two floats in the water," interrupted JP.

"Where did the floats go and approximately how fast did they move?" the Professor asked.

"The navcomm should tell you that. I, of course, couldn't see with my eyes where they went. I mean but the scanner recorded them going east for about a minute and a half. Then we lost the signal. The second one did the same thing."

There was a stir in the professor's room, but JP couldn't hear what was being said.

"The wall on the eastern side, it was about what, two hundred yards away?"

"Yes," replied JP. "I would say that's about right. Of course, the navcomm would have the exact measurements."

Someone pressed the mute button because the sound went off. It came back on after two minutes. Jensen was the first to speak.

"Okay, here's the game plan. Guys, we want you to seal up the cave with the pressure door that Yuri brought with him in his self made cart. We will be sending a new machine on the next drop." Jensen's face was replaced with a diagram.

"It's a mini remote-controlled aqua rover with light and submersible read application. You are to attach the navcomm unit to it. Dr. Werner will explain."

Dr Werner approached the camera.

"We would like to have a way to investigate the water and the current flow. With this device, it will allow us to do so. It has been suggested here that because the water under the ice is flowing at a moderate rate, that this cave and the cave where you are getting your water might be connected by an underground river. What's more, it may go all the way to the South

Pole, which is some 12,800 miles away. We need to find out if this is true. If it is true, then we are dealing with a lost ocean, a lot more water than what we have found as of yet. This would provide proof of a theory that we have been considering for some time."

"Back millions of years ago, Mars was in volcanic upheaval. This would be when the Tharsis Region which contains the three sisters and Olympus Mons, were being formed. Hot magma was being forced to the surface, causing a tectonic plate shift in the planetary structure which created the Marineris Valles. This is not uncommon. The Grand Canyon in the United States and the Marianas Trench in the Pacific Ocean are products of large tectonic plate shifts. When a tectonic plate shift like that happens as a result of volcanic activity, red hot magma or lava from the mantle surges to fill the hole, which it does to some extent. However, in your case on Mars, you had four volcanoes erupting in a central location on the northwest end of the Valles. The split or Valle is running to the southeast. This tells us that the shift started in the northwest section. What's even more evident is that if you look at a topographic map, you see that the Chryse, Utopia and the Amazonis Planitia may at one time have held water. The three Planitias are connected. Together they make up over one third of the Martian surface which would be a rather large Ocean."

"These Regions are approximately the same depth as the Marineris Valles. In which case, when the plates split, the rising lava was met by water pouring down into the trench from the oceans, rapidly cooling the lava and stopping its flow. The water would have had tremendous pressure. As the water stopped the flow of the magma, it formed caves from the pressure excreted by the downward flow. At this point, we are not talking about a small amount of water here. We are talking about an ocean of water with three miles in depth and pressure."

"The thing about this type of activity is that the original split, which you see displayed by the shape of the Marineris Valles may be like an iceberg whereas; only a part of the split is present on the surface. The original split may be much larger than the Marineris Valles which we see on the surface, which as you know is over three thousand miles long. If this is so, the evidence you have found here may indicate that the ocean that disappeared may be under the surface. Of course, when the water hit the magma, a large quantity of it would have been turned into steam. When the split occurred, and if the events are as we described, then that split may go thousands of miles in length and thousands of miles in depth. This would explain a lot about the orbit of Mars. A large shift in the mantle like that may have created a pocket of air inside the mantle which, would defiantly have an effect on the planets orbit it would be like rolling a ball with a weight embedded off center in its core, the ball will warble."

"Of course, that would be to say that these little caves you are finding are just little holes caused by the pressure of the water. There may be larger caverns which we have not found yet. Where these caves then exposed the underground water to an atmosphere, which is minus 100 to minus 180 degrees. This would cause a layer of ice to form over the surface. But, I want to add that this event of rapid cooling may have caused a shift in the planets mantle temperature and may have had an effect on what gives Mars its unusual orbit. Such a large-scale activity in the mantle could very easily upset the magnetic polarity of the planet's structural mass and thus alter the orbit. The image of the Melas Chasma shows that it is the center of the Valles and that it is where the lava was rising from the mantle during the split. The incoming water caused the mantle to cool rapidly, changing the structural density of the internal mass. Look, here's a topographical map with the highest and lowest points marked with the exception of Hellas crater, which we believe to have been caused or formed by an unstable asteroid impact. You see the areas in blue, which would be the former ocean, are connected to the eastern side of the Valles through the Chyrse Planitia. This ocean would have been three to four miles deep and tens of thousands of miles in diameter. The fluctuation of the orbit may have changed the ability of the planet to hold to water on the surface, thus allowing the water to achieve enough velocity to leave the planet's atmosphere, converting to ice when it hit space. Anyhow, that's the theory, but when we see evidence that would support this theory in the data and pictures like this . . ." The screen changed again.

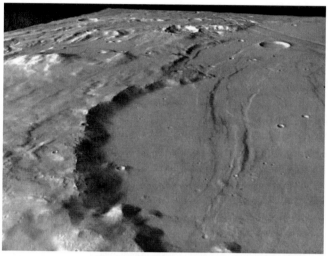

"That tells me that at one time Mars definitely did have water, possibly life as well, and this thesis is our attempt to explain what happened to it. The most prominent elements on the surface are carbon dioxide and iron, which give Mars its red color. It is quite possible that there was a change in orbit in a way that the planet could no longer retain molecules under a specific density. Whereas, the atomic weight of Carbon dioxide is 22 and Iron is 26, Oxygen (O2) is 16, and water is 10. So the elements that have an atomic weight less than let's say 20 cannot be retained on the surface unless bonded with a heavier element, such as the bond between Iron and Oxygen, which produces Ferrous Oxide, with a weight of 34."

"There is another theory being batted around that in this process of a huge amount of ice from Mars entering our planet's atmosphere may have created an effect that may have been responsible for the Ice Age on Earth.

But enough of that, we do need something. We need to know why the water in that cave flows. Where this water is coming from and where it is going to? So here's our plan. When you dropped those float sensors in the water, after it goes past a certain point, you no longer get a signal. This is because of the ferrous oxide that is about everywhere on the planet, blocks the transmission. Our first attempt to figure this out is to get the robots to drill a hole where your water supply in the other cave is coming out and insert a sensor probe." Dr. Werner concluded.

"Well, what do you think Yuri?" asked Jensen.

"We can put the wall and seal on the Cavern tomorrow," said Yuri. "Afterwards, we will have to go back to the base to test the samples. Okay we're about eight hundred miles from the base on the western side of Melas Chasma, so that's about twenty-five hours and I don't have any idea how long it will take to drill out our water supply spring. I'll have to call Xiao and have him fill all the tanks before we start because I have seen it before, where during a drilling, the water stops completely and disappears. If that happens, we won't have a supply of water at the base. Other than that, it sounds okay."

"That's the spirit. So what, then? Talk to you in a couple of days?" suggested Jensen.

"**Да хороший** (yes, good)," replied Yuri. They turned the comm off, and Yuri turned to look at John

He did not have a smile on his face.

"What's a matter Yuri you don't think their sensor will work?" John questioned.

"That's not what I'm concerned about, John," Yuri replied. "Their idea of drilling the spring is a high-risk gamble. If we lose that water supply, we could be in real trouble. They are playing with our lives here. When I worked in the Siberian mines we drilled a spring like the one we have here. We lost the water flow and were not able to recover it. If that happens here, we will lose the spring by the base."

"Well we could always come here to get the water," John replied.

"John, it is 800 miles to the cavern from the base that's two days away but you're right if we have to, we have to. We don't really have a choice." Yuri agreed.

They put the framework up the next morning, unloaded the cart, and installed the air pressure door before heading back to the base. They arrived at the base the late the second day, only earlier than Yuri quoted because he took over driving when it was John's turn to sleep, instead of going half of the way on autopilot. Before anyone did anything, they all needed a drink. The module was okay as far as comfort, but it was sometimes hard to sleep in while it was moving. Some of them decided to take a nap, namely John. John woke up about the next morning. He looked around for Yuri and found him in the lab.

"What are you doing?" John asked.

"I'm going over this diagram they sent us. We can build it, but we may have to fabricate some of these parts and the main structure ourselves, and that increases the complexity of the assembly. We don't have the correct parts to fabricate the entire device ourselves."

"We should just wait for the drop, leave it to the engineers on Earth," John suggested.

"Just thought I could save everyone some time," said Yuri.

John saw Yuri at lunch that afternoon.

"Have you heard from Jensen yet?" John asked.

"No, I haven't. He was unavailable last night, but I'm going to run the sample tests soon. We should hear from him sometime today. I'll be in the lab running the samples."

John helped Yuri for a couple of hours, and then it was time for his shift in the control room. He had been there for about forty minutes when a call came in over the navcomm. Ah, thought John, Jensen finally. But it wasn't Jensen; it was deputy Administrator Jason Greene.

"John, long time no see. Where's Yuri?"

"He's in the lab running tests on the samples we got from the Cavern," John replied.

"Well," said Jason, "I need to speak to both of you, so give him a call."

Yuri showed up at the control room a few minutes later.

Jason started, "We have made some changes to your schedules. First of all, stop what you're doing. As far as the underwater probe, we are going to manufacture the unit component here and ship it to you during the next drop. Secondly, about the next drop, you have two weeks to decide if there's anything you need up there. Anything that you may need to be included in the shopping list, the last CMP is leaving in two weeks. Anything that is not on the shopping list in the next fourteen days will not be included in the drop. The first CMPs will start to arrive in orbit in six months. This is a rather healthy drop. However, most of it is going to Yuri's base."

"Now here's the other news. John, you and your crew have been doing surface exploration to the south of the Marineris Valles. You are to continue, as far as a Marineris Cavern is concerned; it's on hold till after the drop. Okay, now as far as Yuri's crew goes, the Chinese sponsorship has suggested that perhaps Xiao should be allowed to make a discovery on Mars. Understand the Chinese government is a big supporter of this ISA project, so naturally we said okay. The next order of business as far as your crew goes is to include Xiao in the next exploration mission, which after a combined discussion of what was left to be done. It was decided that the mapping of Candor and Ophir Chasma should be the mission. Now Candor and Ophir Chasmas are to the north of the Melas Chasma, which is that large flat section approximately eight hundred miles from your location, as you know. According to data from navcomm index, the Chasmas are approximately one thousand miles in diameter. Candor is first and Ophir is to the north, approximately one thousand two hundred miles away with the same type of diameter."

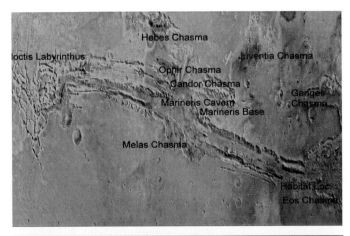

Ophir Chasma

"The surface is too rough for a module, so the crew will have to spend a couple of nights in balloons. When they get closer to the base, they can come home at night. John, you and JP can return to your habitat and continue your operation regarding the craters to the south. I'd like Alex to stay at the base with Yuri's crew for a while. Now Xiao cannot go on this mission alone. Either Andre or Alex will have to go with him, or they can alternate, depending on their location. This mission will require both Ariel's and supplies. They are not to leave the base without a balloon. The mapping should take approximately two months. Navcomm will supervise the navigation inside the Chasma. And they will have to return occasionally to the base for supplies and fuel. It might be a smart idea to stock the Chasma with supplies that they can access without having to return all the way back to the base for Oxygen and food. They are to place in the center of the Chasma an M-series navcomm and then scan the side walls with the two H-series handheld units."

"John, in the upcoming drop will be the equipment you require for your crater exploration, which should not take very long. However, here's the big news. When you are through, we are going to move your module to the base. We are abandoning your cave. Yuri and his crew will help you in the process. You will help them organize the base after the drop. Okay, that's the long and short of it. Are there any questions? And listen, you are not to disclose any of the information on why Xiao was picked for this mission. Yuri, just say it's his turn. Okay, so except for that mission, you guys are on vacation till the drop."

Alex had just walked in the room and had overheard part of the conversation. Jason signed off. Yuri and John explained the facts disclosed in Jason's message.

"So what, I'm going to be living in bubbles again with Xiao as my backup?" complained Alex.

"Yes, Alex," John replied. "Looks that way, but you can take turns with Andre."

John and JP left the next morning in the rover because the Ariel had to stay at the base. It was a three-day trip back to their habitat. For the next three months, John and JP took their vacation seriously. They used the rover for small explorations of Eos and Ganges Chasmas and the Argyre Planitia near the habitat, with nothing much to show for it. John kept up with the reports from Yuri and Alex on the progress of the mapping mission of the northern Chasmas of Candor and Ophir. Alex returned after seventy-two days with the Ariel and remarked how happy he was to be back at the habitat. He was tired of sleeping in bubbles. The exploration of Candor and Ophir had revealed three caves in Candor and two in Ophir, however none with water. But on the upside, Xiao had gotten recognition for the discoveries.

Chapter 10

The Drop

Three and a half months later, the drop started. Although nothing had come down yet, the CMPs were starting to line up in the approach orbit. He had talked to Yuri and found out that the robots had stopped working in Cave 2 shortly after they left. They were now in the Melas Chasma, west of the base, smoothing out another drop zone. According to navcomm, there were eight CMPs in orbit, ready to go, and soon the drop started. It took fourteen days for the drop to complete. The CMPs could only drop so fast, and they had to hit the target. Otherwise, you could lose the cargo. Also, a storm occurred the second day, which temporarily stopped the drop, but when it was over, John and Alex took the rover and went to the habitat landing site to open some bubbles. The robots were already there. They had come over two nights earlier and had stayed in their bunker during the storm. They were already opening one of the balloons.

"What is it?" asked Alex.

"Looks like the other cart," John replied

The balloon pack had ruptured during landing and spilled a bunch of parts with four tires out onto the landing strip.

The robots were stacking the cart pieces in groups.

Alex and John watched them for a few minutes until they had finished stacking. They then started to put the cart together. Alex said, "How do they know how to do that and how did they know the sorting order of the parts?"

"The bubbles have identification cards on them and the cart construction program must have been sent to them last night over navcomm. Let's wait till they finish, and then we'll call Jensen," John suggested.

Alex agreed and they sat there until the robots finished the cart. As soon as the robots finished, they started opening another bubble. John called Jensen, who answered, and by the look of his face, had just been awakened.

"What is it, John?"

"Ah, we're at the drop site now in the rover watching the robots build the cart, and now they're opening another bubble. What are they doing?"

"Honestly, John, you should ask your robots. They know more about it than I do, but now that I'm up, let me tell you what I know. The cart is for you to put the capsule on to transport it back to the habitat. The robots will bring in the rest of the gear when you get back to the habitat. You need to place the capsule inside the habitat with you for the time being. You must take good care of the capsule. It is your only way home, and Yuri's crew is to use it for their trip home. So, if you mess it up or put it together wrong and it don't work right. Besides you blowing up or crashing into the surface and dying. Your crew and Yuri's crew will be stuck there for at least another four years. Also, it might be a point to note that you have to assemble the SRBs yourself, and for any reason you can't obtain orbit, you will crash back on the surface anyhow. So, make sure you assemble them right. That craft is meant only to obtain a low orbit and hold it for two to four rotations. Your return vehicle, which is a converted CMP, will intercept the capsule, and you will transfer to it for the trip home. Okay, anything else you want to know?"

"Ah no thanks, we'll let you get back to sleep."

"JP, are you paying attention?" asked John.

"Yes, John," JP replied over the comm from the habitat.

"How do you talk to the robots? I've forgotten."

"Communications with the robots is like talking to any computer; however their vocabulary and what you can ask is primitive and limited. I think that it was done on purpose. Why don't you tell me what you want to ask and I'll type the question?"

"Ask them what they're doing."

John waited while JP entered < code: (then) what in progress /> JP

< removing return capsule /> Robot 1

< next? /> JP

< attach unit CRT 42 to rover /> Robot 1

< next?/> JP

< secure capsule to CRT 42 /> Robot 1

<next? /> JP

< unpack balloon 27 transport contents to home site />Robot 1

<next? /> JP

Robot 1

<next? /> JP

Robot 1

<next?> JP

Robot 1

"Well, John, that's what they are doing. So now you know," replied JP.

"JP, ask them where the rest of the capsule is."

JP

Robot 1

"Okay, now we know," John replied.

"Look, they have gotten the capsule out, and they have started removing the balloon and the protective drop pack," announced Alex.

The rover started moving toward the position on its own with John and Alex inside. When it got close to the capsule, the rover turned around and backed in. The robots attached the cart to the rover and expanded it to 12 feet. Then placed the capsule inside the cart, they attached the binding straps to secure the capsule. When they were finished, the rover started up and headed for home, still with John and Alex inside.

"I don't even know why we came along," remarked John turning to look at Alex.

They got back home about two hours later, and John said he had enough for the day. Alex agreed, so that was it. JP asked how the trip went. John repeated what he said before and added that he wasn't going back out the next time. He didn't have to worry about that because when he got up the next day, the robots were gone. He got a cup of coffee and staggered out to the control room. JP was on duty.

"Did you see the robots take off this morning?"

"Yes," commented JP. "I saw them pull the rover out of the storage booth, attach the cart to it, and take off with them inside the cart."

John nearly spit up his coffee. "They what, oh this is getting to be too much! Now the robots are joyriding around Mars in our rover."

"Well, kind of makes you think about what you said yesterday, doesn't it?" replied JP. "You know, why we are here anyway? That got me thinking why we are here at all, they could have done most of this with robots."

"I don't know the answer JP. Maybe we should ask Jensen. It's my watch; I'll wake you up when the bots get back with the supplies." John sat down at the control panel. JP excused himself and went out of the module to work with the hydroponics for a while before turning in. For about four hours, nothing happened, so John activated the mobile link and went out into the cave to go over the capsule. It was exactly what it was: a capsule, no wings, no heat resistant tiles, no Kevlar, no control panel. However, there was a power supply heater and a mini navcomm link and mini Tri-Starr unit.

He sat down to read the instructions of the assembly. John kept a slow eye on the robots. Then, they seemed done with what they were doing and appeared to be returning to the module. It would take them three hours to get back. When they got back, the crew put on outer suits and went out to help bring the supplies inside the cave. The robots brought in their loads, which were mostly food and water. However, the cart was loaded with 100-lb (38 lb Mars) bags labeled CL20, which they stacked next to the capsule. There were over two hundred CL20 bags and other bags with other ingredients labeled Dinitrogen tetroxide and MMH, plus a liquid oxygen tank. All were stacked next to the capsule. The robots helped bring in some of the bags and had unloaded most of the food. Also in their load was a package that contained tether wire and the float sensors for the hole. JP started unloading the crater diving equipment. John was stacking the capsule components, preparing to put them in a bubble when JP said,

"Hey, John look at this."

John came over to take a look.

"What is it?" John asked JP, who was standing there with a two a half foot fiber rod which kind of resembled a tuning fork.

"According to this sheet that was enclosed in the packing, it's a navcomm Ariel float frame. Let's see, two navcomm units fit into the inside of this bracket," JP said, holding up the bracket.

"These navcomm units go inside this frame, and the frame has two small motors built into the sides, which can control the navcomm units to go up or down.

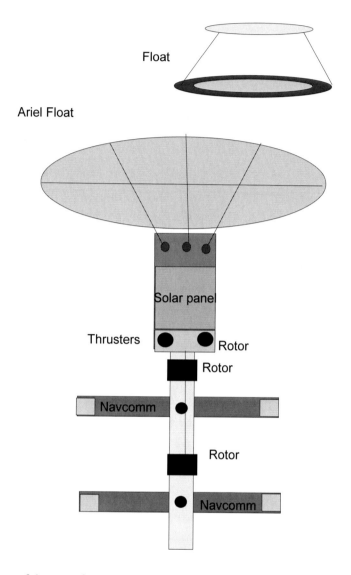

The top of the unit fits to this circular cylinder, which contains a Helium tank, transceiver, power supply and balloon like the Ariel. So evidently, the unit is self-guiding through navcomm and can be used anywhere. John, I'm thinking this might solve our crater problem. Not only that, if I read these instructions right, this unit can be used to do other things including air reconnaissance," JP replied.

"That's great; we will have to test it out." Then John suggested they break for dinner before assembling the capsule structure, and this sounded like a good idea. So they adjourned from the cave to the module. While they were eating, the comm chimed. It was Jensen.

"Hey Mark, we just got the capsule inside, and after dinner we're going to start to put it together," John replied during bites.

"Wrong, John," said Jensen. "You are not to put the return vehicle together. One reason you will notice that the SRB fuel containers are not there. They are at Yuri's. It was done deliberately so that you wouldn't put the vehicle together. Look, you won't be using it for two years. That vehicle is specially designed to get you into a low Mars orbit. According to calculations here, it has enough fuel to do so. If you had the cylinders there, you would most probably assemble the capsule and then fuel it, and that would be a problem. The design engineers don't want it standing for two years loaded with fuel. You will start assembly two months before your lift date. Damn, John, the thing just snaps together. Don't make a big deal out of it. When it comes time, we have a crew here to help you with the hook ups and fuel systems. For right now, I want you to wrap a bubble over the fuel and the other components so that conditions in the cave don't affect them. Also, separate the fuel so that there can be no blending of product, okay? Now let's go over your schedule. We want you to finish up with the crater hole exploration. We sent you some special equipment and three miles of tether line, it looks like a fish line. You are to send this down the hole. Then, we will discuss the next step. Actually, I'm not looking for any earth-shaking news as to the holes content however, the exploration has been approved. So, when during this week, do you plan to start?"

"How about Thursday," asked John? Which was still two days a way, "We still have some things to do in the habitat to get ready for the trip."

"That's fine," replied Jensen. "And who's going to do the exploration?"

"JP found the hole. I think this should be his baby," replied John.

"да,"(yes) agreed Alex.

"Okay, well give me a call when you get into position so that we'll be able to coordinate the information," Jensen replied.

"Mr. Jensen, I've got a question."

"Go ahead, JP. What's your question?"

"This new device that we got in the drop, it's like a bracket and holds two H-series navcomm units. Are we supposed to send that into the hole, or what?"

"Okay, JP, let me explain. You actually have two brackets there, one on top and one on the bottom. The navcomm units fit into the brackets, one on top one and one on the bottom. The brackets come with screws that attach the navcomm units. The separator between the top and the bottom is really a motorized rotator. There is a cord coming out of it. Place the navcomm units in the bracket and attach the cylinder to the top. Plug the cords from the rotator into the cylinder and press 'Activate.' The balloon will inflate and can be controlled through the navcomm interface to do mapping. It works just like the Ariel's do. For directional navigation, it has micro tubes which act as micro-thrusters. But the device has short range application just a few miles, mostly line of sight. That's about it, the device comes with a few additions such as the aqua float, which allows it to suspend itself in water, the cylinder above water, and the two navcomm units suspended underwater. Yes, this is what we'll use for the crater hole. We wish to implant the navcomm sensor readers under the surface. However JP, you need to look over the unit to make sure you understand it before we go to the crater, and don't forget any parts."

"Can do," replied JP. And the screen blinked off. Two days later, John helped JP on with the Ariel, and JP took off for the crater. Jensen came online before he left and asked JP to check the utility pack just to be sure he had everything. JP thought it was odd that one of the components was a tripod. Alex and John watched the event over the navcomm and the Ariel link. JP landed in the crater and parked and anchored the Ariel. He secured the anchor tether and the utility pack to the tether and carefully approached the hole.

Jensen came online a few seconds later. "Hey, JP, are we ready?" Jensen asked.

"Yes, Mr. Jensen. We are A-OK. Now I've attached the probe onto the bracket like you said. Also, I have attached a tether line to the bracket. I'm going to lower the unit into the hole."

"JP go ahead, but I want you far enough back so that you don't fall in. Once navcomm gets the weights right, it will start to lower the probe one foot every three seconds. That's the speed we need for the map," Jensen instructed.

"How does that work anyway?" John asked.

"The float operates the same way the Ariel does. It has an internal heater/ cooler in the float balloon that uses the temperature of the pressurized helium gas to raise and lower the unit. It works just like any navcomm unit, with one exception. When you scan with a regular 'H' series hand scanner, the scan can be used to create a three-dimensional image map. When you scan with two scanners at the same time, such as with this bracket, their images can produce a 3-D panorama, which can be used to create a 3D virtual map. This map can then be loaded through a program that lets you take a virtual panoramic tour of the cave, including under the water. Wait till we're done, you'll see. Also, the probe rotates in a circle at the speed of one foot every three seconds. When the unit turns, navcomm will direct it to the bottom in a slow downward spiral or a circular pattern then bring it back up. The virtual program will then stitch the images together," Jensen explained.

JP crept toward the opening and slowly pressed the probe into the open hole, then retracted, holding the tether.

"You guys getting signal?" JP asked. Both John and Jensen said yes and instructed JP to release the tether.

"Okay," Jensen continued. "Now set up the tripod over the hole with the third navcomm unit, 'H' series pointing down into the crater hole. We don't want to lose the float because of signal loss."

JP went to the utility pack and unpacked the tripod and the other scanner, then affixed the tripod over the hole with the scanner in position.

"At this rate, it will take 4.4 hours to descend to the bottom. JP, you might as well go back to the module and come back out tomorrow to complete Phase 2. We already know the tunnel to be deeper than two miles," Jensen commented. "But leave the utility pack in the crater so we don't need to bring it back out tomorrow."

"I agree. There's no reason to stay out there for four hours JP," John replied.

"Yeah, you're right. I'm coming in," JP went to suit the Ariel for the trip back. He returned to the module forty-five minutes later, and they watched the progress of the probe on the monitor. At approximately quarter of a mile down, the radar went large, showing an enlargement of the cavern walls, at first five hundred feet then larger to half a mile.

Yuri and the other crew chimed in.

"Is this the great hole exploration?" Yuri asked.

"Yep, we're a little over a quarter mile deep, but it seems that the caverns is widening out," John replied.

The crew watched the next four hours till the probe bottomed out at 2.4 miles deep. By that time, it was 6:00 p.m. and dinnertime. Jensen commented that the imaging received by the probe was good enough to make the 3-D panorama virtual map of the cavern, and that they could view it tomorrow. When completed, it would join the rest of the Mars maps, and they were going to title it HAshita1013_subterrianium cavern, which surely had to make JP happy. They agreed to an early start the next day, so when the chime from Jensen went off at 6:00 a.m., no one was surprised.

"Is JP ready to go? I've got some news."

"He's eating breakfast, but go ahead. He can hear you," John replied.

"The laser distance monitor has detected some kind of bottom at two and a half miles down. Also, the cavern becomes larger in one direction more than the other, creating a line of expansion from the northwest to southeast, sound familiar? This means that JP needs to stay out there till we reach the bottom today."

"Did you hear that, JP?" yelled John. Alex was in bed; he had taken JP's shift last night.

"Yes, I heard it, but I don't like hanging out in that crater for four-plus hours," JP replied.

"Neither do I," agreed John. "Why don't we take the rover and put the Ariel in the cart. Then we can sit in the rover and watch the probe from there. We can be in position by nine and be at the bottom by one or so and be back here by four or so. How's that sound?" suggested John.

"It won't be four hours more like two because the mapping is done but, if you want to take the rover, its okay," replied Jensen. "I forgot we now have that extra cart. Give me a chime when you're ready to go. I'm going to have some special people here, and I have to give them a time frame, Jensen out."

The screen went blank. JP finished his breakfast. John was packing a cooler with snacks when JP asked him what he was doing, turning this into a picnic lunch, to which John replied,

"I'm not missing lunch over this."

They loaded the Ariel and were on their way within thirty minutes. It was 160 miles to the crater, which would take the rover a little over three hours to get there. Even though the crater entrance was marked on navcomm, the terrain was rough, and John had to maintain the wheel and speed. They arrived at the crater at 11:23, and John helped JP put on the Ariel for the ascension up and over the ridge into the crater, which was eighty feet high. JP lifted and skirted up the wall, disappearing over the top. A few seconds later the Ariel appeared again, this time with no passenger and landed next to the rover. John grabbed onto it and suited it and was up over the wall and into the crater in a few seconds. JP was over by the entrance hole. The probe had come out of the hole and was lying on the ground next to the tripod with its bag deflated. John anchored and deflated the Ariel and went to join JP. Jensen came online. John pressed his accept.

"Now, this is Phase 2. With the data from the sensor unit, it appears there is a false bottom at the bottom of the hole. We suspect that it is ice. The scanner gives a real bottom measurement of a little over 2.8 miles. However, the false bottom measurement is 2.3. That means we have a half mile of something down there which we think is either water or ice. We're going to recharge the probe and send it back down. Pull the recharge unit out of the utility bag and attach the probe. Also, in the bag you packed the aqua float, which is a large Styrofoam ring. You need to attach that to the probe as well. The ring should be four inches lower than the cylinder. Also, there is a circular disk inside the utility bag attach it to the bottom of the bracket. This is an underwater sonar sensor, current flow indicator, water temperature, and contains a small propeller which allows the unit to navigate in the water. When the probe is recharged, secure one of the packets labeled C-4 from the utility bag. This is a plastic explosive. You are to take it to the hole, turn it on, and drop it in."

JP assembled the probe and secured the C-4 from the utility bag. About ten minutes later, the probe beeped signaling that it was recharged.

"Okay JP, take the probe to the hole, but don't toss it in yet." JP took the probe to the hole, placing it on the ground next to the hole. Jensen continued, "Okay JP, take the C-4. There was a switch on the side. Turn it on. It should light the up the LED on the front."

JP said, "AOK, Mr. Jensen."

"Okay," said Jensen. "Go ahead drop it in."

JP was cautious not to get too close to the hole, and he tossed the C-4 into the abyss. Jensen paused for about a minute. Then he instructed John and JP to go to the side of the crater. Thirty seconds later, there was a marked explosion in the hole.

"Gee," John said. "Do you think they used enough explosives?"

Jensen continued, "In the bag are the two submersible mini navcomm units. Turn them on and toss them in as well."

John located the units and tossed them in.

"Okay, now lower the probe back into the hole with the tether and wait till I confirm we have go signal."

JP lowered the probe into the hole, Jensen confirmed, and JP released the tether.

"Okay, here's what's going to happen. The probe is going to sink rapidly toward the bottom, eventually coming in contact with the water. The two navcomm units will be submerged underwater, and the cylinder will rest above the water on the float. The underwater units will scan the underwater surface. Navcomm will then pick the best place for the unit and use the propeller to move and hold the unit at that spot. The temperature right now is minus 118 degrees Fahrenheit; the temperature will very quickly refreeze the surface, holding the unit in place. With no activity, the unit will go into inert or sleep mode in about 3 minutes. Ordinarily, the power generation is mainly secured by the solar panel on the exterior of the navcomm units. It provides the power to start up the regenerative power supply. However, there is no light in that cave. That's why I had you set up the tripod. When in sleep mode, the probe continues to scan and uses some power but not very much. It depends on the tripod unit to supply a navcomm signal, which it can use to recharge its batteries. It will remain in sleep mode and recharge as long as there is no other motion. If one of our scanners should enter the water source, the submerged units will detect the scanner and wake up. It will then transmit the upload code and gather the data. Then send the data to the tripod unit, which will send it over the navcomm link to us."

"Okay, you guys are done there. You can go back to the module. We won't have any conclusive test results for a few hours," Jensen replied.

They returned to the module which took three hours, and John was making a pot of coffee when Jensen chimed back in. "Guys, Dr. Werner and a group of geological specialists will be coming up on the monitor to discuss the recent current events."

Dr. Werner's image came onto the display.

"Good morning boys, or should I say good afternoon," There were seven scientist seated at the table, the scientists were introduced by Dr. Werner. John guessed from the accents that they were from different countries, most probably Europe.

"We have gone over the data from the two probes and the float sensor that accessed the water source in the crater hole. The data shows that there is current flow in the water. This is both good and confusing because the probes also showed us that the entrance on the northwest side is deep and quite large. Water has a trait. It seeks the path of least resistance, which means the water in the bottom of the crater hole is there because it's the easiest path," Dr. Werner continued.

"As the fissure extends southwest toward the outlet, it becomes shallower, meaning that the flow into the crater pond is not large in volume, and the exit point is shallow, meaning that the water is a retentive volume. Thus, the current flow is not strong; however the water is not stagnant. So, the question is where does the water go? And now take a look at Eos Chasma and Solis Planum in the same general area. If we took the water out of the oceans here on Earth, don't you think it would show landscaping like this? Mr. Alexander, your habitat is located where?"

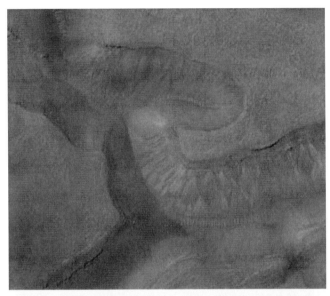

Eos Chasma (The Habitat Area)

"Our habitat is located in the Eos Chasma, about two hundred miles from the Valles southeastern entrance," replied John.

"During your exploration, have you seen areas that look like they, at one time, may have held water?"

"Yes, as well as in the Solis Planum," JP replied.

"Where is the other habitat? I know it's in the Valles, but exactly where in the Valles, Mr. Jensen?" asked the professor.

"The second habitat, you're correct, is in the Marineris Valles, approximately 1,500 miles from the southern entrance, near the Melas Chasma on your map. Start at the two lines which is the Valles entrance and end just before the center expansion of the Melas Chasma. It is on the northern cliff."

One of the geologists named Dr. Ellis stood up and said, "My theory is the following, that the tectonic plate split did create the Valles Marineris. However, during the shift, the water which was contained in the Solis Planum and the Eos Chasma rushed into the cavern, cooling the lava rising from the mantle. This would mean that the actual split is much larger under the surface than is shown by the Valles, and I am becoming convinced that we are not dealing with a lost ocean but several lost oceans of immense proportions. Of course, we all realize that if the split had never happened. The water would be still on the surface.

However, in such a case, the water would form top layers of solid ice because of the planets surface temperature. That means the split occurred before the change of the solar rotation. However, what caused it is still unclear, and we won't have any scientific proof without carbon dating the lava of the Mons and the Valles. Suppose that at one time, Mars had a circular orbit similar to the other planets in the solar system. Something happened to cause the orbit to change this orbit into the egg orbit it currently has. Here, look." Dr. Ellis took a compass, placing it on the middle of the sun on a map displaying the solar orbit of the planets.

"The Martian orbit is the closest point to the sun at 206.6 million miles. Suppose this was a circular orbit before the orbit changed. The change created the farthest point or Aphelion, which is 249.2 million miles. This represents a change in the orbit circumference of five hundred million miles, thus bringing the planet closer to Jupiter and the asteroid belt. Which, we all believe at one time to be the remains of the mysterious 5th planet. It is clear that during this time, the change in the orbit of Mars had an effect on the Martian surface. Then there is Hellas Planitia."

Werner interrupted, "Doctor, you're not suggesting that the change in the planet's orbit and the volcanic activity was caused by the impact of an asteroid collision?"

"No," replied Ellis. "However, it may have created the tectonic shift, and the shift once in progress, split the surface, creating the Valles trench. The mantle rose to fill the gap but, the split also opened a conduit to the Chryse Planitia which is connected in depth with the Utopia Planitia and the Amazonis Planitia. This would represent a large mass of water which would create a tremendous amount of pressure. When the water rushed in filling the Eros and Ganges chasmas and the Marineris trench, the pressure pushed the hot magma to the northwest area of the split. The magma was then pushed up through surface fissures in the northwest Tharsis region because of the pressure of the water. This may offer some understanding of how Olympus Mons and the three sisters were formed. Olympus Mons, because of it is at the most northwest point would have continued to erupt being the farthest from the water. The magma would have cooled from the southeast to the northwest." This caused a stirring in the room.

"This could be quite possible, but as always, we have no proof." Werner turned to the camera.

"Boys, I understand you are coming back in two years. We would very much like a few samples for carbon dating. The samples don't have to be very large a couple of centimeters, but be sure to label the location where you found them, and we will be posting a full analysis in a few days. We would like to thank you for your assistance. Come and see us when you get back. It's 5 pm, let's break for dinner and go over the data again."

Jensen turned back to say something to John, who he noticed was eating a sandwich. The screen went blank. Only Jensen remained. "Good work, guys. Get some rest, it's moving day tomorrow."

Chapter 11

The Move

The next day, the comm chimed. It was Yuri.

"Привет (Hello) John, we're on our way over to see you. Xiao and I will be leaving in our module shortly. It's a forty-hour trip. However, Lefluere will be taking off shortly in our Ariel and should be there this afternoon. We won't get there till the morning of the day after tomorrow. Here is what I am hoping. I am hoping that the loading is done and that getting you on the road doesn't take more than six hours. I'd like to be on the way back that afternoon. We're thinking that JP and Lefluere will take the Ariel's back. We will load the robots in our module and send your rover on autopilot back here. Xiao and I will follow you and Alex in our module on the trip back, if that's okay with you?"

"Yeah sure, that's fine. We are not going to pop the seal until tomorrow, because after that, there's not much left to do except reset the cave and reattach the seal."

JP and Alex were busy stacking trays up on the inside of the cave when the comm chimed again, it was Jensen.

"Hi John, would you get JP for me?"

"He's outside. Hang on a minute," John replied.

JP came in and sat down at the control panel.

"We got too many plants, Mr. Jensen. We don't have room for all these plants, and as much work as I've put in them, I hate to just leave them."

"JP, listen to me. You have some fifty-five gallon containers that we shipped food in, clean them out. Take the water and plants out of the trays and put them in the containers. Hook the light strips onto the top and the handler lines on the bottom. You should be able to get six to eight trays in each one. Any plants with ripe food product should be harvested. Only take your best plants, leave the older plants. Then tomorrow, before you blow the seal, stack them inside the module. You are to leave in the cave the following: air handler, four tanks of Oxygen, 110 gallons of water, three tanks of Hydrogen, the mobile hydro handler with empty tanks, a Sterling engine, a heater, the portable power supply, mobile navcomm hooked up, one of the exterior solar power suppliers and the exterior navcomm, and the capsule and its equipment. Everything else should be going with you. And let me say that when you're loaded, you'll be heavy. So because of this, the autopilot on the trip to the base is out of the question. John, Yuri or Alex should be at the controls whenever the module is moving. If you need more space, dump a few more empty air tanks. As a matter of fact, dump all the empties, but hook them up to the handler before you leave. JP, look I wish I could say that you could leave a robot as well, but it's not on the menu. You're going to need those bots when you get to the base. Now, when you're loaded, you're not going to have much space, so I wouldn't load until tomorrow night. Give me a call if you need any further assistance, Jenson out."

"JP," John said, "I need Alex to help me load some equipment. Can you spare him?"

JP agreed, eight hours later Lefluere arrived and joined JP in loading the hydroponics into barrels. The next day, they started loading the module. Everyone was in outer suits. The module was fully loaded by one, and Jensen was right. There wasn't much room. They couldn't use the kitchen. It was full, and there was only a two-foot walk space to the pods and the bathroom. At 2:00 p.m., it was decided that it was time to blow the seal in order to drive the module out of the cave. They extracted and liquefied most of the oxygen inside the cave. The atmosphere was mostly Nitrogen and Carbon dioxide. However it produced a hiss when it was vented. They had to remove the panels and most of the framework, as well as the air lock, which would require the assistance of the robots. All of the remaining plants were encased in a bubble, and the handler lines were connected. Everyone gathered at the entrance to prepare to remove the panels.

"Okay, the panels are sealed to the framework with an epoxy ceramic adhesive. We are going to have to cut the adhesive to unfasten the panels with a hot knife."

It was slow going, and after two hours, they had managed to remove four of the eight panels. They continued until all the required panels were removed. With the panels removed, the robots came and picked up the air lock, removing it to an area where it would be out of the way. Then with JP and Lefluere outside and Alex at the back door as guides, John started up the module and eased it out of the entrance onto the surface outside. John parked the module on the artificial road, that the bots had built that went to the entrance door of the Valles. By that time, everyone was exhausted and wanted to get out of their suits, so they broke for the day. The next morning, they started back with it by bringing the rover out of its underground chamber. They attached the cart and loaded the exterior solar power generator and one of the two exterior navcomm units and other supplies that were to go.

At about 10:00 a.m. Yuri and Xiao arrived in their module and joined in re-assembly of the panels. The robots replaced the air lock, and things were back the way they were originally, except that the cave had to be resealed which JP, Lefluere and the robots handled. With everything hooked up and the air lock functional, the atmosphere was re-established and the heat was turned on. JP and Xiao took the interior plants out of the bubbles, and they were ready to go. JP and Lefluere took off in a joint flight with the Ariel's at around three that afternoon. They would be back at the base about nine or so. Yuri loaded the robots in his module and they were ready. Half an hour later, John started the module with Xiao aboard and Yuri and Alex followed them in Module 2. The rover had already left three hours earlier and was already at the Valles entrance on its way to the base. The trip was uneventful except for the storm that kicked up the second day, but the module was already inside the Valles, and the storm didn't affect them much because of the Valles walls. They arrived at the base's eastern side two days later, and John was surprised that the rovers weren't standing outside. Then he noticed that the rover storage garage had been enlarged. He asked Yuri about it, and Yuri confirmed that they had enlarged the garage before they had left for John's site. With the expansion had enlarged the garage to 24x32 feet, it was now able to hold both rovers plus the four robots. The base looked a lot larger. John parked his XPLM module outside and Yuri and Alex pulled in behind him, everyone donned outer suits to take the forty-foot walk from the module airlock to the base airlock. Once inside, they were greeted by JP and Lefluere, who had been there for the last two days. JP was preoccupied with getting the plants inside.

"Give us a couple of hours before we start that JP" John recommended.

Yuri caught John's attention and signaled John to follow him. They went down the hallway, took a right, and walked through the dining room, which John thought might be the destination. However, Yuri kept walking.

"While you guys were hole diving in the crater, we were busy here. I didn't say anything about it, but take a look." He had taken another left past the lab and came to a door that opened into a room that he was holding open. John looked into the room to notice a pressure door on the far wall which John thought was the western side airlock

Yuri pointed to the door, "go ahead John open it."

John went over to the door and pulled it open. Inside was a room identical to the one he was in with another pressure door on the far side. Yuri was behind him and nodded. So, John proceeded to cross the room to the other door. Upon opening it, he viewed another room and a hallway identical to the one they had just come out of.

"We built it shortly after we got the drop two weeks ago." Yuri said "It's identical to the other base unit as far as internal and external dimensions. However, internal structure is a little different. The control room is smaller. The lab area is bigger. It has a dining room and kitchen, which are smaller. Unit 1 has twelve rooms. This unit has fourteen. Everyone's going to move into this unit except for the officers, meaning you and me."

"Let me show you what they sent." Yuri opened a door to show a 16ft. × 12ft. room. In the center of the room were two tables with computer chairs.

"This is the office and meeting room. Nice, huh, and this," he said. "Is the control room, it's half the size of Unit 1, in other words 8 × 16. Here, we have two storage rooms, 8 ×12, and of course, the dining room and the kitchen. All the others are the private 8×12 rooms."

"Wow, this is really something. You guys must have worked your asses off," exclaimed John.

"Actually, John, the first day, the robots did all the work, the foundation plates and bottom framework. The next day, we started at nine, we were finished by three. We returned the next two days to do hookups and coatings. Turned out pretty good, but we are not done. We still have bubbles left to unpack at our drop site, which is about an eighty-mile trip, but now, we have two carts and four robots, so it shouldn't be a problem. Tomorrow, we are all going to the site with the rovers and the robots and carts to retrieve the rest of the supplies."

"How much is left?" John inquired.

"26 bubbles, however four of them are food, nineteen of them are this." Yuri toggled a wallboard image.

John had to look twice. "What is that?" John asked.

"It's more panels, except they're different. They're glass, they're new, and they're called clear reflection panels. You see our normal panels as well as the module walls are designed with the idea of low heat conductivity so that we can keep residual heat inside. These panels are designed to help us do this. But they are also designed to reflect heat with the Dewar effect and a special coating. However, even though we can't achieve complete insulation, we can get close to it without sacrificing structural integrity. These panels are made for the hydroponics and so that light can be made to travel through them. They have special glass with a polarized reflector, that lets light in and amplifies it by 200 percent above normal light, plus they supply heat generation. It's kind of like firing a laser off inside a mirrored room with mirrored walls. The laser bounces until it runs out of energy these panels do the same thing to regular light. They are structured just like the other panels, and we have to put them together. Along with that is a bunch of specialized equipment, for instance, two Sterling engines, two air handlers, fans, and a pump system. I'm depending on you guys to help with it. When we get done, we're going to turn JP loose in there. He's become quite handy in the hydro area. It's nice to have someone around who knows what they're doing. Lefluere's good at what he does but that's limited, but I'd trade you Xiao for JP in a second."

"How big is this thing supposed to be when it's finished?"

"The structure is 120ft. × 64ft. or 526 panels, counting the roof, about the size of both base units combined. It's going to take more than a couple of days to complete, but when it's done, it will out-produce the cave. We should be sitting pretty. This is a major step forward. Not only will we be able to feed ourselves, but we will have Oxygen in abundance."

The next morning, everyone suited up for the trip to the drop zone to retrieve the remaining supplies. Both rovers went along with the four robots riding in the carts. The robots were normally slower than the rovers except in rough terrain. The robots had acquired a new habit of riding in the carts. John made a mental note to find out who programmed the robots and have a little talk with him when he got back to Earth. Yuri and the rest of the crew followed in the XPLM module. They arrived at the site about two hours later and proceeded to unzip the bubbles. Yuri had the list printed out so that they knew what was what. They first unpacked the food, then equipment packs, which they loaded on the rover cart. Yuri had the robots take the food pallets and go straight back to the base. The robots and the carts came back four hours later. All the bubbles were then unzipped, and Yuri was using the boom crane to load what they could in the module. Yuri suggested that they could return to the base and let the bots handle the remaining supplies. Those bubbles contained the panels for the hydro unit and the airlock which would require the robots anyway, so they returned to the base. JP went to check on his plants in the module. Yuri went to the cave and asked JP to join him after he got done with his work. John, Alex, Lefluere, and Xiao spent the rest of the day transporting the supplies in the rover garage for storage. John worked with Xiao in the garage, checking the food items in.

"Okay, Xiao, let's check them off: (2) 55-gallon drums Kool-Aid powder, 12 drums of soda syrup, 3 drums of instant coffee, 2 drums of tea, 5 drums of pork product, 5 pallets of chicken, 6 pallets of beef product, 8 drums of flour, 4 drums of turkey product, 3 drums of fish product, 4 drums of biscuits, 4 drums of rice, 5 drums of pasta, 4 drums of instant potatoes, 8 drums of wheat flour, 3 drums of spices, 1 drum of assorted vegetables, 2 pallets of butter, 3 pallets of sausage and bacon, 6 drums of powdered eggs, 6 drums of cereals, 4 drums of assorted fruit, 4 drums of assorted luncheon meats, 1 pallet of yeast, 1 drum of sweetener, 5 drums of powdered milk, 2 drums of chocolate, 3 drums of ice cream mix, 4 assorted drums, 1 drum medical, 1 drum nutrition, 4 drums of paste."

Xiao was checking them off as they went.

"Okay, that looks like that's it for the food," said John.

"Where are we supposed to store all this? You think we can get all of this in the 12×16 foot storage room?" questioned Xiao.

"We will have to stack them," replied John.

Yuri stuck his nose in to see how it was going. He and JP had just gotten back from Cave 1.

"You see this? They gave us only one drum of vegetables. It's only going to hold us for about three months," John complained.

"I think that they are expecting us to make our own vegetables now. And as a matter of fact, with the vegetables you brought, we have now a small surplus. And we have a crop coming ripe in what, Xiao, a month?" Xiao nodded. "So, we'll do all right anyhow. You know where they go, right in the storage room behind the kitchen."

"Mr. Yuri, I'm not so sure that all of this will fit in that room. We already have some Oxygen tanks and two 250-gallon water tanks in there," Xiao stated.

"Well store what we need for right now, and what we don't have room for, take through the air lock into building 2 but, if you break the seal, it will have to stay here. So don't break any drum seals which we won't immediately use."

"All right, let's take a look at the storage area and get the dolly to transfer the products," John suggested.

This process took about an hour. Then they had to leave the garage while Lefluere, Alex, and JP loaded it with the clear hydro panels. When the robots arrived, Yuri went out to help, supervise was more like it. The glass units and framework arrived, and they were left outside because the garage was fully loaded. However, a group of items were brought in that surprised all of them.

"Hey, look" said Yuri. "They sent me the gem polisher and buffer I ordered."

"And a laser cutter," added JP.

It was getting late, and Alex suggested that they wrap up for dinner and resume the next day.

Everyone agreed, and Yuri said that there would be a meeting in the dining room after dinner.

Dinner was good: hamburger, real baked potatoes and gravy, salad, vegetables and biscuits one of John's favorite meals. After dinner, Yuri poured the drinks and started the meeting.

"We need to establish a schedule and duty file so that we can get organized. We have a lot of work that needs yet to get done. Tomorrow morning, we are sending three of the robots and the carts to the drop site to retrieve the remaining supplies which is mostly panels. I hope that we at least get the structure framework done tomorrow. Also, as you probably know, the ISA requires that there be an operator in the control room at all times when there are operations being conducted outside, the same as with the module. Now John, I understand that your crew divided the service into eight-hour shifts, and I think that is a good plan and one we should keep. So, as soon as we are done with the hydro unit construction, Xiao will take the first combined crew shift at 8:00 a.m. till 4:00 p.m. Then, I'll take the 4:00 p.m. till 12:00 a.m. shift, JP for the 12:00 a.m. to 4:00 a.m. shift, Lefluere for the next shift, then John and Alex for the last two shifts."

"When you're not in the control room, I expect you to be working with the others. I'm putting JP in charge of the hydroponics units and setup. He will require a lot of assistance even after the unit is completed. The ISA has made it a priority that the hydroponics are to be up and running as soon as possible. JP, if you need to hold a class to orientate the helpers on the procedures and facts that they need to know, pick a time that doesn't conflict with the work. I want this combined unit to work like a well-oiled machine. I mean, this isn't our first assembly. We should know how to do these assemblies by now. John, why don't you take over installation and system connections on the hydro addition?"

The next morning, John got up when the alarm chimed. It was a little after eight, and he went to the dining room. Someone had made breakfast in the auto cooker. There were eggs, bacon, sausage, coffee, orange drink, cereal, and waffles. Most everyone was there except for Lefluere, who Yuri had to chime again. John asked Yuri what the schedule was and was surprised to find out that the robots had left at about six and were at the drop site as they spoke.

"It won't take them long to load and start back. They should show up between ten and eleven. The bottom struts are already outside. They were brought in yesterday." The one robot that was still here was already preparing the surface for the foundation anchors. Yuri suggested that when the robots got back with the last of the glass panels. Two members should assemble them in the garage and that the other three place them in the structural framework. Everyone followed Yuri outside to the construction site. The robot had done a pretty good job of leveling out the foundation and was pre-drilling out holes for the frame anchors. It used a laser measure to gauge the correct positions and were already about half done.

Yuri instructed the robot to use the laser to generate a guide line to correct the framework. Then he instructed the crew to place the adjustable foundation supports in line with the beams, where the robots had already drilled. The procedure was to line them up and then place weight on them to make sure that the foundation didn't sink. Alex and JP were standing on them. Yuri was bouncing up and down on his. John decided to use Yuri's approach. After that, they had to reset them with a leveler again, then pump the magic Goop in the holes, replace the support in position, and then insert the frame and the anchors. While they were doing that, the robot began drilling the other side. After an hour, the robot was way ahead of them. It had already completed the other sixty-four foot section and was halfway done with the last side.

Goop mixed with sand would be pumped underneath any gaps between the framework and the Martian surface. The frameworks were eight-foot, expandable, clip lock struts, so it wasn't long before the bottom unit was completed. Just as they were finishing, the robots from the drop site arrived. Everyone stopped working to watch them pass the work site and proceed to the Unit 1 garage. Yuri suggested that they break for a half hour and grab a snack while the robots unloaded the clear panels to the inside of the garage for assembly. John and Lefluere volunteered to be co-assemblers. The rest of the crew adjourned to make some final adjustments outside. John opened the first stack, which contained both interior and exterior panels. Even though they were inside the garage, they were in inner suits on with helmets and gloves nearby. The rovers had been pulled outside so there would be room for the assembly. John and Lefluere set up the table to lay the panels on.

"Okay, let me see if I got this straight. First, we assemble the panel structural supports, which snap together. Then, we place the exterior panel in the frame, flip it over, and place the interior panel in on the other side."

Lefluere had a strange look on his face. "*Monsieur*, did you read the instructions? Evidently no,—First, we assemble three sides of the frame. Then, we slide the exterior panel into the groove. Then, we slide in the interior sheet into the interior groove and attach the last side by lining up the grooves and pressing it in place."

"Let's try one," John suggested. "I'll get the hang of it."

Andre brought three eight-foot crystal struts to the table. John followed his lead and pressed the struts together on his side. The click lock snapped in place. Then, John helped him carry an exterior panel over to the table, which they placed on a foam blanket so that they didn't scratch the glass, and pushed the pane into the grooved slots. Andre pulled out a device, which turned out to be a Goop gun. However, it looked more like a caulk gun, and he ran seal along the edges. Then, they slid in the interior panel. The final side was then put in place with a snap. Andre ran the Goop seal on all interior and exterior sides, and they were done. They moved the panel to the side of the room and started the next one.

"How long does it take for your caulk to set up and seal the glass?" asked John.

Lefluere had that look on his face again.

"First of all John, the sealant that I'm placing on the seams is not caulking but an epoxy adhesive ceramic resin like the goop, which takes about twenty minutes to set up under any condition. Secondly, the 'glass' is not glass, like silica glass. It is amorphous metal, which is made to have super low thermal conductivity, which means resistance to the transference of temperature. Notice the joining spots between the two sides. See the seam in the center. It's a temperature block separating the exterior from the interior as far as the temperature. You might also be interested to know that this 'glass' is actually tougher and stronger than steel and titanium. And you might also take note that the interior panels are different than the exterior panels.

"The reason why is, the interior panels have a lens attached to them that effectively turns them into one-way convex mirrors. Thus, light goes through the exterior panel into the Dewar's effect vacuum and in through the interior panel, where it is amplified by the convex lens and then trapped inside by a mirror effect film. Even though the light losses are about 50 percent illumination, by passing through the film, once inside the mirror room the light bounces around working as a second amplifier. This increases the photonic illumination 200 to 300 percent, not to mention what it does to light from an interior light bulb inside the mirror room. This effect and the fact that there is no thermal conductivity, which is secured by the Dewar's effect, secure an optimum photonic yield. A Sterling engine and an air handler regulate the atmosphere, the light and the internal temperature creates a hot room effect that stimulates plant growth. It can be minus 180 degrees on the outside, and it will be 80 degrees inside the hot room and stay that way without much effort or power loss."

Yuri stuck his head in the door. "How's it going? We're about ready for the panels."

Andre pointed to the stack of panels and replied, "Help yourself."

"I'm going to send the robots in to carry the panels out to the site you should close your face shields or take a break." said Yuri

Once they got the hang of it, Andre and John started putting the panels together rather quickly. As a matter of fact, they were completing a panel every minute and a half. The crew came in for lunch. John and Andre kept working. They took lunch after the crew had finished. They were seeing the end of the assembly. They had produced 150 panels in a little over four hours. However, there were over 50 panels left, which they finished about an hour later. They then put on outer suits and went to help the crew outside. They were also pretty well along with over half of the structure done. Yuri suggested that they work inside, putting up the internal roof support struts. The roof required a structural support every sixteen feet, which meant fourteen struts. The roof framework was then installed and the panels slid into place.

Approximately two hours later, they were finished, but they still had to set up the internal systems. The Sterling engine was put in a special compartment. Lights had to be installed and so did two pressure air locks:

fans, tubes, tray racks, sensors, spot heaters, aqua liners, and pumps. Before they started with the internal systems, everyone stopped while Yuri attached the pump line to a valve in the air handler and started pumping the atmosphere into the interior to achieve 10 psi. Watching the gauge, he announced, "We have a leak."

JP and Alex picked up carbon dioxide detectors and began scanning the interior walls. Andre attached one to an extension pole and was checking the interior roof. JP found one and patched it with goop. Andre found one, and Alex found two on the roof. They ran again and found some more. Suddenly, the pressure stabilized. They put the tools inside and called it a day. Yuri turned the valve on the oxygen tank and took a pressure and content reading.

Xiao had prepared a little dinner: pork chops, rice, salad, green beans, and biscuits.

Yuri was quite pleased with the results of that day's development and remarked,

"We did it. I told you we could do it. The basic structure is completed. We'll be completely finished the day after tomorrow, but I've added an extra task. The hydro unit is behind the base on the western side, and I don't like the fact that every time we need to go to the unit, we have to suit up. I would like to build a walkway to the unit. The distance will have to be measured to see whether we have enough panels left over. If not, then we will need to dig a tunnel to the unit."

"I don't know what you had left over after you put together Unit 2, but we have twelve crystal panels left in the garage," John added.

"Does anyone know how many?" questioned Yuri.

"About eleven," answered Xiao.

"That should be enough. Now, this walkway will have to come off the walkway between Units 1 and 2 or the pressure door on the other side of 2."

"I recommend the pressure door on 2. It's a shorter distance. Fewer panels," suggested JP.

"Yuri, you don't have to measure the distance. The navcomm can tell you that," JP said.

After dinner, Yuri and JP went to the control panel to calculate the construction. JP had a sad look on his face when they returned.

"We don't have enough panels. We're short sixteen feet."

"Well," said Yuri. "It will have to be a tunnel then. Tomorrow, we will be setting up the hydro systems and components. Alex, you and Andre are in charge of the tunnel, but remember, it has to be airtight." They both nodded. The next day JP and the rest of the crew set out to finish the hydro unit. They still had connections to plug in, internal lights to be hung, sensors to be installed, wallboard to be hung, fans and irrigation to be connected, plus Yuri had to re-test the internal pressure. When they entered, the sun was already in the sky, and it was warm inside the unit.

"The pressure says we still have an internal leak." Yuri bumped up the pressure to 2 normal Martian atmospheres and then released a purple smoke bomb. The smoke pointed to the left corner. Xiao and JP went to find it and they did. Then Yuri had everyone go outside while he pressurized the vacuum panels and released a second smoke bomb into the vacuum section to test for outside leaks. They could see some color coming out of the roof. So, they sent Xiao up on the roof with some sealer to fix them.

"How much do you think Xiao weighs?" John asked Yuri.

"On Earth, I'd say he weighs about 130 to 140 lbs. Here, he probably weighs about 50 to 60 lbs. or so," replied Yuri.

"You think that that roof will hold him?" questioned John.

"John, the structural supports are made of the same material the panels are. Let me assure you, not only will it support him, but you could probably go up there and jump up and down on it. It's some pretty tough stuff."

John had been watching Alex and the robot working behind him. They were on the outside, on the side of Unit 2's air lock. The robot had the dozer bucket attachment on, and Alex had a tube coming out of the ground with sand coming out of it he was using to fill the bucket with. John tapped Yuri, who took a look and stated.

"I don't care as long as it's airtight."

The structural supports when unpacked were expandable, which allowed then to be raised to eight feet two inches and the tension could be adjusted for structural support of the ceilings. The struts were placed on intersecting frames every sixteen feet. This secured the ceiling, and they started setting up the plant racks using the struts as support. The rack clipped into the wall framework and support frames. Every wall had a rack system containing one tray at two feet, four feet, and six feet. Plus, the trays needed to have light strips attached to their undersides and irrigation intake and output lines attached. They were moving along pretty well, and it was about noon. Yuri had opened a can of Oxygen and everyone had their face shields open. They were getting ready to break for lunch when they noticed Alex come through the lock.

"хороший, looks good."

"Are you guys about done in there?" asked Yuri.

"About done ha! Watch this," Alex replied.

Alex went to the first panel on the left-hand side of the airlock and unfastened the panel. Everyone closed their face shields. Alex removed the panel and Andre walked out.

"There is still some work to be done. We have to make the stairs, but we took some of the extra panels and struts and made the ceiling, it is safe to walk in. The robot had no problem digging out the tunnel. The tunnel is six feet under the surface with an eight-foot walkway. It connects to the Unit 2 interior square. We will have to pull the 8×8 foot panel here and put in a pressure seal on both sides and seal it with goop."

"Agreed," Yuri said with a tone of approval in his voice. "Let's go to lunch." They all went through the tunnel to see the product of Alex's and Andre's work. Not too bad. They had put the expandable ladders at each end, so it was already usable. Lefluere, who had dug with the robots, said he didn't know where he was until he heard the crew talking and then just followed the sound of their voices.

Yuri commented that he liked the fact that the tunnel ended in the Unit 2 garden, but it would definitely need a pressure door for safety. Lunch was no big deal. Andre had made a loaf of bread while digging the tunnel. There wasn't much to making the bread loaf. You put flour, oil, salt, and water with a ½ yeast packet, let it churn for five minutes, knead it, and let it sit in the auto cooker for half an hour, knead again, and press "Cook." When done, place it in the cutter, and you've got bread. The cutter was set at twelve slices, and each slice was about half an inch thick. So, lunch was sandwiches, onion and potato soup, and some fried rice from the night before. After lunch, they returned to the hydro unit to set up the tubs. The tubs were six foot squares and were expandable plastic units which were used for food production.

The next day, they were still working on the hydro unit. JP was supervising the installment of the plants and trays from the habitat XPLM. Some of the algae had grown in the six days they had been in the drums. The algae was separated and divided into equal amounts for each tray. Algae had to be brought from Cave 1 to complete the process along with other plants. It took a few days, but eventually, everything was done. At the conclusion of the hydro unit construction, Yuri poured the evening drink and invited everyone out to the hydro plant to bask in the blue glow of the grow lamps, which cast an eerie blue effect on the Martian surface.

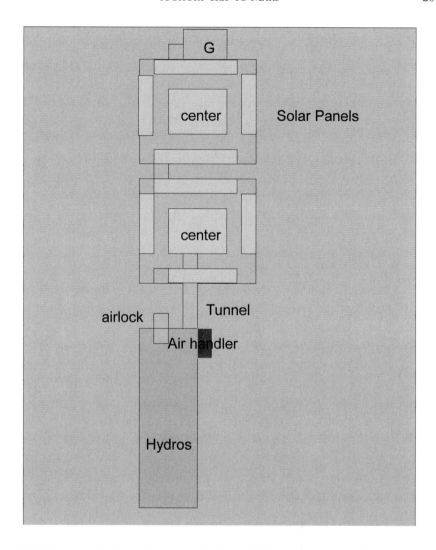

"It's hard to believe that we're finished," Yuri remarked. "This is a real accomplishment. When this gets into full production, we should be quite well set up. JP, how much will this increase our Oxygen production?"

"The sheet says that during normal breathing, a person uses 555 liters of Oxygen per day. This plant, when fully developed, should produce about three thousand-plus liters per day. That and the Oxygen production from Cave 1 will probably yield about two thousand plus liters per day. I give those rates because sometimes the yield will vary depending on conditions. Anyhow, for the first two to four months, we will be running on just enough for us with nothing extra. Then, we should start having a surplus, which we can use to fill the cryo tanks for the Ariel and the rovers. Oh also, we need to build a 16×16 foot storage containment garage for the full canisters with a Sterling engine, heat exchangers, and a multi-coupler or two."

During the next three months, they worked around the base with a trip to Cave 2 every other day. They were still mining it and had turned up some nice finds. Then Yuri suggested that they should start the first mission because they had built up enough reserves, he called for an after-dinner conference.

"Tomorrow, the module is taking off for your famous Marineris Cavern for a few days. Who's going besides me, John, and JP?" Yuri announced looking at Andre, Alex, and Xiao.

Andre paused and then said, "I think I'll stay here with Cave 2, if that's okay?"

"I'm going," volunteered Alex.

"I'll stay here. Someone has to be on the console," Xiao replied.

"Okay me, John, Alex and JP. Let's gather some equipment tonight so we don't have as much to do tomorrow morning," Yuri concluded.

Alex was looking at the tubes on the table.

"John, are these the probes for the Cavern? How do they work?"

"The tubes are standard micro R-series navcomm responders that have been modified to operate underwater. Once the units are activated and released, they start recording. They continue recording until de-activated by a coded navcomm signal. The distance between the cavern and the crater is 1785 + 150 + 800, or 2,735 miles. The responders will record the entire trip and hopefully will end up at a point where the data can be retrieved. So, not only will we know where the water goes, but we will have data as to the dimensions and the volume of the water, including current, velocity, and depth of the channel, which is significant. From this information, we can calculate the amount of water that exists under the surface. The probes are regenerating power supply units and will run years on their own. We release these six units in sequence so that the units will follow one another. In such a displacement the units will pass the information from the first to the last probe."

"The units which are small, only five centimeters in width by twenty-five centimeters length, they contain: the navcomm transceiver, a CPU, a 20 GB flash drive, a laser imager, regenerating power supply, clock, and micro motor and propeller. The units fit into this," John held up a frame with a balloon.

"The float, balloon is filled and regulated by a metering valve and a pump. The balloon works as a ballast control. The balloons pressure causes the sensor to raise and lower itself. If the sensor gets stuck, the navcomm units of the other sensors will assist it in finding a way out. The main thing about these units is if they get stuck in a spot with heavy current, it doesn't have much of an ability to get itself out. It has a small rotational propeller system and directional control but not enough to fight a really strong current. It would then become stuck and probably non-retrievable. However, it will transfer all its data to the rest of the units so, that if we recover one unit, we will have all the information. By recover, I mean re-establish a navcomm code connection with the sensor. We are probably not going to actually recover the units," John concluded.

"Suppose we are correct and one of the units makes to the navcomm unit in the crater and sends its data. What happens then?" Alex asked with a puzzled look on his face.

"I guess the units will just keep going, following the current, you know the path of least resistance" John offered.

"Okay, but to where?" asked Alex. "I mean if the water is connected and if the sensors complete the journey, they will have traveled nearly 3,000 miles, which is some great distance for as small a device as they are. Then it enters the crater pool and is activated by the navcomm there and transmits the data. Then what? It just keeps going? Okay, but going to where? Look at the map. Draw a line from the cavern to the crater. The line is diagonal, starting northwest and ending in the southeast. There is no noticeable depression southeast of the crater that we know of. Everything shows that the water is flowing to the southeast. Perhaps it turns south past Argyre Planitium. For all we know, it may wind up at the South Pole."

"I know, Alex," said John. "That's why we're dropping the probes, but I get your point. Three months from now, we may go to Hellas Planitium and take a look around, find a cave and pond in it, and find one the probes stuck between two rocks. I mean, it would activate to our suit navcomm unit as soon as we were close enough. The trouble with this planet is that it has too much Iron Oxide in the surface, which inhibits the navcomm signal. But we should take a trip to Hellas Planitium anyhow, just to look over it. After all, it is the lowest spot on the planet."

"Navcomm said there is nothing there, John," interrupted Yuri. "That's why we haven't been so far. Besides, it's over six thousand miles from here. Olympus Mons is closer. It would take you two days to get there by Ariel, over two a half weeks by module, with no road and some really rough terrain."

"Suppose," John said pointing to the map. "Instead of taking a direct route over the rocky hills, we take an indirect route through the Chryse Planitia, where the terrain would not be so bad and we could make better time."

"You would be increasing the distance by over five thousand miles," Yuri pointed out. "But I feel you're right because it would be safer for the module. If you have a mechanical problem on the way, the only thing that can get you back is the Ariel. It would be advisable also to take one of them with you, but I think one Ariel should be left here, just in case we have to come rescue you."

"If we have a problem, Yuri, and we have both Ariel's, we can put the module on auto and take the Ariel's back," John stated.

"John, what if it's an engine problem or the module won't move for some reason? What are you going to do? Abandon the module?" Yuri asked.

"Yes, and take the Ariel's back and return later and fix the module," defended John.

"Well, I don't like it because something tells me it is an unsafe plan, but it's not my decision. After we return from the cavern, take it up with Jensen, and if he says okay, I'll help," Yuri replied.

That being settled, they proceeded to gather equipment for the next day. Jensen called and instructed that they were to carry the M-series navcomm unit and a large RS unit. He also instructed them to carry a wire reel. They left the next morning at eight and were halfway there when they lost daylight. They could run the module on autopilot at night because they where on a navcomm road. However, both John and Yuri agreed that they were in no hurry to get to the Cavern, and decided to dock the module for the night. They got an early start the next morning and arrived at the cavern a little after 4 pm that afternoon. The robots had built a roadway to the Caverns entrance which joined the Marineris Valles roadway. JP was the first to suit and go through the lock, Alex was second. It took John and Yuri a little longer because they had to contact Jensen and gather up some of the equipment. They were just about to walk out of the module airlock when they bumped into JP and Alex coming back in. JP was the first to say something.

"Evidently, when we sealed the cave and the water, we didn't plan on the heat inside the cavern increasing, but we haven't been here in nine months and the water has defrosted, there is no ice. However, the navcomm is still on the opposite side and acknowledged me when I came through the tunnel."

"None at all?" John questioned with a tone of disbelief in his voice.

"Well, what there is left, I wouldn't trust to walk on," JP said with a negative reflection in his voice. Yuri had his outer suit on.

"That just makes our job easier. No ice means, no opposition. All we have to do is activate the sensors and toss them in from the cliff. Great!"

They followed Yuri out of the air lock to the entrance of the cave. There was no atmosphere inside the cavern, so an air lock was not required for the seal, just a pressure door. Yuri vented and opened the door and they proceeded inside.

"It is minus 80 degrees Fahrenheit at the door," he announced. Once they were inside, Yuri took another reading. "It is 10 degrees in the outer cave. That's a difference of 90 degrees Fahrenheit."

They headed for the tunnel. The cliff on the other side of the tunnel was just enough to support the four of them. Yuri looked down at the lake. Movement could be seen in the reflection of the light. The navcomm unit was generating from the opposite shore.

Yuri sent the code to start the unit's download.

"You're right, JP. That looks like water, and I don't imagine you want to go swimming," Yuri pointed out.

Yuri instructed, "The first thing we need to do is set up the tripod on the cliff and introduce it to the navcomm on the opposite shore line. When it says A-OK, you have the correct position, and then we can deploy the sensors."

They set up the navcomm tripod unit, and then Yuri reached into his utility bag and extracted the six sensor units. He activated the first one. After the first one activated, he tossed it over the cliff. They heard it hit the water. The suit navcomm receiver and the receiver on the other shore kept track of the sensor as it circumnavigated the lake. The signal beeped, Yuri threw in the second one over the side and so on until all six were deployed. The first one disappeared into the exit point of the lake on the southeast side. The second one followed about a minute later. The data recorded by the first one was transferred to the last unit. In this way, a map of the lakes underwater structure was formed. When the fourth one entered the lake exit, it reported that the first unit had been blocked by an obstruction. Twenty seconds later, the fifth and sixth unit reported that Unit 1 had freed itself and was now following Unit 2. Forty-five seconds after Unit 6 went into the tunnel, the signal was lost. After the sensors were deployed,

Yuri suggested they returned to the module upload the data to Jensen and prepare for the ride home. However, Jensen had instructed them to run the wire from the cliff unit inside the cavern to the cave entrance. Jensen also instructed them to set up the RS unit approximately one hundred feet from the entrance and attach the internal cave wires to it. This would join the unit inside of the cavern with the Rs unit outside making a connection with navcomm. Now they could monitor activity inside the cavern. After the connection was made they returned to the module. Yuri briefed Jensen on the sensor deployment and said that they had the upload from the cavern's unit. While Yuri was uploading the sensor data, John seized the opportunity to introduce the Hellas expedition. After he got through describing the exploration and the procedures that had already been discussed, he asked Jensen for a recommendation.

Jensen sat back and said, "Let me see if I understand this concept. You're going to take one of the modules to Hellas Planitium, but instead of taking the direct route to Hellas, which is an uphill voyage over harsh surface area. You're going to use the module to get within range and then leave the module and take the Ariel's to the location and spend a day or two scanning and investigating the Hellas Planitium. Then, when you're finished, return to the module and take the same course back. Okay, the first question is who's going on this exploration?"

"Well, I was thinking me and JP and Alex," John said as he looked around.

"Ah, John, I don't want to go. I'm training Xiao in hydroponics and computer encoding, so he will be able to handle the systems after we're gone by himself," JP announced.

"I can't go. I need to monitor our experiment and I have a few other things to do in Cave 2. But you might ask Andre," said Yuri.

John then focused on Alex. "So, Alex, it's you and me, last adventure before the trip home. What do you say? We may discover something and get another marker."

"I'm in, John. I want to see if I'm right about Hellas, and I agree we may discover something."

"We'll ask Andre, but let's just say for right now, it's me and Alex," John replied.

"Yuri, how long will it take to get a module ready for this trip?" Jensen asked.

"The food and water are not a problem. I will have to burn some water for the cryo tanks and replace a couple of the battery packs and other supplies like bubbles for an overnight stay in Hellas. I would say about four days from after the time we get back to base."

"Okay well; this I approve. You will delay this expedition until both navcomm and Yuri give it their A-OK's. Secondly, I approve the vehicle route and the approach to Hellas Planitium upon navcomm's approval. The extended stay inside the crater, this is something we haven't fully discussed yet, because it caught us off guard. But it came to our attention when we read the report on the Olympus Mons expedition. It has to do with what happened to Andre. The ISA administration put the matter into an inquiry. Seems nobody foresaw the crater effects of wind currents in relation to a bubble parked inside. If they did they didn't mention it. It was suggested that it was overlooked because of the height of the Mons heavy air currents were not expected. However, it is now advised that if you post a bubble inside a crater, any crater, that the bubble is anchored by a mesh net, and I mean anchored well. You can build one out of tether wire we have sent. Design instructions are on file. I'll post it with the approved navcomm route."

"The incident with Andre may have seemed funny at the time because he was not hurt. The principle has been demonstrated in a wind tunnel on Earth. A wind in an abrupt depression can develop a vortex wave and literally pick a bubble up and transport it, in some cases great distances. It would be extremely dangerous for any person inside the bubble, suit or no suit. Also, taking the Planitia route is good, but you have no road, so there will be no navcomm guide. That means no auto-drive, and no driving at night. I don't like that so, I'm going to require that you send two robots on the route to give navcomm a better idea of the surface. To remove any irregularities, plus plant some navcomm reflectors along the way. Now, just a quick look at the map here tells me that this mission will be a minimum two-month trip, one month there approximately and one month back plus whatever time you spend at the location."

"After navcomm picks the route, it will dispatch the bots. You can figure their general speed to be twenty-five miles an hour. The map says that the trip will be about eight thousand miles. That means it will take the bots over a month possibly two to get to the other end. Even though the bots can travel at night, they have to recharge, so I'm going to figure a little more than one month. I'll have to contact navcomm control to get the T-111s to change their orbits to keep the bots progress monitored. But I can safely say that after you get back to the base, that there will be a one-month delay before you can start, and you will have to pick up the robots when you get to Isidis Planitia (the Cup) for the return trip. Say, you guys have never volunteered for a mission before or even offered a mission suggestion before, so what's up?"

"Mark, we have nine months left here. If everything goes right, this will probably be the last thing we do as far as exploring, so we'd like to take this shot," John replied.

"Okay, can't argue with that. The ISA wanted that section mapped up close but said it was too far away, but since you volunteered . . ."

They had dinner, and then John asked if it would be okay to start for the base the next morning because he didn't want to travel at night. Everyone agreed, so departure was delayed until the next morning. It was evening two days later when they arrived at the base. Traveling in the module was okay. You had comfortable lounging, including the pods with memory foam beds and direct media feed. The kitchen with auto cooker and the food was the same as you would get at the base. Oxygen and electricity were good. The only thing was the constant movement of the module on the road. The road had improved greatly through usage, and every time the bots traveled on it, they upgraded the surface. John and Yuri had taken turns with the driving, which was mostly controlled by the navcomm unit. However the module, after a few days, became a little cramped because there was nowhere to walk. JP and Alex had started playing cards in the dining room which they had done on the trip to Mars, and John had joined in on a few hands but everyone was happy to be home.

Yuri's first stop after entering the base was the control room manned by Xiao, to get up-to-date, not that there was anything new. As long as there was a navcomm unit within range, they were in contact with the base. There were a total of four T-111s in orbit around Mars plus the base navcomm, the Mars Platform navcomm, and the relay station on Phobos. When you were out of range, navcomm would beep, and the signal light would go off. When you came back in range, the navcomm light would beep and the signal light would re-light (signal recognition). The navcomm units had an encrypted identification code that they transmitted which let the other units know what navcomm unit they were. An example of this is when a unit is operational; a log on the navcomm systems keeps track of it and the data it comes in contact with. When contact is lost and a unit becomes reactivated, navcomm knows how long the unit was out of communication and updates the files when contact is re-established.

The unit was then brought up-to-date and the information was stored in the Tri-Starr system. Xiao and Andre joined them in the dining room/

lounge for drinks. While they were gone, the two gallons of moonshine was locked up in the dining room security booth, and Yuri had the only key. But that didn't bother Xiao and Andre, who had access to the still and the hydroponics and had produced an extra gallon while they were gone, which was two-thirds empty. Yuri held it up, looked at it, then looked at Xiao, and said,

"Well, I see you guys haven't been idle."

"Yuri, you've been gone five days, so that's about right," Lefluere added.

Yuri looked again and shrugged, pouring everyone a glass. It was halfway through the second drink when Xiao spilled the beans. He suddenly turned to Lefluere and said,

"Are you going to tell them or what?"

"Tell us what?" inquired John.

Andre bellied up. "While you gentlemen were at the Cavern, I talked to Jensen about the spring in Cave 1. I asked him if he thought we might get a reading if we sent a couple of floats into the drain. He Okayed the idea and sent me the code for the sensors so that navcomm would know who they were. I turned them loose into the hole. He also suggested that I run the water open for three days to aid them in whatever course they would take, which I did. So now, there are eight floats in play, two with separate identification codes."

Yuri was just standing there staring at Andre.

"Since Jensen Okayed it, I have no objection. I don't think we'll hear from those sensors again, but I could be wrong. But how come you or Jensen didn't let us know? What was it, a secret?" Yuri had a frown on his face.

"No, we thought you might call it foolish, so we decided not to bring it up until and if we hear from them. That's all."

John detected that Yuri was in a good mood because he poured everyone a third drink before calling it a night. The next two weeks went by slowly. The crew was checking every day for the sensors. JP was working in hydros with Xiao. Alex and John were going with Yuri to Cave 2 on occasion. The robots for the Hellas mission had left the day before they got back and navcomm was recording their progress as well as sending live feed from their online cameras. They were having a hard time clearing a pathway through the section between the southeast entrance and the Chryse Planitia, not even halfway yet. However once they reached the main body of the Planitia the surface would be easier to handle and their speed would increase. Two more weeks went by, and they still hadn't heard anything from the sensors.

John and Alex started to prepare the module for the Hellas mission, which would start in about, according to the robots progress, a week or two. They were boiling water and compressing oxygen and hydrogen for the module tanks and portable canisters, which they would use during the investigation of Hellas. John was asleep in his room when the alarm went off. John was first a little confused, since he had never heard the base alarm before. At first, he thought that maybe they were being invaded by aliens. He jumped out of bed, adjusted his inner suit, and went to the control room. Lefluere was on the control panel.

"What's going on? Are the Martians attacking?" John asked.

"Sorry John I pressed the wrong button. I've got a sensor contact."

"Where at the crater?" John asked as he took a seat.

"No in the Valles; about four hundred miles from here, on the right-hand side cliff. John, it's my code, which means it's from the spring."

John was getting a cup of coffee from the control room coffeemaker.

He turned and replied, "One of yours, huh, where's Yuri?"

"He's with Alex at Cave 2. They've been gone about three hours," Andre replied. "And I can't raise them on the comm they must be in the cave."

"We will wait until they get back and discuss what the procedure for retrieval will be. Have you gotten any information yet?" John asked.

"No, John. The probe is embedded here on the south cliff going out, but we looked over that area when we did the scan of the Valles and didn't find any caves there. Anyhow, the thing that picked up the probe's signal was a road marker 'C' unit that the bots had placed on the roadway when they built it. Those C unit marker sensors aren't programmed or built for data retrieval. All they do is acknowledge a navcomm signal location. They are solar-powered and have no other form of power generation. They are inert until they receive a signal like from a rover or a module approaching on the road. Then, it sends the identification number down the line to here. It then hits the base navcomm that alerts everyone, including the T-111s, that there is a signal coming from this location. And a Trex will come to see where it is, using triangulation. In order to retrieve the information, we will have to send a robot, rover, Ariel, or a module to that location and send the activation code, and then it will tell its story."

John agreed, "Yes, I know, and it won't be long before we get a call from Jensen. If the identification got to us, our system sent it to Earth station via the Starr. And if it got there, navcomm will send a Trex to get a maximum read as far as the sending location, and if it's accessibility. The Trex will automatically send a bot which will activate the data drop. Look, here is the grid map for that area of the cliff. Now, do you see a cave entrance? No well, neither do I, so we'll wait for the conference before making a decision as to what to do about it. All I'm saying is it's mighty strange that the probe has taken five weeks to go four hundred miles and now it's sending a signal through a rock wall. How many signals have you got?"

"Just one John you remember I put two in," Andre affirmed.

"There's your next mystery. Where's the other probe?" John offered. "Let me know when Yuri and Alex get here and don't notify me if Jensen calls. Tell him to call back for the conference."

"*Oui*, John," Andre replied.

John left the control room and went to the dining room to get breakfast. Yuri and Alex arrived two and a half hours later. Andre notified John, who was in the shower, when they returned. John instructed Andre to advise Yuri that the conference would start in the dining room in ten minutes. Ten minutes later, everyone was seated, and the wall displayed the signal generation and the mystery as to the location of the probe. Jensen and the ISA geologists, including Dr. Werner were on split screen. John signaled Andre to tell the story, who went on to describe the sequence of events concerning the signal

"We have a photographic imagery of the area and the navcomm reading from when it was scanned, and the data doesn't reveal any cave or dimensional abnormalities. We think the probe may be somehow embedded in the cliff," John added.

"John if that were true, how is this probe sending a signal that can be traced by an outside sensor?" Jensen questioned.

John had to admit he didn't have the answer, "I don't know. We are thinking that we can send a robot down there to extract the data."

Jensen hesitated, "Just a second, John."

The sound on the screen went off. They could see Jensen talking to Dr. Werner and the doctor talking back. It lasted for about a minute, and then the volume came back on.

Jensen started, "John, you are scheduled to start the Hellas mission in what, four days? I wish to suggest you could leave as soon as possible and that you do the investigation of the probe. You might spend the night at the location. However I suggest you take a few specialized items: tether, reel, power signal booster, micro transceiver, and a few blast charges, about three just in case. We have our reasons. Dr. Werner and I concur that it would be better to have a person there instead of a robot. If you can, you will attempt to recover the probe. If recovery can't be accomplished, you are to extract the information twice. How's the module and when do you think it will be able to go?"

"The module is fully stocked and ready to go now. We can leave tomorrow morning. We should arrive at the cliff in the late afternoon," replied John.

"Great, before you approach the probe's position, call us so we can watch. Okay, Jensen out." And the screen went blank. John turned and stared at Alex, who nodded. Yuri commented that he had planned to have a going away party before they left. But since they were leaving in the morning, the party would have to be tonight. They should have a drink or two that night and wish them good trip. He unlocked the cabinet and pulled two gallons out, pouring them a drink and handing the second gallon to John saying,

"It's for you and Alex. After all, you're going to be gone for a month, maybe more. Besides, you won't be here, so that means there is more for us," he said which got a laugh.

They were up fairly early the next day and did a full systems check and gathered the equipment that Jensen had mentioned. They left the base around 9:00 a.m. so that they could make it to the cliff while there was still light. It would take about ten hours. Everyone said good-bye, and they started out. On the road, the module was a little more convenient with just two people on board. John took the pilot seat and Alex took the co-pilot seat next to him. They were having a nice discussion about the probe when Alex said something that caught John as funny.

"You don't think that when I was getting water to burn, that the water going down the drain had anything to do with the probe surfacing, do you?"

"No, I don't think so, Alex," he thought for a second. Then he said, "How much water did you dump down the drain?"

"Well, I don't know exactly. Well, I mean I didn't keep count, but a lot more than normal. I mean, we're supposed to have an unlimited amount, so I didn't think it would matter. But when I filled the first 250 gallon container, I let the water run while I took it upstairs, came back and filled the second one," Alex admitted. "Really, John, I didn't think it would have any effect." There was a silence.

John looked as if he was adding up a variable table. Then he said,

"If your water drainage had something to do with the probe reappearing, then you did a good thing. It may be the only one of those probes to actually reappear. You know the thought grabs me that the probe could have been stuck and your water may have allowed it to get free. Also, that might explain the current position of the probe, because as soon as the water had contact with the outside atmosphere, it would freeze, thus blocking the tunnel, but we won't know till we get there."

They where still going down the road. It was approaching 8:00 p.m. when the navcomm alert started beeping.

John said to Alex, "We're getting close." Then it locked. "We're here."

John pulled the module to the right and turned it off. They went to the kitchen for coffee and to watch the late news. Then they called the base. JP was on duty and they advised him that they had arrived at the destination. The next morning, they had a lazy breakfast, waiting for the light to filter into the Valles. The cliff was still two miles away from the road. They suited up the Ariel's and grabbed the utility bags, and then called Jensen. They waited till he came on screen.

"You guys about ready? Remember to wait until we agreed before you start doing anything risky. We could actually receive the data without actually going there. If the road sensor can pick up the probe's signal, so should you're module, but the probe in its position may not be able to receive from the road. The module's onboard laser will pinpoint the probe's signal location when you get closer. So watch for the beam and turn your hand scanners on."

They sleeved on their harnesses and punched "Activate." Navcomm already had the location, and they arrived at the cliff-side within three minutes. When the Ariel came down, John shed his harness and started looking for the laser beam. Alex approached with the hand scanners and gave John one. They followed the signal till it stopped, but there was no beam.

"I don't understand this," John remarked. "The beam should be here. Are we standing on it?" He turned and looked at Alex, who was looking up and pointing.

"There, John." About twenty feet above them was the beam.

"How did the probe get up there? And I don't see any cave entrance."

Jensen came over the comm,

"Okay, guys, let's take this one step at a time. First, we are going to use the Ariel to get up there. You're going to need a piece of tether twice as long as the distance between the ground and the laser point."

Alex pulled out the tether and cut a forty-foot length.

"Next, attach the micro scanner to the remaining wire tether and the other end to your hand scanner." Alex attached the micro scanner, which was about the same size as a cigar, to the output side of the reel. John attached the reel to the harness and the hand scanner to the end of the tether.

Jensen approved,

"Okay, John, attach that line that Alex cut to your harness. The navcomm already has the signal's location, so as soon as you're ready, press 'Activate.' Alex, hold the line of tether you cut so that John doesn't drift, in case a sudden gust of wind comes up. We don't need John slammed into the wall, but don't pull on it. Got me?"

Alex affirmed and looked at John. John nodded and pressed 'Activate' and the Ariel sat there for a few seconds and then began to rise. The Ariel held him out from the wall by two feet. However, the tether kept him in place. John reached the outcrop and raised himself a little above it so he could get a good look. The top of the structure was a hole about 2.5 feet wide and 1.5 feet high.

Jensen came over the comm,

"John, place your micro scanner into the hole and lower it until I say stop."

John followed the instructions and started lowering the scanner. He had passed thirty feet when Jensen told him stop.

"Hold it there, John. We got a good signal. The data download will take about three minutes." John held his position in midair looking down at Alex below him.

After a short time, Jensen said, "Okay, that's it. You guys can go back to the module. We will let you know when the information is placed in form and readable. It will take a little while, so you can go ahead with your trip to Hellas Planitia."

Alex attached his Ariel harness and they were off back to the module, which only took a couple of minutes with the Ariel's. When they got back, they started up the engines and proceeded down the roadway to the Valles southeast entrance, which was approximately eight hundred miles away. It should take them just under two days to get to the southeast exit point. Upon leaving the Valles, the roadway would turn south to the position of the original habitat cave, and they and the module would be going north toward the canyon, following the line the robots had cleared out. The surface was considered rough and hilly. John's objective was to stay as level as he could throughout the journey, to get to the Chryse Planitia, they didn't need any hill climbing in their way. The map showed a blue streak, which represented about 2.5 to 3 miles below the mean Martian surface, which was about the depth of the Valles. The idea was to follow the pathway heading north till it emptied out into the Planitia. Then the pathway which the robots had excavated would turn east till they came to a section which they had named the cup (Isidis Planitia), which was on the south side. They would enter the cup and proceed to the south end, where the robots were waiting. This was the closest position to Hellas Planitia. On the south side of Chryse, the surface rose to about 1.25 miles in altitude. The objective was to stay away from that area until they arrived at the cup entrance. The pathway to the Chryse after they turned north was almost as long as the Valles, which meant two weeks of travel time to reach the Planitia and three weeks-plus travel time to reach the cup, so they should be at Hellas in a month and a half or so.

Alex settled into the seat next to John. "You know, John, I like the fact you and I are on this adventure together. You know, just us. It's a good adventure, and it's nice and slow and we don't have to put up with other people," Alex pointed out.

"Well you're right, Alex. It's kind of peaceful, but we've got a long way to go. We'll be making the turn in the morning two days from now. We should try to put in fourteen hours a day. As Mars comes closer to the Sun, we will have summer weather, which means more sunlight. I've activated the solar light exterior monitor to notify us when the light level drops to one quarter normal. Also, because it is summer, there will be more storms. We haven't been on the Planitia yet during a storm, but we should take precautions to find particle shelter when they approach. Especially vortex effects when we are in Hellas."

Alex smiled and looked at John, who looked back.

"Hey," he said. "Where's Andre when you need him?" They both got a laugh out of that. The next day, the peace and quiet except for the engine and the interruption by Jensen, who had just finished the evaluation of the probe's data.

"Well, Mark, what's the story?" asked John.

"It's kind of a strange story, guys. I'm sending you the 3-D composite map of the probes journey. But to make it simple, the probe became caught in an underground gulley, which was filled partway with water or ice. However, the exit from the gulley was on the top, and the probe couldn't get to it because the water wasn't high enough. But something happened around a week ago in the gully. The water level rose and the probe was able to escape. It continued through the tunnels until it arrived where you found it. The metal contained in the rock of the fissure worked as a sounding board to reflect the signal up through the fissure. And because of the curved top, the signal was projected toward the center of the Valles, where the roadway sensor picked it up. Its current location is about sixty feet below the hole where you were. It is frozen in ice, which is what happened as the water it was traveling in came in contact with the external atmosphere through the hole. I hate to say this, but we won't be able to recover the probe, and we will have to deactivate it because it will continue to emit a signal. It reports that the last time it linked with the other probe was in the gulley about a week ago. And the data did not confirm the other probe making it out of the gulley."

John looked at Alex and said, "You better tell them. If you don't, I will."

Alex repeated the story, explaining that he had placed a lot of water in the drain hole of the spring when loading for the trip about a week ago.

"Thanks for telling me because that explains a lot. Let's see if I can put it together. When we first found the spring, the water was flowing in and draining out at about a gallon every ten seconds. We found out that was because the water was coming through a fissure in the rock which was connected to a larger water source. The water was then going through another fissure which served as a drain, which according to the probe, empties into an underground gulley. When we sealed the water, there was no more flow, so the gulley became stagnant and probably froze over. When Andre released the probes, he ran water which was enough to get them into the gulley. The water, if I remember, had a temperature of about 50 degrees. Maybe some of the conduits were iced, and it took time to melt the ice so that the probe could get through. Eventually it made it to the gulley where it sat until you dumped that water down the drain probably on ice. The probe was then able to escape; continuing down the pathway till it reached that fissure. It would probably have continued down the underground river to a final point, which may be the crater but the water stopped when you turned off the supply, stranding the probe inside the fissure. We would have to dump a large amount of hot water down the drain, which may free the caught probe, probably the other probe as well. I'll have to run this past Dr. Werner to see what he thinks. We should do this, but listen, guys. No more secrets, okay? Alex?"

"Yes, sir, I apologize. I didn't think it was important," Alex replied.

"Look, I hate to say this, but let's let the scientists do the thinking. That's what we pay them for, but good work anyhow. Now, there's something I what to talk to you about. Northeast of the cups entrance is a Mons called Elysium Mons with good altitude. We'd like you to place a navcomm M-series on the top of the Caldera. The reason for this is it will be able to scan the entire pathway and Hellas and a good position over most of the Planitia. This would give us a web link with Olympus and the rest of the navcomm units of over fifteen thousand miles in two directions, plus one inside Hellas and one on the edge S-series. Place the unit on the northeast edge. Navcomm will show you the locations. You can test it for the link with the M unit."

"Well, that would be great, Mark, and you know there is nothing we would enjoy more," John nudged Alex under the table, "but we don't have any probes onboard."

"That's odd," replied Jensen. "Because I'm sure Yuri told me he loaded them. I'll check back tomorrow night, Jensen out."

Alex got up and went to the storage room in the back. He returned with an affirmed look on his face. "That Yuri, you just can't trust him."

Chapter 12

Hellas Planitia

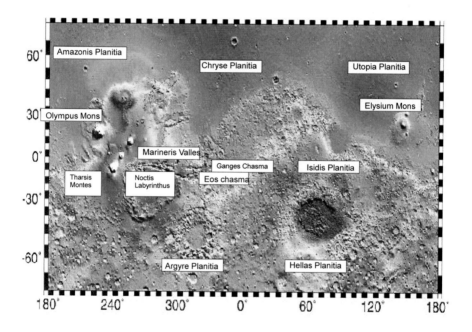

The morning two days later brought them to the end of the Valles roadway. John could see the pathway the bots had carved out and turned the module north, following the pathway through the narrow passage. The pathway of the Chryse region and surrounding surface area were quite a bit rougher than the Valles roadway. Progress slowed to about twenty-five miles per hour. They pushed on. In some areas, the pathway was in good condition and they could pick up speed, in other areas, not so good. They were averaging about 320 miles per day, which in ten days, brought them to the edge of the Chryse Planitia. It spun out in front of them for as far as their eyes could see. Not more than a few miles from where they were, the surface started to drop, which enhanced the view. John paused the module to have lunch and let the module's navcomm get a good scan. This would be the first scan of the Mare from a horizontal angle. A matter of fact, it hadn't crossed John's mind till then, but the rest of the exploration would become historical documentation for centuries. Everyone chimed in to make a comment about the Mare.

After lunch, they took a sharp right and continued along the pathway east. The speed increased and they started to average four to five hundred miles a day, scanning the Mare and the side wall as they went. On the sixth day, they approached a small but deep crater a little north of the pathway, and there was no roadway. However, the surface was smooth in the Mare, after getting the okay from Jensen; they took a left to arrive at the edge of the crater. Jensen wanted an internal scan of the walls so they both suited up and got the Ariel's ready for the trip. Each carrying hand scanners, they proceeded up and over the edge, dropping rapidly. The crater was almost two miles deep. John had his scanner activated and signaled Alex to scan the other side on their way down to the center of the bottom. The scanners were set on auto-synch so they were operating as a single unit. The images of John and Alex would be erased in the composite image. JP s voice came over the comm he was on the base control panel and was watching through navcomm evidently there was a Trex in the neighborhood.

"Hey JP is everyone there with you?" John asked.

"No John, Yuri is at cave two, Andre is in the hydroponics, and Xiao is asleep in his room. I just tuned in because you have a T-111 in orbit above you."

The center of the crater was rocky and rough. John warned Alex to watch his step.

"What we don't need is a torn suit right now, and these rocks seem more than capable of doing just that, so no casual walking around. If you trip and fall, this could very quickly turn into an unpleasant story."

Alex agreed and added, "Yes John, lots of snags."

"We are going to start a composite scan. Let me program the navigation. We'll start by circling the crater floor and then start a series of slow spirals upward. You will be one hundred yards above me, so that it will take approximately let's see, twelve spirals to reach the surface. You will be scanning up and my scanner will be scanning down, okay now."

Alex interrupted, "Hey, John, what's that?"

John looked in the direction he was pointing, on the ground about five feet to the left. He turned his head. There seemed to be some sort of mark on one of the rocks.

"Stay where you are. I'll go see." John maneuvered his way across the uneven surface. When he got to the spot, he realized what he was looking at and was in a slight state of shock. Alex's voice came over the comm,

"Well, what is it?"

John reached for his rock pickaxe, striking the stone on the top. After a few swings, a slab split off the side. Alex heard him say, "Got it in one piece." Then he watched as John put away the pick and picked up the fragment and headed back toward him. Alex could see through John's face shield that John had a big smile on his face as he handed the fragment to him. Imprinted on the stone was the image of a small, about 1.5 inches in length, insect.

"It's just a guess on my part, Alex, but I'd say we got a fossil. It kind of resembles a trilobite, like we had during the beginning on Earth. But it's a fossil, all right, and seeing as where we are, I'd say a fossil of an aquatic animal from millions of years ago. There is probably more around here. There may be fossils of other animals as well. Maybe on the way back, we could stop and spend a day or so looking around. This is a major find, and it's all yours, Alex. After all, you found it.

"John" interrupted JP "are you kidding a real fossil Alex let me see."

Alex held up the fragment to the camera. John heard JP utter a gasp, but John was becoming more uncomfortable with the crater and suggested that they start the ascent.

But JP interrupted again.

"John you would do better using one of those Ariel Floats to map the crater. The virtual map that they created of the crater hole was really good with the virtual map you can pilot around the crater and magnify the interesting point on the sides. In fact you can do a complete investigation of the crater walls at close proximity with good resolution of specific details. Haven't you seen the file of HAshita 1013?"

"No JP I haven't, I saw the first scan but not the completed virtual map," John replied.

"Say Alex, when you were back in the storage area of the module, did you notice any of those Ariel reconnaissance brackets?"

"Yes John, there are four or five of them. I guess Yuri must have stuck them in there when he planted the navcomms."

"Let's use them to do the wall map of this crater. It will take us over an hour to scan this crater with the handhelds. And you heard JP it's creates a better map. We can go back to the module and prepare a presentation and call Jensen. This fossil will give Dr. Werner something to get excited about, believe me! We probably won't hear the end of the speculation until after we get back to Earth. We have just found the answer to whether there was ever life on Mars."

JP agreed and Alex placed the sample in his pouch and adjusted his harness.

"Are you ready? You'll be first?"

Alex nodded and John pressed "Activate." Alex rose from the surface. John's Ariel followed a few seconds later. On the trip upstairs, they weren't required to do anything. The entire trip was controlled by navcomm. They reached the top within a few minutes, and after they were back in the module, John suggested that Alex look up the fossil and compare it to Earth's fossils for the presentation, while he prepared the float. Once John had the float assembled, he took it outside and waited till it powered up. The float, paused a few seconds, and then headed for the crater. John went back inside the module. Alex was on the computer. JP chimed in to say that the T111 was going out of range and he would be out of direct communications until the next Trex came into range in about twenty minutes. John signed him off.

"What did you say was the name of that Earth animal again?" Alex asked.

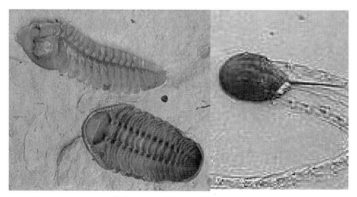

Trilobite and Horseshoe crab

"A trilobite, Alex, it was one of the first forms of life on Earth. They know this through carbon dating the DNA structure left on the stones."

"John, look at this." Alex came forward to the control panel and toggled the viewer. He had pulled up the computer page on trilobites. He was holding the fossil in his hand. "Look, there are several different types of trilobites with scientific names."

John leaned back in his seat to get a better look.

"The one that is the most famous Alex, is that one there" John said pointing to the picture "kind of looks like a horseshoe crab. But you're right; I don't see anything that resembles our fossil. There are several different types, aren't there? Let me see the fossil."

Alex handed over the stone and said, "What's a horseshoe crab?"

John toggled the computer. The horseshoe crab image and script came up. Alex was comparing the images while John was comparing the fossil image to the known trilobites on Earth. He came to a conclusion and said,

"It definitely comes from the same family, but it doesn't match any of the Earth species. It has an extended front section and these," he said, pointing to the fossil, "Look like mini legs, like a centipede would have."

He turned and looked at Alex, who said, "The Earth trilobite does resemble a horseshoe crab. Do you think that horseshoe crabs evolved from trilobites?" asked Alex.

"I don't know, but you can ask Dr. Werner when he calls back. In the meantime, you need to prepare the presentation. You need to burn a piece of the stone to get the exact composition and a full image scan and a micro scan so we can send it. Plus, we'll send the crater map when the Ariel scanner returns."

"John," asked Alex. "How did you know so much about trilobites?"

"I was big into dinosaurs when I was young and studied them and the trilobites at that time. I've actually seen a trilobite fossil at the Museum of Natural History when I was about 12."

Alex nodded and took the fossil to the back to the spectrograph and the micro scanner. The next morning, they sent the information. It didn't take long for a response. First, it was Jensen, then Werner, and a new face who John learned was a prominent Earth paleontologist. John could tell from the tone that they were pretty excited about the find.

Werner started the conversation, "Boys, I want to thank you for this latest discovery. Everyone here is pretty excited about it. We haven't released any public information about it as of yet, but I think that you need to know what this discovery means. We knew when you were on your way to Mars that there would be discoveries, of course, but this was unexpected.

The finding of the fossil proves beyond a shadow of a doubt that at one time, there was life on the planet and oceans. Dr. Shaw will explain."

"Gentlemen, I'm Dr. Julius Shaw. I'm a paleontologist. My job is the study of primitive or early life structures, which includes fossils and primitive life forms. It appears that the fossil you discovered is the fossil of an Arthropod. Arthropods appeared on Earth over five hundred million years ago, during the Cambrian period. This species existed in the oceans of Earth for over 250 million years. Finally, the species came to extinction in the Paleozoic Period, about three hundred million years ago. There are over 1,000,000 different types of arthropods, which are classify into nine separate arthropod groups, however that's not what I'm here to tell you about. Arthropods are primarily aquatic, living off ocean alga and plankton and require water to live. Your find says two rather important things. And that is, at one time the area you are in as well as all the Planitias most probably contained water, and that the oceans contained biological life, and vegetable life. Now, the place you are going is the lowest point on Mars, over five miles in depth but it is presumed to have been created by an asteroid impact, not naturally formed. We've been going over a topographic map here, and it looks like the deepest sections of the Chryse, Utopia, and Amazonis Planitia obtain a depth of seven thousand meters or a little over four miles from the mean surface depth, which is no small ocean. The oceans are pretty much the same as the oceans on Earth's as far as depth, except for the Marianas Trench on earth which is seven miles deep. Anyhow, I'll let Dr. Werner explain the rest."

Werner started once again, "Boys, you remember my theory of tectonic plate shifting on Mars regarding the formation of the Marineris Valles. Your discovery of water and the fossil have added credibility to my theory. There is now another theory being propagated and gaining popular opinion in the scientific community. I will try to explain. It is being suggested that at one time, a planet existed between Mars and Jupiter and that this planet's remains are responsible for the asteroid belt."

"It is also being suggested that a collision with a large mass produced an explosion that broke the planet apart. I don't have to tell you it would take a tremendous amount of mass to destroy a planet. Also suggested is an impact with a comet. The impact could have happened when the planets were first being formed. Besides leaving a large amount of mass in orbit, the manta from the planet's center was sent outward into space in a circular orbital rotation. It is theorized that it may have caused the manta to harden and form into a sphere, creating moons on Earth, Jupiter,

Saturn, Uranus, and Mars. This theory propagates the idea that the moons in our solar system maybe formed from by this explosion, not by the planets themselves. This theory is also suggesting that Mars had a collision with a large mass generated by this explosion which maybe related to the Hellas Planitia. The idea behind this is not proven, however you are going to Hellas Crater."

"The Hellas Crater is not a small-impact structure. The crater measures over three thousand miles in diameter. It is quite large. From the center section, you cannot see the other side because of the curvature of the planet. Anyhow, about your find, we now can be pretty sure that something changed the orbit of the planet, which destroyed the ability for the surface to retain water. As the water was disappearing from the surface, the arthropods seeking to survive gathered in that crater because it was the only available water left. We don't know the exact sequence of events. Whether it was the tectonic plate shift or the impact that happened first or whether they happened at the same time is not known. It is suggested that this event occurred three to four billion years ago a long time before any form of life was known to be on Earth. However, we don't know for sure, carbon dating will tell us more as to when this happened. Thank you, boys, and remember to bring the stone with you when you come back."

Jensen interrupted, "Guys, how far away are you from the cup (Isidis Planitia)?"

"We're about four days from the entrance of the cup," replied John.

"Okay, be sure and give me a call when you get there, Jensen out." The screen went blank.

John continued on his way down the pathway toward the entrance to the cup. Four days later, the pathway took a sharp turn to the right. John knew that this was the beginning of the cup. Although it didn't look like much on the map, the cup was a day and a half of traveling time to the other side by the Hellas Planitium. The road surface inside the cup was not as smooth as the Mare, but they made good time. Arriving on the other side, the first item they noticed was the robots. The navcomm had steered the module to their location. They were parked near the edge just as the surface started to rise.

John parked the module and they stayed on the edge of the cup that night. Before they retired, John used the boom crane to load the robots into the module. He and Alex spent some time doing routine maintenance because the robot had been outside for over a month. The next morning, Alex and John gathered equipment for the trip. They pulled out the Ariel's and began loading supplies. They would spend four days in the Hellas crater. They loaded the scanners, food, water, and one bubble apiece, and Oxygen canisters. They didn't leave that day. They went back inside and went over the plan so they would be up bright and early the next morning for the journey to the crater, which was over a thousand miles away. It would take them four hours to get to the edge of the crater. Before leaving the next morning, John checked the navcomm for estimation of the weather, it looked good. So at 7:00 a.m. the next morning, they took off. Navcomm had picked the spot for the placement of the first navcomm unit. They arrived at the crater around eleven and set the scanner up so that it had a good view of the interior of the crater. It would be another eight hundred miles to the crater center or approximately three hours.

After planting the sensor at its designated position, they proceeded to the crater's center. They were scanning the crater's interior on the way in. When they reached the center of the crater, John noticed that the surface was pretty much the same as the other crater. It was rough, with many sharp out crops of rock. John and Alex stood for a while in the center, revolving the scanners to get a good collection of data. John cautioned Alex that he didn't expect to make any major finds inside the crater itself but stressed that they should keep their eyes open for anything that was unusual. According to the plan, they were going to take a spiral orbit from the center out to the edge and around. Alex would start first; John would follow, putting a distance of one hundred yards between them. They would retain a speed of twenty miles an hour and an altitude of forty feet. Alex remarked that it was going to be a hard time to find a soft enough area to set the bubbles up for the evening, John agreed. Alex left first, John left two minutes later. The navcomm was controlling the orbit. Six hours later, they had completed one third of the crater's surface and with light failing, set about finding a place to set the bubbles for the evening.

John instructed Alex to make sure that he anchored his bubble. They climbed in and inflated the bubbles. Alex had a hard time because the two and a half foot entrance didn't exactly match his structure but success was achieved. Hot food that night was out of the question. As long as they had their helmets on, they could communicate with each other through the bubbles. They settled in for the night. They could watch TV and talk to the base through their outer suit navcomm, which they did. They had a foam mattress which wasn't really all that comfortable, but it was better than nothing. They were awake the next day rather early because it was hard to sleep in a bubble after the sun came out. The bubble's skin seemed to intensify the sunlight, and the heat inside the bubble was a bit much after 9:00 a.m. at a temperature of 90 degrees.

They continued their scan of the crater. However, all they found were more rocks. They started collecting samples, and by the time they were done the second day, they had a bagful. John suggested that they return to the module and use an Ariel float to map the rest of the crater. It didn't take long for Alex to agree. It would be dark by the time they got back to the module, but Alex voted to go back to the module that night. They arrived at the module about 9:00 p.m. that night. John suggested that they could use a drink. Alex agreed. The floats returned to the module two days later. That part of the mission was done. They got under way to Elysium Mons around 10:00 a.m. the next morning. They were carrying an M-series navcomm scanner. The M-series was a lot heavier and larger than the Rs-series that they had used in the crater. The trip to the Mons was a four day journey but a pleasurable experience because the altitude gave them a good view over the Mare. Ever since they had entered the cup they had been in the Utopia Planitia They arrived at the Mons which navcomm identified as Elysium Mons four days later around 2:00 p.m. and implanted the M-series unit at the location navcomm had selected. It was a downhill flight back to the module. They arrived a little after 6:00 p.m. as light was disappearing.

The next morning after breakfast John started the module and turned to Alex. "Next stop, Marineris base, then Earth," John said and smiled.

"You are forgetting," said Alex, "that we agreed to stop at the other crater before going back, for a fossil dive."

"Okay," said John. "But just one day."

"John," asked Alex. "What's this mark on the map just past the other crater on the left side?"

"Oh, yeah," John replied. "I was looking at that the other day. That's the Pathfinder probe. It's been here since the turn of the century."

"Can we stop and see it?" asked Alex.

"Well, if we do, we will have to take the Ariel's. It is a few miles off the roadway and a thousand feet above us, but I'll see what Jensen says."

The next day they talked to Jensen about a trip to the Pathfinder.

"Most of the equipment of the Pathfinder is obsolete," Jensen explained. "You have to remember, it is over thirty years old, and even with the Ariel's, you wouldn't be able to transport very much of it back. Not that a good scan of the unit and its current condition wouldn't be a good addition to the Achieve. You also have the Voyagers a little father away, Voyager 1 and

Voyager 2. However, there is something you might be able to use from the Pathfinder. The Pathfinder had a component known as the IMP, which is a stereoscopic camera which might have an application which we can use. I can't confirm that it could be made to work. Like I said, it's over thirty years old. But I'll send the Pathfinder files to you tomorrow. Take Alex there. He'll get the thing apart."

They reached the fossil crater in approximately a week and a half. They put on outer suits and descended into the crater's center. Once down there they used the virtual map crated by the float to locate objects they thought would make good samples. They took out their pickaxes and scaled the bottom surface with extreme care. They had guessed correctly and found three more fossils, not all of the same type. John knew that this crater would become a major site of archaeological research. They returned to the top of the crater and continued on their trip back to the base. Two days later, they attached their outer suits and headed out to locate the Pathfinder. The Pathfinder was located in an area called the Ares Vallis, which was not in the Mare bed. The unit had landed in the upper section, which was three hundred miles south from the edge of the Mare and a mile above the module's position. Navcomm had a mark on the location, so after an hour, the navcomm landed them at the site. The thirty years had done its damage on the exterior of the probe. The storms had practically buried it with sand, and there was rust forming on the exterior sides of the probe. Alex had studied the components and assembly from the files Jensen had sent. They took an all-surface scan of the unit. It took Alex all of twenty minutes to remove the IMP; he complained that the bolts were frozen. They wouldn't be able to tell whether it could be made to work until they got back to the base.

Once that was completed, John noticed Alex walking around, surveying the ground. He just had to ask,

"Alex, what are you looking for?"

"John, I am looking for the rover," Alex replied.

"What rover?" asked John.

"The Pathfinder had a rover with it that did atmospheric and soil testing. It was a small rover called the Sojourner rover. I'd like to find it," stressed Alex. "This IMP is nothing. It's like an antique navcomm imager, but the rover may be useful."

"Well, if the condition of the Pathfinder is any indication, the rover is probably buried under the sand." John reached into his utility bag and pulled out a small device which turned out to be a metal detector.

"Where was the last place it was recorded?"

"A few hundred feet north of the probe heading toward the Mare," Alex replied.

"Okay, you space out ten feet, and we'll take a walk," John suggested.

Twenty minutes later, John got a read from the detector, and Alex assisted him in digging up the rover. The weather hadn't had as much of an effect on the unit, probably because it had been buried in sand.

"John, there's not supposed to be any air moisture here on Mars. So, how come the Pathfinder was rusted?" Alex asked.

"Alex, I don't really know, but it is like Jensen said. Thirty years is a long time. I would guess that the sand blasts from the storms destroyed the probe's protective coating and the CO_2, and what little vapor there is did the rest," John replied.

Alex wrapped up the rover and placed it in the carry basket on the Ariel. John took the IMP and they headed back to the module. On the way back to base, Alex prepared the presentation of the fossils and submitted it to Earth station. There was another talk with Jensen, a talk with Jason, and a talk with Dr. Werner and his associates, who were very insistent that the crew bring the samples back to Earth to be carbon-dated. The trip back to Marineris base took approximately six and a half weeks. It was easier going back than it was the first time coming out. John now knew what to expect as far as the pathway's variations. They arrived at the base and pulled the module up to the garage and disembarked.

Yuri, JP, Andre, and Xiao were glad to see them and prepared a small party. Liftoff back to Earth was less than four months away. Alex brought in the IMP and the rover and set them up in the lab. John walked in a few hours later. JP was assisting Alex in the examination and they had taken the units apart and JP was shaking his head.

"Well can you fix them, JP?" John asked.

"There isn't any point to fixing the IMP imager," JP replied. "The device may have been a highly sophisticated concept in 1997. However our H-series navcomm is an overall better unit. The only thing I could use from the device is maybe the lenses. The Sojourner rover however, may have an application. We can actually use a device like this for exploration. Unfortunately, it too is very out of date. We could use a device like this to explore areas that we can't access, such as small cave openings. But we could build a better unit which is more versatile than this with a small navcomm, electric motor, regenerating power supply, Geiger counter, atmospheric sensor, and spectrographic sampler. I mean, we have the electric components in the electronic package they shipped in the drop before last. And we have a small dc motor, but there's one thing we don't have, John."

"What's that, JP?"

"Wheels, John. They didn't give us any wheels the right size. We have wheels for the modules, the rovers, wheels for the robots, but no six-inch or eight-inch wheels for something like this. If we had the right equipment, we could build a hundred of these units and have them circumnavigate the planet, collecting all the data we need. But without wheels, they won't be going anywhere. Problem is that the planet is mostly sand and rock. The best tires for this application are wide, double-set units, like we have on the module but smaller. So if we can fix this unit, which seems to have an electronic and power supply problem, the best this unit will be able to do is about twenty miles. Do you know why it quit working?"

"No why?" asked John.

"The battery died," replied JP

Well, it's too late to get tires. We will be on our way home, so do what you want with it."

JP and Alex nodded.

Chapter 13

The Capsule

The call came in from Jensen a few months later. It was time to assemble the capsule. The crew and Yuri arrived at the old cave early in the morning, three days later, in the module which the crew had lived in for four years. They passed though the air lock into the habitat cave which they had once called home. Alex carried a handheld navcomm with him as instructed. They removed their helmets after checking the oxygen. The cave was a mess. You could tell that nobody had been there in a long time. The hydro tanks were overflowing and there was a stench to the air.

"The atmosphere is enriched, meaning the Oxygen level is at 24 percent, so no sparks," Yuri emphasized. Alex plugged in the navcomm unit to the auxiliary plug in the air handler. John signaled Jensen, who was waiting for their call.

"Hey, glad to hear from you guys. You're right on time. I have some people who designed the capsule here and some experts waiting to give you instructions on putting that thing together, so without taking up anymore time."

The screen split to reveal a conference room with six people seated around a table. A rather large gentleman came toward the camera.

"Hi, I'm Robert James. I'm an engineer with the company that built the equipment. I and Mark Stevens, a man seated at the table raised his hand, designed and built the launch vehicle you're about to assemble. The other gentlemen here are ISA engineers of the following fields: Dr. Griffin, propulsion, Dr. McAlister, mechanical engineering, Dr. Smith, electronic engineering, and Dr. Hansen, systems engineering. It's our job to get you home. Both Stevens and I know the vehicle works. We assembled and fired it twice here on Earth. Of course, here it did not attain orbit because the fuel pack is too small to attain even a Low Earth Orbit. But the tests were conclusive that it does have enough punch to put you into orbit over Mars. This, as Dr. Griffin will explain, is all you need to catch your ride home. Dr. Griffin . . ."

Griffin stood up. "Okay, here's the long and short of it. We calculated the weight of the craft including the capsule and the payload, which we gave to be a thousand pounds, which would be you three plus four hundred pounds. Then we calculated the amount of thrust based on the gravitational pull of the planet and its atmospheric density to accurately determine the amount of thrust needed, to attain a limited or Low Mars Orbit (LMO), which according to the plan is all you need to accomplish. You need to achieve a minimum of thirty miles in altitude. Once you get into orbit, your return vehicle which is a CMP currently in orbit, will match your velocity, altitude, and direction to dock with your vehicle in space. You will then transfer to the return CMP for the trip back to Earth. However, we don't exactly know what your altitude will be. If all things go right, the CMP should dock with you on your first orbit. If not, it should correct its data and pick you up shortly thereafter."

"Ah, Dr. Griffin, how many orbits will they have before they start to re-enter the atmosphere?" asked Yuri.

"The capsule or lift vehicle has a small ion pulse engine and maneuvering engines attached to it, and you guys are going to attach the fuel canisters before launch. That may be enough to keep you in orbit for three or more days, but you will run out of Oxygen in about one and a half days. Now, as a fail-safe program where the CMP doesn't dock, the navcomm will attempt to direct the capsule and frame to the Mars Platform," said Griffin.

"That's what we don't exactly know, is how many orbits the capsule will be able to do. That would depend upon the altitude and velocity achieved during liftoff. There are a number of factors which are represented as variables in the mix. As a safeguard, the incoming crew will be on the Mars Platform for a rescue operation if needed. Hopefully, everything will go right. All you have to do is get the capsule into orbit."

Robert James then took over. "Okay, now that we know what the plan is, let's go ahead and get an understanding of what the vehicle is and how it works. There are five basic parts to this vehicle. There is the framework to which everything is attached, two Solid Rocket Booster (SRB) engines, the containment tanks, the capsule which you ride in, and the integrated systems and its components. The SRB units are your main source of propulsion.

They have a burn time of a little over one minute and contain six basic parts: the fuel, the fuel canister the pump, the igniter, the nozzle, and in this vehicle design an expansion chamber which fits between the pump and the igniter. If you want to get home, you must assemble these units correctly. The SRBs attach to the framework and the capsule which contains your: navcomm unit, the mini Tri-Starr, internal handler, maneuvering thruster and thruster controller, emergency separator, and cryogenic harness. Unlike earlier modules produced thirty years ago, the SRB units do not get jettisoned from the craft when exhausted. They remain with the craft, if possible. The only thing that drops from the craft is the LOX tank, which is used to oxidize the solid propellant during the burn in the exciter. The other two much smaller tanks are for your maneuvering system, which is also LOX mix.

"You will also be attaching a Hydrogen tank to the framework. The capsule has a secondary Oxygen tank, but it's your Oxygen supply if needed. The capsule has micro-maneuvering engines, which are as is everything else, controlled by navcomm. If the framework is completely out of fuel and a large rock is headed toward you, there is a manual control switch. The emergency separator will separate the capsule from the framework. The volume of propellant from the capsule maneuvering system is not enough to do much for you, so try not to do that. Okay, let's get into knowing our parts. You have four ten-foot containers. These are your outer container shells for your SRBs. They are metal a composite or alloy. They fit together with a type of O-ring clip lock assembly. They are made of titanium and a beryllium alloy. They are the SRB unit's exterior case. You also have two ceramic metal mesh tubes or bags with ceramic ends. They are what hold the solid propellant. Notice that the fittings on each end, one side has an input port and on the other side is an export valve to your pump. The export valve connects to the pump input tube, which connects to the orbital expansion chamber or exciter module. The exciter module plugs into the dual igniter and then to the nozzle. Now, the exciter also acts as your part of your auto gimble (launch navigation), so these components must be assembled correctly."

"All right, now line up the twenty-foot bags, which are made with a mesh metal and polymer ceramic fiber, and stretch them out. Next, assemble the table which is composed of four stands and two foldout plates that need to be joined together, making a table of twenty-four feet. Your first stand should be at two feet, you're second and third should be at every six feet, and your last stand should be two to three feet from the other end.

Lay the mesh tube on top of the table. Thread the bottom of the mesh tube through the bottom part of the containment shell. Connect the top of the shell to the bottom, making sure that the input valve extends out the top. The mesh tube valves should lock into the input and export holes of the shell. Close the export valve and attach the mix to the input valve. Connect the pump to the export valve of the internal tube. The pump should lock to the export valve of the propellant tube and the framework of the shell. On the side of the pump is a small release tube. Attach the vacuum hose from the air handler to the release valve and withdraw all the air out. Check all your settings and turn the mix on. The propellant bag inside the shell will fill and expand. Wait until the mix pump stops and remove the air on the top end. Replace the input cap, sealing the unit. Next and in this order, attach the pump, the expansion module, the igniter, and the nozzle and the electronic components that go with it." James had a assembly display projected on the viewer.

James paused until the task was completed. "Okay, that's one SRB. Now, do the second one the same way." The two robots moved toward the completed canister, one taking the bottom and the other taking the top and removed it from the table, transporting it to the side. James continued, "Each one of those bags you put in weighs 100 lbs on Earth. On Mars, they weigh approximately 38 lbs. The SRB units you assembled carry forty-eight bags apiece, which would be an Earth weight of 4,800 lbs (1824lbs Mars), just under a ton on Mars, which require the robots to move them."

Alex attached the hose to the pump, and Yuri attached the hose from the mix to the input valve at the top of the canister. John turned on the mix pump. The propellant started filling the tube inside the shell. The assembly of the both SRB units was successfully completed in about two hours. The crew broke two hours for lunch. When they returned with the robots, it took a few minutes to get restarted. Then James took the stage again. "The frame is already assembled. It just has to be unfolded and the lines connected," James said. "That process won't occur until the capsule is transported to the launch site in five weeks.

"According to our calculations, that 9,600 lbs of fuel should be enough to get you into orbit at about fifty miles which is twenty miles more than you need. Prior to your launch, a Trex and your return CMP will be coming into orbit south of you. The T-111 and all other navcomm units in the area will assist the CMP to match speed and altitude. Tomorrow, we will be doing work at the launch site. You have mixed in the supplies five ten-foot pipes. Bring them with you."

JP held one up. "You mean these?"

"Yep, that's it. Attach the cart. I'll see you at 10:00 am tomorrow at the site. The robots will be there also. As soon as you convert them to a drilling glove, we can start the construction. Place any unused fuel in a bubble and vacuum seal it."

They arrived at the site the next morning at 9:30 a.m. It was about half an hour before Jensen would queue the link. Yuri had driven the module over and decided that it was time for coffee. He slid out of the command seat to join the crew at the dining table, except for Alex, who was still a sleep in his pod.

John looked up as he sat down.

"Yuri, what do you think of this capsule idea? I don't mean the capsule but the propulsion and the construction. I mean, do you think it will do what they say?"

"I don't know, John. I came along on this trip so I could learn how to put this thing together, because in two years I'll be in your position. I don't really care what it looks like, and I don't know that much about the propulsion systems. I read the manual, which says that the engine nozzle allows only enough fuel to create a 1.25-minute burn. If everything goes as it should and the vehicle is able to achieve orbit. I have confidence that the intercept vehicle will be able to make the interception because I have faith in the navcomm system. However, cut my tongue out for saying this, but if something goes wrong, I won't be using the vehicle two years from now. You see capsule and parts are supposed to go to Mars Platform after the CPM your taking back to Earth achieves correct altitude to realize the capsule to the platform. The team on the platform will disassemble it and store it in their XPLM and bring it with them when they land on the surface. Of course, you guys will be on your way back to Earth by then. So let's try and think good thoughts, okay? The capsule only has to gain thirty miles to go into a temporary orbit, and I think this vehicle can do that." But Yuri could tell that John was nervous.

John could hear a racket outside and went to the window. "I see the robots are already drilling. Does anyone know what they are making?" asked John.

"They are making the launch gantry," JP replied.

The comm chimed Jensen had just activated and James was with him.

"Looks like the robots are making good time," said James. "I guess you want to know what's going on. One of the pipes had a bit head attached to it. The robots are drilling a starter hole. Then they are going to drill the pipe into the ground and sink the pipe 9.5 feet. When they are done, they will attach four of the other poles to make a forty-foot launch pole. You will need to have someone with a harness and the boom crane to attach the last two poles, because the robots can't reach over twenty-four feet in height. When the first pole is in place, you need to pour ten gallons of goop down the interior to make a positive seal. When the gantry is completed, you're done and you can go home."

The robots will let you know when it's time to get busy. So for half an hour, they watched the robots drill. Alex had awoken and was wandering around the kitchen.

John said, "Alex, as soon as you're done, put on your outer and JP get him a harness. You have got to set the poles."

"How come me?" he said turning around to point at JP.

"JP has already been out helping the robots this morning," John lied, "and I have to run the crane and Yuri is our guest so, besides it's your turn."

Alex said something in Russian and Yuri said something back and twenty minutes later, Alex was outside. James was still on the comm.

"You'll first want to mix the Goop. You're going to need about ten gallons, that's pretty simple. Add four parts A to one part B and stir for two minutes. Then use a high-pressure pump to feed the goop into the lower pipe. The pipe has holes in it and will allow the goop to form an exterior seal with the pre-existing sand, strengthening the support of the pole, this is very important. Then you'll let it set. Goop has a setup time of about two hours. The robots will set the first and second extensions. You will have to set the third and fourth extensions with the crane."

Alex and JP had mixed the Goop and started loading it into the pole. One of the robots was pouring sand down the sides of the pole. When they finished the first container, the robot stopped and waited till the second container started pouring to resume the loading the sand, which evidently bothered Alex because he stopped pouring and said, "What's he doing?"

James replied, "I told you the pole has holes in it, so as you pour, the robot is adding the sand to make a more solid foundation by making a bonded support with the existing sand on the sides of the pole."

"Oh, well," said Alex, "that explains it."

They finished adding the Goop and reported that they had about a gallon and a half left. The robot approached with a pole inserted into the coupling and turned the clip lock, the unit clicked. Then it picked up the five-gallon empty plastic bucket and proceeded to cut the bottom off it and did a nice job too. The robot extended its extension arm to eleven feet with the bucket and placed it over the pole, dropping it top side down. The bucket arrived at the bottom upside down and then the robot beeped at Alex.

"What, what's it want?"

JP, who was standing a few yards away, said,

"It wants you to add sand. I think it means for you to add mixed sand to the leftover Goop and pour it in the bucket. But it just says 'add sand.'"

Alex started adding sand in the bucket with the remaining 1.5 gallons of goop. JP went to get the mixing paddle they had used to mix the Goop, and Alex stirred the mix. Second beep,

"It says, 'Pour,'" offered JP. Alex poured the mix into the upside-down container at the base of the pole. Third beep, Alex looked at JP. "It says, 'Leave,'" and the robot turned and headed toward the solar power supply for a small recharge.

Yuri came on, "James had something to do and left. He said to tell you to take a two-hour break. He'll be back."

Alex could hear John laughing in the background.

"Okay, coming in," Alex replied. "Stupid robot."

When they got in, Yuri asked Alex what the problem was.

"I don't think we should have given the robots that upgrade plug-in. They now want to argue and are giving orders," replied Alex.

"Well, the plug in was a navcomm signal amplifier and program updater, which gave them a larger vocabulary," replied JP. "It is a multiple language formatter, but I'd go easy on the bots. They could someday save your life."

As they were waiting for the two hours to pass, the comm. chimed an incoming call. Yuri looked down.

John asked, "Jensen?"

Yuri shook his head and said, "*Nyet,*" as he pressed the accept button.

A familiar face filled the screen.

"Hey, John, Alex, JP, Yuri thought I'd give you a call just to see what's going on. I called the base, and Xiao told me you guys were out on assignment. What are you doing? I told them not to alert you. I wanted it to be a surprise."

It was Samuel Johnson, John's roommate during training. Of course, everybody knew him. They had taken classes together.

"Sam you old dog, how are you?" prompted John.

"I'm on my way to see you. We should be at Mars Platform within the month. We are the next drop crew. Of course, according to the schedule, we won't be dropping until after you're gone, John. So I won't get to see you in person, but we will be moving to the base for an unspecified amount of time."

Yuri interrupted, "Sam, who's with you?"

"We have eight Yuri; their profiles are in the drop pack 3/4456 file, not from the school. I'm the only one from the old class. These guys are mainly engineers. They have been in training for two years prior to you guys finding the Marineris Cavern. Our assignment is to renovate the cavern and make a fully functional habitat out of it. You know you guys are famous, right? I mean, really famous. Everyone knows who John Alexander is in America and the same with the other members, including Alex and Yuri and JP. You guys are as famous as the Wright brothers on Earth. The story of your progress has already been published."

"My god Sam, have you been in training for seven years?" John asked.

"Sort of, after Yuri's crew left, there was a restructure of the program, and a lot of the original people were sent back. I wanted to stay, I didn't like jail. The training was good and the food was good, and after you guys discovered the first cave, I knew I wanted to be part of this. So, I buckled down and amped the program. However, they no longer offer trips back. What they offer is a ten-year term on Mars with the possibility of a form of transportation to be offered later, maybe, no guarantees. That doesn't bother me. I got no family, so I don't care. John you remember my parents died in that car wreck, I never married, and my grandparents died three years ago. There wasn't really much here for me, and then you know the life sentence. Well, it was all downhill. So, I decided to make the effort and perhaps become famous, like you guys. You know, Mars is the 'Brave New World'. There are still a lot of things to be discovered. Maybe I can get my name on something. Anyhow, the drop that's coming with us is huge, over three times Yuri's last drop, all going to the cavern."

The comm chimed. It was Jensen.

"Oh hi Sam, How's it going?"

"You guys know each other?" John asked with a little surprise in his voice.

"Sam was here for about four months. He left five and a half months ago. I was his trainer on module systems. He's mission commander for his crew. Okay Sam, the guys need to complete the next phase of the launch pole so that they can go home. However, you can watch if you want."

Sam's image disappeared and James's image reappeared.

Jensen continued "There's something I need to discuss with you. I was waiting for the right time and I think this is it. I'm going back to Earth after you guys launch. I won't be here when you get to Luna City. I mean, I've been here six years and my term is up. They'll have somebody taking over for me. On your way back, if you have any problems, that's who you'll be talking to. I'm going to Earth, but I'm going to be at the Cape. When you get back, come and see me."

James took over "Okay, guys, the Goop should be ready. We need to get the boom crane extended and a harness on and implant the two remaining poles. When these poles are connected, we should have a launch pole forty feet high."

Alex and JP still had their outer suits on. They attached their helmets and gloves and went outside. John was working the boom crane and had the boom extended over the pole site. JP hooked Alex's harness to the cable and handed him the pole. John raised Alex to the top and Alex inserted the pole, and the same with the next pole. Then, Jensen said they were finished and they could go home. John lifted the robots into the module's storage bay and put the unit in high gear for the trip back to the base.

It took them four days to get back to the base. As soon as they arrived, the beginning of the drop started. However, the drop wasn't at the landing site but in the Marineris site, about eighty miles west of the base in the Melas Chasma. Until it was over, the cavern was off limits. John kept up with Sam and his crew's progress as they approached the Mars Platform, finally docking. After they had docked, John had a conversation with Sam.

"The drop is only about halfway through. The CMPs are stacked up here. I watch them at night, when I'm on duty, we have four CMPs here at the platform. They have given us an assignment of converting the rail section of one of the CMPs with a web net inside the load bay plus a lot of other things and updates. I think it's your return vehicle. Also, they told us that after you're through with the capsule, it will be coming here. We are to make modifications to it so that we can transport it to the surface. We are going to take it apart and place it in our storage containment. In other words, the SRBs will need to be taken apart."

John now knew the procedure by heart, so this was no news to him.

Chapter 14

Going Up

Six days before the launch, the crew fired up the module to return to the habitat cave. They arrived at the cave three days later, with two robots, the capsule cart, and a module. Andre was with them, he was to take the module back to the base after the launch. Yuri and Xiao had stayed at the base. They had said their goodbyes there. Yuri had given them two gallons of shine for the trip and a one hundred-pound bag of gems and the collection of samples that the ISA wanted transported. Also, he had given John a can of shaving cream, to which John said,

"What's this?"

"It's our gems, John. I cut the bottom out and re-fabricated it to carry the stones. Press the top." John did and shaving cream came out.

"Place it in with your personal gear, it will pass. It contains my personal collection, plus your dark green stone, which is yours for the risk. We will divide the rest between the crew. I will attempt to bring another one with me. When I come back two years from now, we will meet for a reunion and complete the transaction then. You will have to hold on to them till then."

"Okay, can do," They shook hands and said good-bye.

When they arrived at the habitat, the robots opened the airlock and carried out the framework, capsule, and the two SRB units and loaded them on the cart. When everything was loaded, it was strapped down and they proceeded to the launch site. They arrived late and spent the night at the site. The next morning, they started the final assembly of the craft. The vehicle stand was attached to the pole, then the framework and capsule, and finally the SRB units. They spent the rest of the day attaching and checking connections. When they called it a day, all that was left was to attach the gas canisters, which would happen the next morning. They were being chilled inside the module.

The crew was up earlier the next morning. They had spent the night in the module parked next to the launch site two hundred miles from the habitat cave. It was five o'clock a.m. Andre helped attach the gas canisters to the framework, and then they checked the connections again. The launch program had been entered into navcomm. They were awaiting confirmation which according to Jensen would come sometime around noon. At nine, Yuri was on the comm along with the new crew from the Mars Platform.

"John," said Yuri, "we wish you the best on your trip back. It's an extra month on the return, because Earths orbit was one month out of sink. But I guess you're going home and you don't care."

Alex came over to say, "When I get home, I'm going to get big food with family and lots of vodka."

John looked out to the lift craft. It was the strangest looking craft he had ever seen, the two SRB units rising on each side twenty feet in the air and the framework and capsule standing twelve feet high in the center.

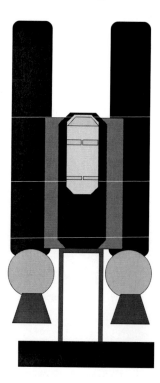

It wasn't very big. The two SRBs were small in height but wide. It didn't look like much either, but it would not be returning to the surface. The capsule was poised on the vehicle stand and gantry pole.

The screen split, Jensen's face loomed in. "You guys ready to go?"

John and Alex affirmed. JP was making another pot of coffee.

"Okay, here's how it goes. Soon the navcomm will send the alert. You will put on outer suits with M series 2 liter cryo canisters and proceed to board the capsule. Andre will help you seat the capsule using the module's boom crane if necessary. Once inside the capsule, you will activate the launch sequence. You will have approximately an hour before the launch. You see the alert is the one-hour notification to the window. You must be in the capsule half an hour before the launch time in order to activate so don't be late or you won't be going home today. Also Andre, the crew from the Mars station will be dropping in two days. I'd like you to wait there for them and take them back to the Valles. Okay with you, Andre?"

Andre was drinking coffee with JP but managed to call out, "*Oui.*"

They spent the next couple of hours talking about things. Alex was visibly stressed out and hadn't slept much the night before. He said he would sleep when they were in the return vehicle on the way home. When at 11:58 the alert button sounded, the crew changed into "outers," while Andre drove the XPLM over to within twenty feet of the launch vehicle. John, Alex, and JP climbed up the ladder to board the capsule. Once on board, Andre removed the ladder and extracted the module.

"Well, here we go," stated John to no one in particular as he hit the "Activate" button. The panels lit up and John went through the procedure of system activation. The countdown started at forty-eight minutes, and the comm came on. Everybody on navcomm could see the same thing John could. So then it was just a matter of time to wait it out.

Jensen was still narrating, "Okay, you're going to launch in forty-six minutes. The craft will be active for 1.25 minutes or eighty-five seconds, and then the SRBs will stop and you will be hopefully in orbit. You should then link with the return vehicle that is currently in orbit around the planet, which you will use to return to Earth. Now, you shouldn't have to do anything. You should link with the CMP through navcomm. However, if you do not link, you are to proceed to the Mars Platform if you can and we will send the CMP there."

"Yeah," said Johnson, currently on the platform, "you can come over and see us."

"As much as I would like that, Sam," John replied, "I would just like to get in flight on the way home."

Alex and JP affirmed that statement. Alex added, "I just hope we put this thing together correctly. I don't want to become a permanent part of the Martian landscape."

Jensen came through John's comm,

"John, I'm on a restricted line. No one can hear me but you. If something does go wrong during the launch, you will only have a couple of seconds to react. For instance, if the launch should go sour, like one of the SRBs fails or jams and the capsule should go off course; don't hesitate to press the emergency separation button. This will separate the capsule from the framework. It may not give you a safe landing, but you won't be with the frame when it blows up or impacts the surface. It may save your life."

"I understand," replied John.

The countdown clock had just shifted to three minutes. The closer they got, the quieter it got until—10, 9, 8, 7, 6, 5, 4, the SRB igniter started, 3, 2, 1, 0, lift. The vehicle soared into the Martian sky. After 1.25 minutes, the SRBs cutoff. John looked at his navcomm altitude gauge. They had attained a fifty-eight-mile orbit. The view plate had turned into the darkness of space. The comm came back to life.

Sam interrupted, "John, looks like you're about ten minutes to link."

John looked down on the panel. Sam was right. The navcomm panel showed the CMP approaching them from the rear. The module would pass them and then slow slightly to match velocity and bring the capsule on board through the rails load bay.

It went like clockwork, and in fifteen minutes, they docked in the rail section of the CMP through the upper 16×32 foot load hatch. They went immediately to the cockpit, the propulsion alarm sounded, and the CMP thrusters fired thirty seconds later. The CMP was increasing its orbital rotation by pushing in short pulses called 'nudging'. John activated the communication display panel. Everybody was there, Yuri, Andre, Sam, Jensen, and some ISA staff, and it was a sure bet that it was being channeled on all ISA links as well as WGNN.

Jensen chimed in, "Congratulations! Guess I'll be seeing you here on Earth in about eight months. I live near the Cape, so maybe after you land, we could have lunch or something. I'll put in an info pack for you at the center. Okay, guys, have a nice trip back."

The screen blinked and a new face appeared. "Hi, I'm Carl Monroe I'm your current Luna City operator. When you get here, there will be a debriefing here at Luna City and a few meetings before you go back to Earth. So, I'll be also expecting to see you in eight months. All you need to do now is make sure the capsule gets to the Mars Platform, and you're on your way home. Yuri's crew will be using it next time two years from now. Once again, you don't have to do anything. Navcomm will do it all."

Within a day's time, the approach proximity No. 2 alarm sounded. Alex was asleep. John and JP were in the control room.

"We are approaching Mars Platform," said John. Fifty minutes later, the platform loomed into view. The CMP module slowed, the rail top load panel opened, and the capsule was launched out of the bay. John had toggled the exterior cameras to watch the capsule maneuvering engines fire and adjust course for the dock with the platform. Sam came over the comm,

"Thanks, John. We got it. Have a nice trip back."

As John was going to bed that night, he found it hard to believe that he was actually on the way home. To him, it was kind of like a dream. Eight months later the proximity No. 2 alarm sounded. Everyone on board knew what that meant. It meant that the craft was within twenty-four hours of docking. Everyone got out of their pods to take a look. The image of the Moon loomed large in the display. The comm signaled incoming message. John hit the transmission 'Accept' button to see Carl Monroe come on screen.

"Well, guys, welcome back. You've got a lot of people here waiting for you to arrive, a few media crews and ISA representatives. You're going to be very busy for quite some time. Okay, here's the schedule for the docking. We are bringing your module in to dock at the Lunar Platform. It will dock in the repair bay. When you disembark, you will be greeted by ISA administration personnel and the current heads of the council. The only media that will be present will be ISA. Within an hour, you will be transported to the Luna City, where you will attend a formal dinner and a debriefing over the next couple of days and then leave for the Earth Platform in about a week, and then Earth. The whole procedure should take about 10 days. Sometime after that, you should be standing in the bank making a withdrawal. The money you were promised for your participation has been deposited in a bank near the Cape, with instructions to transfer it to any bank you wish. There are several media groups that wish you to appear on public programs. The ISA has appointed a legal and financial consultant to assist you in any capacity you may require to have handled. I will see you the first night during the dinner. They got some kind of big shindig planned for your first night here. The Lunar station, which is now called Luna City, has changed and the Lunar Starr is gone. It contains two structures and can accommodate over two hundred occupants and growing. While you guys were up on Mars, there have been some developments that have made living on the Moon easier. Look, there's a map and description of the development on your computer. But I'm going to leave you guys alone to allow you to prepare yourselves and I'll see you tomorrow night."

JP interjected, "Mr. Monroe, what happened to the Lunar Starr?"

"Part of it's still here. It's just not at the same location; one of the CMPs is now the Jumper lift station. Look, view the presentation. We will talk later."

The screen went blank John commented that he didn't like Monroe as well as Jensen. JP got the impression that Monroe didn't really care. But Alex said to give him a break he was just doing his job. Meanwhile, JP dialed up the file on the Moons history, entitled Lunar Starr to Present. The file opened with a picture of the Lunar Starr as they remembered it and went on to show the development. The Starr's original landing of the first CMP and the eventual development of the Starr's structure.

Suddenly, Alex said, "Hey, look! It's us."

"That's three days before we launched. Look, there is footage of us launching," said John.

In the next sequence, John got the answer to the question he had asked Jason six years ago. The image showed the encapsulation of a crater which, they were working on when John and crew had left for Mars. The next series showed the construction of the modular building which was located next to the crater. The construction enveloped the encapsulation of two small craters and installation of platform construction. The modular buildings were 162 × 162 feet square. Completely enclosed, similar to the base structure they had helped build on Mars, except they were three stories or twenty-eight feet high. Part of the Lunar Starr had been moved to the location next to the Luna City. The 'A' section was gone as well as two of the CMPs that made up the Starr. They could grasp the development of the structure but the next scene which brought the presentation up to date showed where the project is now and a concept representation of what was to become a possible future of the lunar station. The construction of the next building which was being considered was shown in an artist's conception of the finished structure. It was one building the size of the two other buildings combined, 324 × 324 feet. and three stories high. The text explained how upon completion, the three buildings would be joined by an internal walkway and would supply accommodations for over 120 people with the other two structures. It would bring the occupancy level to 450. The text also talked about manufacturing and drilling under the surface. The boys stared at it in disbelief.

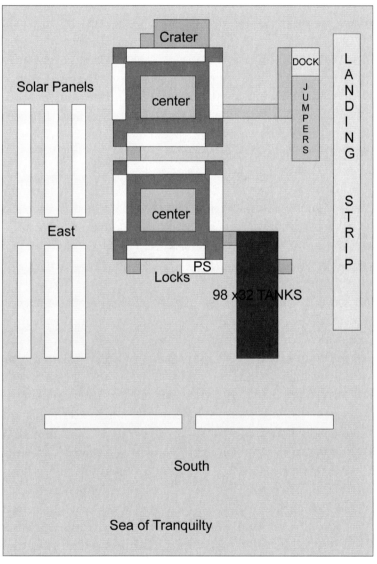

Lunar City

Alex uttered, "They've been busy since we've been gone."
John agreed, "Yes, they have."

"Are you sure we were only gone seven and a half years?" JP asked.

JP seemed confused. "How much do you think this project of theirs is going to cost?"

"A lot," confirmed Alex.

The next day, the ship docked with the platform. The crews stepped out into the repair bay and were greeted by twenty of the onboard crew and some media. After about an twenty minutes of ceremony and interviews, they were transported by Jumper to the Moon's surface and Luna City. They landed at the Starr section, and the air lock door opened to reveal the enclosed walkway to the Starr module. Once inside the Starr module, they were escorted by ISA agents and Carl Monroe to the main section which they entered through a tunnel which had been drilled under the surface. It took them to one of the two modular panel buildings that were featured in the presentation. There, they were greeted by public media representatives and ISA administration representatives and would have been there quite some time if Monroe hadn't stopped the proceedings by convincing the crowd to hold their questions until after the dinner that night and rustled the boys off to their accommodations. Monroe directed John to his room and handed him the pass key card and said,

"See you in a couple of hours."

John entered the room. It was divided by an interior wall into two rooms, each 12 ×16 feet. The first room was the public room. To the right of the door was the kitchenette with small refrigerator, sink, auto-cooker, microwave, and other appliances. Behind it going toward the back wall was a small dinning table with four chairs and then the living room or greeting room, which had an internal space of 8×16 feet and a fifty-six-inch HD wallboard with 3-D and stereo, a couch and coffee table. On the right in the center of the wall was a door that went into the second room or bedroom, which contained: a six-foot bed, a closet, a dresser, a small wallboard, and the bathroom. The shower was almost twice the size of the module's showers but with the same technology. The entire room was nice. It even had a touch of luxury. John noticed a circular switch on the wall next to the opaque glass wall on the exterior side of the room the Bedroom had one also. John twisted the switch the wall, which was 16x8 feet in dimension, became clear giving a maximum view of the lit surface of the moon, the same for the Bedroom. You could see several miles across the lunar surface. John settled in to watch a little TV. He turned on the wallboard and flipped through the channels until he came across a channel showing pictures of their docking at the platform. He halted for a second and raised the volume.

"Here is the crew disembarking from their return module that transported them back to Earth. This is similar to the module that they landed and lived in for their time on Mars."

John watched the clip for another eight minutes, which showed them being greeted by the ISA representatives and the personal interviews. Then he decided to watch something more entertaining until dinner later that night.

Chapter 15

Luna City

The wallboard chimed little after 5 it was Monroe.

"John, I'll be over to escort you and the guys to the main hall in about a half an hour, so be ready."

John was ready early and decided to step outside on the walkway to wait. He exited the room onto the exterior four foot walkway. They were on the third story which had a nice view of the center section. The four foot sealed walkway extended along the exterior on all three levels. The interior distance from to the opposite side was 130 feet. In the center of the second and third levels was a suspended platform containing plants and the elevator, built with clear panels. The interior platform measured 92x92 feet with a 24 foot gap from the walkway. Four enclosed conduits from the platform connected the walkway to the platform. In the square on the ground floor as well as the platforms were a large amount of what John knew to be Oxygen-producing plants and trees. Alex and JP came out of their rooms and joined him on the walkway.

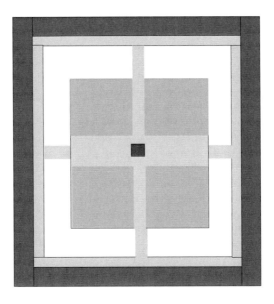

"This place is really fantastic and the rooms definitely upscale," remarked Alex.

JP agreed "Yes, I wouldn't mind spending some time here it's quite nice."

"JP, take a look at the hydroponics design. You think that those plants are enough to supply this entire building with oxygen?" John pointed out.

"To answer your question John, no," offered JP. "You remember the book said that it would require four hundred plants to provide enough Oxygen for one person per day. Well, my math may be a little off, but that only looks like about six hundred, and I think I heard someone mention that this unit has twenty rooms like ours per floor. Let's see, three levels, that's 60 rooms, and the other building has the same. That's 120 rooms, some of them double-occupied, which means a maximum capacity of 240 people, which means 96,000 plants, and when you figure in that the structure that they are building now, which is about the same as these two structures combined, you're talking a total of 432 people and 172,800 plants, and that's a lot of plants. But however it's done; the air here seems of good quality."

In a few minutes, Monroe arrived.

"Okay, guys, ready? Follow me." They went and crossed the walkway conduit to the platform continuing till they came to the elevator. The elevator was a 8x8 clear panel construction. JP was agog everywhere on the platform were plants including flowers which gave the atmosphere of the platform a nice fragrant scent.

"Mr. Monroe what is that scent, I've smelled it before?"

"Let's see were on building two, level three. I think its night blooming Jasmine JP."

Monroe pushed a button and the elevator arrived. They got in and were lowered to the second floor. They followed Monroe to another walkway, which they found out was an enclosed 120-foot walkway between building #1 and building #2. It was also made out of clear panels and posted a good view of the Moon's surface.

John asked, "Is that the Sea of Tranquility?"

Monroe confirmed that it was.

Upon reaching the other building, they took the elevator there to the ground floor, then down a hallway, where they entered a large dining room. John estimated the room to be at least eighty feet in length.

John heard JP say, "There must be over 160 people here," and JP was right. The place was packed. John reasoned, according to JP's calculations that it would be just about everyone who was currently at Luna City.

Monroe showed them to their chairs next to the ISA delegates, and Monroe took the seat to their left. As they were waiting for the service to begin, a familiar face called out to them.

"Hi boys, glad to see you made it back." It was Joanne.

"Give me a hug," everyone hugged Joanne.

"Joanne, what are you doing here?" remarked John. They had talked to Joanne every year while they were on Mars, the same with Yuri's crew.

"It was an option in my contract. If you came back, I got a trip to Luna City, if I wanted it. I'm glad I took it now. This place is fantastic. I especially like the low gravity. Have you been to the trampoline room yet? Oh, of course not, you've just arrived. Well, don't miss it. It's a real experience."

"Is Jason here?" asked JP.

"Mr. Greene is no longer with the ISA directly. About a year ago, he accepted a lucrative offer by a group of sponsors to manage their interest in space applications. I was surprised not to see him here today. And your mission supervisor, Jensen, got kicked upstairs to administration and works at the Cape. You'll see him when you get back to Earth. They have some kind of celebration planned for your return, and you guys are the guests of honor. Oh, I've got to take my seat. They are getting ready to start."

They said good-bye to Joanne, who replied, "Oh, you'll see me in a couple of minutes. I have to give a small speech about you three, nothing embarrassing, like JP's phobia of being eaten by space aliens or anything. See you in a few minutes." She rushed off to take her seat.

John and Alex turned and stared at JP, who was obviously embarrassed.

"Eaten by space aliens, JP? Really?" remarked John.

The ISA delegates spoke and there was a presentation of a group and individual plaques and awards of merit. Alex got his tech operator pin; JP got a system specialist pin; and John got the successful mission commander award. The crew answered questions and talked about the wonders of Mars and survival on the angry red planet. About halfway through the dinner, a man approached and said something to Monroe, who turned to the boys and said,

"Look, guys, there is something that I need to attend to. Ah, my aide will take you back to your rooms when you're done here, excuse me."

Alan Brooke sat down in the empty seat to take Monroe's place. The ceremonies lasted about two hours, and then they followed Brooke back to the rooms. On the way, JP asked Alan about the Oxygen supply and how they could supply the structures with enough Oxygen to support the air conditions of the two buildings.

Brooke replied, "Oh, that's right. You haven't been to the craters yet. Normally, we produce more than we need plus and the CMPs deliver a large supply of cryo-Oxy when they dock, which we store in the cryo tanks outside. This creates a storage reserve which feeds the Jumpers and the modules with what they need. We have no problem here with long-term cryogenic storage like they do on Earth. Look, Mr. Monroe will be taking you tomorrow on a tour of the City and the craters. He will explain everything to you then." Brooke dropped them at their doors and bid them goodnight.

Monroe called early, about 8:30 EST. "I'll be over in about ten minutes for breakfast and to take you guys on the tour." John was already up and had made himself a pot of coffee in the kitchenette.

Monroe showed up ten minutes later. The crew followed him to the elevator and the return to the dining room for breakfast. Carl instructed them to grab a tray and make their selection from the buffet, which was how breakfast, they found out, was done. The food was excellent and a good selection, and JP thought it would be appropriate to mention the fact. To which Monroe commented that the food was a little fancier than usual because of all the ISA brass currently onboard. After breakfast, the crew followed Monroe to the elevator a short distance from the dining room. They bundled into an elevator, but the elevator didn't go up. Instead, it went down. They found themselves under the surface in a sub-level, which opened into an underground tunnel walkway. They followed Munroe down the tunnel approximately a quarter of a mile till Monroe announced.

"Welcome to Crater 1. I believe that this was being built when you were launching on your way to Mars. However, it has changed. I'll attempt to explain the improvements in stages."

John looked over the interior of the encapsulated crater to view the most incredible hydroponics garden he had ever seen. As far as the eye could see was nothing but plants. The sides had algae-bearing tray racks stacked ten feet tall, the same kind of racks they had used on Mars. Above them was a clear panel ceiling. Monroe took them over to another glass elevator and they proceeded up to the second story. Meanwhile, Monroe continued his orientation speech.

"The crater was encapsulated just before you arrived here seven years ago. That is what the hubbub was about at that time. The encapsulation was easier and turned out to be cheaper than anticipated. Once the crater had a roof on it, an atmosphere was added. It was originally intended to make the crater Luna City, but three things changed that. One was the expansion. The original structure had sixty rooms, like the rooms you're staying in. However, in order to supply enough air for the personnel it required more hydroponic space. This crater is a little over one fifth of a mile in diameter or 1200 feet and has four levels which are mostly Oxygen-producing plant life. If you look across to the other side, you can see the original housing that was constructed over six years ago."

John looked across and gazed at the panel building, which showed thirty panel rooms which were attached to the side of the crater.

"The original structure only had fifty of the sixty rooms available for habitation. The rest were storage and administration rooms. Then, plants were grown on the base floor. At that time, it only produced one quarter of the oxygen that was needed. With the combination of the Lunar Starr which provided an additional thirty-six pods and had its own Oxygen generation. The facilities could sustain a habitat for about eighty people. The life systems had to produce 44,400 liters of oxygen per day and half a gallon of water per person per day needed to be supplied. That's forty gallons a day. So, even if we solved the oxygen problem, we still had a problem with the portable water."

"A little math here: each person needs two liters of water a day minimum. Eighty people using ½ gallon a day, 40 gallons × 365 days = 14,600 gallons a year and that is a lot of water, at 8.35 pounds per gallon gave us an Earth lift weight of approximately 120,000 pounds. That is what they call an extended payload. So, what was needed was a way to supply a large quantity of water somewhere around 20,000 gallons per year. That would support approximately 120 people with drinking water and for other water systems such as bathroom and hydroponics water. So then, they decided to drill a tunnel from this crater to the next crater, which is a little larger, and encapsulate it. That went fairly well, and with the added space, they had solved our oxygen problem."

"Around the same time that this was being done, a scientific group was drilling up in the poles and found a little water, well ice. Though not potable it could be filtered and used in the service systems like the hydroponics. It was processed and a lot was used as supply in different water systems, well it paid off. They found a sealed pond of several thousand gallons and later a few more. That, plus the fact that they found a new way to lift water and other essentials, helped considerably. As you know, a CMP has the ability to lift a maximum payload of about 100,000 lb. safely, and at a cost of 1.2 billion a piece, it was a major expense to lift water."

"So, they built a different type of vehicle which lifts 160,000 lb. of primary supplies. It's new and in production right now. You see, the station gets three lifts a year. That represents around five billion in cost per year. So, since you've been gone, this station has cost in excess of 25 billion, plus add-ons like panel structure, equipment, and miscellaneous materials. The new payload vehicles aren't like a CMP. They don't have space for people, except for a two-passenger emergency cockpit. The reason is the vehicles, which are basically just shells, and are reusable and a low cost application. They lift to the Earth Platform, where they wait for a CMP to bring them to the Lunar Platform. Once they are unloaded, they can be sent back or transported in tow back to Earth."

"Suddenly, there was investment capital being offered for expansion. That's when the outside panel buildings were suggested. The idea was to move everything into the panel buildings because they were cheaper to build and well, I don't know. Someone liked the concept better. I think what they realized, was that they don't get enough light being inside the crater; all of the light inside the crater is synthetic. In the panel buildings, every room unit has a view window in both the living and bedroom rooms, which is something that everyone seems to like. You couldn't do that with the craters. The view of Tranquility Base is quite spectacular during the lit period."

"Could you imagine the complexity of drilling eighty window units in the side of the crater? It took six months to do the crater, but only one month to complete a panel unit building. Even though the panel buildings have twenty habitat units on each floor that represents sixty units per building only 100 units are habitat rooms. The downstairs of both buildings is consumed by research and utility rooms like the dinning room and kitchen. When you add the eighty-unit structure remaining here in the crater mostly occupied by ISA staff, it makes a grand total of 180 units. However, 25 percent of these units are office units designed for administration purposes, mechanic shops, work shops and private company offices, and utility rooms leaving 140 habitat units. In the two habitat buildings and Crater #1 there are three chemical labs, two machine shops, a recreation area, and a doctor's office. The entire station is run by about sixty people as staff, so figure it. One hundred people here a year, tourists, sponsors, and ISA staff, which require water, food, and air. In the crater right now, we recycle our water through a cleaning process, and whatever we don't have application for winds up here," Carl said, pointing to the hydroponic tray.

"After the water cycles around for a few rotations, it winds up at the water processing plant in the second crater, which we will be going to shortly. But before we do, I want to show you something." Carl led the way back toward the center of the second-story platform and the elevator. Carl took the crew up to the fourth level. They saw that the third and fourth platforms were half sections, having a partial floor like the panel buildings. Carl stopped at the fourth level. The door opened to reveal a circular suspended platform 16 feet in diameter around the elevator with a rail that stopped visitors from falling over and a conduit walkway to the platform.

Carl continued, "The floor panels on the second, third, and fourth levels are clear to allow light to generate throughout the structure. Notice the dissimilarity of the flora plants here. The levels are arranged for plants that require a lot of light, while downstairs are plants that don't require as much, such as mushrooms. I believe I heard a rumor that the inside structure is going to be upgraded soon. However, the basic structure will remain the same. Okay, let's go so we can get to Crater 2."

They boarded the elevator again, but instead of going down, they went up. John could see that the elevator shaft disappeared through the top of the crater's seal. Sure enough, they were outside the crater above the seal in the next couple of seconds. The shaft kept going up. Suddenly, they were above the crater walls. The elevator shaft finally stopped twenty feet above the top edge of the crater. The elevator halted at a platform like the one on the fourth level, except this one had a dome enclosure on it. Carl smiled,

"I just had to show you this. It was built when they first built the crater thinking, I guess, that people would be satisfied with it for the view of the surface. Now, they have an observation rooms on each of the panel buildings, but they are not as high as this one nor is the view as impressive." The Sun produced a luminescence over the landscape of the Sea of Tranquility. You could see miles across the lunar surface in every direction and the two panel buildings below them. Suddenly, JP yelled,

"Hey, look! There's a Trex."

Everyone looked to see a T-111 drift across the sky in orbit. They joined Carl for the journey back downstairs, where he led the way toward an abstract crater wall. When they got to the wall, they found a set of stairs that led downward into another tunnel, which ran down about half a mile to another set of stairs. He continued the description as they were walking in the tunnel.

"We are walking in the connection tunnel to Crater 2. The encapsulation of Crater 2 started a year after the completion of Crater 1, after you landed on Mars. The whole construction process took ten months to complete, if you include the plant cultivation. Completion took about two years to get it to where it is now. This crater is very important. Crater 1 contains a majority of air-producing plants, whereas Crater 2, which is larger, contains more food-producing plants that supplement the nutritional requirements of the City's diet. After this was completed, the construction of the two panel buildings was started, although the structures only took about one month per building. There were three months involved in installing the interior, so the buildings are only about, well, less than three years old."

They started up the stairs, and as they came up to the floor level, John was in a state of shock. It looked like a jungle in the sky. There were several levels, all with clear floor panels. The upper levels were half platforms, and the crater walls were coated with a silver reflective gloss. The temperature was about 80 degrees with a wind which alternated in pulse. Later, they found out that the wind was created by a series of rotating turbo fans from the ceiling level. Carl led them to a side table near the stairs, where he picked up and dispensed a group of sunglasses. The reflected light inside the crater was extremely bright.

"Okay, let's take the walk. Notice that the ground is a combination of Moon dust and enriched top soil with a fiber. That product was designed by a scientific company on Earth. We sent them a sample of the Moon dust, and they sent us this back. We mix it one gallon to five gallons of moon dust. Works really well as a plant able ground cover, as you can see." They were walking down rows of plants. There were melons squash, onions, strawberries, lettuce, cabbage, carrots, peppers, tomatoes, green beans, broccoli, and others.

"Carl" interrupted John "what are these." John had noticed a large section covered by one particular type of plant."

"That's a type of soy bean John; here we grow our own soy, coffee and tea and chickpeas. Soy and the chickpeas are necessary nutrients and very popular here. We are big on chickpea and soy products such as from chickpea flour, curry, hummus and from the soy, tofu and soy milk. In the dining room you can find several soy or chickpea products. The entire first floor is mostly soy, chickpea tea and coffee cultivation and of course garlic, saffron, and herbs. Some things we can grow here and some things we can not such as, wheat and rice because too much space is required to produce a significant yield."

Carl was still explaining that the plants were hybrid, quick-generation plants, which were staged to supply a continuous supply for the City. They passed a man picking tomatoes and placing them in a basket. Tom, as he was introduced, turned toward them as they approached.

"Let's watch this. Can we?" Carl requested.

The gentleman, who was also wearing sunglasses, nodded.

"Hi, guys. Welcome home. Okay I'm picking vegetables here in Section 'A'. When I have a full basket, I send it to the City via this rail system." He pointed to a cart which was poised before a hatch door like a rabbit hole.

"I guess I can send one." He went to the cart and placed the basket in the tray. He then closed the hood over the top, opened the rabbit hole, and pushed a button. The rabbit hole opened and the cart slid in.

"This is the air lock sled to the processing room. The product will arrive in the City's building 1 processing room in about less than a minute. Then, some of it goes to preparation, and some is processed and flash frozen, and some are stored in cc (climate controlled) storage for use in the near future."

"The vegetables are grown in stages. Stage A comes due this month, B next month, and C on month three. When I'm through with this section, I must replace the harvested vegetables with new plants, which are growing now in the germinator pod," he said, pointing to a very large tray by the side of the Crater. "There is something I want to show you Carl and Tom led them to a section of the crater. This is the chicken coop we have over 300 chickens here which produce our eggs supply. Many animals we can't raise here such as cows, horses, and fish however, it has been proposed that we can raise pig and poultry. Carl suggested that they continue the tour by returning to Luna City. So, they said goodbye to Tom and backtracked their way through the tunnel to Crater 1 and then back through the entrance tunnel to Luna City building #1.

As they came out of the tunnel, Carl made a sharp right, which led them down a hallway about fifty feet. He opened a door and stepped in. It was a long room, about sixty feet in length and 12 feet wide. Carl then turned them around to walk them back the same fifty feet. Most of the room contained what looked like refrigerators until the last twenty feet, which contained machinery. There was a man working there who Carl introduced as Bill, and Carl asked him to explain the work done at his station. Bill started with a brief explanation of his duties.

"First, I take the baskets out of the tray and separate them into sections, wash them, and look on the preparation sheet to see which ones will be prepared tonight. See," he said pointing at the screen. "That's how much and what gets sent to the cooker today. So, I pick out the best selection and put them in the basket. Now, tonight it looks like they are going to serve a salad, which is normal. So, in this basket, I'm going to put 30 lbs. of tomatoes, 15 lb. onions, 15 lb. cucumber, 30 carrots, 20 heads of lettuce, and so on, and in the basket behind it, I'll put broccoli, squash, and peppers. Then I send the carts to the cooker. The product that's in good condition that is not needed for tonight goes to cc, and the product that's not in particular good condition gets juiced or processed for the freeze dryer. It looks like we're having spaghetti tonight." Bill went to one of the refrigeration units and started pulling out large bags of tomato sauce, which would have weighed eighty pounds on Earth but only twelve pounds here.

"The big meal was last night for your welcome home dinner," Bill continued. "The ISA shipped extra supplies such as tonight's pasta, for your stay here. You see, our normal occupancy at Luna City is approximately a hundred people. For this week, the figure is more like 160. That's sixty more people than we normally feed, and although we do a pretty good supply of products, sixty extra people eat a lot of food. Now, as far as what you saw in Crater 2, that's what we produce. However, we are still dependent on shipments from Earth for certain other products. We, for one reason or another, can't produce food such as cheese, milk, butter, bread or wheat, syrup, mixes, and of course, meat products. What we do produce is vegetables, fruits, nuts, yeast, potatoes, glucose, and proteins, ah, and eggs. What the Craters produce cuts the product bulk lift mass. Because we produce a lot of the food product here that leaves lift space for specialized product like hot chocolate mix and other specialties."

"Moreover, it makes the base semi independent. If something would happen and supply would be interrupted, with what we have in stock and what we generate, we would still be able to survive here quite well. We produce enough air and food to survive. However, water would still be the problem. Has Carl shown you the storage depot yet?"

Carl shook his head. Bill took them to the exterior wall panel, where there was a window.

"This was built after the unit was built." Bill said pointing to an exterior structure not far from the processing room. "The building contains food storage and containment rooms, and the very large tanks you see in the back contain Hydrogen, Oxygen, and Nitrogen and other essential cryo gases. The H2O tanks are located under the surface in a thermal jacket. The majority of the Oxygen contained in the storage tanks was generated here, and if we cut off the crater, there is enough air stored in the tanks to support the atmosphere for three months which is about 2,500 gallons for one hundred people."

Carl gave regards to Bill and mentioned that the next stop should be lunch. The guys said good-bye to Bill and followed Carl toward the main dining room, but Carl went straight to the back, opening a door and stating,

"Welcome to the Cooker. Hey Doris, I brought them over for lunch."

A stocky woman came up and introduced herself.

"Hi, I'm Doris I told Carl that if he didn't bring you boys over that he would regret it in his food ration. Well anyhow, boys, this is the food prep station, commonly called 'The Cooker'. Here, we prepare the standard meals for all the people at the Luna City Base. We prepare breakfast from six to ten, lunch from ten to two, and dinner from five to eight. There is also a smaller prep for midnight and 4:00 am. Of the one hundred people that are normally here, thirty of them are ISA workers, like me, the hydroponics personnel and the maintenance crew. Thirty are scientific personnel involved in research, twenty are ISA administration personnel, and usually twenty to forty are tourists or temporary visitors."

"Here is where we cook the food. It starts out simple. In the morning, we make coffee, which is available all night and mix up the juice in the machines. Then we have eggs, bacon, sausage, muffins, grits, pancakes, and potatoes, and cereals are offered on a single-server menu. Sometimes there is a problem with visitors, as they don't understand why they can't have a fourth cup of coffee. And so, they have to be told about the water rationing, two liters per person per day. We actually make that three here, but you have to draw the line somewhere, so we have cards."

"Now, there is a store, lower level building #2, where people can go and buy groceries and sodas or two liters of water, but they are costly. For instance, a gallon of water costs about twenty dollars, but the non-liquid food supplies are fairly economical, sandwich meat, chips, and canned foods, and so on. For the last year, lifting supplies has gotten extremely cheaper. You know, it's funny, we drink an average of 3.5 lb. of water a day, but we only eat 3 lb. of food a day. Well, its lunchtime, actually after lunchtime."

John looked at the clock. It was after two, Moon time.

"But seeing that you're with an ISA administrator, I think that it would be okay," she smiled. "We have sandwiches, salad bar, soda, a couple of salads, potato, macaroni, chicken, eggs, but this will be on the cuff. What would you boys like?"

Alex chimed in, "I'd like a steak."

"Okay," said Doris, "and what about the rest of you? Steak and potatoes all round? What about you, Carl? Writing this one off?" Carl nodded. "Okay, go take a seat. It will be about twenty minutes." They went out to the dining area and took a seat. Lunch was officially over, so there wasn't anyone but them in the room.

"After lunch," Carl suggested. "We should go over to Building 2 and visit with some of the researchers and some more of the administration faculty."

Doris came out of the kitchen. She held in her hand a container about two feet in length. "I wanted to show you this. Last night we feed 180 servings of boneless chicken breast, broccoli, and potatoes with a salad. We supplied the broccoli, potatoes, and the salad. The 180 chicken breasts came from Earth. This pack contains sixty breasts. They are packed on their sides, the same as the steaks which are in fifty packs. They come on pallets of four hundred packs a piece. We get between forty to eighty pallets every four months with bacon, beef, pork, pork chops, fish, and other meat products. They wouldn't be able to supply us with as much as they do with vegetables or other products that we use because of the bulk. Okay, how do you want your steaks?"

Everyone voted medium rare. Doris went back to the kitchen.

"You see, when you guys discovered water on Mars, you may not realize this, but you changed the future of space exploration. It now shows that we can colonize Mars. You see, because we can develop everything that is here under the surface of the planet, making it self-sustaining. In doing so, it may become a more independent structure. One can only guess what it will become in the future, say a hundred years from now. But I suggest that Mars will become an underground community with hydro pods on the surface. One reason is the protection from radiation an underground would provides. The inhabitants will probably become vegetarians however," said Carl.

JP interrupted,

"I noticed when we were in the craters this morning that all the light was synthetic and so is the light and usage of electricity inside the City. How do you get enough power to supply all this?"

Carl laughed, "You're right JP that was a problem. Luna City has a power supply variation on a 28 day rotation, meaning that we have 7 days of direct 24 hour sunlight during the lit period and 14 days of indirect sunlight. During the unlit period we have 7 days of earth reflection light which isn't enough to meet with the power requirements needed to support the Cities usage. Our power supply during that time is generated by an integrated combination of sources. We get power from solar panels outside, fuel cells, and a few other sources. Looking at power generation is like looking at water. You have a glass which is empty and a gallon of water. Does it take the entire gallon to fill the glass? No, it doesn't, and if you tried to do that, you would waste the water. This morning, we used the elevator to go to the observation platform in Crater 1. Well, as you were going up and down in the elevator, you were actually making electricity. True, you were using electricity, but you made more than you used. Because as the electric engine was turning to lift you up or down, it was also turning a generator that was producing over twice the electric energy that you were using, so you were making electricity by using electricity.

"There are a lot of re-generative devices here like that in the design of basic structures. When you were on Mars, your module had a re-generative power source. Navcomm devices also have a re-generative power source, and it doesn't take much to get them started. I took a course on re-generative units when I was in college. They demonstrated how a re-generative power supply could power an electric engine with a battery that had no charge on it. A good example of this is in your room, when you turn on the light in your room, you are generating more electricity than your light uses. It's because of the light bulbs and the panels. It's new technology, a space-applied technology. We'll talk to some of the researchers about it they may have a better perspective and explanation. Anyhow, the steaks are here."

Doris came over and presented the meal off a cart along with beverages. The steaks were good, only seven ounces; however there were enough potatoes and salad to make it a splendid meal. After lunch, they thanked Doris, who said as they were leaving,

"Yawl come back now, you hear." Which got a laugh because; there was nowhere else to go.

The crew accompanied Monroe across the exterior walkway to Building 2, where they spent the rest of the day visiting the research stations, talking with various scientists who seemed more interested in things they had done on Mars. John felt some of the questions were odd. One of them wanted to know all about the operational efficiency of the Sterling pump and gas containment on the surface. They also visited with a scientist who was trying to make a Carbon/Oxygen separator a reality. The crew realized immediately its implications for the Mars atmosphere which is Carbon dioxide. At the end, they wound up at Carl's office which was located on the suspension platform second level of building #2. There a meeting was taking place in the conference room next door between the ISA administrators and some engineers. They all said hello, and the crew was shuttled off to Carl's office, where they met Debra, his secretary. As they walked in the room, John noticed a model on the table, so did JP, who asked, "Hey, Mr. Monroe what's this?"

Carl didn't hesitate with the answer.

"It's what's being discussed at the meeting in the other room. It's the next building to be built at Luna City. It's called the 'Glass House,' it is a specially designed, with double-insulated glass panels and one-way reflective panels on the sides and roof. It will supply both heat and light for hydroponics and other systems. It will be, when completed, twice as large as both of these buildings. The unit will be able to supply heat and power to the base as well."

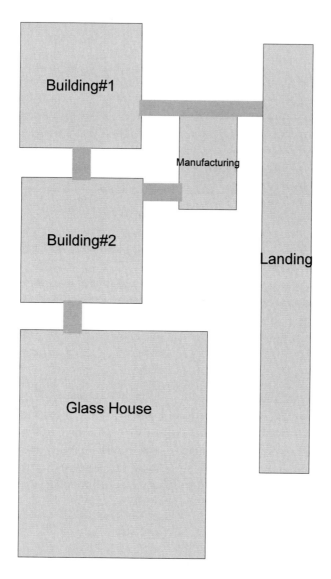

"But I thought that the next building was going to be another habitat building," replied John.

"I know that's what the majority of the people here think but, you see we just don't need anymore people here. If we wanted right now, we could accommodate 180 people-plus, but water is the main problem. Water is the most important substance in space, believe it. If we didn't have to import water, this station could become almost self-sufficient; of course we would all be vegetarians. But by finding water underneath the surface on the moon, would mean they could drop the supply run by one lift, which would lower the upkeep costs of the City considerably. But I'm afraid that the finding of a large amount of water under the surface here is like wishing on a star. The moon is composed of igneous rock not like Mars and this makes mining tough. Anyhow, if we find another source of confined water or if our molecular chemist is successful, then maybe we might and I say might, put together another habitat building. This will probably be the last structure for a while. You see, the Starr did okay for what it was, a habitat for thirty-two people, which was adequate for general purposes."

"It didn't produce enough air or food to be considered an independently sustaining structure. They thought that the crater would be a solution, and they were partially right. If they had just left it there, it would have been good. Or let's say they didn't do the crater at all and instead kept the Starr as it was and built the glass house for the hydroponics and food and left it at that. That would have been good. At the time the Starr was operational, it was supplied three times a year at a cost of five billion dollars a year. Now the cost is twice that and going up. If you what to know what I see in the future for the Moon, it is a reduction of staff here from sixty to forty. The addition of the Glass House, and that's about it, I'm sorry to say. When you guys found water below the surface of Mars, it means that they can develop a self-sustaining base on Mars, and if done correctly, it may become fully independent. The talk now is to start the construction of a colony under the surface by drilling out a structural area to support the construction. Mars is not made of igneous rock except for the volcano's lava and drilling there would not be as difficult. The term being thrown around about Mars now is 'Red Australia'. I'm sorry, boys, I didn't mean to say that . . . ."

"No offense taken, but do you mean that they are going to make it into a penal colony?" John asked.

"I don't know. It's just a rumor, and that probably won't be decided for several years. Well, if it does happen, you can be thankful that you got to come back. No, that model is a concept model for the presentation in two days. What's going on in the other room is the cost and application meeting. They are deciding how much and how soon they want to stage construction for this package. I imagine that they will eventuality complete the development, when and how I don't know. There is also a large contract being discussed where Luna City will be granted contract to supply products to other communities such as Mars, Jupiter, Saturn, and beyond. And by product, I mean food, panels, and power equipment which can be manufactured and assembled here and shipped direct. This would mean a lot for Luna City and a lot for the remote stations and the ISA as far as costs are concerned. Private sponsors are now involved. John, those gems you found on Mars helped to increase interest in overall space exploration. You know, not too far in the future, that model and a platform around the moons of Neptune could become a reality, mark my words. Now I have to make a presence next door. However, you guys enjoy yourselves while you're here."

"Okay, but there is nothing to do," remarked Alex.

"Oh, wrong you are, Alex. There's the trampoline and recreation room, or you could schedule for a trip to the mining operations at the poles. Or you could get a rocket pack or an Ariel for the day and go to the dark side and have a paste picnic lunch. Also, there is the media room. It's a social meeting area. You know, we do have some unmarried females onboard here. My secretary Debra is one of them. Hey, John, you might get lucky. You guys have the key to the city till you leave for Earth, so enjoy yourselves."

There was a silence and the tour was over for that day. The crew went back to their rooms to get ready for dinner. Now that they were known, dinner went fairly well except for the fact that they had to eat at the ISA administration table with the administration visitors, who John understood were going to be leaving in the next couple of days. The ISA was sending a special shuttle for them, which they would board from the Lunar Platform. John also found that during the time they had been on Mars, the Constellation class vehicles had been upgraded to an eighteen-person carrier called the Andromeda class re-entry vehicle, of which there were two, plus the five of the original eight-passenger constellation shuttles that were still operational. The representatives would be going to the Earth on board one of the Andromeda class vehicles which they would catch at the Earth Orbital Platform. John and the crew would go the next week on a Constellation class vehicle.

Chapter 16

Homeward Bound

John slept late the next morning and got up around ten. He stopped by Alex and JP's room to see what their schedule was. They had both gotten up earlier and had already had breakfast. So John went to the dining room by himself to see what was available. He had already missed breakfast but lunch may be available. He got a BLT and egg sandwich and a cup of coffee. He was seated at the table when a gentleman approached with a food tray in his hands.

"You're John Alexander, right? Hi, I'm Robert Bose, ISA administrative engineer. I'm sorry that I missed your ceremony Tuesday but we all have to sleep sometime. My shift is 4 a.m. till 2 p.m. I'm in charge of some of the ISA Research Project Lab being developed here at the City. Do you mind if I sit?" John gestured that he didn't and offered Bob a seat.

"I wanted to talk to you about your experience on Mars and what you think could be improved. In particular the panel constructions that you did and anything else you think could be an improvement."

"The panel construction was fine. The glass house we built for the hydroponics turned out really well, no complaints there. The temperature became an ambient 80 degrees Fahrenheit during the day, and the regenerative power supply did well keeping it at that temperature during the nights, which sometimes dipped as low as minus 180 degrees. The base was interconnected through an air handling system that kept the entire base temperature stable, the hydros at 80 degrees and the internal habitat atmosphere at 72," said John.

"John, as administrative engineer, I'm in charge of the panel development here. We are currently in negotiations with the ISA and private concerns to secure a contract to supply products for Mars and other deep space applications. You know the asteroid belt, Jupiter, Saturn, Uranus, and Neptune and points beyond. We want to take over the supply of panels, food, and other products for future deep space explorations. Now, the panels that I have been told are called by some glass panels are not silicon glass like we are familiar with on Earth, but amorphous liquid metal alloy. Liquid metal is poured and hardened rapidly in a cold temperature to produce these clear solid plates which we call 'glasses'. This product is expensive to manufacture on Earth. In order for the liquid metal to be produced in a clear state, the elements need to be heated and then cooled very rapidly. This process costs money."

"We however, don't have a problem with that here. When we want to cool something, we just stick it outside for a minute. Plus, after they are made on Earth, they still have to be lifted here, which increases their cost. In the lab, we are working on designing new applications and processes for panel construction. Our focus right now is internal panel layers. John, we have designed over sixteen different panels, and we are now trying to integrate them into one main application panel, you know one panel that we can produce that does everything so we can mass produce it. To do this, we've been experimenting with layering. We are now at a point where we had to create a new framework to support the layers. The panel's characteristics are a clear panel, with Dewar's effect and interior magnification, polarized grid for radiation shielding, and to incorporate an electronic detective. Also in the framework, we wish to incorporate a functional internal system handler."

"We had an electronic detective in the XPLM we took to Mars," John replied. "It was one of the major components of the hull repair and EOS system, which I studied in great detail on the trip to Mars but you, might want to talk to JP about it. He seems to understand the electronic systems better than anybody."

"Okay deal, why don't you and JP come over tomorrow morning and sit in with us? Maybe you could suggest some ideas."

"We don't really have anything to do until next week when we leave for Earth. So I guess it would be okay, but I'm not coming without JP. So he has the final word."

"See if you can talk him into it. Besides, some of the other staff members who couldn't make it to your return ceremony would like to meet you. I've got to go I have some things to do. Hope to see you tomorrow." John said good-bye and realized that Bob was probably on his way to bed. John returned to his room and went to JP's room to relay the appointment information, but JP was not at home. He went to Alex's room to find both of them watching TV and drinking vodka.

"Isn't it a little early for that?" John said.

"John look, we are millionaires. There is 2.75 million dollars American money waiting for us when we touch down at the Cape. I haven't had any good Russian vodka in eight years, and that stuff Yuri's crew was making was okay for Mars, but we are not on Mars anymore."

"Okay, so how much did that bottle cost?"

"In Moscow, I would get a bottle like this for about $40 USD. Here, it cost $120, but who cares? I want to have some. Go ahead, John. Have one."

John thought he knew Alex pretty well after six years, but he had never met rich Alex before. John informed JP of the offer for the next morning and JP agreed.

"So," said Alex, "tomorrow we will go to lab early?"

"Well gee, Alex. They didn't say anything about you," said John while he was pouring himself a drink. "I don't know whether it would be okay for you to come."

Alex had the look on his face of a dog that was being denied a doggie treat.

JP muttered, "John."

John said, "What? Oh okay Alex, yes you can come, what can they do but throw us out."

The next morning, the boys had breakfast early. They were on their way to the lab by eight o'clock. John had gotten the location from the ISA index, which gave the address as Building # 2 Unit 101. The engineering lab was a 32 x16 foot room at the end of the level one hallway. They entered the doorway to see four people at work inside the lab. Bob introduced them to everyone who was there. He then proceeded to explain their current point of development. They had some demonstration panels which were 4' x 4' feet with which they were doing experimental reconstruction. Bob showed them a model of their current application.

"This model," explained Bob "is a model of our current stage of development. The exterior panel is amorphous liquid metal plates separated by plastic sheets. We are hoping to put the electronic detector in this position using chemical etching. The Dewar's effect is contained in the center of the panel by two isolated interior sheets. These sheets need to be strengthened, which we hope to accomplish by using what's known as stress manufacturing or pressure forming. The two sheets form a vacuum seal, and high-energy plasma is pumped through this containment. The interior panel has a polymerized lead added to the alloy. Over here, we have an X-ray generator, which we are using to test the effectiveness of the panel. Of course, gamma rays have a higher density and are more difficult to stop. Last week, we had successful results, whereas we intensified the plasma frequency. It lowered the penetration of the X-ray particles to fewer than 50 percent. What we're trying to accomplish is to build an energy field inside the panel that will repel exterior radiation, such as cosmic rays."

John needed to say something, "Bob, I noticed that the completed panel is approximately eight inches thick, which is almost four inches more than the ones that we used on Mars. Is this going to affect their basic construction?"

"John, they are eight inches in width because that is what we made the framework. When we get our final product, we hope to reduce the framework by at least two inches."

"Mr. Bose," JP added, "what's the advantage of the layering the panels?"

"One of the most important aspects of space exploration is radiation shielding. Radiation can have long-term effects on the human body in space. When you were on Mars, you were in a cave that protected you. On Earth, we are protected by the atmosphere, and the base you built had an anti-radiation shielding. What we are trying to do is to construct a panel that works as a mirror to the radiation and make the cosmic rays work for us. Radiation can also be used to produce heat and power, which means that the radiation comes in and does not get out. In other words, blocking the reflected radiation and amplifying it, providing heat and power to a structure as a source.

"Our goal is to build a panel structure that is self-sufficient and independent of actual integrated systems, in other words, panel units which provide a needed function by design and are self-supporting. Example, you are adrift in space. Your vehicle has been damaged, and the electricity is off. You're in an inner suit but without any electricity. The heat is gone. You would most probably freeze to death, but your vehicle is made from these panels, which keep you from freezing."

Bob turned his attention to Alex "Alex have you got any ideas or was there anything on your trip to Mars that you might want improved that we can work on."

Alex looked like he was thinking then he said "Yes there is, you know Mr. Bose of all the people that were on Mars I was the person who spent the most nights in a bubble. The bubble itself wasn't uncomfortable because of the double pressure seal and the foam mattress and you could watch media over navcomm if you had a contact. However, you had to sleep in you suit. But one thing that could be improved is the food. While you were in a bubble you couldn't have hot food. In the module we had a microwave and an auto-cooker. I was thinking that we could have a portable way of heating the food in the bubble including hot beverages, paste gets a little old after a month."

"You see," Bob said to John. "That's the kind of input I'm looking for. I'll see what we can do, okay?"

The crew spent another couple of hours at the lab before going back to their rooms. JP seemed visibly impressed by the development work going on in the lab and returned several times before they left for Earth.

It was about three days before John was to leave for Earth. He had been with JP and Bob in Engineering for most of the morning. It was a little past lunch time he decided to go to the dining room to see what was available. Alex was in his room and JP had decided to stay at the lab. He came through the line after selecting his meal and took a seat at one of the tables. About a minute later John noticed Carl Monroe at the serving counter. He called out to Carl who waved and after selecting his food came over to join him.

"Hey John you'll be going back to Earth in and a few days, like three isn't it?"

"Yes in just about three days we will be on our way to the Earth Orbital Platform. How did the meeting go with the ISA as far as the construction of the Glass House?"

Carl paused and got a funny look on his face.

"Well John, it didn't go like I thought it would." Carl replied.

"What do you mean did you get a contract or what?" John inquired.

"Yes and no" Carl replied. "So far no actual contract however, we do have an understanding. They are going to go ahead with construction of the Glass House, which is good. However, the actual details and the time frame are still a little cloudy."

"Oh, how so?" said John.

"Well, they don't know exactly when they will start, they don't know exactly how long it will take and they don't know how many houses they wish to build. You see John amorphous metal is a combination alloy resulting in a variety of metals being fused together to obtain the final product. Essential metals are Zinc, Copper, Beryllium, Boron and Titanium. This presents a problem because so far we have not found an abundance of these metals here on the Moon. In fact we haven't found an abundance of any metals mostly just rock. We've of course have found some metal however, not in significant quantities. This means that the raw metals will have to be shipped from Earth which of course increases the cost. I mean don't get me wrong, we secured some type of agreement which is good and they seemed to be behind the expansion and upgrade of the City but, the ISA has a way of making decisions without other peoples concerns being addressed. You know John I'm supposed to be partly responsible for the operation of this station. You know that I'm an ISA employee you would think that being in an administrative position that it would allow me to have some say so as to project development of the City. I went into the conference two days after your visit with the understanding that it was going to be about construction of the Glass House and the timescale of the contract production. However, I left with no contract and iffy time scale. I went into the conference attempting to get approval for the construction of one Glass House. However, I find out they don't want to build one Glass House they want to build three. But before we can do that, they want us to build a panel manufacturing plant. They are going to load one of these new vehicles called a CTU or Cargo Transport Unit with the machinery required. The smelter, vacuum press, cooler, conveyer belt, and the lift machinery and it should arrive within the next three to six months. We are to set it up and prepare it for operation. A second unit will be arriving shortly there after. We are to join these two units together to form the panel construction plant.

"Well that's good I mean that's what you wanted right?" John questioned.

"Not exactly John, their plan is that we shall build the amorphous panels here on the Moon and that we will construct the Glass Houses in stages. They will be shipping the metal product to us in stages. Every time they send one of these CTUs to us we will produce the panels and build another Glass House that part is fine. I mean, with the manufacturing lab we shouldn't have a problem and this plan will mean a change in personnel here. We will have specialized engineers arriving to handle the procedure."

"You know John; I was in sink with entire game plan until Robert Bose got up to do his presentation, then things got confusing. He started talking about his recent developments in panel assembly then mentioned a new development in the lab which he claimed if successful will revolutionize panel construction and application. That's when JP's name was mentioned.

"JP what's he got to do with this?" John responded.

"According to Bob that's where they got the idea from. Bob promised that they were working on an idea that JP had brought to their attention which showed a solution to their Universal panel application. And according to Bob if the research turns out to be successful, they would be able to develop a panel that has ability as a radiation shield, thermal insulator, and solar generator to create a power supply function. He also hinted that this unit would be able to store electrical power like a battery. But he didn't stop there he claimed that they may be able to create a super panel, which could be developed and integrated with different layers for different applications. This of course got a definite reaction from the ISA representatives. They adjourned for a day and scheduled another session for today which I'm coming from now. Look, this is their concept of what Lunar City will look like in two years" Carl said placing a layout page on the table.

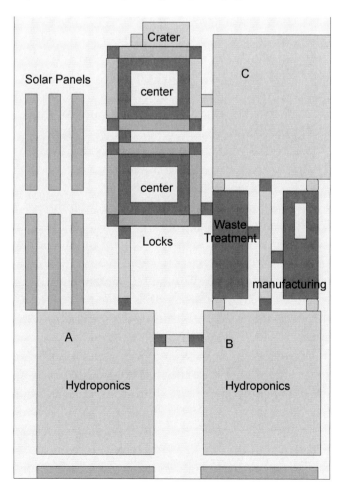

"What you're looking at is about 12 billion dollars using CTUs maybe, a little more depending on what they ship. The Glass Houses will be 3 stories high or 28 feet. With this amount of hydro-product generation we will have enough product to supply Mars, the Earth Orbital Platform, and the orbital platforms on Jupiter and Saturn.

"Carl, what can you tell me about these new CTU devices," asked John.

"Well John, I don't know much about them but they're not exactly like the CMPs. Their payload weight is estimated at 140 to 160,000 pounds and they have no large scale propulsion engines. They do have a medium power ion plasma engine. The CTUs are convertible, in other words modifiable, they are like shells. The entire cockpit of a CTU is contained in the first section which is 8 x 16 feet and includes: a rack for four pods, Tri-Star and navcomm unit station, and a six by eight foot kitchen and bathroom. They are not equipped for any long-term application as far as a people transport vehicle unless converted. The CTUs are 100 feet in length 16 x 16' height and width like a CMP. The extra space gives the CTU a storage capacity of 24,000 cubic feet and that is a lot of cargo space. You could load the unit with over 4000 completed panels, enough to build a 400 foot square hydro building, like the Glass House so, for every lift one Glass House. But the CTU it self is just a shell with a control system and a very small maneuvering system. The reason that these units will replace CMPs is because, except for the unit's nose, they are built with standard panels which make them super cheap."

"Wait did you say panels what kind of panels?" questioned John.

"Panels like you used on Mars when you built the base structure and hydro-unit on the surface. You know regular metal and the clear amorphous panels, just like the ones were going to build here, in the Moon factory. After we get through building the glass houses, we are going to start building CTUs here. When they are completed we're going to load it and park it at the LP where it will be joined by other units to form a train. This is for deep space application. A CMP will then work as the locomotive pulling the chain of CTUs into deep space to supply Jupiter and Saturn and form the orbital platforms for Uranus, Neptune, and the Kuiper Belt. Of course, we won't be sending any components that we don't have, such as water. Earth will have to supply that but having clear panels could create a crystal clear vehicle. CTUs come with attachments and can be converted which make them more versatile than the CMP's. They have a frame component called the SLED which attaches to their undercarriage. The SLED is simply a cart with built in components. They contain a navcomm unit, landing wheels, EOS system, fuel tanks and landing thrusters. This allows the CTU to land here or back on Earth making the craft re-usable. Many of the units won't ever need them because they won't be re-used. The crystal units we make will be integrated into platforms.

"You know John, between the period of 2024 and now, 2036 twenty eight CMPs were built."

"One is here at the City, operational as the landing bay and there are four CMPs forming the LP. They're four making up the Mars Orbital Platform there's four at Jupiter, and 4 on there way to Saturn. Oh yes, and six forming the Earth Orbital Platform. But the structural design of the CTU's is smarter and they will probably phase out the CMPs as the main cargo vehicles. The CMPs will become the engines for the CTU trains."

"But you said that these CTUs don't have any engines much to speak of. How do they get from the Earth to here?" John asked.

"The two extra CMPs that are docked at the EOP will operate as tow engines. Once the CTU is in orbit a CMP will link with them and bring them here and release them into orbit around the Moon. They will have Sleds attached and will be able to land on the surface. Then they will be unloaded and once empty they can be sent back to Earth. Others will be linked in a train using a CMP as an engine and sent into deep space. They will be carrying Oxygen (LOX), water, replacement parts, food product (meat products) from Earth and our products which will be clear panels and vegetables.

"How many CTUs are in a train Carl?" John asked.

That is not specified, so I don't know exactly but, they said that the trains could be multi-packed with separate loads for separate stations. For example a train can leave from here with a multiple load every year or so containing a shipment for Neptune, Uranus, Jupiter, Saturn and Mars. The main asset of the CTUs is that they can easily be converted to habitat vehicles. A CTU when converted can host 22 eight by twelve rooms but twenty would be more accurate. Plus the CTUs can be linked together; they have extendable linking conduits in the front and rear ends. This allows them to link together to form a habitat platforms. Also, when the CTUs are used to form a platform they can use a connector to link eight units together in a sort of circle or an 8 sided Octagon because these connectors have an adjustable 45 degree angle differential.

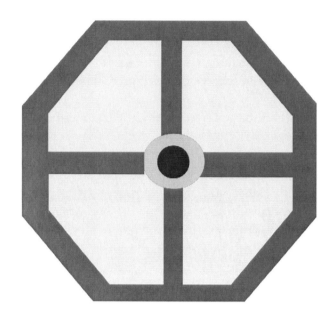

Once constructed the Octagon can be rotated or spun to create an artificial gravity like Von Brauns Space Station. The Octagon is connected to a central hub. Twelve CTUs and one hub make a platform which can be developed in layers to create multilevel structure. Also after the Octagon is operational two of the pre-existing CMPs that this system replaces won't be needed and will be sent back to the LP to be updated and re-fitted. What I like about this is the load capacity of 160,000 lbs is almost enough to supply this City with the water required for a year."

"Let me get this straight Carl" John replied. "So, you're going to build these CTUs here and then produce and load product. Lift it into orbit so that it can be integrated into a train and sent to stations in deep space. They will then be converted into platform components including habitat and performance units, okay. But Carl you're talking about going into Jovian space. To get to Mars only takes 7 months but to Jupiter it's 2.5 years away, Saturn is 5 years, Uranus is 10 years and Neptune is 13. It takes 26 years under current conditions to get to Neptune and come back. So, I don't really see a big advantage to this program."

"John you're forgetting navcomm can take the trains into Jovian space without human occupancy and you just said the magic words under current conditions. Well, the CTUs all come with a medium power ion plasma engines which are mounted on the roof at the rear of these units. The CMPs have two main engines so imagine a train of a hundred CTUs all equipped with plasma engine propulsion. The propulsion would be 400 to 500 times greater than a single unit thus reducing the travel time tremendously. This may make getting to Neptune and the Kuiper belt more practical. Of course, you'll have to account for the time it will take to slow down. I think a train of 100 units would be a bit much; a closer estimate would be 12 units per planet to form a platform on the first run, probably the same for the second run. That would be 60 units plus five CMPS unmanned of course. Human habitation will have to come later but that's a good look at the future of space exploration," Carl remarked.

"I know that they were already building a CTU on Earth and it will probably get here within the next 6 months to create the manufacturing plant and they will probably build a few more to run the plants raw material supplies. I'm just concerned that what Bose said may have delayed the train project. They may decide to wait until Bose produces his super panel before they start producing these deep space vehicles."

"Well that's a pretty unusual viewpoint of the future," John remarked. "What your suggesting is when the first people get to Jupiter or Neptune stations that there will be a two story 24 units habitat waiting for them with a fueled return vehicle including a abundance of food, water, and oxygen. How long do you think it will take for them to launch the first train and how much do you think it will cost."

"It's about 3 to 4 years away. As far as the cost goes; it costs 1.5 billion to build, load, and launch a CMP. From what I understand these CTU are about 700 million for everything the fuel, the load, and the lift so let's see about 50 billion maybe a little more. I'd say 80 to be on the safe side. But when the second train goes we will have mastered the solar system with navcomm as our maintenance and watchdog regulator. So the cost for three trains somewhere around 240 billion? I think for what we're getting that's cheap the whole process should take about 10 years from the first launch. The more trains that are launched the bigger the network will become. So you see, we've got the plan what we need is a new form of propulsion which can get us to Neptune in two years. But that would be over 100,000 miles per hour. Traveling at that speed we would need some type of shield to protect the vehicle our current advanced warning system wouldn't be effective at that speed."

"I agree Carl" there was a pause then they both laughed

Lunch was now defiantly over John said goodbye to Carl and went to empty his tray the idea came to him that maybe he'd give the Trampoline room a try.

That night John retired early however, woke up at what the clock told him was 4:00 a.m. He decided to go for a walk and thought he would take advantage of a look over the Sea of Tranquility at night. The city was already in its dark period and the blue growth lights gave an eerie blue light to the interior of the building. There was an observation platform on the top of their unit. John went outside the room to the hallway and proceeded down the hallway to the stairs that connected the observation unit. Even though there was light in the distance, the city was in total darkness. John noticed as he walked down the hallway that the lights seemed to follow him. The panel he was standing on was lit up and the panels ahead of him and behind him were also lit.

As he proceeded down the hallway, the hallway continued light up as he approached. He reminded himself to ask someone how that was done later. He reached the observation deck and proceeded up the stairs to the top. The observation deck gave a good view of the Sea of Tranquility at night. In the dark period, there was no day or night. It was dark all day and would remain in that condition for approximately fourteen days. John sat up there taking it all in for about an hour. He noticed a T-111 passing over the base, and he caught a view of the Lunar Platform as it passed on its orbital rotation. He returned to his room shortly thereafter. They would be leaving on a Jumper in one and a half days at 2:00 p.m. for the trip home. At nine o'clock, he decided to go downstairs to the dining room and see what he could get for breakfast. Doris noticed him when he entered.

She came over to the table. "John, you're still in time for breakfast and a little early for lunch. I have some Salisbury steak and mashed potatoes with brown gravy and a couple of eggs over medium with toast. How does that sound?"

"That sounds great, Doris," John replied.

"Orange juice and coffee with that, John?" Doris asked.

"Even better," John replied.

Doris disappeared to the kitchen. A few minutes later, John noticed Bob enter the dining room. Bob grabbed a cup of coffee from the counter and came in his direction. He placed his coffee on the table and sat down.

"Hey, John, how's it going? I understand you're leaving us in a day or two. JP is becoming a member of the crew, bright boy. He has suggested integrating clear metal alloy fibers into the framework to serve as a clear alloy battery. I don't know why we didn't think of it, but we are working on it now, after we gained the understanding of what he was suggesting. We realized that if we changed the mix, we could do exactly that. We are smelting a mix now to produce a demonstrator for experimentation. This type of technology is exactly what we were looking for. It was then suggested that we could build the panels with a regenerative power supply and battery backup. We are going to ask the ISA if he can stay up here with us till the project's done in about six months. He's already agreed that he would be happy to do so, and I'm sure it will be approved. So it looks like just you and Alex will be returning to Earth by yourselves, if that's okay with you?"

"Sure, if he wants to stay it's fine with me. Say Bob listen, the other night I was on the walkway with no one else present. And the lights turned on and off as I walked. How's that done?" John asked.

Bob smiled. "That's one of our panel inserts John. The insert is a piezoelectric plate that generates a little amount of electricity when you step on it, not much, but enough to operate a switch. This turns the light on when you step on it and off when there's no pressure. All the floor panels in the building are piezoelectric, even inside the rooms. So when you move around in your room, you are creating electricity. The lights have a timer and a switching system that operates in the following manner. The panel you're standing on is lit, the panel behind you is lit, and the panel in front of you is lit. When you step to the next panel, the panel behind you that was lit goes out. With just one person, we actually lose power in the operation, but with people using it all day, we come out ahead. If JP's idea works out, and I'll have to say it looks extremely good on paper, it will change that process, making the power generation much more efficient."

Doris had arrived with John's plate.

"That looks pretty good, Doris, Is there any more?"

"Yes," replied Doris. "You want a plate, Bob?"

Bob nodded and Doris went back to the kitchen.

John had a question, "Bob, how is the billing done for the meals?"

"Well, if you're ISA, the meals are included in your contract, same with the tourists. However, it's part of Doris's job to keep track of what is prepared and what is served. Here, let me give you an example." Bob pointed at the meal in front of John. "On Earth, a meal like that would cost you in an American restaurant about eight dollars. You could buy it in a grocery and cook it yourself for about four dollars. How much do you think it costs for you to have that meal here?"

John shrugged. "I don't know."

"Here's a quick figure," Bob pulled out his calculator. "Whatever it costs on Earth, multiply by one thousand, and that's not exact but close.

So that meal would cost approximately eight thousand dollars. Space has never been cheap. A CMP can lift about 110,000 lb. in payload safely. Luna City receives three supply CMPs a year. In order to support the one hundred people here, it takes 18,250 gallons of water per year which weighs 8.35 lbs a gallon, the lift weight is152,387 lbs The average person eats about 2.5 lbs. of food a day. So, for a year 100 people would need 91,250 lbs. They also require 9,600 gallons of LOX at one liter per person a day. Lift weight 91,500 lbs, so we add it up: 152 + 91 + 81 = 324,000 lb, and remember, we gave the total lift weight for the three CMPs at 330,000 lb. so that we have a little leeway of around 6,000 lbs to play with. However, it's not that simple. There's also packaging and additional supplies. But with the modifications we have made, mainly the hydroponics, we have cut the food and Oxygen usage down 40 percent. So now, based on our previous figures, we gain 38,000 lb. on the Oxygen and 40,000 lb. on the food. We could cut one shipment, but what we save they replace with water and equipment like the food processor or the metal we use to make the glass. Any extras we have go into storage. We have no problem keeping our cryogenics cold and our food supplies in long-term storage. The big problem is the water. You see, it cost 1.2 billion dollars to build, load and launch a CMP, in other words, 3.6 billion dollars a year to keep this base operational and that's a low estimate. So, if you've done the math, it cost 12.3 million per day to support Luna City and its inhabitants, or $98,630 per person per day. Now divide that into three equal parts, one for food, one for air, and one for water, and you get 32,876 dollars for food per day, and you just ate one of your three meals. Well John, you must be rich, because you just ate a 10,958 dollar Salisbury steak dinner. And that's not counting your coffee and your orange juice. We either need to find a way to lift cheaper or learn to produce the products we need."

John gasped. "Bob, I find that hard to believe. I don't think that meal was worth over $2,000."

Doris was approaching with Bob's tray and overheard John.

"No, I'm sorry, Doris. I didn't mean it. It was a good meal. It's just that Bob—."

"I know," Doris interrupted. "It's one of Bob's little jokes. He pulls it on the tourists and newcomers. However, I have heard that they are charging the tourists a price of 5 million for a one-week stay here at the City; it's just a paper game. But, when you and your crew discovered water on Mars, it put a whole new light on space exploration. Suddenly, they're talking about developing a colony on Mars. And they started talking about expansion of the city. As a matter of fact, right after you found it. We got twenty extra employees and the second housing unit. If they agree, we will start producing the components for the platforms and Mars. We can send a CMP from here for just a few million. One of the main products is what Bob's working on, the panels for construction. From a cost effective analysis, I don't see them refusing us the contract. We don't need to ship food, Oxygen, or water to Mars, maybe to the developing platforms yes, but not Mars. I've heard they are already calling Mars 'Red Australia.'"

Bob looked up from his lunch. "Yes, I've heard that mentioned as well."

"Bob do you think that these new CTUs will be the answer?"

"The new CTU vehicles will greatly reduce the cost of lifting supplies into space, including water. They should be able to lift an entire year's water supply in one lift. But of course that wouldn't leave anything for the EOP which depends on water to be lifted in the same way the City does just not in as great a quantity. I think they will probably build a CTU capable of lifting 15,000 gallons per lift. This would mean a lift weight of 125,000 lbs and would supply both the city and the EOP giving us 22,000 gallons and 8,000 gallons for the EOP. Yes, I believe that would solve the problem. Plus, they could send the LOX with it to make up the weight differential. Remember, what I said about your meal costing 10,000 dollars. If these units turn out to be as good as they say it will cut operational cost of the City in half, in other words it will reduce your Salisbury steak dinner to 6.5 thousand.

When lunch was over, John returned to his room. Bob went to get some sleep. John went and tapped on Alex's door.

When Alex answered, John said, "We need to talk to JP."

John then tapped on JP's door and heard JP answer,

"Come in."

He and Alex entered the room. JP was on the couch watching the news.

John started, "What's this I hear about you staying here?"

That, of course, was news to Alex, who seemed to be having a hard time understanding what was just said.

JP stammered, "I told Bob and the rest of the crew I would. They think my idea will work, and I want to see it through. They said it would only be six more months, and I don't mind so much. Stuff like this has been coming to me since I started this project. You might say I've found my groove besides this place is nice."

Then Alex found his voice, "You mean that tomorrow it will be just me and John going home. But why JP? You've already spent seven years in space. Why would you want to stay longer?" Alex asked.

"First of all, this isn't Mars and it isn't space. It's Luna City and I feel it's important and it's something I want to do. Who knows? I may continue with the ISA as an engineer it has been mentioned," said JP.

He was interrupted by Alex, whose hand was pointed at the wallboard, "Look, it's us."

John turned to see his image on the display "Turn it up, JP."

"The first men on Mars will be leaving Luna City tomorrow for their return to Earth. They will be taking a Jumper from Lunar City to arrive at the Earth Orbital Platform in three days. They will board a re-entry vehicle to land at the Cape after being in space for over seven years. The captain, John Alexander, and Alex Gorkov will be onboard for the Friday afternoon landing. Hitu Ashitu of Japan will be staying at Luna City to do consulting work on a current ISA project and will return in six months. In other Mars news, a probe launched over eighteen months ago has surfaced inside a crater south of the Martian equator. The probe that was launched with five other probes has made a journey of over five thousand miles and, contains data on the underground structure of the Martian surface. The probe, which was an aquatic submersible vehicle, recorded data to make a map of the underground canals that exist under the Martian surface. The probe surfaced last week inside a crater in the southern hemisphere of Mars."

"Well, what do you know about that? The probe, I don't believe it," said John.

"It sure took a long time to get there. I mean, I know it is five thousand miles, but it's almost been two years," said Alex. "They will get a lot of data of the canals from that probe, and it will make Dr. Werner very happy."

"It will make a lot of people very happy, Alex," JP agreed.

"Well, I guess it's settled. JP, we're going to miss you, buddy. When you drop in six months, give us a call and we'll get together."

JP agreed and then replied. "Oh, Alex Bob asked me to give that to you," he said pointing at the table.

There was a box sitting on the table. Alex crossed the room and opened the box. He pulled out the enclosed object.

"A weightless cup what do I need with a weightless cup?"

"It's not your ordinary weightless cup Alex. Notice the bottom they put in a re-generative power supply and a receiver which operates of a navcomm signal. Remember you asked Bob to make a device that would allow you to have hot food in a bubble well that's it. He thought you should have one after all it was your idea. Here's how it works it doesn't matter whether your in a gravity or a weightless condition if you can receive a navcomm signal you can have hot food. That means because your outer suit sends a navcomm signal you can have hot food in a bubble, watch." JP came over and unscrewed the lid

"When you take a food packet out of the refrigerator its frozen right? Just place the product in the cup screw the lid back on and add water with the water injector. Now coffee, I don't have any condensed coffee here but I got some instant." JP placed a tablespoon instant in the cup and screwed the top back on.

"Okay we are not on a ship if we were you would use the water injector to produce the coffee. But let's suppose we are on Mars." JP reached into the box and produced a bubble with a injector tube coming out of one side he unscrewed the top and filled the bubble with water once the bubble was filed he turned to Alex and asked

"Do you what sugar with that?"

"Da," Alex replied. "Two."

JP added two sweetener packets recapped the bubble and shook it then connected the bubble injector hose to the injector intake valve on the top of the cup he squeezed the bubble and the cup filled with water.

"Okay now just turn it on and wait a little while, it will work here because there is a navcomm signal."

"There's one for you too John," JP said. As he went to the kitchen and came back holding another box.

"Well, that's good but we're going back to Earth, JP. I'm afraid I won't have much use for it there."

"Look John," JP had that look on his face that he got when John didn't understand something. "It has a plug in for AC electrical outlet and DC auto. You can use it on Earth besides; you can use it on the Jumper on the trip to the EOP. "

John looked over at Alex who was taking a sip out of his.

"Does it work?" He asked.

Alex nodded but replied "Now I'm mad, we could have had this the entire time I wouldn't have had to eat all that paste"

John and Alex said good-bye to JP. The next day, they had to be at the Jumper station at noon for the 2:00 p.m. lift off. They had to put on outer suits and wait for the navcomm signal. John's personal items, which weren't much, were in a carry-on bag, including his shaving cream. They suited and entered the Jumper. An ISA tech operator came in to see if everyone was on board. There were six other people going with them. John asked the tech where the pilot was, to which the tech replied, "If you go into the bathroom and look over the sink at that shiny thing on the wall, you can see him." He paused for a second. "You and Gorkov got this one," the tech said, pointing at them.

"Pilot, co-pilot, got it?"

John and Alex settled into their seats in the cockpit. Ten minutes before liftoff, JP appeared at the window. John saw him and waved. He tapped Alex, who looked up and waved. At exactly 2:00 p.m., the navcomm signal activated, and the Jumper lifted on its way to the EOP and then to Earth.

Epilogue 1147-01/D
(colonization)

The concept of the exploration of Mars and the development of its colonization is of course fictional at the current time. However, not to say the approach to the idea of developing a permanent self-sustaining base and colony on Mars is impractical. One thing that is required for colonization is water. Without water there can be no colonization only exploration. To place 1000 people into space requires 500 gallons of water a day or 182,500 gallons of water a year without which the colonies would not survive. The actual equation is 182.5 gallons a year per person plus 20% or 219 gallons a year. Our current technology allows us to colonize only the Planet of Mars and large primary moons such as Ganymede, Io, Callisto, and Europa on Jupiter and Titian, Tethys, Dione, and Rhea on Saturn. There are also the dwarf planets of the Kuiper Belt, Pluto and Makemake and others. If there is no water discovered at these locations the establishing a large scale base of operations is pointless. All water would have to be supplied by Earth. Planets such as Mercury, Venus, Jupiter Saturn Uranus and Neptune because of either tempeture or Mass are out of the question at this time. In the story **Jovian Space: The Space Train (JS:TST 1147-01/E)** we introduce the concept of field effect radiation shielding which would be required for any permanent base structure including any long term presence in space (a major concern). The exposure to gamma and cosmic radiations can have dangerous effects upon the human bio-structure resulting in severe health issues. The idea represented in the (**ASTTM**) habitat Cave is smart. The Marineris Valles is over 4 miles deep although the ground is lava which is an igneous rock, and hard to drill. The sides are the remains of the surface rock. The lava which has been covered by sand left from storms for over the past millions of years. Probably contains a top sand layer of many feet. A permanent base structure can beat the radiation problem by developing habitat structures under the ground. If the location contains metal deposits the habitat can produces it own panels and structural supports. It has been suggested that metal deposits in great quantity can be found on the asteroids of the belt. It has even been suggested that large deposits of Gold and Platinum are available. The **(JS: TST 1147-01/E)** story warns of altering the suspension of orbital mass regardless of density or size which should be taken seriously. However, the problem is still water, it was suggested by one of the AADG consultants that in the future it may be possible to synthesize water with a plasma field and the components of 2 parts Hydrogen and 1part Oxygen. Of course, it was also suggested that if we wanted to visit Venus or Jupiter. We could do so by developing a force field that would create a bubble shield that would allow us to travel the surface without having to worry about massive gravitation and extreme temperatures affecting us.

Such a concept would also introduce a new propulsion system. This could be a possible vision of the future.

The story 'A Short Trip to Mars' **(ASTTM)** brings up several concepts which give this idea a more practical understanding. Two of these concepts are the Navcomm and the EOS Systems. The Navcomm System is a **must have device** needed to journey great distances in space. The system supplies all these benefits such as Solar Security, Tracking, Vehicle Navigation for manned and un-manned vehicles, early warning detection, rescue and the identification of hazardous development and corrective avoidance, explained in Jovian Space: The Space Train (JS:TST 1147-01/E). The EOS system is a **fail-safe system** which protects the vehicle in a manned and un-manned states This system operates with a different group of protocols which regard what's best overall for ship and/or crew. The two stories are produced as a puzzle demonstrating concepts which should be applied and mistakes which should be avoided. Not all the assets of the 1147-01 Project are explained in the stories. Information as to the project or a PDF copy of the book can be found at http://1147-01.aadg.info

Bio

Fcreyer is the current owner of Altered Atmospheric Design Group and Gismoworks Ltd. and has lived in the Space Coast of Central Florida for over twenty-four years. He is educated in communications, computers systems, electronic engineering, design engineering, and mechatronic engineering and is currently involved in the development of a M-tronic conversion database for M-tronic system integration in Seattle, Washington.

Book Description

Plot

The story starts with Deputy Assistant Jason Greene at the International Space Administration building in Montreal, Canada, where top level conferencing is under way for an international effort to have the first manned landing on Mars. The mission is to last six years because of the two-year, uneven orbit of Mars. The point was brought up that no one would want to be marooned on Mars for that length of time but that there was a lot of pressure building for the mission and two years would not be enough time to explore the surface adequately. A plot was contrived for the major governments, Russia, China, USA, Japan, and Europe (combined) to select three candidates from their criminal incarceration to become the mission crew of three and the first men on Mars. For their participation, they were offered a pardon for their crimes plus financial compensation. If for some reason they didn't come back, compensation would be paid to their selected beneficiaries. In order to qualify for this, the candidate must be sentenced to a life sentence or long term incarceration and undergo an interview, sign a contract, and undergo a psychological examination. Jason meets with a psychiatrist working for the Justice Department to pick the three USA candidates. The three are picked but everything is hushed up under instruction by ISA security until two months before the launch, when the mission details are announced to the public. The crew becomes instant celebrities, but security is tight. The American whose name is John Alexander is assigned as mission commander because he had pilot training in the US Marine Corp. The second pick is a Russian from the Ukraine named Alex Gorkov, who was a machinist in the Russian navy, and the third pick is a Japanese candidate whose nickname is JP, who was a computer hacker.

They launch after training and arrive on the Earth Orbital Platform (EOP), which replaced the ISS when the permanent lunar station (the Lunar Starr) was completed. The crew catches the lunar shuttle to their destination the Lunar Starr. Three days later, they arrive. They stay at Lunar Starr for 2 days, Earth time. Then they are transported to LP (Lunar Platform) for orientation with their mission module, where they will spend the next seven months on their way to Mars, which occurs in a few days. The module goes from the LP to MOP (Mars Orbital Platform), where they wait for the drop to the surface. Three weeks later, it's a go. A lot of supplies were already dropped to the surface ahead of them, so after they land, they have to unpack. The supplies were dropped over the last six years and contain food, water, specialized gear, plus two robots that have been digging a cave for the last 4.5 years to house the module in to protect the crew from the harsh conditions, to preserve oxygen, and act as a radiation shield (lots of technical stuff). Once on the surface, they go through a series of adventures, the most prominent the exploration of the Valles Mariners and the Polar Regions. They are then joined by the second team that has its own mission, based on what they had already discovered. They exist there with the second team for four more years. The last supply drop included a return vehicle which they must assemble for their return to Earth in two years. They do and leave Mars for the return to the Lunar Starr. However, the Lunar Starr is gone. It has been replaced by Luna City. A lot had changed. The project is based on information gained by the space shuttle, Lunar Lander, ISS, and Mars probes, and the information offered is factual on that basis. The Ariel, which is a method of transportation made available to the crew, achieves a high-end velocity of 350 mph using an ion engine currently under development by a former astronaut, who has established a development firm in Costa Rica. The engine is called the mini ion and will be implanted on the ISS this year. Many of the devices presented in the story are real. The story may be fictional but the project it's based on is not. The project is called the 1147-01 Project, which contains five step program related to space exploration and introduces over sixty new products The story is also a learning experience for people who don't know much about the planet Mars.

AADG fcreyer

Index

NCES (Navcomm Central Earth Station), 56
Neptune, XII, XVII, 272, 274, 280–83

O

Olympus Mons, IX, 83, 85, 87, 133, 138, 141–42, 148, 159–63, 166, 172, 174, 195, 211, 225–26
Ophir Chasmata, 179

P

Pathfinder probe, 234–36
Pavonis Mons, 147–48, 160, 162
Petrov, Representative, 3
Phobos, 72–73, 161, 216
pods, 58

R

radiation, 276
rail, 32, 34
Red Australia, 271, 287
Robins, Jeff, 46–47
Russia, 30, 105, 133, 295
Russians, 2, 23, 30, 106

S

Saturn, XII–I, XVII, 38, 232, 271, 274, 280–82
Saturn Platforms, 37
Sea of Tranquility, 258, 263, 284
Security Council, 2
Shaw, Dr., 231
Shaw, Julius, 231
Smith, Dr., 238
Sojourner rover, 235–36

Solis Planum, 194
Space Commission, 1
SRBs (Solid Rocket Booster), 183, 239–41, 246, 249–50
Sterling engine, 19
Stevens, Mark, 238

T

T-111 mapping probes (Trex), XI, 49, 52–53, 64, 68, 72, 108, 111, 148, 161, 163, 215–16, 218, 241, 263
theory
  existence of planet between Mars and Jupiter, 231
  existence of water in Mars, 175
  ice in Mars causing Ice Age on Earth, 176
  tectonic plate shifting on Mars regarding the Marineris Valles, 231
Titan, 38
Todd, Alan, 3–5
Tom (Luna City garden worker), 264–65
Trex. *See* T-111
trilobites, 228–30
Tri-Starr, 36, 55–56, 58, 61, 68, 74, 98, 101, 216

U

Uranus, XII, XVII, 232, 274, 280–82

V

Valles Marineris, 25, 29, 83, 138, 194
Vexsler, Yuri, 15–16, 105–7, 111–14, 116–17, 120–40, 158, 161,

Edwards Brothers, Inc.
Thorofare, NJ USA
March 29, 2012